Praise for *New York Times* bestselling author

CANDACE CAMP

A Perfect Gentleman

"[T]he real fun to be had in reading *A Perfect Gentleman* is Graeme's slow, unwilling tumble into love."

—*Heroes and Heartbreakers*

"The dialogue is witty, the plot is engrossing, and the construction of place is rich. . . . I closed the book with a happy sigh."

—*All About Romance*

Praise for the thrilling Scottish trilogy

Secrets of the Loch

Book Three

ENRAPTURED

"With heated love scenes, sensuality and poignancy, this fast-paced read is Camp at her very best."

—*RT Book Reviews* (4½ stars, Top Pick)

"*Enraptured* captivates with compelling escapades and engaging characters." —*Single Titles*

"In many ways this book was like the perfect romance. It had deeply moving chemistry, a grand adventure, and a sharply witted heroine." —*Night Owl Romance*

Book Two

PLEASURED

"Candace Camp never disappoints and only gets better with each story." —*Single Titles*

"Once again, Camp populates a romance with interesting characters . . . [in this] steamy Scottish historical."

—*Booklist*

Book One

TREASURED

"Sweet. . . . Entertaining. . . . A Highlands version of small-town charm."

—*Publishers Weekly*

"*Treasured* demonstrates Candace Camp's ability to draw her readers in with strong, well-drawn characters. A legend of hidden treasure, a man who hides behind many façades, and a woman who fights for her birthright form the tapestry of this poignant, sensual, and emotion-packed romance."

—*RT Book Reviews* (Top Pick)

And praise for Candace Camp's acclaimed trilogy

Legend of St. Dwynwen

THE MARRYING SEASON
A SUMMER SEDUCTION
A WINTER SCANDAL

"Sensuality, intrigue, and Camp's trademark romantic sparring. . . . Delightful."

—*Publishers Weekly*

"A charming courtship. . . . Readers will be captivated."

—*Booklist* (starred review)

"Sexy and sweet! Beautifully written, with just the right touch of mystery and a generous helping of a scandalous romance."

—*Coffee Time Romance*

Be sure to read Candace Camp's dazzling Willowmere novels. . . . Critics adore this breathtaking Regency trilogy of the unforgettable Bascombe sisters!

AN AFFAIR WITHOUT END

"Delightful romantic mystery. . . . With clever and witty banter, sharp attention to detail, and utterly likable characters, Camp is at the top of her game."

—*Publishers Weekly* (starred review)

"Sprightly dialogue . . . [and] a simmering sensuality that adds just enough spice to this fast-paced, well-rendered love story."

—*RT Book Reviews* (4½ stars)

A GENTLEMAN ALWAYS REMEMBERS

"Intensely passionate and sexually charged. . . . A well-crafted, delightful read."

—*Romantic Times (4 stars)*

"A delightful romp. . . . Camp has a way with truly likable characters who become like friends."

—*Romance Junkies*

"Where the Bascombe sisters go, things are never dull. Candace Camp delivers another witty, heartwarming, and fast-paced novel."

—*A Romance Review*

A LADY NEVER TELLS

"This steamy romp . . . will entertain readers."

—*Publishers Weekly*

"Well-crafted and enchanting."

—*Romantic Times* (4½ stars)

"Superbly written and well paced, *A Lady Never Tells* thoroughly entertains as it follows the escapades of the Bascombe 'bouquet' of Marigold, Rose, Camellia, and Lily in the endeavor to make their way in upper-crust London society."

—*Romance Reviews Today*

"One of those rare finds you don't want to put down. . . . Candace Camp brings a refreshing voice to the romance genre."

—*Winter Haven News Chief*

"Filled with humor and charm. . . . Fine writing."

—*A Romance Review* (4 roses)

Also from Candace Camp and Pocket Books

A Perfect Gentleman

The Secrets of the Loch Series

Enraptured

Pleasured

Treasured

The Legend of St. Dwynwen Series

The Marrying Season

A Summer Seduction

A Winter Scandal

The Willowmere Series

An Affair Without End

A Gentleman Always Remembers

A Lady Never Tells

A MOMENTARY *Marriage*

CANDACE CAMP

Pocket Books
New York London Toronto Sydney New Delhi

Pocket Books
An Imprint of Simon & Schuster, Inc.
1230 Avenue of the Americas
New York, NY 10020

First Pocket Books paperback edition August 2017

Manufactured in the United States of America

10 9 8 7 6 5 4 3 2

ISBN 978-1-5011-4162-1
ISBN 978-1-5011-4163-8 (ebook)

For Anastasia—you're the best

I always thank the same group, but they're the ones who always make my book possible.

Anastasia for her research and suggestions and being my sounding board.

Abby for helping me resolve the dilemmas and fill the gaps, as well as separating the wheat from the chaff.

Marla and all the rest of the team at Pocket for all they do to get this book out there—that's a lot of work, people, and I appreciate it!

Maria and the folks at Maria Carvainis Agency for their support and expertise.

A MOMENTARY *Marriage*

1882

Sir James de Vere was going home to die.

He would end his life as he had lived it, alone in the midst of his family. It was a bleak prospect, but even so, not as bad as spending his last days here in the gray and grimy city. At least at Grace Hill, he would have the beauty of his gardens. And Dem would enjoy the freedom of the country.

He glanced over at the huge dog, stretched out in the sunlight coming through the window. As if he had heard his master's thoughts, the brindle mastiff raised his head and looked at James, then, apparently satisfied that all was in order, lay back down again.

"Sir?" the man on the other side of his desk said uneasily.

James turned back to his man of business. Obviously he had missed whatever the fellow had said. He found it more and more difficult to maintain his focus—indeed, to think of anything but the stab of pain behind his eye. "I beg your pardon. I didn't hear you."

"I was asking if there was anything else, sir." The man's

tone was deferential, but James knew he was itching to leave. James was never sure if Johnson was more uneasy about incurring James's displeasure or that of his dog. He had kept sneaking glances over at the mastiff throughout their conversation. In fact, Dem had a pleasant, even sweet nature, but James had never seen a reason to ease anyone's mind about it.

"No. I think that's everything." He had wrapped up every detail; there should be no confusion or encumbrances or dangling ends in his estate. Even though he wouldn't be here to see it, James disliked a lack of order. If he left it to his family, they would muck it up and eventually toss it all in Graeme's lap to untangle. There was no point in subjecting his cousin to that.

"Um . . ." The agent shifted on his feet. "Mrs. Hobart?"

"Ah, yes. Mrs. Hobart . . ." James had forgotten about her—and wouldn't that have sent that brown-eyed beauty into a snit if she had known?

"Yes, sir. She, ah, came by the office last week."

"Did she now? How enterprising of her."

"She'd heard you were in the city. I said you were not; I assumed you would not, um, that you, ah . . ."

"You assumed correctly."

Dem let out a deep bark, which made Mr. Johnson jump. The animal surged to his feet, facing the doorway, on alert. There were footsteps in the hall, and James's cousin appeared in the doorway. The mastiff gave a wag of his tail and padded over to regally offer his head for a pat.

James's visitor obliged, saying, "Hallo, Dem, I believe you've grown even more enormous since I saw you last."

"Hello, Graeme."

"James." Graeme's blue gaze went to James's agent, and he hesitated.

"Johnson, sir," the man supplied.

"Yes, of course. How are you? I believe last time I saw you, you were awaiting a happy event."

"Were you?" James glanced at his agent. Trust Graeme to remember such niceties.

"Yes, sir." Johnson beamed. "Thank you for asking. We have a bouncing baby boy, healthy as an ox, I'm happy to say. And you, my lord, I believe you and Lady Montclair have been blessed as well."

"Indeed."

James watched as an equally fatuous smile spread across his cousin's face. He resigned himself to a discussion of the wonders of infants. It did little to distract him from the knife of pain behind his right eye. His fingers twitched, and he curled them into his palm.

Graeme, glancing over at James, broke off his effusions. "But I have interrupted you. I apologize. I shall return later."

"No." James straightened. "Stay. We are finished here." He turned to Johnson. "Buy Mrs. Hobart some jewelry, a necklace and earrings." He paused. He had been with her for some time; it tended to raise expectations. "Maybe a bracelet as well. You'll know what to get better than I."

"Certainly, sir." Johnson paused, then went on delicately, "You'll wish to add a note?"

"Oh. Yes." That was the last thing he wanted to do with his head in this vise. But of course he must. It was expected. Seizing a piece of paper from a drawer in his desk, James frowned for a moment over the page, then scribbled a few words and signed it. Hastily, he blew on the ink to dry it, folded the note, and handed it to Johnson.

Graeme watched the procedure, his face a study in astonishment, and when the agent had exited the room, he swung back to James, saying, "You are, I take it, breaking it off with your mistress?"

"Obviously." James lifted a brow. "I don't know why you're surprised. It's been months."

"Yes, but I would have thought—it's just—you're not going to tell her good-bye?"

"I just did."

"With a note."

"And some very nice diamonds. Believe me, she'll appreciate those far more than a few words from me." He gave Graeme a half smile. "Don't worry about bruising Ellie Hobart's heart, coz. She doesn't have one. That's why I choose not to indulge in romantic encounters. There's no emotion involved, only cash. No fuss and no tears."

"No affection."

James shrugged. "I don't keep a mistress for affection. Come. Sit down. Would you care for a drink? Whiskey?" Graeme agreed, taking a seat in one of the armchairs before the fireplace as James crossed to the decanters. "What are you doing in London? I would have thought you couldn't tear yourself away from domestic bliss."

"It wasn't easy." Graeme took the glass James held out to him, his concerned gaze on James's face. "I had to come to the city for business. I already miss Abby and Anna like the devil."

"Of course." James knew Graeme was speaking only the truth, astonishing as it was to James that anyone would prefer to live with a squalling infant.

"You should see her, James." Graeme's eyes lit up. "A full head of hair, jet black, just like Abby's. She looks like her."

James had seen the baby in question and as he remembered, she had not looked like much of anyone, only a tiny red wailing thing with a madly wobbling chin. He did recall, however, a burst of black hair spiking out all over her head like the raised hackles of a dog.

"It's been only three months since you've seen her, but you cannot imagine how much she's grown." Graeme went on to enthusiastically detail the many changes.

Fortunately, Graeme did not require much response from his listener, for James heard only half of what he said through the pain that gripped him. The headaches came more and more frequently now, until at times he wanted to bash his head against the wall in search of blissful unconsciousness.

Graeme, watching him, stopped his flow of words. "James. What's the matter? You look terrible."

"Why, thank you, cousin. I am glad to know you don't feel the need to flatter me."

"You know what I mean. You look as if you haven't slept in a week."

"I probably haven't." He gave Graeme a thin smile. "I've had a little trouble sleeping lately."

"I'd wager it's more than that. You've lost weight as well. Are you ill? What is it?"

"Apparently, the doctors can't agree on that. I've discovered recently the true depth of medical ignorance."

Graeme frowned. "How many doctors have you seen? How long has this been going on? Does Aunt Tessa know about it?"

"God, Graeme, what in the world do you think my mother could do?"

"Point taken. But, really, James, you can't just sit here and suffer."

"Sadly, I have discovered that I can."

"You should go see Dr. Hinsdale."

"Who? You mean *your* Miss Hinsdale's father?"

"She's not *my* Miss Hinsdale. But yes. His family views him as a bit of a disgrace since he chose to actually do something useful with his life, but he's one of the brightest men I know. Always up on the latest thing."

"Thank you, but I suspect I'd be lucky to survive passing through his door, if the lovely Laura is there."

"Don't be absurd. Laura may, um . . ."

"Despise me?"

"Don't be daft. Laura isn't the sort to hold grudges. She knew you were only speaking the truth."

"Mm. But truth is not something many people relish hearing."

"Trust me. However she may feel about you, she would never turn you away. She is much too fair, not to mention kind."

"Doesn't your wife object to your blatant admiration for Miss Hinsdale?"

"Abby is much too fair, as well."

James had to chuckle, despite the pounding in his head. "All your women are paragons."

Graeme grinned. "Yes, I know. I'm a lucky man. But Laura is not mine. And Abby knows that I feel about Laura as one would about a sister."

"Of course . . . if one had wanted to marry one's sister."

"That was eleven years ago. I was too green to understand what I felt. What I'm saying is, Abby knows I love only her. And stop trying to get me off the subject. We're talking about you seeing Dr. Hinsdale."

"Must we?"

"Yes. If anyone can find what's wrong with you and fix it, Dr. Hinsdale can."

"I'm tired of chasing a magical cure. I think I shall go home soon. Things are in order here."

"In order? What are you talking about?" Graeme's voice rose in alarm. "You sound as if—James, you're frightening me." He paused, then added, "It's not like you to give up."

James huffed out an exasperated laugh. "You're bringing out the heavy artillery now. Next you'll be telling me it's for queen and country."

"Don't be a buffoon. You know very well it's for me. For all of us who love you. I don't want to lose you, James. Go see Dr. Hinsdale."

"You're bloody persistent." James sighed. He was tired of hope; he was tired of fighting. And he was most excessively tired of keeping a stiff upper lip. "Where is this medical miracle worker?"

"You know where. You went there to talk Laura into breaking our engagement."

"Ah. Yes. Close to Canterbury. Rather out of the way."

"It's not the ends of the earth. An easy day's trip from here. I'll take you."

"No! No." James saw the faint hurt on the other man's face, but he couldn't explain why he'd rather be alone. It was simply easier not to have to maintain the façade of stoicism. He tried to soften his abrupt words. "You have business to do, and you must get back to your wife and daughter. I'll go to Canterbury before I return home."

"Promise?"

"Yes, yes. I'll take a bloody oath on it. Now can we talk about something else?"

Satisfied, Graeme left the tender subject and returned to more raptures on the bliss of fatherhood, relieving James of the burden of conversation or, indeed, of even really listening. James leaned back, letting the familiar tones of his cousin's voice wash over him.

James came to with a start, his heart pounding, his breath jerking in a gasp that set off a paroxysm of coughing. Graeme was gone. Thank God. At least he had not witnessed the wracking cough. It was embarrassing enough that James had fallen asleep in front of his cousin, like some decrepit ancient. The rest of the time he could not sleep, yearning to slip into oblivion, yet today, with someone there, he could not keep his eyes open.

With a snort of disgust, James pushed up from his chair. The butler would appear soon, no doubt, to pester him with afternoon tea, laying out an array of delicacies with his ever-hopeful expression. James thought of escaping, but there was nowhere else to go, nothing to be done. He had just spoken to the only person whom he would regret never seeing again.

Dem heaved to his feet and padded after James as he left the study and walked down the hall. He stopped at a door that was smaller, plainer than most in the house, for the small room inside had been refashioned from what had once been the butler's pantry.

Dem sat down, letting out an almost human sigh. James smiled faintly and brushed a hand over the top of the dog's blocky head. "That's right. It's the place you cannot enter." He rubbed his thumb across the wrinkles that gave the dog his perpetually grave look. "I apologize."

James stepped inside, closing the door behind him,

and turned on the low gaslight. It was a small space, filled with several glass-fronted cabinets, too cramped, really, for his tastes. But it was imperative that the room be windowless and unventilated, sheltered from the touch of sunlight, air, and dampness that would ruin the ancient pages.

Not long ago, he had spent hours at a time here, carefully preserving his collection of medieval writings. Now he merely strolled past the cabinets, drinking in the beauty of the illuminated manuscripts, the gilt and jewel-like colors of the ornate letters, the cunning drawings hidden among the curlicues. Studying these painstaking works of countless monks never failed to soothe him.

Was it faith or art that fueled their efforts?

Cynically he had always assumed that it was a love of beauty that inspired the monks, the same joy and yearning that swelled in his chest as he gazed at them. But perhaps, in the good brothers, at least, that sweet ache had been faith. James was not well enough acquainted with such things to know.

He leaned his forehead against the cool glass of a display case, the vicious pain in his head increasing. His heart began its now-familiar pounding, stuttering in that way that shot a spear of panic through him. It would pass, he knew, but deep down he could not quite suppress the fear that this time it would not.

This was the last time he would see the manuscripts. He hated to leave them, but they were too delicate to pack and cart about the countryside. And his longing for the verdant gardens and spacious rooms of Grace Hill was stronger than his love of any art. It was time to go there.

But first he had to go to bloody, benighted Canterbury.

Why had he been so weak as to agree to Graeme's urgings? But he knew the answer to that—deep down inside him there still grew a tender green shoot of hope. Futile though it would doubtless turn out to be, James was unable to ignore it.

He would seek out Laura Hinsdale's father. And some irrepressible sense of mischief, some spark of humor that refused to leave him, made him smile, thinking of the look on Miss Hinsdale's face when he crossed her threshold again.

Laura gazed at the cluttered room. She had packed most of their remaining belongings, but she had not had the heart to enter her father's study. Now, looking at his books and papers haphazardly stacked and fallen and wedged in wherever they would go, the long scarred table on which sat beakers and dishes and various pots and jars, tears clogged her throat anew.

It was so unfair, so vastly unfair that a good, kind, intelligent man like her father, a man who had spent his life healing others, should be taken away at his young age when so many other men far less worthy than he survived. Venal, brutal men like Sid Merton.

She scowled at the thought of their landlord. He would be coming around today, wanting his money in full—no matter that her father had been in his grave less than two weeks. She had sold everything she could the past few days, but not many people wanted medical tomes or old, well-worn furniture. A doctor in the next village had purchased her father's instruments, and she thought one of the men with whom her father had corresponded might buy some of his library, but it was scarcely enough to pay her father's debts.

She could only hope that she could stave off Merton with

it, allowing her time to try to find the rest of the money . . . though God only knew how she would manage that feat. Panic seized her as it had several times since her father's death, flooding her chest and throat as if to choke her. What was she to do?

A heavy succession of thuds against the door of the cottage made her jump. It would be Merton. Who else would hammer so gracelessly at a house in mourning?

Laura opened the door with all the calm and dignity she could muster and faced Sid Merton. Tall and broad, he was accustomed to intimidating everyone with his size. The fact that neither Laura nor her father had allowed him to bully them had offended Merton and seemingly made him determined to prove that he was to be feared.

He started inside, but Laura neatly sidestepped him, slipping out of the house and into the yard, so that to talk to her Merton had to turn away from the door. She waited for him to speak, her face set in the calm aristocratic mask she knew he hated.

She could hear faint noises from the street in the background—the rumble of a wagon farther down the road, the swish of a broom sweeping the stoop across the street, a child's high-pitched laughter. She hoped even Sid Merton would think twice about threatening her in public view.

"Have you got it, then? I want my money." Merton scowled, thrusting out his hand.

"I have sold some of Papa's things." Laura reached into her pocket and pulled out a coin purse, opening it and pouring the contents into his outstretched palm.

"This?" He stared at the pitifully small pile in the center of his beefy hand. "This is what you're giving me?"

Laura reached into her other pocket, withdrawing two

paper pound notes, and laid them on top of the coins. "And this. It's all I've been able to get so far, but I'm sure I'll manage more if you will but give me a little time."

"That's not even half what you owe me. And that's only for the note your father signed. You're also behind in your rent. Four weeks behind." He held up his other hand, fingers spread and thumb tucked in, to demonstrate.

"Yes. I am aware how many four is," Laura retorted. "But—"

"Are you mocking me?" He took a long step forward, looming over her. "D'ya think this is a joke?"

"Believe me, I find nothing humorous in my situation."

"You think I should just let you stay here for free?"

"I'm not asking for that." Laura's hand curled her fingers into her skirts, struggling to maintain her calm. "But my father passed quite recently, as you know. It will take a bit of time for me to settle his affairs. I'll find a way to pay you the rest if you would only—"

"Oh, I could let you stay here." Merton smiled in a way that sent a shiver of dread down her spine. He reached out to wrap his thick fingers around her wrist. "If you were a bit nicer to me, maybe."

Laura stiffened, fury coursing through her. Behind her she heard the jingle of horses in harness and the roll of wheels, but she paid no attention. "I'd sooner go to debtors' prison than be 'nice' to you."

"Fine by me." He yanked her forward, and she slammed against his broad chest. Jerking her arm up behind her back, he bent over her. "I like a bit of a fight."

"Stop!" Laura wedged her other arm between them and pushed with all her strength, turning her head aside. A sharp pain shot up her twisted arm. "Let go of me!"

Behind them a man loudly cleared his voice. "I beg your pardon."

Merton straightened to glare over Laura's head at the man who had dared interrupt him. His grip slackened enough for Laura to turn, easing the pain in her shoulder, and edge away from Merton.

A tall, thin man, his face shadowed by a hat, stood at the edge of their yard, a team of horses and a carriage behind him. His pose was studiedly careless, weight on one leg and a hand resting lightly on the head of a gold-knobbed cane. In a cool, faintly bored voice, steeped in aristocratic hauteur, he went on, "It appears your suit is unwelcome to the lady."

"What business is it of yours?" Merton snarled.

"Well, you see, I have come to speak with her father." He swept off his hat and sketched a bow to Laura. "Good afternoon, Miss Hinsdale. I hope I have not arrived at an inopportune time."

"James de Vere?" Laura stared. Graeme's cousin was the last person she expected to see in her yard. He looked older and thinner than the last time she'd seen him, when he'd come to inform her that she must give up the man she loved. But he was just as coldly handsome, his tone as supercilious. It was humiliating that he of all people should find her grappling with Sid Merton in front of her house. Even more humiliating, given her current situation, she must hope for his help.

Beside her, Merton let out a short, harsh laugh. "I wish you luck with that."

Sir James's brows lifted faintly at the words, but he ignored Merton, saying, "If you would be so kind, Miss Hinsdale, I would appreciate a bit of your time. If, of course, you are not otherwise occupied."

"I am perfectly free." Laura took another step away, jerking her arm as hard as she could. Merton's grip did not loosen.

"You're not going anywhere," Merton growled.

James turned a disdainful gaze on him. "You, my good man, are becoming tiresome."

"Tiresome!" Merton gaped at him.

"Time you left, don't you think?"

"No, I don't think." Merton tossed back James's words in a smug, singsong mockery.

"Mm. Clearly."

The large man flushed with anger. Naturally, Sir James would come to one's rescue in an irritating manner. Even the way he stood was insulting, too certain he would have his way to bother bracing for a fight. His arrogance would probably cow many men, but Sid Merton was a bully used to relying on his size and his fists to get what he wanted. It would take more than a haughty attitude to intimidate him.

"Sir James . . ." Laura began in a conciliatory fashion, hoping she could convey to him the need to tread lightly.

Both men ignored her.

"You're the one who's leaving." Merton scowled menacingly, his free hand knotting into a fist.

"I think not. For the last time, release Miss Hinsdale and go."

Merton let out a scornful laugh, making a show of looking the other man up and down. "You think you're going to make me?"

"No." James smiled thinly. He snapped his fingers, and the largest dog Laura had ever seen jumped out of the open carriage door. "He is."

chapter 3

There was a dead silence as both Laura and Merton gaped at the dog. The top of his square head was level with James's waist—and James was a tall man. The animal's muscular body was a mottled combination of black and yellowish tan, but the muzzle and face were entirely black, as if he wore a mask, and it rendered his eyes barely visible, giving him an even more sinister appearance.

James flicked his hand toward Laura. "Guard her."

The dog stalked over—he was even more terrifying at close range—and took up a stance beside Laura, fixing Merton with his unswerving gaze. Color drained from the big man's face and he dropped Laura's arm. Shooting her a final vicious look, Merton whirled and strode away, not glancing in Sir James's direction.

Laura's stunned gaze followed him for a moment, then went to James. Gratitude mingled awkwardly with her years-old dislike. "I, um, thank you."

Sir James gave a careless shrug and strolled toward her. As he drew close, she could see that purplish shadows were smudged beneath his eyes and his face was etched with lines of weariness. "I could hardly allow the churl to accost you. And he was annoying me."

Obviously Sir James accepted gratitude as gracelessly as he did everything else. Laura looked down at the dog. Her gaze hadn't very far to go. The animal regarded her gravely, the thick wrinkles above his eyes giving him a worried look.

"And thank you," she told the dog. He accepted the compliment better than his master, giving a single wag of his tail as he continued to study her. Laura was someone who generally liked dogs, but this one made her a trifle wary. "May I pet him?"

"You're wise to ask." James might look older and more worn, but his voice was the same, delivering whatever he said in a cool, faintly ironic tone, dipping now and then into ice but never warming. She remembered it well; their last conversation had lingered in her thoughts for a long time. "But, yes, you may touch him. He's not likely to bite your hand off."

"Not likely? That's reassuring." She stroked her hand across the wrinkled head. He allowed her caress without losing any of his dignity—no tail-beating, rear-end-wiggling, hand-licking response from him. His calm steady gaze was a trifle unnerving. "Trust you to have a pet that terrifies people."

She thought the noise James made was a chuckle. "Trust you not to back away from him."

Had he just given her a compliment? It seemed unlikely. "What's his name?"

"Demosthenes."

"Demosthenes?" Her eyes flicked up to his. "The orator?"

"And seeker of truth." James gave her a faint smile that didn't reach his eyes; it was the only kind she had ever seen on his face. "He has a knack for pulling the truth out of people."

"Mm. I imagine he can be very persuasive." Laura smiled.

James shifted and cleared his throat. "Miss Hinsdale . . . as I told that oaf, I've come to see your father. Is Dr. Hinsdale in?"

Unexpectedly, tears filled Laura's eyes. She had not cried for a few days, but somehow now, at his casual mention of her father's name, she was pierced all anew. She could see James's eyes widen slightly, his faint but unmistakable pulling back.

"What—" he began, but left the sentence dangling.

"Papa died two weeks ago," she told him baldly. No need to couch things in a genteel manner with this man.

Despair gazed back at her for an instant before the mask descended once again on James's face. "I see." His hand tightened on the head of his cane and he appeared to lean on it now rather than use it as a whim of fashion. "Well, that's that, then." He glanced away. "My condolences." Then, awkwardly, "I am sorry, Laura."

"Thank you." The use of her given name startled her; he had not addressed her so since they were children. Though he was Graeme's cousin, he had never been Laura's friend. But there was a genuineness to his brief statement that unexpectedly touched her. "Would you like to come in?"

He looked as if he needed to sit down.

"Oh. Well." James's face was tinged with an uncertainty she had never seen in him. "Yes, thank you."

He followed her into the house, pausing at the doorway. "Perhaps you'd rather Dem not enter."

"Why?" She looked over at the dog. "He was my rescuer, after all."

"He is also rather large, and he has a deplorable tendency to, um, salivate."

As if to demonstrate, Dem shook himself vigorously, sending slobber flying from his drooping jowls. Laura laughed. Somehow it made the impassive dog less intimidating.

"I see what you mean. Still, he deserves a treat, don't you think? I suspect we can handle a bit of a shower."

Both man and dog trailed after her as she went into the kitchen. Filling a large bowl with water, she set it down on the floor. While Demosthenes lapped up water, she fished through a pan on the stove, coming up with a bone, which she placed on a plate beside the dog.

"You have made a friend for life."

At James's words, Laura turned toward him. He stood in the doorway, still perfectly straight, but there was something unutterably weary in his face. He was ill; that would be why he had come to see her father. It must be something dire to have led him here. Not, of course, that he would deign to tell her. She gestured toward the kitchen table.

"Won't you sit down? Or perhaps you'd rather sit in the parlor." Sir James was not the sort of man who visited in the kitchen.

"This is fine."

"Would you care for tea?" She moved to the stove to heat the kettle without waiting for an answer.

"Thank you, no," he replied, but when she set the cups down on the table a few minutes later, he took a sip.

It was exceedingly strange to be sitting at the kitchen table with Sir James de Vere, sharing tea. Laura cast about for something to say. "I'm sorry you came all this way. Can I help you, perhaps, or . . ." Laura trailed off.

"Thank you, no," he said again, with as little emotion as he had earlier rejected her offer of tea. "It was a professional matter. Graeme suggested it. Clearly, he was not aware of your father's passing."

"No." Laura shook her head. "I haven't written his mother yet. It must be such a happy time at Lydcombe Hall, with the new baby. I hated to bring up anything sad."

"I am sure Aunt Mirabelle would want to know, however. And Graeme."

"Yes, she's always been very kind to me. She and my mother were close friends."

"I remember. I shall tell them, if you wish, when I reach Grace Hill."

"Thank you. Pray tell her that I will write soon."

Another silence fell. The dog's crunching of the bone seemed inordinately loud.

"What sort of dog is he?" Laura dredged up another topic.

"A mastiff. He's a good watchdog, though not as fierce as he looks."

"I would think his appearance would suffice."

James smiled faintly. "Generally." He glanced around at the emptied cabinets and filled boxes. "What will you do now?"

"I haven't decided. Perhaps I'll go to my father's relatives." Laura could not entirely keep her distaste for that idea from coloring her voice, so she forced a smile to negate it.

"I am sure Aunt Mirabelle would be happy for you to visit, um . . ." He cleared his throat. Laura suspected he had belatedly realized the awkwardness of Laura's presence in the house of the man who had once loved her.

"Yes, Lady Montclair is very kind, but the situation is—it hardly seems the time to intrude upon them. The new baby . . ."

"Of course. Well, I . . ." He pushed up from the table. "I should go."

She stood up, as well, relieved to be rid of him—though she would rather miss the reassuring presence of the enormous dog stretched out on her kitchen floor, gnawing at the soup bone. For a moment her home felt warm again, as it had on so many nights when she sat with her father in this very room, talking about his research or an unusual medical case.

James hesitated. "About that fellow . . . will he return?"

"I feel sure he learned his lesson." That was a lie. Merton would doubtless be back tomorrow; he wouldn't give up the money her father owed him. But she wasn't about to reveal all the miserable details of her life to James de Vere. She would simply have to manage to stay out of Merton's clutches.

"But . . ." From the way he frowned, she suspected James didn't believe her. He would probably also guess that the man had been hounding her for money. He had seen the small cottage and its rather shabby furniture. It made her cringe to imagine what his thoughts were.

"I'll be fine." Laura squared her shoulders, smiling determinedly. "Thank you once again."

Her tone was dismissive, and after a moment's hesitation, James bowed and took his leave of her, slapping his hand against his thigh to summon Demosthenes. The dog arose ponderously and followed him, bone still clenched between his teeth.

Laura stood in the doorway, watching her visitors depart. Sir James attempted to dissuade the mastiff from bringing his prize into the carriage, but finally he lifted his hands in a gesture of defeat and motioned for Demosthenes to jump in, bone and all. Apparently Demosthenes's powers of persuasion worked on his master, as well. It was almost enough to make one like the man. Almost.

She shut the door and turned the lock. Drifting to the window in the parlor, she stood, looking out at their minuscule garden. But she did not see the tall spikes of purple irises or the riot of red roses climbing the trellis.

All she could see was Sir James in this room eleven years ago as he hammered the nineteen-year-old Laura's dreams of a life with Graeme into dust. It was unfair to blame him. Sir James had not forced her to give up Graeme. He could not have compelled his cousin to marry an American heiress.

He had simply told her, as swift and sharp as a knife, that her continued engagement to the man she loved would ruin him. Graeme was too much a gentleman to break off their engagement himself, so Laura must do it. James had ripped aside the rosy veil through which Laura had been viewing the world those last few months and made her face the truth.

And for that, she could not like him. She had managed to avoid seeing him again, an easy enough task given that Laura was in London only infrequently and James scorned the social whirl. Time had covered the old wound. Passion subsided and memories faded. Her love for Graeme had not died, exactly, but it had settled down to present regard and a wistful memory.

Laura was truly glad that he had come to love his wife . . . though she was human enough to wish sometimes that his wife were not quite so stunning. She found it was possible to live a happy life without Graeme. For companionship, she had had her father—and indeed, what would the man have done without her there to see his socks were darned, his schedules met, and his meals cooked? As for the rest of the emotions she had felt during those brief months of love with Graeme so long ago: the heat, the yearning, the uprush of joy, well, she had managed without them.

Still, it was something of a shock to see Sir James, a painful relic from her past rising up to disturb her in the here and now. She wondered what disease was eating away at his vitality. However cold, he had been a figure of power, of strength—tall, leanly muscled, implacable. Something like his dog, now that she thought about it. It was strangely disturbing to see him ill. She could not help but remember when she had told him her father was not there and for a brief moment his face had been unguarded—and utterly hopeless.

Laura grimaced and turned away from the window. Why was she standing here thinking about James de Vere? She ought to be worrying about her own situation, which was decidedly bleak. Her father was dead, whatever pittance of income she had now gone. Even if she managed to sell all their possessions, it would not pull her completely out of debt. And the man to whom she owed money was a remorseless pig.

Sir James de Vere didn't matter. She would never see him again.

James let out a sigh and leaned his head back against the seat. He'd managed to escape Laura's home without completely humiliating himself. It had been a harsh blow to discover that even the ephemeral hope of Graeme's medical marvel, Dr. Hinsdale, was gone. For a moment, he'd felt weak, and he had feared he was about to ignominiously crumple to the ground under Miss Hinsdale's disapproving gaze.

"Do you think the lovely Miss Hinsdale was telling the truth about that oaf?" he asked Dem. The dog cast a glance up at him and went back to his bone. "No, neither do I. He'll be back to bother her. No doubt her father left her in debt. That's generally the way with saints."

He would have to take care of it. Graeme and his mother would want it. Truth was, James himself had disliked the sight of those meaty fingers wrapped around Laura's arm. He was, after all, a man who appreciated beauty. And however prickly Miss Hinsdale was, there was no denying her loveliness—the porcelain skin, the crown of golden hair, the deep blue eyes. He might be sick, but he wasn't blind.

The prospect of browbeating the large man cheered

James a little. But he could not manage it tonight. His head was throbbing . . . and now that blasted hand was starting to shake. He gazed down in a detached way at his fingers jerking and twitching on the seat beside him, as if operated by some unseen puppeteer.

Muttering a curse, James rapped his gold-knobbed cane against the ceiling, and when the carriage rolled to a halt, he told the coachman, "Turn around. We'll spend the night here. I saw an inn at the edge of the village."

It was doubtless shabby and furnished with lumpy mattresses, but it scarcely mattered. He could lie awake staring at the ceiling there as easily as anywhere else. At least he wouldn't be jouncing about in the coach. Lately his joints had begun to ache like an old man's.

Bloody hell. He would *not* dwell on his condition. He turned his thoughts instead to Laura Hinsdale. He wondered why she had never married. It would have been disastrous for Graeme to wed her, of course, but surely there must have been a number of wealthy men who would want her for her face and form even with her lack of fortune.

She probably wouldn't have landed an earl, but Miss Hinsdale didn't seem to covet a title. Perhaps she was just too choosy about her offers. Or still in love with his cousin. That idea struck James as absurd, but then, most things about love did. Attraction he could understand; even he had been swept by passion. Fondness. Affection. A preference for a certain person's company. But he had never really grasped the desire to tie oneself to someone, to give over one's heart.

His mouth twitched up at one corner. Of course, there were those who said James de Vere did not possess a heart. He would have been inclined to agree if only that organ did not thunder and clench inside his chest as if about to cease altogether.

The innkeeper looked somewhat askance at the enormous dog at James's side, but graciously admitted him when James offered an extra coin. James climbed the stairs to his room, using his cane for aid rather than fashion since there was no one here to see it.

The room was small, but Demosthenes managed to turn around in it enough times to satisfy himself before he curled up on the floor. To James's surprise, the place was clean if somewhat shabby, and it had a window. James gazed out at the dusk settling over the town.

It was well and truly over now. He had to face it. Who would have thought that thirty-four would be the sum of his years?

He had always assumed he had years and years to live out his life, that there would be plenty of time before he had to buckle himself to a wife and produce children. He'd meant to leave Grace Hill to a son. But now it looked as though he'd have to leave it all to his brother Claude.

James turned away and began to undress. He'd never had a valet. It seemed idiotic to pay for the irritation of someone fussing over him. A time would come when he would have to hire one, of course, to do all the things he would no longer be able to. But not yet. He could still avoid that humiliation.

He climbed into bed, knowing he was unlikely to fall asleep, and if he did manage it, he would doubtless awaken after an hour or two. But one clung to the structures of one's life. As he lay there, drifting in that netherworld between wakefulness and sleep, a new thought came to him. And he smiled into the darkness.

Laura marched into her father's study the next morning, determined to make up for the pitiful effort she had put into clearing it out yesterday. She worked in her usual organized fashion. Journals went into a trunk—no one would want to purchase those and she couldn't bear to throw them away. Loose papers she scanned and usually tossed into the ashcan. Only now and then, when she happened across her father's pipe or found his favorite woolen scarf beneath a pile of books, did tears blind her vision.

She had to keep on. It was the one constructive thing she could do. She would not think about the piano that would have to be sold. She ought to sell her violin, too, but, oh, how could she bear to? It was small, and surely she could keep one thing she loved.

Nor would she dwell on the fact that she would never again have a home of her own. At thirty, she was long past the age of marrying. As a penniless single female, she would be thrown on the mercy of her relatives, part object of pity, part unsalaried employee. Her only other recourse was to become a governess, trying to shove knowledge into the minds of wealthy children, a future that seemed equally unappealing.

There were few other occupations for a woman. She could sell hats in a millinery shop or try to make a living as a seamstress. But her needlework left much to be desired, and one had only to look at her own plain bonnet to realize she had no talent there.

She supposed she could become a nurse; she had helped her father enough, after all. The furor it would cause among her father's relatives was almost enough to make it appealing. But it would appall and embarrass her aunt, as well, and she wouldn't do that to her mother's dear sister. Besides, it hadn't been dealing with people's illnesses that she had enjoyed as much as aiding her father's research—and, admittedly, organizing his life.

Unfortunately, there was no career in managing lives, and her one gift, that of music, was a poor way to earn a living, even for a man. No, she was doomed to spend the rest of her life as a companion or governess.

Laura was startled from her gloomy thoughts by a sharp rapping at the front door. Her heart leapt into her throat. Merton must have come back. She rose to her feet, smoothing down her skirts and giving her nerves a moment to settle before she went to open it.

The knock sounded again, followed this time by an unexpected voice. "Miss Hinsdale? It is I. De Vere."

"Sir James?" Laura opened the door. It was indeed him, the enormous dog sitting beside him. For a moment all three of them simply stared at each other.

"Miss Hinsdale?" He raised one black eyebrow. "Have I come at an inopportune time?"

"Oh." She stepped back. "I beg your pardon. I was surprised to see you again. Please, come in."

Demosthenes slipped past James with surprising agility for an animal so large and headed toward the kitchen. At the door, the dog turned to gaze back at Laura with an expression so humanly expectant that she chuckled.

"I hope you have another soup bone hidden about or Demosthenes will be severely disappointed," James told her.

"I imagine I can find him something." She followed Dem into the kitchen and rummaged around, finally coming up with a bone. The mastiff took it neatly from her hand, and flopped down on the stone floor to enjoy his gift. Laura, a smile lingering on her lips, looked back to James. "Did you come just for the bone?"

"No." A corner of his mouth twitched in what she thought might be amusement. "I have a question to ask of you."

"Very well."

He glanced about. "Perhaps we could sit somewhere more, um . . ."

"Formal?"

"I was going to say, more suited to the, ah, moment."

"What moment?" Laura asked warily.

"Are you always so suspicious?"

"No, but I have had conversations with you before."

"Oh, the devil." The hint of amusement on his face turned to irritation. "I'm not here to blight your life. I have come to propose an arrangement of mutual benefit."

Laura stared, her mind reeling. "Pardon? Are you—are you offering to make me your mistress?"

He was the one who stared now. "Good God!" To her amazement, a flush rose in his cheeks. "No, Miss Hinsdale, I am not here to purchase your nubile body, entrancing as I am sure it is."

Laura crossed her arms over her chest. "Just what *are* you here for?"

"I have come to ask for your hand in marriage."

Laura plopped down onto the nearest chair, his words so far from anything she expected to hear from him that she could hardly grasp it. Finally, weakly, she asked, "Are you joking?"

"I rarely jest about marriage, I assure you."

She blinked. "I . . . uh . . . why?"

"I would think the advantages are clear. I hope it is not

vain of me to point out that you would have a much more agreeable future than the one you are currently facing, which offers penury and the less-than-alluring prospect of throwing yourself on your relatives' generosity. I can give you a gracious home, a generous allowance, and a respectable, dare I say honored, name."

He sounded as if he were offering her employment. "No. I mean why would *you* want to? What possible reason could you have for proposing to me?" Long-buried resentment bubbled in her. Laura popped back up. "If I was not good enough to be Graeme's wife, as you so kindly told me, how could I possibly be acceptable as yours?"

It was some balm to her feelings that James looked taken aback. "I never said you were unworthy. The only issue was saving the Montclair estate. I can assure you I did not question your character. In fact, it was precisely your good character I counted on. Once you understood how ruinous it would be for Graeme to wed you, you would break it off. I knew I could use your sense of honor against you."

"What a cold and calculating man you are." His words were mollifying, at least in regard to his opinion of her, but it amazed her that he would admit it. "It's hard to believe you're related to Graeme."

"It's a wonder, is it not? But I have never tried to appear anything except what I am."

"I don't know that that makes it any better." She studied him. "I must say, however, that I fail to see any cold calculation in proposing to me."

He gave her a wry look. "I would guess that most women would regard marriage to me a cold thing indeed."

"No doubt. But that's not an explanation. It isn't as if you like me. You barely know me. And I am relatively certain I am not the sort of woman whom you would choose."

"You're right," he shot back, annoyed. "You are not at all the sort of woman I planned to marry. However, at the moment my choices are rather limited."

"I can understand why if this is your manner of wooing."

"I have not tried to 'woo' anyone else."

Laura stared. "I am your first attempt at a proposal?"

"Yes."

"But why? Why would you choose *me*?"

"I am beginning to wonder that myself." When Laura said nothing, merely crossed her arms and waited, James continued, "I chose you because I thought you were in such exigent circumstances you would agree."

"Well, at least you are candid."

"I usually am."

"Then let me be equally straightforward. I may be in exigent circumstances, but I would rather remain in my penniless state, here in my ungracious home, with my unrespectable name, than share your bed."

He let out a dry laugh, surprising her. "Trust me, Miss Hinsdale, the way I feel now, lust is the furthest thing from my mind."

"What about in the future?"

He looked at her flatly. "There won't be any future."

Nonplussed, Laura simply stared at him. James released a long sigh and sank onto one of the chairs at the table, gesturing wearily at the other. "Please, sit down. Let me begin again."

"Very well." She sat down on the edge of the seat, as if any action might break the fragile truce.

James looked straight into her eyes. "I am dying."

Laura sucked in her breath. "You are sure? That's why you came to see Papa?"

"Yes, on both counts. I have spent the past several weeks going from one doctor to another. I have been diagnosed with everything from a bad heart to brain fever to tumors. But all are agreed on one thing: I am not long for this world." He delivered his news with a flat calm, almost as if he were discussing someone else.

"Oh." Laura's face softened.

"I don't want your pity." His voice was sharp and cold. "I am telling you this so you understand I have no intention of robbing you of your virtue. I won't demand my husbandly rights. And you will not have to be my wife long before you are my widow. At that time you will inherit nearly everything except the title and the estate attached to it, which must go to my brother Claude. In short, I am offering you a golden opportunity."

"But why?" she asked softly. "Why would you wish to leave all that to me?"

"What I wish is to *not* leave all that to them."

"Who?"

"My family."

"You intend to disinherit your family?" She gaped at him. "You feel nothing for them?"

"Little that is good."

"Well." Laura sat back. "I suppose I shouldn't be surprised, given your reputation for caring for no one."

"That's not entirely true. I care for my dog. And I am entrusting him to you."

He really meant it, Laura realized. He was dying. And however bizarre it was, however impersonal, he was offering to marry her. "This is absurd."

"I had some difficulty believing it myself."

Laura blushed. "I'm sorry. I didn't mean—"

"No need to apologize. As I've said, I prefer straight speech."

"It's just—this is so odd, so—I cannot help but think you are making sport of me."

James leaned forward, resting one arm on the table. His eyes were silver in their intensity, and the piercing gaze he directed at her caused an odd, uneasy feeling in her very center.

"I don't play games, Miss Hinsdale. However low you may think me, I do not lie. Did I deceive you when I told you Graeme's circumstances? Did I try to soften it in any way when I said you must give him up?"

"No, you certainly did not." She felt on more solid ground here. "But neither do you do anything without good reason."

"Perhaps I'm hoping to atone for my past sins," he told her lightly. He turned to look out the window, his face momentarily bleak. "Or maybe I just don't want to face the end alone."

He stood up abruptly, his chair scraping across the stone. "Much as I relish sitting here exchanging barbs with you, Miss Hinsdale, as you might guess, I haven't the time to spare. What is your answer?" He went on in a needling tone, "Will you throw yourself off the wall, like a perfect heroine of Scott's, rather than marry this black-hearted villain?"

Laura glared. The moment one began to feel a bit of sympathy for the man, he immediately trampled all over it with his sarcastic goading. She would have liked to throw his offer back in his face, just to thwart him. But she was all too aware of the hard, lonely future that awaited her and, admittedly, too pragmatic to let annoyance rule her.

"No. I mean, yes. Oh, bother. What I'm trying to say is I am no romantic heroine. And however mad you may be, I accept your offer of marriage."

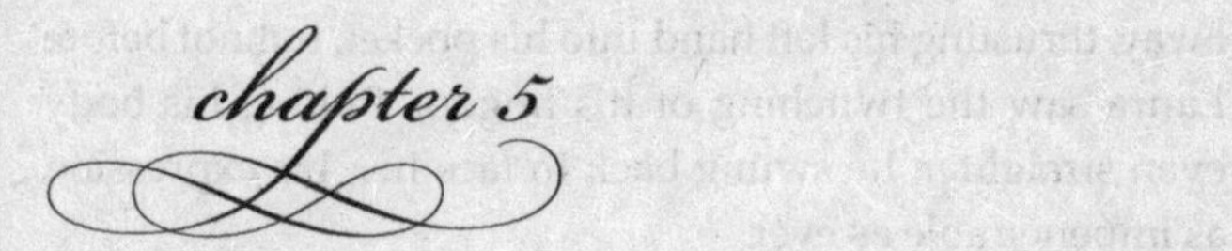

chapter 5

"You do me great honor." James made her an elegant bow, but there was no mistaking the irritating smugness that danced in his gray eyes. He straightened, all business again. "Fortunately, Canterbury is close, so I can obtain the special license this afternoon. I shall make arrangements for the ceremony tomorrow, if that meets your approval. I presume you would prefer it done in the church."

"Yes, I suppose," she replied, a trifle dazed by his swift disposition of her life.

"You may find the haste unseemly, but I see no reason to cool our heels here for two weeks, waiting for the banns to be read. Besides, best to tie it up now, lest you have to roll me down the aisle in a bath chair, drooling."

"Sir James!"

"What?" He raised his brows. "You may as well get used to it."

"Used to what?" she retorted. "Your drooling or your irritating manner?"

"Why, both, I suppose." A grin flashed across his face.

It struck Laura suddenly how very handsome James de Vere was. She had known he was good-looking, but she had viewed him too much as an enemy to see him as a man. A blush tinted her cheeks at the thought.

Fortunately, James was not looking at her. He turned away, thrusting his left hand into his pocket, but not before Laura saw the twitching of his fingers. Pulling his body even straighter, he swung back to face her, his expression as impenetrable as ever.

"Hire someone to help you pack whatever you want to keep. I'd prefer to leave after the ceremony tomorrow morning." James reached inside his jacket and pulled out a coin purse, tossing it onto the table. "There's a bit of money to pay them and take care of any outstanding accounts. If you need more, I shall see to it when I return. No need to bother with Merton. I've talked to him."

Laura stared. "You paid that debt?"

"I can hardly have my wife owing money all over the countryside."

"You did it before you knew whether I would accept your proposal." The thought of his generosity warmed her.

"It would have been a handy lever in case you refused."

"So you intended to use it to coerce my agreement."

"Only if it was necessary." He quirked a brow. "Come, come, Miss Hinsdale. The fact that I'm dying doesn't mean I'm virtuous."

Laura grimaced. "Well, at least you make it less upsetting to watch you die."

"Indeed. You might even come to enjoy it." He turned aside without waiting for her response. "I shall leave Dem with you." At the mention of his name, the dog came to his feet and padded across the room. James's face softened fractionally. "No, boy, you're staying here. You must look after Miss Hinsdale." James reached out and took Laura's hand, startling her. He placed it atop the dog's blocky head, covering her hand with his own. "Guard her, Dem. She is ours now."

Laura stood perfectly still. His words sent the oddest sensation through her. She kept her gaze on the dog, unable to look into James's face. She wasn't sure what she feared he would see there, but with James, it was wise not to give anything away.

"Good day, Miss Hinsdale. I shall see you later this afternoon." With a perfunctory nod, James turned and left the room.

"Well." Laura felt numb and strangely removed.

It had unsettled her to notice how attractive James was. She wasn't sure why, exactly; perhaps it made him a person instead of a conveniently featureless villain from her past. A real person whose eyes could dance with amusement, whose thick black lashes could make a woman sigh with envy . . . or desire.

One would assume illness would mar his looks, but instead, the lines of pain and the shadows beneath his eyes had softened the cold perfection of his features, and though he was much thinner than he should be, that had only heightened the soaring cheekbones. It was as if the disease had burned away any softening layers, leaving behind only the fierce beauty of bone and skin.

But it was not his looks that left her troubled, nor her unexpected involuntary reaction to them. It wasn't even the odd way he had taken her hand and told Dem she belonged to them. No, the problem was she had betrayed her beliefs.

Laura had sworn she would marry for love, not position or wealth or even companionship. When that dream was thwarted eleven years ago, she had resigned herself to life as a spinster. Over the years, even as her youthful passion faded, she had clung to the idea that she could marry only for love.

Yet here she was, tying herself to a man with barely a flicker of consideration in order to secure a comfortable life for herself. Oh, she could defend her decision. She was not deceiving James by pretending she loved him. Nor was she selling her body; he had promised her that, and however she felt about James, she was certain he would keep his word. It was a bargain, pure and simple, and eminently practical on both sides.

Still, it was lowering to acknowledge that she was marrying for pragmatic reasons, not love. But when she thought of the alternative—a life spent scrabbling to make ends meet, burdened with her father's debts, and always at the beck and call of others—she knew that if given the choice again, she would do the same thing. She had made a bargain, and not with the devil, only with an annoying man. All she could do now was get on with it.

Laura turned and found herself facing the giant dog. Demosthenes sat in the middle of the hall, regarding her patiently. She felt a twinge of unease at being alone with the animal. He could snap her arm with a single bite. At the same time, his presence was reassuring. She need not worry about Sid Merton today.

Returning to the kitchen, Demosthenes at her heels, she picked up the coin purse James had left for her. She could hire Mrs. Mitchell, their sometime housekeeper, to help her pack. Laura opened the purse, and her jaw dropped.

Obviously she and Sir James had vastly different ideas of what was meant by "a bit of money." She could hire a host of helpers with these coins, as well as pay off her accounts at the butcher's and apothecary. She felt vaguely guilty about accepting so much money from him.

But tomorrow she would be his wife—that thought set up a fluttering in her stomach—so it was only practical to use his money today to take care of necessary tasks. Laura could well imagine James's biting comments if he was delayed a day because of Laura's qualms about propriety.

Laura set off on her errands, Demosthenes by her side. She hooked her hand into Dem's collar . . . though she had no idea how she could stop the muscular dog, who must outweigh her by close to a hundred pounds, if he decided to charge off.

It did not take long to hire Mrs. Mitchell and her half-grown son, then pay the apothecary and butcher. Whatever misgivings she might have about marrying Sir James, her spirits grew lighter with every step. The day seemed brighter, warmer, more sweet smelling. She felt wonderfully freed; she had not realized till now how much her father's debt had weighed on her.

While Mrs. Mitchell and her son worked upstairs, Laura started again on her father's study. Demosthenes thoroughly investigated every nook and cranny before sprawling in the center of the room and watching her with grave interest. Laura found herself addressing him now and then as she pondered what to toss, what to keep, and what might be worth selling.

As she worked, she thought about the man she was about to marry. Had James really paid off Merton with the intent of pressuring her to agree to his proposal? She had taken his statement at face value. But the fact was, he had done it without any assurance she would be his wife. He could not have forced her to marry him if she chose not to. Perhaps it really had been, as she first thought, an act of kindness—but in that case, it seemed peculiar that he had tried to convince her otherwise.

What if she had misjudged him all these years? Maybe he was not as cold as he wanted everyone to believe. After all, it wasn't as if he had set out to hurt her eleven years ago. She could hardly fault him for doing whatever he could to save his cousin. The fact that he could have done it in a gentler, kinder manner didn't make him wicked.

Mrs. Mitchell and son had finished up and returned home to fix supper, and Laura, her work in the study finished, was in the parlor practicing her violin when Demosthenes suddenly raised his head, then jumped up and trotted out of the room. Laura set aside her instrument and followed. She had left the front door open to admit the evening breeze, and the mastiff bounded out, loping across the yard toward James.

James bent to greet the dog, whose dignity had given way to all the wriggling, wagging enthusiasm he had refrained from till now. James smiled, talking to him as he scratched behind Dem's ears, and even laughed when Dem ended his greeting by giving a full-bodied shake that flapped his jowls wildly and sent saliva flying.

If the ladies of London had thought him handsome before, Laura thought, heaven help them if they could see James's features now, laughing and warm. As if he'd sensed the thought, James turned toward the door and saw her. He started forward, and as he walked, the laughter faded from his face, revealing his weariness.

"Miss Hinsdale." James bowed, sweeping off his hat. "I take it you and Dem survived the experience."

"We had a very nice time. I hope your trip was not too tiring."

He shrugged. "More boring than anything else. I did little but sit about."

She didn't dispute him, though the lines of his face said otherwise. She had seen enough of her father's patients to recognize pain. But clearly it was not a topic he cared to discuss.

"Please, come in. Will you have some tea?"

"Another cozy family gathering about the kitchen table?"

"No, I thought we would sit in the parlor." She was determined to remain pleasant. "However, I have made some soup, so if you would like to have a—"

"Miss Hinsdale, there is no need to play nursemaid. I assure you, neither tea nor soup will cure what ails me."

"I beg your pardon," she replied in a chilly voice, her earlier cordial feelings about the man having fled. Sir James had an extraordinary ability to irritate. "I did not mean to presume."

"Egad, don't turn missish on me now." They had reached the door of the parlor, and he stopped, propping his shoulder against the doorjamb in a pose of negligent lounging. Laura wondered how much was a pose and how much a need for support.

She crossed her arms. "Perhaps you should delineate the rules of our marriage so I'll know what is too concerned or too missish. I wouldn't want to play my role incorrectly."

Surprisingly, he chuckled and slanted a teasing look at her. "Ah . . . now there you have it. No retreat. No quarter given."

There it was again, an odd little rippling sensation in her

core. Laura turned her face away. "I'm sure I don't know what you mean."

James grasped her chin between his thumb and fingers, turning her face up so that she looked into his eyes. In this light they were the color of pewter. Her flesh tingled where he touched her, anticipation welling in her chest.

"I have no need for any role from you. I know you, and that is all I ask." He dropped his hand and took a step back. "I shall put a lump sum of money in a bank account in your name when we return home. That way you'll have money to buy whatever you like."

Laura stared. "James, you don't need to *pay* me."

He raised a brow. "You think a married woman shouldn't have money of her own to manage?"

"No! Of course I don't think that."

"So your objection is that *you* won't be capable of managing it. If you'd rather come to me for money each time you want to purchase something, I have no objection, though it is a bit of a bother."

"Stop it! You know that's not what I meant."

"It's eminently practical. It will make you independent. I trust you to use your money wisely, and it will provide you with ample funds while the estate is being settled. What is your objection?"

He paused for a reply. It was supremely irritating that Laura didn't have one. All she could do was glare.

"Then that's settled. Excellent. Here is a bit of pin money until your account is established." He handed her a sheaf of bills that made her eyes widen.

"That's a great deal of pins."

His mouth twitched up on one side, but he said only, "Now, as for the rest of it: I obtained the special license and arranged with the vicar to marry us tomorrow morning at eight o'clock."

"And I suppose *I* am to have nothing to say about the matter?" She wasn't sure why she felt so annoyed . . . and vaguely disappointed.

"Did you wish for a later time? Eight thirty? Nine o'clock? I thought you understood there is a need for haste."

"Yes, of course, but . . ."

"I see no reason to tarry." He glanced around dismissively. "If you wish to take some of these things, I'll—"

"Yes, I wish to take some of *these things*," Laura snapped. "However paltry they may seem to you, they are important to me."

"Then naturally you can—"

Laura plowed on, determined to have her say. "But that is not the point, anyway."

"Indeed? May I ask what is?"

"Your high-handed, dictatorial manner. Your assumption that the only thing that matters is what you want. I agreed to marry you, not to be your slave. I don't intend to sit about with my hands folded and my mouth shut, meekly going along with whatever you say."

"And here I was so sure you would." His eyes glimmered in amusement.

"Don't you dare laugh at me." She balled her hands on her hips.

"I wouldn't think of it."

"Hah!"

"Are you going to hit me now?" He eyed her clenched fists. "I'll need to brace myself . . . my condition, you see . . ."

"What?" She gaped at him, dropping her hands to her

sides, temper suddenly gone. "How can you joke about that?"

"How can I not?" He gave her a wry smile. "Miss Hinsdale, please accept my abject apologies for having offended you." He made an elegant bow. "I fear I am too accustomed to making decisions for myself alone. When, pray tell, will it be convenient for you to be married?"

"Stop." Laura tried to glare, but her mouth rebelliously curled up at the corner. "Eight is fine, if the vicar doesn't mind."

"The vicar thinks the whole matter is splendid, especially the new pulpit in your father's name."

"James! You didn't."

"He seemed to have some reservations about my taking advantage of you in your bereaved state."

"It's none of his business. You needn't let him push you into giving the church money."

"*You* are accusing me of being too soft? Miss Hinsdale, I'm astonished."

"Truthfully, so am I."

"I didn't want him plaguing you about it or looking like doom all through the ceremony. It's scarcely the wedding young girls dream of as it is."

"Well, I . . . thank you. For having Father's name remembered." Laura added, a little hesitantly, "I would like to take my father's books and some of his other things with me. It's rather a lot, I know, but I—"

"Take whatever you like. I'll make arrangements to have it shipped. Except that piano. There's a far better one at Grace Hill."

"Thank you."

"I'm not a tyrant, you know," he told her mildly. "Merely a bit high-handed."

She chuckled. "I am glad to hear it."

"Then . . . you intend to go on with it? You haven't decided to cancel our agreement?"

"Of course," she said, surprised. "I don't go back on my word."

He gave her a short, sharp nod. "Good. Then I shall see you tomorrow morning at the church."

chapter 6

Laura wore black to her wedding. With her father dead only two weeks, she was still in mourning. James cast a sardonic glance down her dress and leaned in to murmur, "How appropriate. Practical, as well—you can use it again for the funeral."

Laura sent him a quelling look and turned to the vicar. The best way to deal with James's goading remarks was not to answer. It felt very strange to stand beside James like this, linking her life to his . . . and even stranger to know that it would not last long. It was hard to reconcile this tall, commanding man with the idea that life was slipping away from him.

She glanced up at James, and he turned his head to her. It was hard to tell what he thought; his gaze seemed always assessing. Even harder to guess what he might feel. He must feel something, despite his careless dismissal of emotion.

When they came to the point in the ceremony where James was to put a ring upon her hand, Laura realized he would not have one, given how impulsive the decision had been. But she had misjudged him, for he took her hand in his and pulled a ring from his pocket. Three blood-red rubies were set into the gold circle, separated by two diamonds.

James slid the ring along her finger, the cool metal caressing her skin. Her stomach fluttered at his touch. The tumult inside her grew even worse as his words followed, twining all through her: "With this ring I thee wed, with my body I thee worship, and with all my worldly goods I thee endow."

James raised his head as he finished, his eyes glinting, as though he knew the sensations that ran through her and was faintly amused by them. When the vicar pronounced them man and wife and said to kiss the bride, Laura's stomach jumped. She had not considered this, either.

He cupped her face with his free hand, and Laura wondered wildly if he thought he must hold her in place to keep her from avoiding him. He bent toward her, and she closed her eyes, maddeningly aware that she was trembling. His lips touched hers, soft and warm, and her heart began to slam in her chest. But he did not linger, just lifted his head and gazed down into her eyes for a moment.

He drew back, keeping his fingers interlaced with hers as they walked up the aisle. Laura wasn't sure whether he did it to annoy her or to conceal the faint trembling that had begun in his hand. It was odd indeed to have any part of her flesh against the skin of this man, whom a week ago she would have said she disliked. Yet it stirred a curious sense of excitement in her, as well.

He did not speak until they were at the carriage. There he bowed slightly as he handed her up into the vehicle. "Lady de Vere."

Laura drew in a little skipping breath. She was no longer Laura Hinsdale, but this man's wife. Unreal as it all seemed, her life had changed in an instant. Forever.

"Regrets already?" That eyebrow lifted, inciting the familiar spurt of irritation in her.

It occurred to Laura that he did it for exactly that reason—to ignite a flash of temper, however small. In the next moment, she understood why. It was to deflect her attention from him, a quick and easy distraction.

"No. Simply absorbing the fact." She refused to let him draw her. What, she wondered, did he want her not to see in him? She took in the pinched lines at the corner of his mouth, the dull pain in his eyes. The ceremony, however short the vicar had made it, had taken a toll on him. His hand was trembling more, and he thrust it into the pocket of his jacket.

"I must spend a few minutes at the house before we go on," she told him. "To change into my carriage dress."

Was that a faint glimpse of relief in his expression? "Very well."

He followed her into the house and settled down in the parlor with Demosthenes. Laura changed into a dress better suited for traveling, then slipped into the kitchen to make tea. Minutes later, she reentered the parlor, carrying a tray laden with teapot, cups, and scones.

James, who had been leaning back in the wing chair, opened his eyes. "Now it's tea?"

"I was too nervous this morning to eat." She was getting the hang of dealing with him. "I was sure you would not mind."

"Naturally." His voice was heavy with irony.

"Try one of these scones. My neighbor brought them this morning as a farewell gesture. They're quite delicious."

He broke off a piece and began to eat. "I didn't realize you were such a managing sort. Perhaps I should have inquired before I proposed."

"Probably a wise idea," she agreed blandly, not rising to his jab, as she set a scone on the hearth for Dem. "I fear I'm unlikely to change now. I've been at it for years; Papa, you see, usually had his mind on more important things than food or billing his patients."

She felt rather triumphant when James ate half the scone and drank his tea. His face was somewhat less drawn, though there was still a pinch of pain between his eyes. "Have you a headache? I could get you something for it. My father's bag of remedies—"

"It would not help. Believe me, I have taken medicines by the score." He set down his cup with a rattle. "I think it's time we left."

She had made a misstep there. However, Laura was not one to give up easily. She went along with him, but as soon as they were settled in the carriage, Dem sprawled on the floor between their seats, Laura took up the subject again.

"You did not tell me what your illness was."

"No, I did not."

She crossed her arms and gazed levelly at him. "It's a long ride to spend in silence."

He returned her stare for a moment, then muttered, "The devil with it." He continued in a crisp impersonal tone, "I have a cough. Headaches. My heart beats irregularly. Lately my hand . . ." He unconsciously rubbed his left hand. "Food often nauseates me. I cannot sleep, and when I manage to do so, I frequently have odd, vivid dreams. The other day I—I could not remember where the bank was located." He turned his head to stare out the window, setting his jaw. "There. Does that satisfy you?"

Laura tamped down the pity that rose in her. James, she suspected, would close the topic immediately if she offered sympathy. "What was the diagnosis?"

"Lord, but you are persistent. Let me see . . . the first doctor said catarrh. Another suspected consumption. Next, a bad heart. When my hand began to shake, they thought it palsy. One doctor suggested brain fever and offered trepanning as a cure. I have tonics to inhale to aid my cough and pills to combat the headaches. I gave up the pills because they made me feel worse, and I've no desire to let them cut open my head and go exploring. In the end, they decided on brain tumor. Apparently one growing at a rather rapid rate."

"I suppose that would explain the varied symptoms."

"It scarcely matters, does it? It's all the same in the end."

Laura swallowed hard. "I'm sorry."

"No reason to be. Not your fault. And nothing to be done about it."

He leaned his head back against the seat and closed his eyes, effectively ending the conversation. Laura studied his face. He was such an unyielding man. One would almost think his will alone would keep him alive. Which was, she reasoned, exactly how he wanted to appear.

She wondered what really drove James. Pride? Sheer contrariness? He had both those in full measure. The face he presented to the world was cold and practical. And perhaps that was all there was to him. Still, she had seen the regret and despair that had flashed in his eyes at unguarded moments, the humor that made its way past his pain, the affection for his dog. He was a puzzle, and she had always been intrigued by puzzles. A little pang went through her; there might not be enough time to figure him out.

As the time passed, Laura could see that the ride wore on James. Trapped in this carriage with her for hours, he could not completely hide the severity of his condition. She saw his hand twitch even though he immediately tucked it under his leg or shoved it into his pocket. She saw the lines of his face deepen, his jaw clench, his face grow paler, his erect posture begin to sag. Once for a short time he slept, and in that state, stripped of pretense, he could not hold back a low moan or hide a wince.

It did not surprise her that he didn't halt the carriage for himself, only for the horses. Laura had learned enough of him not to comment or ask if his pain was worse. Instead, whenever she saw that he was flagging, she told him she needed to rest or take a stroll or have refreshments. James always complied, though once or twice he cast a speculative glance at her.

It was awkward to sit together for hours without talking. But a few general questions brought only brief responses from him. Obviously, James was not a man for idle chitchat. Finally, grasping at conversational straws, Laura asked him about his family.

"They're an uninteresting lot, I assure you. You have met my mother, Tessa."

Laura smiled. "Yes. She's charming."

"She is indeed. But I warn you, if you allow her to, she will have you running her errands constantly. Mother prefers living in London in general, but a few weeks ago she returned to Grace Hill for reasons I did not fully comprehend other than that it involved Lady Cumberton's soiree and a certain dress."

Laura chuckled.

"I have no idea who Mother will have dancing attendance on her. It's too difficult to keep up with her current swains. My brother Claude will be there. He likes to keep an eye on the estate he expects one day to rule."

"What is Claude like?"

He paused, thinking. "Claude is . . . unsatisfied. He is married to a woman so sweet she will make your teeth ache . . . which could, I suppose, explain much of his dissatisfaction with life."

"Some would think sweetness of character a good thing in a wife," Laura countered.

"Not if they had met Adelaide. They have a son, Robbie."

"How old is he?"

"He's—" James stopped, confusion flickering in his eyes. "I'm not sure. Not an infant." He muttered a curse.

Seeing his discomfiture and remembering what he had said about his failing memory, Laura quickly moved on. "You have more than one brother?"

"Another brother and a sister." He seized the conversational diversion. "My sister, Patricia, is given to complaints. Otherwise, she is much like my mother, though less captivating. She is married to Archibald Salstone, whose single virtue is that one day his father will die and Archie will become Lord Salstone. Fortunately, they are not in residence at Grace Hill, but live in some huge and decaying pile of stones in Wiltshire. My youngest brother, Walter, is still at Oxford, though he is as likely to be at home as at school, since he manages to get sent down for something or other regularly."

"Is that everyone?" she asked when he paused.

James shrugged. "There is Cousin Maurice, but as he will tell you more about himself than you would ever want to hear, I see no need to put you through that twice."

"You are very hard on them," Laura said, though she had to laugh at his wry descriptions.

"I assumed you wanted me to be honest."

"What will they think about our marriage? Will your family dislike it?"

He shrugged. "I hadn't considered it, really."

"Of course not." Laura suppressed a sigh. "They are bound to be taken aback."

"Because of the haste in which we wed? Or the inconvenient fact that you are in love with my cousin?"

"James!" Laura stiffened. "Surely you cannot think that I would—would—"

"Cuckold me?" He smiled sardonically. "Of course not. I am not the jealous sort. Though I doubt any man would appreciate knowing another man had kissed his wife, however long ago it happened."

"We didn't!" Laura protested, heat flooding her cheeks. That wasn't exactly the truth, but those few innocent kisses weren't the sort of thing James was implying.

"He never kissed you?" James raised an eyebrow. "What a pity for him." His eyes flickered to her mouth. "I would not have thought even Graeme was so chaste."

"Stop it!" Laura straightened, ignoring her deepening blush, as well as the peculiar dancing nerves in her stomach. "What happened between us is none of your business. And I will not stand for you impugning my reputation—or his."

"Indeed, I would never think of such a thing," James

said gravely. "I know that you and Graeme are both far too saintly to have damaged your reputations—or to do so now. But I see little point in pretending that things are other than they are."

"I am not in love with your cousin," Laura told him flatly. "After eleven years, it's absurd to think that—"

"Is it? And here I believed you quite constant in your affections."

"Of course I care for Graeme," she snapped. It was astonishing, really, how easily James could goad her, but even seeing the lurking amusement in his eyes as her temper flared, she could not manage to remain cool and collected. "But I'm not a fool."

"I never thought you were. Love can make otherwise intelligent people remarkably foolish . . . or so I've heard. I will admit that ours is an imperfect situation." He paused, raising an eyebrow when she snorted indelicately at his words. "Neither of us is our ideal mate, but—"

"Tell me." Laura leaned forward a little pugnaciously. "Who *is* your ideal mate? What paragon of virtue would you have chosen if your options had not been, as you said, so 'limited'?"

"Ah. That stung, did it?" His lips twitched. "Sorry. I was . . . a trifle out of sorts, as I remember."

"That doesn't mean it's not true. Come, tell me. You say what you think, whatever your other faults. What sort of woman would you actually *want* to marry?"

"One who wasn't so bloody curious, for one thing."

His words startled Laura into laughter, her irritation fleeing. James looked at her through his thick dark lashes, his smile wickedly teasing, and Laura's heart stuttered in her chest. She managed to say, "Obviously. What else?"

"Very well, if you must. First . . ." He raised his hand, ticking off his answers on his fingers. "You are much too beautiful."

She stared. "Your desire was to marry an ugly woman?"

"Not hideous, you understand. She would have to be pleasant enough in appearance that it wouldn't be a chore to . . . um . . . look at her daily. But truly stunning women require too much time and effort. It's tiring to be continually paying compliments and fending off admirers."

"Of course it would be." Laura rolled her eyes. "But I'm not stunning."

"There. Already you're fishing for compliments. You see what I mean about beauties?"

"I'm not asking for compliments!" Laura protested, flushing.

"Anyway, you haven't a say in it. It was *my* ideal."

"Very well. So we have a modicum of looks. What are your other requirements?"

"She'd have to come from good lineage. The purpose, after all, is to have an heir. So no mad uncles or ancestors who were hanged or burned at the stake."

"What about one who lost his head on the block in the Tower of London?"

"That might be acceptable," he allowed. "It would mean he was an aristocrat even if a traitor."

"Mm. Or unlucky enough to be married to a king."

"Precisely."

"What next?"

"Money would not be a necessity, though it would be better if she knew how to deal with it. Good taste, obviously. An ability to converse and to navigate the social waters. Pleasant. Competent to manage a household.

Able to handle her social obligations, but not a social butterfly."

"Because that would be too tiring, too?"

He smiled faintly, but shook his head. "No. Because I would hope she would spend much of her time with her children."

"Love would play no part in your perfect marriage?"

"I doubt I could find any woman who could meet that requirement. I am not a man given to tender emotions nor one who inspires them." He shrugged. "Love has always seemed a foolish thing to me."

"More trouble than it's worth."

"Exactly. What I would hope for in a marriage is a mutual understanding, I suppose. A lack of antagonism and drama and obsession. Marriage should be like a business arrangement."

Laura sighed. "I pity the poor woman who would be your wife."

"Ah, but, you see, you *are* that woman."

Laura had to laugh. "Yes, I suppose I am." She paused. "Did you really marry me to thwart your family?"

"I meant it when I said I wished to leave Demosthenes in your care. I have other animals—my horses, the hounds. And over the years I have acquired many objects of beauty. I hate to leave them in the care of my siblings."

"But I am practically a stranger to you."

"I know that you will be fair. You will be kind. You'll have an appreciation for the things I've acquired. It will all be safe in your hands. And that is what matters."

Because of Laura's frequent stops, they did not arrive at James's home until almost dusk. As they passed beneath the shadows of the lime trees lining either side of the drive, the dog suddenly popped up to a sitting position, his ears twitching forward.

"Yes, Dem, we're home."

Demosthenes pressed against the side of the carriage, sticking his great head out the window. On the other side, Laura unashamedly did the same, though she did not sniff the air, only looked for the first sight of the house.

"You've not seen Grace Hill before?"

Laura shook her head. "No, we never drove over here the times I visited Lady Mirabelle. Ohh . . ." She let out a sigh of appreciation as the road curved and the house came into view.

Impressively wide and tall, it was built of sandstone blocks varying in shade from tan to rose to a dusky salmon. Its symmetrical lines and sharply peaked gables were softened by a rounded tower and narrow tall trees that flanked it on either side. A whimsical cupola topped the edifice, its copper roof tarnished to a patina of bluish green. Flowers grew around the house in all directions, buffered by dark green, neatly trimmed hedges.

"It's beautiful," Laura breathed, turning to James.

"I'm glad you like it." For once his smile was not colored by irony or condescension. "Wait until you see the gardens in back."

Dem was out of the carriage as soon as James opened the door. He released a few thunderous barks and raced across the lawn and back before calming down and returning to trot along beside them.

Their arrival surprised the footman, and even the imperturbable butler was taken aback when James introduced Laura as his bride. Simpson recovered enough to tell James that the family had gathered for dinner in what he termed "the blue room." Then he hurried toward the kitchen, Demosthenes trotting after him.

"You can see where Dem's heart is," James commented.

"The kitchen? I've noticed."

James offered her his arm. "Come. We might as well get this over with."

"Hah. Don't pretend you're reluctant." Laura took his arm. "You're looking forward to tossing the cat amongst the pigeons."

"But of course." He led her across the marble-floored hall and into the hallway opposite. A pair of doors stood open, revealing the people inside. "Good God," James murmured. "Patricia and Archie have decided to plague us with their presence."

One young man turned toward the door and saw them walk into the room. "James!"

Just as everyone turned to follow his gaze, Laura felt James's arm jerk, and his hand began to spasm. He let out a low curse. Laura clasped his hand and pulled it down to her side, while at the same time moving closer so that the folds of her skirt concealed their interlaced fingers. James glanced at her sharply.

"Mother. Everyone." He sketched a bow. "I hope you will pardon our unannounced arrival. I was eager to introduce you to my bride."

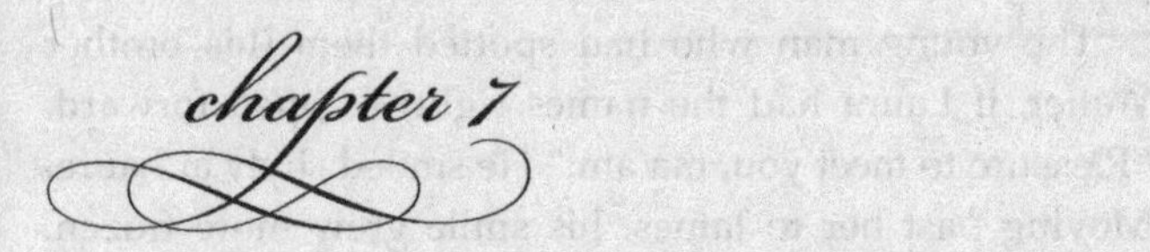

chapter 7

The room quivered with silence. James turned fractionally aside, releasing Laura's hand and placing his trembling arm behind his waist in a formal pose.

"My dear, allow me to introduce you. My mother, whom I believe you already know. My brother Claude, his lovely wife, Adelaide . . ." He went on, listing all the names he had told her about in the carriage, though he stopped on the last person, raising his brows in a look that hovered between inquiry and disdain. "And Mr. . . ."

"Netherly, sir." The man bowed. He was elegantly dressed and his manner polished. His hair was dark, with a dramatic sweep of silver at the temple. "No doubt you don't remember me, but I have been privileged to call upon your mother in London."

"Ah, yes, of course. Mr. Netherly." James inclined his head graciously. Laura was uncertain whether James's inability to remember the man's name was an indication of failing memory or a lack of regard. With James, it could be either.

The usually voluble Tessa was for once too shocked to speak. Her face had paled at their entrance, and something almost like fear shone in her eyes. Claude, too, had gone bone white at his brother's introduction of Laura, but it was anger she saw flash across his face immediately after. Apparently James had drawn the reaction he desired from him.

The young man who had spotted them (his brother Walter, if Laura had the names right) stepped forward. "Pleasure to meet you, ma'am." He smiled shyly at Laura. Moving past her to James, his smile grew more frozen. "Congratulations, James."

"Walter." James nodded pleasantly enough in acceptance of the man's greeting, though he added drily, "Sent down again, eh?"

"Well, uh . . ." The young man blushed. "Yes."

"I'm glad you are here," Laura told Walter, smiling and offering him her hand. "Else I wouldn't have met you."

"Oh. Well, um, thank you."

As Walter stepped back, James leaned in and murmured, "Already a conquest, I see."

Laura sent him a repressive look and went forward to make her curtsey to his mother. Tessa had recovered her composure, and she rose to kiss Laura's cheek.

"What a lovely surprise. Laura, my dear—I hope I may call you that, given our long acquaintance—it is a pleasure to welcome you to the family. We must sit down and have a tête-à-tête. I want to know all the details."

"I look forward to it, Lady de Vere."

"Oh, no, you must call me Tessa. Lady de Vere sounds so *old,* don't you think?"

"I'm sure no one would ever regard you as old," Laura responded gracefully.

Tessa beamed at her, then swung away, wagging a playful finger at her son. "James! You are wicked not to give me even the slightest hint. Here we are without any preparations made." She smiled prettily up at him and patted his cheek.

"No doubt Simpson is adequate to the task."

"Naturally. Still, I'm sure your new bride would have liked to take a rest before being rushed into supper with her brand-new kin."

"I think you'll find Laura is made of sterner stuff," James told her, and the smile he gave his mother was the warmest expression Laura had yet seen on his face. Apparently he was capable of affection, despite his razor-edged comments about his family.

"I confess that a meal sounds excellent to me," Laura said. "If I could just wash away the dust of the road . . ."

"Of course." Tessa flashed the smile that had won her many hearts, and looped her arm companionably through Laura's. "Come, I'll show you the way."

Tessa whisked her out of the room. "Dearest, I cannot tell you how excited I am to see you. I had almost given up hope, you know, because James never showed any partiality for one girl. He is not very sociable, of course, but even when I can drag him to a party, he will dance with a few different girls and chat a bit, but he doesn't seem terribly interested. One would almost think that he is *odd*, if I didn't know that he has always had a string of—" She stopped abruptly. "But that's nothing we need discuss. The problem is just that he is so very *choosy*. It would take a paragon to catch his interest, which, of course, you are."

Laura was not sure what to say to that statement, but fortunately Tessa seemed to need little response from her audience, sailing on to a new topic of conversation. "How is your dear father?" Tessa glanced over and saw Laura's stricken face. She stopped with a gasp, her eyes flickering down to Laura's black dress. "Oh! No! Is Dr. Hinsdale—surely he is not—"

"My father passed away two weeks ago."

"I am so sorry." Tessa's eyes glittered with ready tears. "You must be devastated. But of course, that explains why James said nothing to me beforehand. No doubt he went flying to your side as soon as he heard."

Laura blinked, taken aback at the dramatic picture of James his mother painted.

"He did just right." Tessa patted Laura's arm comfortingly. "I will not scold the boy any further. Naturally he wished to marry you right away so he could take care of you. I do hope your father did not suffer, poor man."

"No, I believe not. He went quite suddenly. It was apoplexy; I did not even hear him cry out."

"Oh, my . . ." Tessa sighed, shaking her head.

Her new mother-in-law continued to talk all the way to the washroom and back, flittering effortlessly from one topic to another and requiring little response from Laura. It was clear Tessa was used to being the center of any social setting and equally clear why she was.

Though her face was softer and more lined than in the days when she had taken London by storm, her dimples were entrancing and her silvery eyes, so like her son's, were vivid. She had a way of tilting up her chin and casting a sideways glance at one that both was charming and, Laura noticed, served to smooth out the wrinkles around her neck. And if Tessa's dark hair owed its color to something other than nature, it was no less shining and dramatic against her pearly skin.

It would be difficult not to be charmed by the woman, but Laura waited with dread for the moment when Tessa asked Laura about James's health. Since James had been in London, she doubted Tessa knew how serious his condition was. Laura would not want to be the one to tell her. That should come from James himself. However, if Tessa asked a direct question, she would find it hard to lie to his mother.

To her surprise, Tessa did not touch on James's thinness or the shadows beneath his eyes and the lines of pain bracketing his mouth. The closest she came to the matter was when she paused for an instant in her monologue, a tiny frown wedging its way between her lovely curving brows, and said, "I knew Mr. Caulfield could not be right. He's partner with James in some business or other, and he saw James in London, and he said—but obviously it was love that afflicted James. It would take him like that, of course. He would fight it." She shook her head at the peculiarities of her eldest son. "But now that he's married, it will be different."

Laura stared at Tessa. Could she really think that James's appearance came from thwarted ardor? That a few nights of love in Laura's bed would make him whole again?

For an instant something peeked out from behind the dimples and smiles, and Tessa's hand tightened on Laura's arm. "He isn't . . . ?" Then Tessa shook her head, letting out a little laugh. "No, I'm being silly. I fear I often am. Laurence used to call me his beautiful, foolish girl." She let out a little sigh at this apparently cherished memory of her late husband. "James is obviously making plans for the future. He's fine; he'll be quite fine."

Laura realized that Tessa did not want to learn what was wrong with James. It would shatter her pretense that all was well. Laura wasn't sure whether she felt more pity or irritation at Tessa's willful blindness.

The others were waiting for them in the anteroom. James gave Laura a searching look as he offered her his arm to escort her into the dining room. "I take it you survived my mother intact."

"Your mother is charming, as you well know."

"Yes, but you are accustomed to an atmosphere of quiet and peace." He seated her at the elegantly laid table before she had a chance to make a riposte.

James assumed his seat at the head of the table, with Laura seated on his left and his brother-in-law, Mr. Salstone, facing her. Salstone was a sandy-haired man who sported a twirled guardsman mustache and muttonchop whiskers so ridiculously wide that Laura had difficulty not staring at him.

His wife, Patricia, seated beside him, resembled her mother, but she lacked Tessa's vivacity, and her eyes were a faded blue rather than Tessa's unusual silver color, so that she looked like a poor copy of the original.

As the first course was served, Laura took the opportunity to study the other diners. James's brother Claude was seated beside her, and the youngest, Walter, was farther along beside the maligned Cousin Maurice. Neither brother greatly resembled James. Like Patricia, their eyes were blue and their hair more brown than black. Claude had a sullen set to his mouth. Walter, nodding along in a bored way as Cousin Maurice talked to him, kept sneaking glances down the table at James and Laura. Once, when Laura caught his gaze, he glanced down hastily.

Laura suspected that Mr. Netherly was one of the "swains" James had mentioned hanging about his mother. Tessa seemed to devote most of her arch glances at him. The other person at the table, Claude's wife, Adelaide, lived up to James's description, her smile almost constant and her voice soft and sweet. Indeed, in all her ribbons and flounces, with her porcelain skin and fluffy blond hair, she looked like a confection herself.

"Lady de Vere."

It took Laura a moment to realize that James's sister was addressing her. A faint flush rose in Laura's cheeks as she said, "Yes, I'm sorry. I am still unused to my new name."

"Of course," Patricia responded with a narrow smile. "I don't believe we have met before, have we?"

"No, I think not. I'm sure I had my come-out before yours," Laura replied.

"Then you do not visit London during the Season?" Patricia went on doggedly.

"Rarely."

"My wife prefers the solitude of the countryside," James told his sister, putting a faint emphasis on the first two words.

"But do you not miss the balls? The plays?"

"Not the balls, but I do enjoy the theater." Laura smiled. "And the museums."

"Oh. How . . . unusual."

"I am sure you would find it so," James agreed. "Laura is peculiarly given to things of the mind."

"Now, James, don't tease your sister," Tessa inserted with the ease of long practice. "I believe Laura often visits her aunt in London, don't you, dear?"

"Sometimes," Laura agreed. "But I preferred to stay at home to help my father."

"Yes," Patricia's husband said in the languid, faintly arch drawl affected by upper-crust young gentlemen. "Your father is a . . . barrister, isn't it?"

"No," Laura replied evenly. "My late father chose to devote himself to medicine, much to the disapproval of his family, who, like many aristocrats, find helping people quite beneath them."

Beside her, James, who had stiffened at Salstone's disdainful tone, relaxed slightly, letting out a chuckle, and Walter hid a sputtering laugh behind his napkin. Even Claude smiled. Patricia's husband was apparently not liked by any of the de Vere males. Unfortunately, from the look on Patricia's and Archibald's faces, Laura suspected she had made enemies of them both.

Tessa once again entered the fray. "I rarely speak ill of people." That brought another quickly hidden smile from her sons. "But I must say, Laura, that I have never really liked your father's family. Your cousin Evesley seems a selfish, unimaginative man."

"Evesley?" Archibald cast a sharp glance at Tessa. "The Earl of Evesley?"

Tessa nodded. "He's Laura's cousin. I pity poor Mariah, having to put up with him. Of course, she was determined to catch him. Her family hadn't a penny; everyone knows her great-grandfather gambled it away. Still . . . I'm sure she never dreamt Evesley would live this long."

Archibald swung his gaze to Laura. "The Earl of Evesley is your cousin?"

"Of some sort. His father and my grandmother were cousins, I believe. I'm not sure what that makes us."

"It makes you the all-important relation to an earl, doesn't it, Archie?" James gave his brother-in-law a smile devoid of humor. "And how is your father, the baron?"

Laura, watching James, thought she would not have wanted to be on the receiving end of his icy smile. Unsurprisingly, after that dampening exchange, conversation limped forward in spurts of polite chitchat. The chill around James was almost palpable, though Salstone, at least, seemed not to notice it. Patricia kept up a resentful silence, and Claude was politely distant.

It was a relief when the meal ended and the women left the men to their port and cigars. Laura, pleading fatigue from the day's journey, retired to the sanctuary of her bedroom. It was, she found, large and furnished with equally massive dark furniture, embodying both grandeur and gloom. But at least it offered solitude, which she badly needed at the moment. With a sigh, Laura plopped down in the chair by the window and rested her head against the back.

What a strange, eventful day it had been. Her wedding day.

Thank heavens it was over.

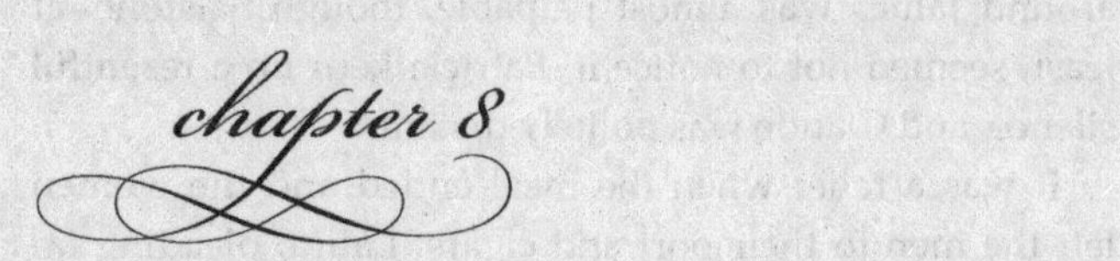

When the butler left the room, having set out the gentlemen's port, James fixed his brother-in-law with a glacial gaze. "Salstone . . . if you ever presume to condescend to my wife again, you will be out of this house on your backside. Do you understand?"

Salstone gaped at him. "I—I—intended no insult."

"Even you are not that stupid. You knew exactly what you were doing and so did Patricia. But no one—" His eyes swept around the table. "*No one* who insults Laura will remain in this house."

"J-James, I would never . . ."

"Not you, Walter." James's glance dismissed him and lit on Claude.

"Unlike Archie, I'm not an idiot," Claude replied scornfully.

"I say, Claude . . ." Salstone began.

"I thought not." James gave his brother a nod before turning toward Salstone. "Archie?"

"Well, of course, beg your pardon. That is to say, misspoke, all that." Salstone took a gulp of his drink.

James turned away. Out of the corner of his eye, he could see Salstone's expression shift to a sullen sneer, but he ignored it. He didn't care if the man hated him. Indeed, he rather enjoyed it. "Well, Walter . . . what brings you down from Oxford this time?"

As Walter began to shift in his seat and hem and haw, Claude asked drily, "Tell me, will it be my turn to be lectured next?"

James gave him a cool look. "Not unless you've done something irredeemably foolish. Nor am I about to lecture Walter." He looked back at the young man. "I was simply curious what rule he'd found to break that he hadn't already."

"Oh, well, it wasn't exactly new. It was just that Ned and I . . . well, you know his brother?" Walter began a convoluted story involving a pig, a don, and an upper-floor room, which James did not try to follow. His head was throbbing and his joints ached, and he worried that his hand might begin to shake in front of the people he would least like to witness that performance.

James wondered how soon he could leave. He had never enjoyed this postdinner ritual, its only advantage being that it meant fewer minutes spent in the company of Adelaide and Patricia. Thank God Cousin Maurice and his mother's admirer had gone with the women.

"Who's this fellow dangling after Mother?" he asked abruptly.

"Our future Byron?" Claude snorted.

"I thought his name was Netherly," Salstone said.

James would have laughed if his head hadn't been throbbing so. He wasn't sure which was more amusing, Salstone's puzzlement or Claude's pained expression. Too bad Laura wasn't here; he would have liked to meet her eyes and see the laughter brimming there.

"I think he's talking about the poet, Archie," Walter explained.

"Oh. Ha! Never much for poetry myself."

"Astonishing," Claude murmured, then said to James, "Surely you've met Netherly. He's one of Mother's admirers. At least he merely skulks around being moody and 'interesting.' It could be worse; Major Bellingham threatened to escort her back from the city."

"Gad." James could see that Salstone was working up to say something, but he gave him no encouragement. He knew the sort of subject the man wanted to broach with him.

"I'm glad you returned, James." Unfortunately, Salstone needed no encouragement.

"Are you?"

"Yes. Benbroke—you know Benbroke, don't you?" he said in a hearty tone. "Cecil's cousin."

"I've heard of him."

"He's on to something capital. I knew you'd want to hear it. It's a canal. In Australia. Brilliant idea, but of course one has to act quickly."

"Archie. Stop. I'm not lending you money."

"Course not," Salstone said in a hurt tone. "Wouldn't think of it. It's Patricia's trust I'm talking about."

"Nor are the trustees giving it to you."

"Trustees!" Archie snorted. "Hah! The others don't matter. You're the one who decides. We all know it."

"I'm surprised you don't also know that I won't allow you to squander the trust's money on some ridiculous scheme."

"It's not ridiculous, I tell you. I've looked at it and—"

"I'm not giving you the money."

"It's not as if it's your money!" Salstone's face darkened with anger. "It belongs to me."

"It's for Patricia, not you."

"Her money is mine."

"That is precisely the reason Sir Laurence left it in a trust," James shot back.

"It's not fair!" The other man jumped to his feet. "Why the hell do you get to control all the money? You aren't even—" He stopped abruptly.

James raised his brows, saying in a silky tone, "I'm not even what?" His brother-in-law simply glared at him, not answering. "I'll tell you what I *am,* Archie. I am the man who controls the trust Sir Laurence left for his wife and children. And I won't permit you or anyone else to squander it."

"It's not fair," Salstone repeated, turning toward Claude. "You know it's not. Why should we have to go begging to him for money that should be ours?"

"Fair doesn't matter. Haven't you learned that yet?" Claude shook his head in disgust. "Really, Archie, have you no sense? You insult the man's wife at dinner, then ask him for money?"

"Don't act as if you weren't all thinking the same thing! She's a nobody. I don't care if he wants to pick up Montclair's leavings, but to—"

James burst up from his chair, grabbing a handful of Archie's ascot and shirt, and shoved him back onto the dining table. Salstone landed with a thud, knocking over the decanter and sending port streaming across the damask. James leaned on the other man, holding him to the table with one hand, his entire weight behind it, and with the other hand twisting the material in a choking grip.

"Don't. Don't you dare even say her name." He rapped Archie's head against the table for good measure.

"James!" Walter grabbed one arm and Claude the other, pulling him back. "Stop. Let go. You'll kill him."

"That's what I'd like to do." James released Salstone.

Salstone, coughing, stood up. "You're a bloody lunatic."

"And you're a bloody fool, Archie," Claude said dispassionately.

James ignored their exchange. "Get out."

"What?" Salstone stared.

"You heard me." James bit off the words. "I want you out of this house."

"You can't toss me out. This is Patricia's home."

"Patricia may stay. *You* are leaving."

"James, wait . . . think . . . the scandal," Walter began.

"I don't care about the bloody scandal!" James turned and strode away.

Behind him he heard Salstone begin to bluster and Claude's scornful reply, "What the hell did you expect, Archie? He *told* you."

Then he was out the door, leaving them behind. Demosthenes, waiting patiently in the hall, followed him. James took the back door onto the terrace, going across it to the steps into the garden. He sat down on the top step, gazing into the darkness. Customarily, he would make a round of the garden with his dog last thing before retiring, but tonight the spurt of rage had drained him, leaving him shaken and dizzy.

This disease was making him a stranger to himself.

Archie Salstone could drive a saint to murder, and there was no way James could have let the insult to Laura stand. But it wasn't like him to be violent. He had always been able to take care of any enemy with a few acidic words. These days, however, anger bubbled in him, seeking release.

Demosthenes, after a single puzzled glance at his master, sat down beside James and stared into the garden with him. James looped his arm around the dog. "Ah, Dem, have I done Laura a grave disfavor?"

He was not an impulsive man normally, yet with Laura, he had jumped in without thinking. He wasn't sure why he'd done it; it wasn't his inclination to examine his inner motives or deep desires. If he wanted something of beauty, he acquired it. If he sought pleasure, he bought it. If something needed to be done, he made sure it was.

It hadn't occurred to him until tonight that he had put Laura in an uncomfortable situation. He had known Claude was bound to resent her, but then his sister and her husband had tried their knives on her at supper. James was accustomed to his family's sniping and usually got in as many shots as he received—well, in truth, probably more. But when they'd started on Laura . . . Anger boiled up inside him again.

Perhaps he should send Laura to his London house, where she would be away from the bitter tongues of his relations. But the idea left him feeling empty. Irritating as Laura's poking and prying was, he perversely enjoyed it, too. And though he would have denied it, he had meant it, at least a little, when he said he didn't want to die alone.

It was peculiar that a virtual stranger could quell the icy fear seeking to take root in his chest. But somehow he felt more at ease when he looked into Laura's calm face, her steady blue gaze. He didn't want to send her away.

Laura had shown tonight that she could handle his relatives' barbs. She had the advantage on them in intelligence. And in chucking out Salstone just now, he'd gotten rid of the worst one. She would have to deal with them after he died anyway. Might as well figure out how to do so while he was still here to step in.

God knows how long he would have the strength to do so. The confrontation with Salstone, coming on the heels of the journey, had left him exhausted. Two months ago, he would have scarcely noticed it. Now he could not summon the energy to even walk the garden with Dem. Indeed, climbing the stairs to bed seemed an enormous effort at the moment.

But, of course, he had to. He must use the steam treatment for his cough tonight. He'd already gone two nights without it while he was at the inn. He hadn't noticed that the treatment had eased his cough, and more than once, he'd thought of simply giving up the tiresome practice. But of course he hadn't. He could not have given up the struggle any more than he could have changed the color of his eyes. He would keep on until the bitter end. It was what one did.

James stood up and started into the house.

chapter 9

Laura awoke in much better spirits. However overwhelming this room was, the massive bed was comfortable, and she had slept the night through. Getting out of bed, she opened the drapes. Her window faced the gardens below, a massive spread of spring flowers, trees, and shrubbery. The house, on the crest of a hill, commanded a view of the countryside. Rolling hills stretched off in the distance, and closer at hand, at the bottom of the hill, she could see the ruins of a stone castle nestled beside a pond.

She dressed quickly, eager to explore the gardens. As she left the room, she heard a door slam down the hall and turned to see Patricia, sobbing hysterically as her mother tried to calm her. Laura hesitated, uncertain whether to go back inside her room, sneak away, or try to help.

Patricia looked up and saw her, and her face twisted. "You!" She flung out an accusing hand at Laura. "It's all your fault!"

"Hush, now, darling," Tessa said in a harried way, patting her daughter's back and looking at Laura apologetically. "Don't fret. I'm sure it will be fine."

"It won't. It won't. I hate him!" Patricia cried as she let her mother sweep her into the room behind her.

Laura stood for a moment, gazing after them. Well . . . life in the de Vere household was certainly not dull.

As she stood there, a small face edged around a corner. When Laura made no move, the boy stepped into the hall, lifting his hand to wave to her. She presumed that he must be Claude's son whom James had mentioned the day before. He looked around six years old, with a mop of blond curls and an angelic face that reinforced the idea that he was Adelaide's child.

Laura went down the hall to him. "I'm—well, I guess I'm now your aunt. Laura is my name."

"Hullo." He looked up at her with great interest and no appearance of shyness. "I'm Robbie. Robert Edward Danforth de Vere."

"My, that's certainly a mouthful. May I simply call you Robbie?"

"Course." He continued to regard her. "You're Uncle James's wife. I heard Mum talking about you."

"Did you?" However sweetly she had spoken to Laura last night, Laura suspected that in private Adelaide's words had been more acidic.

He nodded. "You *are* pretty, though."

Laura wasn't sure how to respond to that.

Robbie seemed to require none, for he went on, "I like you. You're nicer than Aunt Patricia."

"Thank you."

"I like you better than Uncle James, too. He never talks to me."

"I suspect your Uncle James isn't sure what to say to young boys."

"Why not? He was a boy, wasn't he? Papa always says, 'James is just like when we were boys.'" He dropped his voice on the last sentence in imitation of his father.

Laura smiled. "I'm not sure your Uncle James was exactly like other boys."

"Robbie?" a piercing voice called. "Robbie, where are you?" A moment later, a stick-thin woman came into view. "There you are! Come here. I told you not to leave the nursery."

"That's Miss Barstow," Robbie explained to Laura. "She gets upset. I have to go."

He took off down the hall to meet the woman, presumably his governess. She took him by the arm and hustled him back the way she had come, grumbling, "Why do you always run away?"

Laura turned, smiling a little. It seemed Robert Edward Danforth de Vere was a bit of a handful. She hurried back down the hallway to the front stairs, hoping that Patricia wouldn't pop out to hurl more accusations at her. Downstairs, she found that the dining room held only Claude and Cousin Maurice.

Claude glanced up and rose politely, followed by the other man. "Good morning."

"Good morning." She nodded at them. "I thought James might be here."

"Here and gone. You know James."

No, she really didn't. But she could scarcely say that.

"I hope you slept well," Cousin Maurice offered.

"Yes, I did, thank you."

"I only wish I could." Maurice sighed mournfully. "I rarely get a full night's rest. It's my back, you see."

"I'm sorry."

"Just be grateful you're young. The cold and damp are terribly hard on one as one grows older."

"I'm sure they are." He didn't look to be older than his forties. And it was neither raining nor cold.

"I thought it was your stomach kept you awake," Claude put in, his sardonic tone similar to his brother's.

"Oh, it does. My back, as well." Cousin Maurice sighed lugubriously and launched into a description of his ailments that was mercifully cut short by Adelaide entering the dining room.

"Lady de Vere." Adelaide beamed. "I hoped you would be here. Usually I am the only woman at breakfast. Conversation is so dull." She giggled and made a little moue toward her husband. "Sorry, darling."

Claude didn't seem to mind. He stood up, offering the first real smile Laura had seen on the man's face. Taking Adelaide's hand and raising it to his lips, he seated her with the care one would show an invalid. However coolly he presented himself to others, it was clear that with Adelaide he was all warmth. It made Laura more inclined to like him.

"Good morning," Laura answered Adelaide. "And, please, call me Laura."

"Lovely! After all, we are sisters now, are we not? I haven't had the chance to welcome you to the family. I vow I had begun to think Sir James would never marry."

There was a flat note to her last words that made Laura glance at her sharply. Despite Adelaide's overt cheeriness, Laura suspected the woman had in fact been disappointed James had not remained a bachelor. But at least she was attempting to be nice, which was more than could be said for much of James's family.

"It's wonderful that Sir James found someone." Adelaide recovered her pleasant tone as she turned toward her husband. "Isn't it, dear?"

"Wonderful," Claude repeated sourly.

Adelaide leaned forward, laying her hand upon her chest and tittering in a self-deprecating manner. "Though I must admit, I would never have had the nerve myself to marry Sir James. Such a formidable man!" She gave an expressive little shiver. "You must be terribly courageous."

"Um . . ." How was she to respond to that?

Laura was saved from replying by Claude, who drawled, "Oh, I doubt it required courage, my dear, merely clear thinking. After all, James is a far better choice financially than Laura's first fiancé." He turned to Laura, his expression cool and disdainful.

"Claude!" Adelaide gasped.

Laura met the man's gaze levelly, letting a heavy silence build, then said, "I thought that James had gravely underestimated his brother's character, but I can see now that he spoke nothing but the truth."

Claude smirked. "I don't know what he promised you in return for marrying him, but if James thinks to supplant me with an heir, he's left it a little late."

Laura clenched her hands in her lap, aware of a strong desire to drive her fist into Claude's smug face. Controlling herself with an effort, she rose and turned toward the others at the table, ignoring Claude. "Pray excuse me, Adelaide. Cousin Maurice. I find I have lost my appetite."

Laura escaped to the gardens, thankful that she ran into no one on her way. She was too furious to be polite. The gall of that man! The utter, heartless lack of compassion for his dying brother! It was little wonder that James didn't want to leave his dog or anything else to Claude. She hurried down the steps leading from the terrace to a formal garden, too angry at first to even notice the flowers and plants around her. But as she walked, the beauty of the garden began to soothe her. Orderly beds of early spring flowers were arranged around the central fountain, their geometric shapes sharply delineated by low green hedges. In contrast, the lower gardens beyond it were a lush riot of flowers and shrubs. Bright spikes of foxglove were banked by hydrangeas, and spiky purple balls of allium topped tall green stalks like lollipops.

Paths wound through the gardens, tree-shaded benches scattered along the way. At the other end of the colorfully jumbled garden, an arbor covered in lavender wisteria led to yet more steps and a trail shaded by trees. The ground sloped down slightly, and Laura followed its twisting way.

Small paths branched off in different directions, but Laura stayed on the more-trodden walkway, emerging finally into a small green clearing. Here the land fell sharply away. On the far side of the clearing stood a large fountain, and beside it was a stone bench, facing outward to enjoy the vista. The man who sat there turned at the sound of her approach.

"Sir James!" Laura stopped in surprise, then started forward.

He stood up, his smile teasing. "Sir James? Don't you think we should drop the formality?" He leaned in as she stopped beside him. "Considering that we are presumed to 'know the secrets of the boudoir.'"

She quirked a brow at him. "You're merry this morning."

"The gardens affect me that way. Come, look." He took her hand and led her to the fountain.

Below the fountain, wide, shallow steps of white stone marched down the hillside, grouped in tiers. The stairway was bordered on both sides by narrow streams of water that flowed from the fountain. The water tumbled down over black stone steps, creating a series of small waterfalls. The effect was enchanting, filling the air with the soft burbling of a brook and creating a stunning landscape.

At the bottom of the hill lay the stone ruins Laura had glimpsed from her window this morning. She could see now that the pond beside the old castle was actually a wide, irregular moat. The ruins lay on an island in the middle of the water so that one had to cross a small bridge to reach them. They were more extensive than she had realized, consisting of two buildings, partially caved in, and a squat round tower.

Laura drew in a sharp breath. "Oh, James! It's perfect." She turned to him, her face glowing.

He smiled. "I thought you would like it." His eyes moved over her face, and something in the set of his mouth, the look of his eyes, changed subtly. He still held her hand, and now his fingers slipped between hers, their palms pressed together. "Laura . . ."

She was very aware of the pulse hammering in her throat, the rise and fall of the breath in her chest, the touch of his skin against hers.

Suddenly there was a loud thrashing in the brush on the other side of the fountain. They swung around, startled, as Demosthenes burst into view. He loped up to Laura, ears flopping and tongue lolling from one side of his mouth, looking so comical that Laura laughed. She feared for a moment that he was about to throw himself against her in greeting, but James raised a hand, saying sharply, "Down," and Dem stopped short and leaned his head against her.

"I can see you've added another de Vere to your collection," James said lightly. "First me, then Walter, now Dem . . ."

"Dem would be glad to see anyone if they'd fed him soup bones."

"That might be true," James said. "Would you care to sit? Or would you rather I show you the ruins?"

"I think I'd prefer to just admire the view from here today." Laura would have liked to see the fallen castle; she had intended to walk down to it. But she had learned enough of James to know that he would accompany her even if the climb was too taxing.

"What is that place? The de Vere ancestral home?"

"Not ours. It was the original owners' castle. It was tumbled down long before the estate came into de Vere hands. The fact that they built their stronghold at the base instead of using the natural defense of the hilltop will give you some idea why they lost the property."

Laura laughed. "Something a de Vere would never do."

"I wouldn't, at least."

"Dem seems happy to be home," Laura commented.

"Mm. It's easy to be happy here."

"I'm not so sure your sister is happy." She thought it better not to mention Claude's attitude.

"Patricia?" He cut his eyes toward her. "Why? What did she say to you?"

"She was in the hall crying this morning. Your mother was trying to console her."

He cursed softly. "No doubt I'll have them in my study this afternoon, wailing and tearing their hair."

"Why?"

"I tossed Salstone out."

"What?" Laura stared. "Are you serious?"

He shrugged. "Well, not literally, though that was a near thing. But I told him to leave, yes."

"Why?"

"Because he's a bloody fool. Worse, he insists on exposing that fact to everyone."

"James . . ." When he didn't look at her, she slid forward, turning so that he would have to look in her face. "Was it something to do with me?"

"I don't know why you should assume that."

"Because *I* am not a bloody fool, that's why. Besides, Patricia told me it was all my fault."

His mouth tightened. "I'll talk to her."

"No. I didn't tell you so you would fight my battles for me. I just want to know what happened."

"Leave it. It's nothing you need worry about."

She stood up, planting herself squarely in front of him and folding her arms. "Do you really expect me to be satisfied with that?"

"No." James heaved a sigh. "I am certain you won't be satisfied until you've dragged it all out and turned it over twice." He rose to face her. "He was rude. Insulting."

"You mean because of his jabs at me last night at dinner? I took care of him well enough, didn't I?"

"Of course you will win any contest of wits with Salstone. That's not the point. You are my wife, and if he cannot speak of you with respect, he isn't welcome in my house," James said with finality, turning and starting back up the path to the house.

"Wait." Laura caught up with him. "It rather lacks respect, don't you think, to go charging off in the middle of a discussion without so much as a pardon me or good-bye."

He half turned, giving her a slight bow. "Pardon me. Good-bye." He strode away.

"James!" She trotted after him. Blast it, the man was supposed to be sick. Why did he walk so fast? "Will you stop? Just because I agreed to your proposal doesn't mean I'm going to keep silent—"

"I am well aware of that."

"Or let you direct my life. Or treat me as something less than your wife."

"For God's sake." His long legs ate up the ground, and they passed through the wisteria arbor into the lower garden. Glancing up at the terrace, where Tessa and Patricia were now sitting, James cursed again and whipped around to face Laura. "Why can't you leave it alone? I am trying to be courteous."

"Then be rude, as you usually are, and tell me."

"He insulted you!" James's eyes flashed. "Don't you understand? I warned him. I told him what would happen if he behaved that way toward you. Then he had the gall to make a remark that I am *not* going to repeat to you even if you plague me all day." The words spilled forth, his voice low and fierce and almost breathless.

Suddenly his face turned ashen, and he swayed.

chapter 10

"James!" Laura stepped in, wrapping her arms around him and bracing to take his weight as he sagged against her. She clung to him, her body flush against his. "No. You cannot faint on me now. I won't be able to hold you up."

Her head was turned, her ear flat against his chest, and she could hear the rapid pounding of his heart, feel his chest rising and falling as he sucked in air. He rested his head against hers, his arms curving around her. His words came out in short, sharp pants, gusting against her ear. "I. Won't. Faint."

For a moment he wavered, then gradually she felt him straighten, taking more of his own weight. He leaned his forehead against her head in a pose she imagined looked loverlike. "I beg your pardon. I was . . . dizzy for a moment."

"You wouldn't have been if you hadn't been racing away to keep from answering me."

She felt him shake a little in silent laughter. "Laura . . . Laura . . . trust you to get the last jab in."

Raising his head, he gazed down into her face for a long moment. "Thank you. Why did you do that?"

"Did you think I would let you fall without trying to help?"

"No, but you needn't have made it appear we were embracing, either."

"I thought you would rather . . . since there were people watching . . ."

Color returned slightly to his face. His mouth curved up on one side. "Still . . . it's a trifle improper, isn't it, snuggling in plain sight?"

"Snuggling! I like that—I try to help you, and you call me improper."

"I rather liked it, too." He leaned closer, murmuring, "Perhaps we should add to the verisimilitude." His lips touched hers, light as they had been after their vows, but clinging a little this time, then pressing closer. He straightened, his eyes warm, his expression faintly bemused.

Flustered, Laura drew in a quick breath. She could feel her cheeks heating, and she didn't know where to look. "I—there is a bench over there. We should sit down."

"Perhaps we should."

She turned, sliding her arm around his waist, and urged him toward the bench. He went docilely, his arm around her, though his steps were steady enough now. His body was warm against hers, solid beneath the separation of their clothes. Her lips still tingled from his kiss. His taste lingered on her mouth.

Why had he kissed her? What did it mean? He was putting on a show for his family. He was teasing her. But there had been that look on his face, a little surprised, a little amused, even a little wistful.

They sat down, his arm stretched along the back of the bench. Laura's nerves still jumped, and her thoughts skittered around, searching for someplace safe to light.

"James . . ." She turned to face him, which had the added advantage of putting distance between them. "I appreciate your coming to my defense."

"So we're back to that."

"Yes. We are. I understand your reasons. But I have no problem with your family."

"Give them time."

"I don't want to be the cause of trouble between you and your sister."

"You aren't. Archie is the cause of trouble. Always has been."

"But you could overlook his behavior this once. Be the better man."

"Being a better man than Archie Salstone is not a high achievement."

"Maybe not, but I suspect your halo could stand a bit of burnishing." She gave him a pointed look.

"My halo?" James let out a huff of laughter. "I'm not sure where to find that accessory."

" 'The quality of mercy is not strained,' " Laura said, taking another tack.

He snorted. "Don't start quoting Shakespeare at me, or you'll lose whatever foothold you've gained."

"Have I obtained a foothold?"

"A toehold, perhaps."

"You could grant it as a favor to your new bride."

"I don't understand." James looked at her quizzically. "Why do you care? Neither he nor Patricia was pleasant to you."

"No. But I doubt that banishing her husband will endear me to your sister."

He studied her for a long moment, then leaned back against the bench, closing his eyes and sighing. "This marriage business is more complicated than I'd imagined."

"Do you . . . regret marrying me?" Laura was surprised at the twist of hurt inside her.

"No." His eyes popped open and James turned his head toward her. "Not at all. I like—that is to say, I find it harder to wallow in my misery with you bedeviling me."

"That's good, because I'm a dab hand at bedeviling." When he smiled as she had intended, Laura went on. "I'm not asking you to let Mr. Salstone stay so that Patricia won't hate me. It's for you. This creates a terrible rift between you and your sister."

"We were never close."

"Neither were you and I, but here we are, married. One doesn't have to remain at odds with a person forever. I'd hate for you to be estranged from the members of your family."

"You think I should make my peace with them before I die."

"Well . . . yes. I do."

He studied her warily. "You aren't going to start hounding me now to see a clergyman and repent my sins, are you?"

"No." She laughed. "Not that."

"Very well. I'll play the doting bridegroom and give Archie leave to stay." He stood up. "But for you, not them."

James looked around his study, feeling at loose ends. It wasn't like him. This room, with its carefully stacked papers and precise rows of books and the battered desk that he refused to let Tessa replace, was usually where he was most at home. The rest of the house might be filled with his mother's bright chatter and people he'd rather not see, but here it was quiet and comfortable. Welcoming.

He liked to work. He enjoyed running down the lines of figures, totting them up in his head, and seeing the patterns, using them to chart his future course. But this afternoon, he had trouble keeping the numbers straight; they kept tumbling out of his head. He'd hardly heard what the estate manager had told him, distracted by the slant of light coming through the window and the way it sent an arrow of pain into his eyes and straight through to his brain.

It had been a relief when the man finally left. But now he felt restless . . . yet the thought of doing anything seemed far too great an effort. James shoved himself to his feet and wandered to the window.

He wondered where Laura was, what she was doing. His mind kept returning to those moments in the garden this morning. She had felt so soft and warm in his arms; he'd had a cowardly urge to hold on to her and bury his face in her hair.

Her lips had tasted sweet. And for an instant, he had thought that if only he were well . . . but, of course, that was nonsense. He wasn't well, and if he had been, Laura would never have agreed to marry him. Nor, for that matter, would he have wanted a wife.

He turned away from the window, irritated at his wandering mind, and started back toward the desk. His solicitor would arrive tomorrow, and he should get his thoughts in order. But before he reached his chair, he was distracted by the sound of music down the hall.

Curious, he opened the door. Notes danced through the air, light and melodic. He started along the corridor, inexorably drawn to the music, and paused in the open doorway.

Laura was seated at the piano, her fingers moving nimbly across the keys, and his mother stood beside it, one elbow propped on the instrument.

"Oh, lovely! Do play more!" Tessa exclaimed as the giddy tune tumbled to a close.

Laura, smiling, began a ballad, and after a moment, Tessa began to sing. She had a pleasant alto voice, and on the chorus Laura joined in, her bell-toned soprano mingling and twining with Tessa's through the sweet, sad lines. James leaned against the doorjamb, watching them, and his chest swelled with a fierce yearning pleasure.

They finished, and Laura raised her face, beaming at Tessa, her face glowing. Tessa clapped her hands together like a child, crying, "How beautiful!"

"It's Graeme's favorite song," Laura told her.

Of course. She played for Graeme. He should have known.

Laura glanced across the room and saw him. "James!" She smiled and started to stand. "Come in."

"Darling, join us," Tessa added gaily. "Your wife is so talented."

"Yes, I know." James knew he sounded stiff and he added a brief smile to soften it. "You play beautifully, Laura. I should love to stay, but I fear I must return to work."

He turned, retracing his steps. He could still hear her playing if he left the door to his office open. And, really, that was the best option. Safest.

Laura had become a lady of leisure, and she found herself with a great deal of time on her hands. It was a delight, of course, to have ample time for her music, and she spent several hours every day at the piano or her violin.

She chatted politely with Tessa and the other ladies of the house almost every afternoon. Her relations with Patricia were no less strained, but at least they were polite. She saw the boy Robbie now and then, pelting down a hallway or playing in the gardens, but in the way of noble families, the nursery was well separated from the rest of the house.

She strolled in the gardens daily and took longer walks down to the old ruins. She explored the house. The huge library was a delight, but it was the galleries that took her breath away. The long sunny halls were lined with statues and paintings. Indeed, every room seemed to offer another beautiful work.

Laura understood now why James had spoken of the things of beauty he wanted to leave in her care . . . and equally well why he would not consider Tessa or any others of his family adequate caretakers.

Strangely, after that close moment in the garden, James had become more remote. His manner was aloof, and he stayed closed up in his study most of the time, first meeting with his attorney, who came down from London, and after that with the estate manager.

It was clear that James was determined not to accept help and equally determined to give his illness no quarter. His carriage was always straight, his face only rarely showing a flash of pain. He was at dinner every evening though he ate little, mostly pushing food about on his plate. He was the last to retire, sitting on the terrace with Demosthenes after everyone else went to bed. If Laura awakened in the night, she heard him pacing restlessly in his room or up and down the corridor. But when she went out one night to ask if she could help him, he rebuffed her efforts so sharply that she left him to his own devices.

But pretend as James might that all was normal, it was obvious he was rapidly growing more ill. He looked hollowed out—his face drawn and pale, his eyes bruised with shadows. Laura was not sure whether she felt more pity for his condition or irritation at his stubborn refusal to accept sympathy or aid.

One night, unable to sleep, Laura slipped down to the library after everyone else had retired. As she left the library, she saw James climbing the stairs. She hung back in the shadows, watching as he trudged upward, Demosthenes at his side. He gripped the banister, pulling himself up each step, exhaustion in every line of his body.

She knew then why he went to bed after the others. The stairs taxed his strength, and he didn't want anyone to see his weakness. The man was so stubborn and contrary it made her want to scream, but she could not help admiring his dogged determination. James would go down fighting.

Sorrow welled up in her chest. Blast him. She didn't want to feel anything for James. She already missed her father with a steady ache. It seemed most unfair that she must add sorrow for James as well.

He paused on the landing, bracing himself against the railing, his head hanging. Demosthenes gazed up at him and whined softly. Laura could no longer stand still. She darted across the entry and up the stairs. He turned at the noise of her footsteps and frowned.

"What the devil—"

"Don't," she told him crisply. "I am not going to stand by and let you act like a fool just because you're too proud to allow anyone to help you." She lifted his free arm and hooked it over her shoulders, sliding her arm around his waist.

For once James made no protest, just started up the remaining stairs. Demosthenes bounded up before them and stood waiting.

"What happened?" Laura kept her voice crisp, knowing that sympathy would only make James more resistive.

For a moment she thought he wasn't going to answer, but then he said, his whisper quick and harsh, "I felt dizzy, and . . . I couldn't see. For a moment, I was blind."

chapter 11

James leaned more heavily against her as they went, his steps slowing. When they reached his room, Demosthenes took up his post outside James's door, fiercely watching the hall, as if he could keep the danger at bay. Laura blinked tears from her eyes.

They weaved across the floor to his bed, and Laura eased James down on it, grateful for the servants' custom of turning down the bed. He started to lie down, but she grabbed both his arms, stopping him.

"Wait. Let me get your jacket first." She reached out to grasp his lapels.

He pushed weakly at her hand. "No. I can do it."

"Oh, do shut up, James." Laura pulled the garment off him. He was, apparently, feeling too bad to put up any more protest, but sat docilely as she started on his waistcoat and ascot.

"How far do you plan to go?" he asked drily.

"It's encouraging that you feel enough improved to make annoying comments," she told him, giving him a little push back onto the bed. "Where do you hurt?"

"Where do I not?" He lay back, raising his hands to his head and squeezing as if he could crush out the pain. "My head is the worst. Damn it, I wish it would just get it over with."

Laura looked at his drawn face and brushed her hand across his forehead, gently pushing back his hair. "I'll get you something for the pain."

"I don't need—" He stopped and sighed. "Laudanum makes me ill."

"Then I won't give you any." She pulled the covers up over him and crossed to the door. Demosthenes turned to regard her, but did not give way. Laura reached down and stroked the dog's head. "Don't worry. I'm coming back."

She gave his shoulders an extra pat. The mastiff let out a long sigh that sounded much like James's and stood aside, leaving a narrow space open for her to leave. Laura went to her room and pulled her father's bag from the bottom of her wardrobe.

It occurred to her that she should probably put on something besides her nightgown and robe. She had never been around any man but her father in only her nightclothes. But she didn't want to take the time, and it was scarcely as if James would notice or care in his condition.

Picking up the medical kit, she returned to James's room. Demosthenes, who had remained standing at the door, flopped down across the doorway after she entered and laid his head on his paws, closing his eyes. Apparently he had decided it was safe to leave James in her care. Laura shut the door softly behind her and tiptoed across the floor.

"You needn't sneak," a voice said from the dark. "I'm not asleep."

"May I turn on a low light?"

"Whatever you like." James eyed her bag suspiciously. "What is that?"

"Instruments of torture." She was pleased to see his face had recovered a bit of color.

"Ah. Good to know."

"It's what my father took with him when he visited a patient." She pulled out a bottle and poured some of the contents into a glass, adding water. "This isn't laudanum; it's from willow bark, good for headaches."

"Your father dabbled in folk medicine?"

"He wasn't one to discount a remedy merely because it was old." She slid one hand beneath his head to lift it, and he raised up on his elbows.

"I'm not helpless."

"I'm sure you're not. Drink this."

He sipped and made a face. "That tastes terrible."

"Of course it does—it's good for you." She gave him a teasing smile and laid her palm over his forehead. "Now drink the rest of it."

James complied, then lay back down and watched her as she moved about, pouring water from the pitcher into the bowl and dipping a rag into it.

"You feel a trifle hot," she commented. She feared that was the reason for the color in his face. "Are you feverish?"

He shrugged. "Perhaps. I'm no longer sure what I am."

Laura wrung out the rag and bathed his face. He closed his eyes, his features relaxing under her hand. She rewet the rag to cool it and returned to his bedside.

He watched her warily. "Clearly you have some need to nurture someone, but I am not—"

"Oh, for—why do you make such an effort to be obnoxious when you are feeling so ill?" She began to wash his face again.

"I don't like being fussed over."

"It's unfortunate you didn't think of that before you married me," Laura retorted. "I am a doctor's daughter, and I have been in the habit of helping sick people all my life, even those who are annoying. You will simply have to get used to the fact that I'm not going to stand about watching you suffer and do nothing about it."

"I should have known you'd turn out to be a despot," he muttered, closing his eyes. "Graeme has a weakness for overbearing women."

A chuckle escaped Laura. "Insulting to the end, I see." She was pleased to see that his lips curved up in response.

"Will it bother you?" he asked softly. "Being so close to Graeme here? Seeing him frequently? He's bound to come over when he gets back from London."

Laura glanced at him, startled. "No, of course not. I told you—"

"But you must . . . when you see him . . . you surely feel . . ."

"Friendship," Laura said firmly. "That's all." She poured the contents of a bottle into the water and dipped the rag into it. A pleasant scent stole through the air as she wrung out the cloth and laid it across his forehead.

He took a deep breath. "It smells like you."

Laura glanced at him, surprised. "It's lavender—soothing for a headache." She thought he looked a little better. "Will you be able to sleep now?"

He snorted. "I never sleep."

"I hear you walking about at night."

"I get restless. It's madness to be so tired and yet unable to sleep."

She perched on the bed beside him. "I would have kept you company, but you didn't seem to want it."

He slanted a look over at her. "You mean I was rude as the devil."

"Yes. But I expected that. I wasn't sure, though, whether company would make you feel worse or you were just being unpleasant."

He snorted. "I have yet to see you let either of those things slow you down."

She shrugged. "I spent all my life managing a man who took no care of himself."

James scowled. "You're saying I remind you of your father?"

Laura laughed. "Goodness, no. My father was a kind man. A good man."

"Very different then." There was a hint of a smile on his lips. Laura was aware of a peculiar desire to trace her finger across them.

"He was too busy looking after others to take care of himself. I'm not sure why you neglect to do so."

"I take care of myself. Most would say *I* am my greatest concern."

"Perhaps. I don't know you well enough to say. But you refuse to let anyone help you."

He stirred, turning his head away. "It's obvious you don't know me well. I have a great many people who help me."

"You *pay* them to work for you; that's an entirely different thing. What you won't do is allow someone to give it to you freely."

"You're daft."

"Am I?" She curled her legs up on the bed, positioning herself more comfortably.

James frowned. "What are you doing? Are you settling in for a cozy chat?"

"I don't see why not. I'm wide-awake, and you say you never sleep. We might as well talk to each other."

"What if I don't want to chat?" His tone was so close to that of a petulant child that Laura had to smile.

"Then I suppose I shall have to do all the talking, won't I?"

"You probably would." But he turned toward her.

"Why won't you tell your family that you are ill?"

"What do you expect me to do? Stand up at dinner and announce I shall die soon? I'm sure they have figured it out by now. Nobody wants to speak of it."

"Your mother doesn't realize it. She thinks that marrying me shows you're expecting a long life ahead of you."

"Mother likes to be happy. She doesn't want shadows or lurking demons or anything but fine clothes and a pretty reflection in the mirror. And ample men to admire her."

"But what about when you—when it happens?"

"You see?" He quirked an eyebrow at her. "Even you have trouble saying it." He rubbed his hand over his face, knocking the cloth askew, and Laura leaned over to adjust it. "Don't worry yourself over my mother. She will have a grand opportunity to emote. Throw herself across the casket and weep. She has perfected the art of crying without damaging her looks."

"James!" Laura was shocked. "What a horrid thing to say. Do you really believe your mother won't grieve for you? That she doesn't love you?"

"Oh, she cares. Just as she cared for my father. Or Aunt Mirabelle. Or—" He broke off with a shrug. "But she dearly loves the drama of it all, as well."

Laura studied him for a moment. His thick, dark lashes

shielded his gaze from her. He appeared to be intent on the path his fingers took as he traced the pattern on her brocade dressing gown where it spread across the bed coverings.

She wondered if she ought to cease questioning him, but it seemed to her that conversation, even his irritation at her probing, distracted him from his pain.

"If you know that your family has surmised you are ill, why do you try so hard to keep them from seeing it? Why do you hide your tiredness? Your pain?"

"My weakness?" He looked up at her then, his mouth twisting in a mockery of a smile. "Well, one cannot let down the side, can one?"

"What side?"

"I'm not sure," he admitted, the smile falling away. "Very well, if you must know, I cannot bear to have my mother indulge in her tragic role. Crying and bemoaning and asking me every two minutes how I feel. Handkerchief always at the ready, reminding me of every tender moment in my life, real or imagined, pleading with me to be strong and not leave her. It's exhausting."

"I see. But what about the others? Your brothers and sister, their spouses."

"Them?" His jaw tightened. "I wouldn't give them the satisfaction."

"So *they* are the other side."

"Mm. I suppose the other side is everyone except myself."

"You're wrong there," she said in a matter-of-fact voice, reaching out to turn the cloth over so that the cooler side lay against his forehead. "I am your wife. So whether you like it or not, *I* am on your side."

His eyes flew to hers, an odd spasm of emotion so fleeting she couldn't identify it flickering across his features. "I don't need your pity," he told her roughly.

"Maybe not. But you could certainly use my help."

He turned his eyes back to his forefinger tracing a whorl on the brocade. After a moment, in a low voice, he said, "I'm losing my mind."

"What?"

He wet his lips. "I couldn't tot up a column of numbers today. It wasn't just my stupid hand shaking. I couldn't . . . I couldn't remember how to add them. It was hopeless."

"Don't fret over that. Someone else can do it. I'll check them for you if you like."

"Yes, but that's not the point. I've always been good with numbers. I *understand* them. They're fixed, certain. But now . . ." He turned his hand palm up, flexing his fingers as if grasping at air. "I've lost them."

Laura took his hand. "You haven't lost them. They're still there; they still mean the same things. They're just as constant as they were before."

"Yes. It is I who's not." He stroked his thumb idly up and down hers. Sad as his words were, it was the intense heat of his skin that worried her. He was growing more feverish. "I sometimes see . . . things that aren't there."

"What do you see?"

"Nothing important. The other day I saw Mother's cat. Only it died years ago. Last night I dreamed my—I saw Sir Laurence beside my bed. I remember the occasion; I was seven and had a fever. Years later my mother told me they had been afraid I was about to die, too, as my brother Vincent had." His hand tightened on hers as he looked up into her face. "I am not given to imagination or mystical thoughts, Laura."

"I'm sure you are not." Laura's throat burned with tears, but she managed a smile. She had not realized he had had another brother, but this was scarcely the time to question James about Vincent or his death.

His eyes drifted closed, though his thumb continued to slide along her skin. After a moment, it, too, stilled, and his grip loosened. He was asleep. Laura felt a small moment of triumph.

She considered pulling her hand from his and leaving him to sleep, but she feared the movement might awaken him. Her position, however, soon grew tiring, and her eyes kept closing. Finally she moved, and his hand tightened on hers. Her eyes flew to his face; he was still asleep. After a moment, she lay down on her side, curled in a ball in the lower quadrant of the bed, her hand stretched up to his.

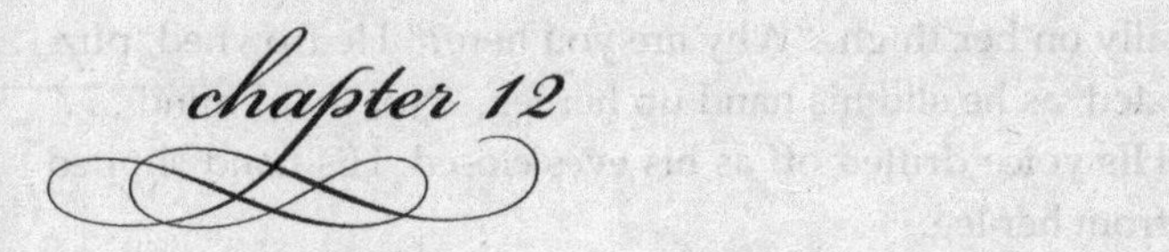

chapter 12

Laura dreamed she was lying beside the fire, its heat strong against her back. She drifted awake, hot and vaguely confused. She lay stretched out on her side, an arm thrown across her, and she was enveloped in heat. Her eyes flew open as she jolted into full awareness. She was lying next to James; it was his arm that curled around her, tucking her into his side.

She went still, scrambling to pull her thoughts together. She had fallen asleep, and sometime during the night, she had shifted around until she now lay next to him. Her face flooded with color. Even with the bedcovers separating their bodies, it was an intimate position. What would James think if he awoke and found her cuddled beside him as if . . . as if they were lovers?

She sat up abruptly, pulling out of his arms, and turned to look down at James. She didn't need to feel his forehead to know he was feverish. She had only to look at his flushed cheeks, the rosy color of his lips. The fever had momentarily given him the mask of health.

He opened his eyes and smiled at her in a lazy way, his eyes bright silver, warm and beckoning. Laura stared, remembering how his lips had felt against hers when he'd pretended to kiss her in the garden the other day.

"Laura . . ." His voice rasped. James laid his hand casually on her thigh. "Why are you here?" He frowned, puzzled, as he slid his hand up her leg. "Not that I mind . . ." His voice drifted off as his eyes closed. His hand slipped from her leg.

Laura stared, shocked by the way her body had reacted to his touch, his smile. For a moment she had wanted to lean down and kiss him, to feel his arms around her again, his heat pouring through her.

Impatiently, she shook off the image. James was obviously burning up with fever. He was delirious. Snatching the damp cloth from the pillow where it had fallen, she wet the rag and wrung it out, then began to wash his face and throat. Draping cool cloths around his wrists and across his forehead, she poured out another dose of the tincture. Laura slid her hand beneath his head, lifting it, and held the drink to his lips.

"Take a sip." He opened his eyes. They were still that combination of hot and hazy that did peculiar things to her stomach. Obediently he swallowed, then screwed up his face and turned his head away. "No, James, now drink it."

"Don't wa—" As soon as he opened his lips to speak, she poured the rest of the liquid in. He swallowed, then pressed his lips tightly together and glared at her.

Laura hid a smile. Who would have thought that the lordly James de Vere could pout like a ten-year-old? She continued to wet the cloth and bathe his face, but his temperature remained stubbornly high. He mumbled, tossing and turning in the bed, and his words were usually unintelligible. But once his eyes flew open and he called her name sharply.

When she turned to him, he reached out toward her, saying hoarsely, "Put it out! Can't you see it? Your hair—the fire—can't you see it?" He swept his hand roughly over her head.

As suddenly as he'd awakened, he pulled his hand away and dug his fingers into his own hair, his face contorted in pain, muttering, "Stop, damn it, stop."

He threw off his covers. His shirt was soaked through with sweat, clinging to his body. Laura opened the top few buttons of his shirt and moved the cool rag down over his throat and into the V of his shirt. Finally she simply unbuttoned it all the way, pulling it from his waistband, and bathed his whole chest.

The sight of his bare chest brought up more of the restless, twisting feeling inside her. He was too thin, his ribs pressing against his skin, but there was something about the broad set of his shoulders, the ridge of his collarbone, that made her vaguely warm and unsatisfied. And when she slid the cloth across his chest, the heat licked higher in her.

Laura was beginning to suspect she was wanton. Even as concerned as she was about James and his fever, she enjoyed stroking him this way. It was stirring and somehow exciting, and when he opened his eyes and looked at her, hunger flaring in her eyes . . . well, she enjoyed that even more.

He clamped one hand around her wrist, stilling it, then pushed her hand downward, leaving the cloth behind. She sucked in her breath, her eyes going wide with astonishment as she felt him move beneath the cloth of trousers, hard and pulsing. James made a low noise and sank his other hand into her hair, pulling her head down to his. Laura didn't resist.

His lips were velvety soft, as hot as she had imagined them, and more aggressive and insistent than his gentle kiss the other day. His mouth moved against hers, opening her lips to his questing tongue. Laura jerked in surprise. This was wrong, surely. This was fierce and hungry, not at all loving. This was . . . delightful.

He no longer held her hand against him, but Laura found she had no desire to pull it away. She moved her fingertips lightly over the buttons of his trousers and felt his flesh surge in a primitively gratifying way.

His hand wandered up her body, hot as a flame wherever it touched. He slid in beneath the lapel of her dressing gown, flesh searing through the thin cotton of her nightshirt, and settled on her breast, and though that, too, was a surprise, she did not flinch. She was growing accustomed to these new and pleasurable things he was doing, and now she waited for them with anticipation.

James groaned and turned, pulling her beneath him. His body was heavy on hers, pressing her into the soft mattress. His mouth left hers to roam down over her throat, and a shudder shook him. Suddenly he let out a low moan of an entirely different sort, a sound of loss and desperation. "No . . . no . . . don't go." He buried his face in her neck, his hand clenching into the sheet beneath them. His breath, already hard and fast, came in pants. "I won't . . ."

He shivered and rolled away from her, throwing his arm up over his eyes and muttering to himself. Laura sat up shakily, struggling to pull her tattered composure into order. He was delirious. She slipped off the bed, straightening her dressing gown and retying the loosened sash.

It was more difficult to pull her thoughts together. She sank down onto the chair, putting her head in her hands. She was a doctor's daughter. She had long been aware of what went on between a man and woman. Or at least she had thought she understood. Clearly the mechanics of it didn't begin to explain what actually happened.

She sat back, leaning her head against the chair, and took a calming breath. Eleven years ago Graeme had kissed her a few times—sweet, stolen kisses that had made her pulse quicken and promised a rosy future.

But it had been nothing like the fierce way James crushed his lips to hers and invaded her mouth. The way his hands roamed her body. She closed her eyes, remembering his palm cupping her breast, his thumb teasing at her nipple through the cloth. His ragged breath as he rolled over, pinning her to the mattress beneath him. The thickened flesh beneath the cloth of his trousers and the way it pulsed against her hand.

Her cheeks flamed at the memory—not just with embarrassment, but with another kind of heat altogether. For however unexpected his kisses had been, they had not been as astonishing as her own reaction. Her entire body had simply burst into flame. She'd wanted to press her body into his; she'd reveled in the weight of him on her, the intensity of his passion.

What in the world did that say about her? Even worse, what did it say that she hadn't wanted him to stop?

The truth was, her pulse was still racing, and she was suffused with heat. Her insides had melted, a low throbbing ache starting deep in her abdomen. If James had not broken it off, his delirium taking him off on another path, there was no telling what she would have done.

If she had not given up Graeme, if they had married, is that what would have passed between them—no, that was too embarrassing to even think of. She could not imagine doing such things with the man who had been her friend since they were children.

Far easier to feel this way about the man who had that wicked smile, whose silver eyes glittered in sardonic amusement at the world, who had no interest in being any better than he was. James de Vere was not a gentleman, which made her less ashamed for not acting like a lady.

Had James even known who she was when he kissed her? He had clearly been delirious; he could have been thinking about some other woman. It was a deflating thought, but it would be better if he had been unaware. It would make it easier to face him again. If, of course, he recovered.

That was what was important. James had a raging fever; he could be near death. This was no time to be sitting around pondering her feelings. She must get to work. Laura stood up, smoothing her hands down her dressing gown, and turned back to the washbasin.

James was shivering now despite the searing heat of his skin. He turned onto his side, huddling into himself, so Laura pulled the covers up and tucked them in around him. Still he shivered. She added the blanket folded at the foot of his bed. He continued to shake, his teeth chattering. She opened the chest at the foot of the bed but found no other blanket. Finally she took off her dressing gown and added that to the pile of coverings atop him.

"Cold," he whispered. "It's so cold."

Not knowing what else to do, Laura slid into bed and wriggled over until she lay behind him. His body was like a furnace, and the pile of coverings added to the smothering heat. Laura snuggled up against his back, holding him close and wrapping her arms around him. Gradually his shaking stopped, and he once more fell into sleep.

It was so hot beneath the covers that it was some time before Laura realized that James's body next to hers was no longer blazing. He had stretched out, no longer trembling. She sat up, propped on her elbow, and felt his forehead. It was clammy and much cooler to the touch.

His fever had broken.

chapter 13

James awoke and stared at the dark green tester high above his bed. He had slept—slept for more hours than he had in weeks, judging from the light coming through the cracks of his curtain. Yet he felt wrung out—weak as a kitten, drained, and thirsty.

What the devil had he done last night? It was a tangle of heat and bright piercing pain, of shivering cold, of color. Laura had been there, her blond hair tumbled down around her shoulders. He had been in a cave of ice, and she had pressed herself against him. No, that was idiotic. A cave of ice? It had been a hallucination, just as the flaming heat and the hunger that had filled him, the heavy, throbbing desire deep in his loins.

It had been one of his dreams. He had, after all, dreamed of Laura at other times these past few days. That day in the garden when she had rescued him in all his humiliating weakness and he had kissed her—he had dreamed of her that night.

He hadn't wanted a woman in weeks. Then Laura had put her arms around him to keep him from falling, and he had kissed her to keep up the pretense of a lover's embrace. No, that wasn't true, not really. He had used that excuse because he wanted to taste her lips. Had wanted to for days. That night he had dreamed that he was well and strong again and they were walking. She'd held his hand and leaned against him—before she turned into a raven and flew away.

The dream was absurd, insane . . . just as it had been last night when he was holding Laura in his arms and kissing her. God, he had been kissing her as if he would consume her, her mouth so hot and wet and welcoming, her body lithe and firm beneath him, the scent of lavender in his nostrils, her hair like corn silk slipping through his fingers.

It had to be a dream. Laura would never have been rolling in this bed with him in a welter of heat and desire. But it had seemed so real, his body hard and eager, her kiss so sweet. His hand tingled with the memory of her breast in his palm. And the scent of lavender still clung to his sheets. He turned his head, breathing in the smell. She *had* been here.

He tried to think back. It was so hard to remember things, his scattered thoughts made even worse by the lancing pain. He remembered sitting out on the terrace with Dem, as he always did, waiting for the others to retire so no one would witness his feeble climb up the stairs. It had been very warm, and he had felt a little dizzy again. And on the stairs—yes, on the landing he had gone weak in the knees, and his vision turned black. For a heart-pounding eternity of seconds, he had been certain he was blind.

That was when Laura had come running up the stairs—rescuing him again, of course. What was the matter with her, anyway? She didn't even like him. Yet there she was, wanting to help him. God knows, he was always tempted to take it. To give in.

Last night he had. He had leaned on her and let her put him to bed like a child. She had given him something foul to drink—that was just like her, too. Then, of course, she had plagued him with her questions. He had been so hot. So tired. The next thing he knew, she was sitting on his bed, her hands cool and caressing on his chest, and he had been aflame for her, aching and eager. He remembered guiding her hand lower as he reached up to pull her down to him.

James closed his eyes. If he had even the slightest bit of energy, he would be hard all over again, remembering it. It had to be real. It couldn't be something he imagined. But Laura wouldn't have kissed him, wouldn't have let him caress her.

Not willingly.

He remembered taking her arm and moving her hand down; he had clamped his hand behind her neck and pulled her down. Perhaps she hadn't wanted it at all. Because he could remember, too, that she left him and he had reached out, trying to pull her back, only she was out of his reach. Then he was running after her, and she was fleeing from him. Had he hurt her? Had he tried? He had been so desperate, so yearning, he would have believed himself capable of almost anything.

The icy dread in him now was enough to make him push up and out of bed. He swayed when he stood up, but he wrapped a hand around the bedpost and managed to stay upright. He looked around. There was a bag on the chair. Yes, that had been what she had carried in here, and there, beside his washbowl, were two damp rags, hanging to dry. He picked up one and brought it to his face. It smelled of lavender.

A knock sounded on his door, and he turned so quickly

he overbalanced and again had to grab the bedpost to keep from toppling over. The door opened a crack, a woman's soft voice, saying, "James."

"Laura!" The word came out in a croak, and he took a step forward, afraid to let go of the post. He looked like a fool, he knew, standing there shirt hanging open and feet bare, clinging to the bedpost and clutching the washcloth in his hand like a spinster about to have a fit of the vapors. But then, he so often looked like a fool these days, he supposed it scarcely mattered.

The door swung wider, and Laura came into the room. She was smiling in that way of hers, calm and serene, but with a glimmer in her eyes that spoke of a readiness to laugh. He had always thought her beautiful in the way a perfect piece of art was, but now he could see how much more intriguing she was than perfection. He wished . . . well, no use wishing anything.

The important thing was she wasn't angry or disgusted or fearful, all the emotions he had feared he might see in her face. The knot in his chest eased. It *had* been a dream.

He took a step toward her and crumpled to the ground.

The dog reached James first, prodding him with his nose and licking his cheek. Laura knelt beside him, pushing Dem aside.

"James?" She laid her hand on his forehead. He wasn't hot again. She shook his shoulder. "James, get up. I need you to get into bed. Please, I can't lift you."

Laura ran to the bell pull and yanked it several times. There was a noise behind her, and the mastiff growled deep in his throat. Laura swung around. Walter stood in the door, staring at James. "Good God. James."

"Don't stand there," Laura snapped. "Come here and help me."

Her orders broke the young man from his paralysis and he hurried to her side. Together they tugged and pulled, but could manage to do no more than get James into a sitting position. Laura cradled him against her breast, holding his head to keep it from lolling back. She stroked her hand across his forehead.

James opened his eyes and blinked owlishly at her. "Laura. Beg pardon."

Laura was perilously close to hysterical tears. What was she to do? A fever she could battle, but she felt lost now. Nodding toward the bell pull, she told Walter, "Go ring again."

But at that moment, Simpson came in, followed by one of the footmen. Between the men, they managed to lift James and put him in the bed. Simpson shoved the pitcher at the footman and told him to fetch more water, and Laura turned to her father's bag.

With shaking fingers, she poured willow bark tincture into a glass, then patted James on the cheek. "James, wake up. Look at me. James." Her voice grew sharper, and her hand against his cheek was a little stinging.

James muttered a curse and opened his eyes. They were clearer now, at least. She managed to get some of the liquid down him, though he gave her a baleful glare. She cupped her hand against his cheek, running her thumb along his cheekbone.

"Stay awake now. Will you?"

He nodded and ran his tongue over his lip. "Thirsty."

The footman brought the pitcher of water, and she gave James a sip. He looked slightly better, though his face was bloodless. The footman retreated to the foot of the bed, but Walter remained on the other side, staring down at his brother. He looked, she thought, quite lost.

"James . . ." he said vaguely, then, gazing up at her, "He can't—he'll be all right, won't he?"

Behind her, more practically, Simpson said, "I'll send for the doctor, ma'am."

"No." James spoke up, though his voice was so lacking in power it scarcely sounded like him. "No doctor." He looked at Laura. "Keep them away from me."

"Yes, of course, if you don't wish him here," she said mildly, taking his hand.

"I wish him to the devil. I wish everyone to the devil." His hand tightened on hers. "Not you."

She glanced at him, surprised, and once again felt tears burning at the backs of her eyes. "My. High praise, indeed."

Demosthenes padded over and reared up, planting his paws on the bed, and stretched his head toward James. James patted him. "It's all right, Dem." To Laura he said, "Get Owen to take him out; he's the only one not scared of him."

"Yes, sir." The footman came around the bed. "That's me, ma'am. I'll take him."

It took some persuasion from Owen, but finally the big dog followed him from the room. Laura turned to the butler. "Sir James had a high fever last night. I think perhaps he simply fainted because he's weak from that. Why don't you bring him a cup of broth or maybe oatmeal? Something strengthening."

"I don't want it," James said behind her.

"Of course not, but I think you should have a little anyway."

"Then doubtless I will." He pushed himself up to a sitting position. "I must use the breathing treatment."

"I can help." Unexpectedly Walter spoke up. "I know where the tonic is. I picked it up at the apothecary."

"Why don't you rest for a bit first?" Laura suggested. "Have some of the broth."

James shook his head. "I'll wait on the treatment. But I must clean up and dress. Mother will be here soon."

"He's right," Walter agreed, turning and rummaging through the dresser. "Word will be all around the servants' hall. If Simpson doesn't tell her, her maid certainly will. Here's a fresh shirt."

"But she won't care that you're rumpled, surely," Laura protested.

Walter snorted. "James? Rumpled? She'll be certain he's at de—" He stopped abruptly, turning brick red.

"Death's door," James finished for him.

"I'm sorry. I—I didn't mean—of course you aren't . . ."

"Stop yammering, Walter, and give me the blasted shirt." James began working on his buttons.

"Yes, of course."

Laura watched the two men in amazement as Walter helped James replace his shirt. There was the sound of agitated voices, then a rush of footsteps in the hallway. James let out a curse and stood up just as Tessa flew into the room.

"James!" She stopped in the doorway, her eyes huge in her face, her hands clutched to her heart.

"Mother." James gave her the ghost of a smile.

"Darling! The maid said—oh, God! It's true!" Tears welled in her eyes and she wailed, "Why didn't you tell me?"

Tessa started forward in a rush, arms extended, as if

to throw herself against James, but Laura, with visions of Tessa knocking him over, nimbly stepped in front of the other woman and took her arm, pulling her to a halt. She leaned in, saying in a low voice, "Don't. He'll fall. He hasn't the strength."

Tessa rolled her eyes toward Laura. "No . . ." It was more a moan than a word. She looked over at her son. "James, no . . ."

"I'm sorry," James said inadequately, and sat down on the bed.

Tessa burst into sobs and threw her arms around Laura. Laura had no doubt that Tessa's distress was real; she saw the stark terror in the woman's eyes. But she could understand why James found Tessa's emotions exhausting. He shoved one hand back through his hair, looking helpless, his face bleak.

"I can't. I can't." Tessa pulled back, her gaze pleading. "He *must* get well. I can't bear to lose another son." She turned to James, but apparently saw no help there, for she swiveled back to Laura. "What's wrong with him? I thought . . . people get better from consumption."

Laura linked her arm through Tessa's, steering her toward the door. She cast a speaking look at James's brother. "Walter . . ."

"What? Oh! Oh, yes." He came up on the other side of Tessa. "Don't cry, Mama."

Tessa patted him on the arm, giving him a tearful smile. "Why didn't he tell me? I'm his mother."

"I'm sure he didn't want to alarm you," Laura told her as she led her into the corridor. "I know it's hard, but you must be strong. For James. He hates to see you cry."

"Yes, of course. For James. He tries to be so hard, you

know, but he cares. He really does." She turned toward her other son. "Doesn't he, Walter?"

"Um . . . yes, yes, of course."

"His father was the same. Poor Laurence. Vincent. And now James . . . oh, I cannot bear it. My sons!" She burst into sobs and threw herself against Walter's chest.

Walter patted his mother's back, and Laura abandoned him to the task, returning to the bedroom. James still sat on the edge of his bed. He offered a wry smile.

"I should have known you would handle Mother." As she drew near, he reached out and wrapped his hand around her wrist. "Promise me you'll keep the rest of them at bay."

"Your family? James, they'll want to see you."

"To bid a fond farewell?"

"Well, yes. Don't you . . . wouldn't you like to see them?"

"Graeme, maybe. If you won't let him get maudlin."

She smiled faintly. "I'll give him instructions."

"If the others have to see me . . ." He shrugged a shoulder. "I suppose you must let them in for a bit. But I don't want them hanging about watching me die, like I'm a performing monkey."

"I won't let them do that. I promise you."

He nodded and turned to lie down. He closed his eyes, and after a moment he said, "Thank you."

And that, almost more than anything, made her want to cry.

Walter returned with Demosthenes, and after the dog checked on James in his bed, he lay down across the door in his usual position. Laura suspected that the mastiff would be the most effective deterrent to anyone visiting James.

Laura got most of a cup of broth down James, and it seemed to give him some strength. James wanted to do his cough treatment on his own, but after a brief verbal tussle with Laura, he agreed to allow Walter or Owen to help him.

Realizing that behind his stubbornness lay embarrassment, Laura left the rooms during his treatment and went out to the gardens. She needed a few minutes to herself. It was frightening how quickly James had gotten worse. He had been pushing himself too hard, and the high fever last night had drained him of his remaining strength.

Were fevers common with tumors in the brain? It seemed odd. Laura wished she knew more about it. She felt helpless to deal with James's illness. How could she sit there idly and watch him die? She thought of her father's medical books. James had said he would send for the rest of her things. Given his usual orderly competence, those boxes from her house should be here by now.

Laura got up and hurried back to the house, reinvigorated by the prospect of doing something constructive. It took only a few minutes with the ever-efficient Simpson to learn that her trunks and crates had indeed arrived and were stored in the cellar. It would be, the butler assured her, no trouble to have the trunks carried to her bedroom.

James's eyes were closed when Laura looked in on him, and she hesitated for a moment, not wanting to wake him. His eyes opened. "Laura. Come in." He shoved himself to a sitting position. "I need to show you my will."

"The will? No, James, that's not important now."

But James was insistent on doing it, and Laura gave in. She was amazed to learn the extent of the fortune he was leaving her, but she had come to know him well enough that it didn't surprise her that he had left a trust to provide for the rest of the family, much as his father had. She did, however, object to the fact that he named her as one of the trustees of that fund.

"Why me? They are bound to resent it. They barely know me. *You* barely know me."

"I know you well enough. I need a third trustee in case of a deadlock. Graeme is far too soft, especially where my mother is concerned, and the other trustee, Caulfield, can be hard. Like me, he understands numbers better than emotions. You, however, can be firm *and* kind. I trust your good sense. Besides . . ." A trace of his wicked smile touched his lips. "You're so skilled at managing everyone."

She brushed his hair back from his forehead. "Yes, well, I'm going to manage you now. You should sleep."

Laura stayed by James's bed throughout the day. Whenever he opened his eyes, he looked for her. She didn't want him to awaken alone. As she sat there, she went through a few of her father's books, looking for answers, but she could find nothing to help her fight a brain tumor.

The members of his family came to see him, all of them looking uneasy and, amazingly, a little shocked. Despite the strong evidence to the contrary, had they all believed that James would recover? She was prepared to move them out the door if they remained too long, but none seemed inclined to linger, nor did they come back frequently. To be fair, that might have had something to do with the fact that Demosthenes continued to lie directly across the doorway and growl whenever anyone approached.

Late in the evening, Laura awoke to find she had fallen asleep in the chair beside his bed. She sat up, heart pounding, and turned to the bed. James lay quietly, his eyes closed, his chest rising and falling shallowly, and she sagged in relief. Asleep, it was easy to see the ravages of James's illness. His pale face was gaunt, weary grooves lining his mouth and eyes. He frowned and muttered in his sleep.

Laura rubbed her temples, where a headache had formed. Her neck was stiff from the position she had fallen asleep in, and she rolled her head, trying to ease it. Laura went to the bed, straightening the covers as she searched his face.

As she turned away from the bed, his hand wrapped around her wrist, startling her. "Stay." Laura looked back at him in surprise. "Please."

"I will." Laura had intended to stay with him through the night anyway. But it was most unlike James to ask for a favor. She laid her hand on his forehead to check for fever.

"I'm not out of my head. I just . . ." His hand began to shake, and he pulled it back. His entire arm spasmed. "I hate this."

"I know."

He turned his head away, saying, "No. Never mind. You should go to your room and sleep. It's foolish for you to stay here."

"Not as foolish as it is for you to pretend you need nothing and no one." She smiled at him. "I'll just go change into my dressing gown. I'll be back soon."

When she returned, James's eyes were still open, and his arm was once again still. Laura sat down on the side of his bed, taking up his hand even though she had no need to check for fever.

"Don't wear black for me," he told her.

"James, really, must you bring this up?"

"Glad to see I can still annoy you." He smiled, but the sight of it on his wasted face sent a chill through Laura.

"If that is all it takes to please you, you should be a happy man indeed." It was hard to maintain her crisp, cool front. But James would hate her growing "maudlin," as he would term it.

"And, please, I beg you, do not let Mother have a daguerreotype made of all of you artistically posed and weeping into your kerchiefs."

Laura couldn't help but chuckle, having seen one or two such mourning mementos. "I promise I will dissuade her."

He fell silent, his thumb tracing a circle on her palm. "I'm sorry."

She glanced at him in surprise, but he kept his gaze on her hand, so that she could see nothing in his eyes. "For what?"

"For . . ." He shrugged. "Ruining your life eleven years ago, I suppose."

"I think you acquired more of your mother's love of

drama than you'll admit." He looked at her then, startled, and she went on. "You didn't ruin my life. You may have noticed I didn't wither and die because I didn't marry Graeme. In any case, you couldn't have forced me to give up Graeme. I chose to do so. You were simply . . . the bearer of bad tidings."

He made a breathy noise that she thought was meant to be a laugh. "Now there's an apt description of me. But I was harsh."

"You aren't prone to softening blows. But maybe that makes it easier in the end, after . . ."

"After the weeping?" He cocked an eyebrow.

"Sometimes it's better to be quick and sure than to be kind. I can tell you that if I had a splinter in my finger, I would go to you to pull it out."

"And I'd be happy to do it." There was a twinkle in his eyes, quickly gone.

After that he was quiet, and Laura took her seat in the chair again. The night wore on. Laura slept now and then, waking to check on him.

Other than changing into a dress the next morning, there was little to distinguish the day from the night. James continued to grow worse. Laura acquired a headache. She was achingly tired. She wished she had someone to whom she could talk. But the truth was, at Grace Hill her closest friend was James's dog.

Late that night, James began a fit of coughing, and guiltily Laura realized she had overlooked his breathing treatment this evening. She was tired, but Owen had just taken Demosthenes out for his bedtime ramble, so it was up to her to help James with the vapor therapy.

Taking out the brown bottle of medicine from the cabinet, she turned to carry it back to the bed. Her foot slipped on the edge of the rug, and she lurched into the dresser, hitting her elbow. The bottle shot from her grasp and crashed to the floor, spilling its contents over the wood floor.

Laura let out a cry of horror and sank to her knees beside the mess. Tears spilled from her eyes. Silly to cry, of course; Walter would get more from the apothecary in the morning. But in her tired state, bombarded by her jumbled emotions, spilling his tonic seemed the last straw.

The wink of something silvery caught her eye. The bottle was brown, as was the liquid inside. What could be silver—she leaned forward to peer at the pool of tonic. Bright amidst the brown medicine lay a silver blob.

Quicksilver.

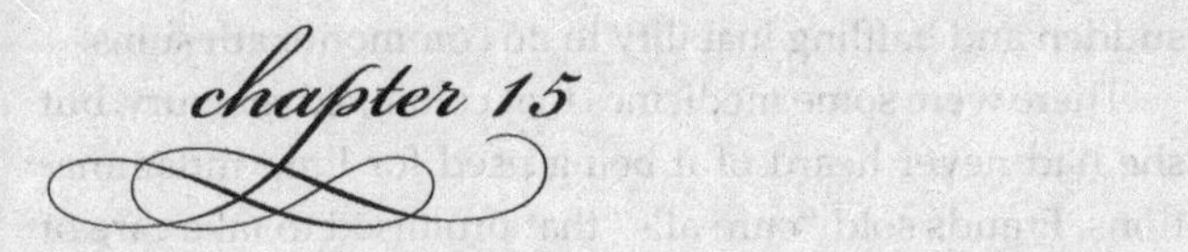

Laura had seen it before. The less dramatic-sounding name was liquid mercury. And it was poisonous. Carefully picking up two pieces of the glass, she scooped up the blob and wrapped a small towel around it. She felt strangely removed from herself, her movements slow, as if she walked through water. Her mind, on the other hand, flashed about, dancing around the horror at the center of it.

Poison. There was poison in James's medicine.

Laura closed the bedroom door and locked it, as if that could keep them safe from danger. She felt icy at the core. Turning the light brighter, she examined her find again. There was no mistaking that it was mercury. Her father had used it in some of his experiments.

Many years before, he had studied a case involving hatters suffering from mercury poisoning. Mercuric nitrate was used as a smoothing agent to treat the fur of small animals in order to make felt. The material, saturated with the chemical, continually released mercury vapor into the air as the workers made hats out of the felt. After years of breathing the toxic air, the hat makers often died. That was where the expression "mad as a hatter" came from; they acted strangely, said mad things. She thought of James telling her that her hair was on fire, the bizarre things she had heard him mumbling. He had said he'd seen his dead father beside his bed and another time a long-dead pet. His sudden and baffling inability to do common math sums.

There were some medicines that contained mercury, but she had never heard of it being used for lung inflammations. Frauds sold "cure-alls" that promised to take care of various illnesses and that had not only ineffective ingredients but even harmful ones. But James hardly seemed the sort to go to quacks or believe in fantastical remedies. Still, when one was dying, she supposed that even a cynic might fall prey to such things.

Perhaps that was it. Otherwise . . . it meant someone was trying to murder James. No, someone *was* murdering him by slow degrees. She began to pace, all weariness having fled.

James had started taking this medicine because he was already sick with headaches and coughing. The mercury in the steam he breathed couldn't have given him the illness, only worsened it. Either he had suffered from an entirely different ailment, which the medicine had exacerbated, or he had already been exposed to mercury some other way, and the tonic had been used to continue or increase the exposure.

Laura looked over at James in his bed. She wished she had the aid of his cool, incisive mind now. He coughed, and somehow that made Laura cough, too. She stiffened. She had coughed a few times today, but had thought nothing of it. Her head ached. She had attributed it to the strain of her situation, the stiff neck from sleeping in the chair.

But what if those symptoms came from something else? She had been closed in this room with James for two days. She hadn't handled the breathing treatment before now; Owen or Walter had helped James. So the treatment couldn't have affected her. She could be only imagining that her mild symptoms were like James's. But if she was not, it would mean that there was something in this room that caused it. Something that had originally made James ill. If she remembered correctly, simply breathing in the vapors was hazardous.

Laura glanced around the room. It wouldn't be in plain sight. Otherwise James would have seen it, or certainly one of the servants would have noticed it when they were cleaning. She opened the wardrobe and each of the drawers in the dresser even though enclosed spaces didn't seem the likeliest place for it. She lay flat on the floor and checked under the highboy and the nightstands. Last, she turned to the bed, aware of a curious reluctance to search under it even though the high bed would be the best place to hide something. She didn't really want to find out.

Irritated by her cowardice, she lay down beside the bed. She could see nothing on the floor underneath the bed, but near the head of it, a shallow square object hung from the frame. The bed was so high off the ground that Laura had no problem sliding beneath it. The object she had seen turned out to be a cast-iron pan hanging from wires fastened to the bed.

Laura's heart hammered. It was too dark to see the contents of the pan, and she had to slide out and set the lamp on the floor beside the bed, then crawl beneath the bed again. It took some contortions to not block the light as she lifted her head to peer into the container. The bottom of the pan was covered with silver liquid.

Laura shot back out as if she had seen a snake. She

would have jumped to her feet except her legs were trembling too much. There could be no doubt. Someone had put the mercury there. He had carefully, intentionally fastened it beneath the upper part of James's bed, where he would breathe it in all night long.

She shuddered with revulsion at the thought of James lying here ill the last few days, all the while breathing in the fatal poison. How could anyone be so cold-blooded?

Even worse, the would-be murderer must be here in the house. A stranger sneaking into James's bedroom with a pan and a bottle of mercury would have been noticed. Of course, it could have been done by an earlier visitor to Grace Hill. One of Tessa's admirers, for instance. Laura had several times seen Mr. Netherly pacing up and down the entire length of the hall, apparently lost in communion with his muse. He could easily have slipped in and out of James's room. But why would he—or any of Tessa's swains—want to kill James? It would hardly endear them to Tessa.

No, the obvious killer was someone in the family.

What was she to do? How could she fight this? Laura was alone. James was too ill to be of any help, and she had no idea whom she could turn to. However awful the idea was, any of the people around her could be the very person trying to kill James. Not his mother, of course, but Tessa would be of no help in a crisis. Graeme's home was not far away, but Tessa had said that Graeme was still in London.

No, it was up to her to protect James. Laura shivered. The house seemed dark and cavernous, looming all around her. She had never felt so small and cold. So alone.

James stirred on the bed, muttering. She pushed herself to her feet and leaned over him. He moved his head restlessly on the pillow. His black hair was damp with sweat from his intermittent fevers, and it clung to his skull, making him appear even more gaunt. A saving anger rose up in her. She was *not* going to let James die.

"James." When he didn't respond, she shook his shoulder, saying his name again. Finally his eyes opened. He blinked at her uncomprehendingly.

"James. Listen to me."

"Laura?" The word was a mere whisper.

"Yes, it's me. This is very important. I don't think you have a tumor or brain fever or any of those things."

He frowned, watching her intently, but in a puzzled way.

"Someone is trying to kill you. You have to help me." She took one of his hands between hers. "You understand? You have to hang on. Don't give in, no matter how hard it is. Because I'm *not* going to let them have you."

In the light of the lamp his eyes flashed with silver, and his hand tightened on hers.

chapter 16

"We need to get you out of here." Even if she removed the pan from the bed, the fumes might linger. Opening the windows to air out the room wasn't an option in a sick man's room. It was spring, but the nights were still cool.

James nodded and pushed himself up and out of the bed. He had to grasp the bedpost to keep from wobbling, but his face was set in an expression Laura was coming to know well. All he said was, "Where?"

"My room. It'll be easiest." She slipped an arm around his waist and they started forward.

Demosthenes jumped up when she opened the door. Seeing James, his tail began to wag and he pressed against him. With the mastiff on one side and Laura on the other, they walked down the hall to Laura's bedchamber. Their progress was slow and slightly weaving, but they made it to her door without running into anything along the way.

Laura left James on the chair just inside her door, Demosthenes beside him, while she returned to his bedroom to set up the scene. She intended to keep her discovery of the poison secret. If the would-be killer realized his trick had been discovered, he might try something else or get rid of evidence. But if he thought this was a temporary move and James would return, he would simply wait. He might even be complacent enough to give himself away.

She removed the evidence of the shattered bottle, wiping up the liquid and wrapping the broken glass in the towel with the mercury, but she left the pan hanging beneath the bed. She had a moment's pause, concerned that others might be exposed to the fumes. But if James was no longer there, no one would go to his room except for the brief time maids might come in to dust.

Next she poured a cup of water from the jug and tossed the contents onto the bed, artfully leaving the cup on its side on the covers. It would be perfectly reasonable to move James if she had clumsily spilled a drink, soaking the mattress.

Casting a last glance around the room, she repacked her medical bag and carried it and the towel containing the ruined bottle back to her own room. Dog and man were waiting patiently by the door, James leaning back against the wall, eyes closed, and Dem sitting with his great head resting on James's lap.

James levered himself up, and they made their halting way to the bed. As she reached out with one hand to whisk down the bedcovers, James said, "Dear Laura, if you wanted me in your bed, you had only to ask."

She grimaced at him. "No doubt you'll go to your maker with a smirk on your face. But I don't intend for that to happen anytime soon."

He eased down onto the bed and closed his eyes. Laura could see the effort the move had cost him in every line of his wan face. Demosthenes, who had followed them to the bed, whined softly.

"I know," Laura told him as she sank down into the

nearest chair, her urgency-fueled strength draining out of her. "It's upsetting to you." Dem sat down, putting one paw on her lap, and gazed earnestly into her face. "I'm so scared, Dem," Laura whispered, laying her cheek against the top of his massive head and curling her arm around his shoulders. Tears spilled from her eyes and melted into his coat. "Thank God I have you with me. What if he's already too far gone? What if I can't handle it? I don't know what to do."

Dem gave her arm a reassuring lick, and somehow that lightened her spirits. With a last pat, she stood up and wiped away her tears. She couldn't afford weakness. She needed to find out how to combat this poison.

She wasn't sure what could be done beyond waiting for the mercury to leave his system and hoping she had caught it in time. But she knew that it could be done. Two of the men her father had treated had lived. And if anyone was stubborn and contrary enough to fight off the poison, it would be James.

The place to start was her father's old medical journals. Thank goodness she had already had them brought up here to her room. Picking up a lamp, she went into the large dressing room. Her few clothes took up little space, leaving ample room for the trunks and boxes from her house.

It didn't take her long to find the trunk containing her father's journals. Fortunately, each was dated. But since she wasn't sure when her father had healed the men, only that it had been before her mother's death, there were several years to be explored.

She started with the year her mother died and worked backward. It turned out to be the year Laura was four that held her answers. No wonder she couldn't remember the events, only her father talking about it years later. Flipping through the pages, her eyes fell on the word *mercury*, and she paged more carefully through it to find the beginning of the case.

"It may present as a catarrh-like illness," her father had written. Upper respiratory symptoms—fever, chills, shortness of breath, pleuritic chest pain. Heart palpitations. Insomnia. Headaches. Tremors. Confusion . . . memory loss . . . irritability.

Laura drew in her breath, her hands trembling. They were all right there. Symptoms easily mistaken for other diseases, neurological indications that could be taken for the effects of a brain tumor. It was an uncommon illness, not a disease but poison, and unless one had treated hatters—an unlikely patient for doctors accustomed to treating the wealthy and the peerage—a physician would not have encountered it.

Squinting in the lamplight to read the faded ink, she followed her father's accounts of "hatters' shakes," vivid dreams and hallucinations, even delusions. The symptoms were apparently many and varied, and not all the men had exhibited the same ones. She was grateful James had not experienced them all, but it made her heart squeeze in her chest to think of him suffering so needlessly.

Anger burned in her at the idea of someone purposely doing this to him. But that, too, she had to put aside. What she needed to focus on now was making sure that the monster didn't achieve his goal.

Tears glittered in her eyes as she read her father's closing remarks on several of the cases: *patient deceased*. But not all of them. Laura took hope from the fact that it seemed that those who had suffered a brief exposure, even if it was severe, recovered more quickly and completely than the men who had breathed in the vapor at a low level for years.

She skimmed the pages, looking for her father's discussion of treatments. It seemed that little had sped up the recovery beyond removing them from the toxic fumes. But surely James, a strong, young, healthy man, would have a better chance of recovering than many of the men her father had treated.

But here . . . she stopped and read more slowly. Her father said he had had some success with administering milk thistle. Popping up, she went to the medical bag she had set on the floor by the bed and looked through it until she found a small bottle of milk thistle. Measuring out the brown liquid, she noted with concern that there was not much left.

It took some effort, but she managed to get the liquid down James. He began to talk in his sleep, his voice so soft and slurred she couldn't make out the words. Then he stopped and opened his eyes and said, "Laura."

"Yes. It's I."

"Lovely Laura." He closed his eyes. His forehead was damp, a faint flush along his cheekbones, and she knew he was feverish again.

Laura bathed his face with cool water, and as she worked, she wondered what to do. Her supply of milk thistle would soon run out. She had to get more. But first, she knew, she must sleep. She was too tired to think clearly.

Demosthenes had been restlessly pacing about. Laura led him to the door of her room. Pointing to the floor, she said firmly, "Guard."

Dem gazed at her for a long moment, then sprawled out

in the hallway across the door. With one of his long-suffering sighs, he laid his head on his paws. Laura bent down to pat him, pleased that he had obeyed her. She felt much safer with the mastiff on watch. Closing the door and locking it made her feel even safer.

She checked on James once more and found him cooler. Laura thought of sleeping in the chair beside her window, but it was a dainty chair not given to comfort. She was too tired to care about the proprieties. She lay down beside James on the bed and immediately sank into sleep.

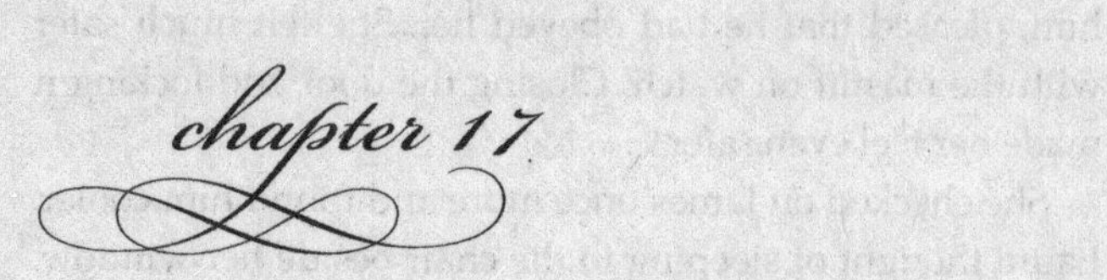

A loud bark outside her door brought Laura out of a deep sleep, and she shot out of bed. Memory flooded back as she threw on her dressing gown and hurried to open the door.

Demosthenes was standing staring down the hallway, his gaze intent on Walter, who hovered outside James's open door. Though the mastiff had not showed his teeth nor even raised his hackles, his warning bark was enough to freeze Walter where he stood.

"L-Laura!" Walter turned his panicked face to her. "Where's James? What's happened? He's not—he's not—"

"No, no," Laura hastened to assure him. "We moved him into my room."

"Oh." Walter relaxed.

Laura reached down to pat Dem, murmuring, "Good boy. It's all right."

Another door opened down the hall and Claude stuck his head out, frowning, then went back inside. At the end of the hall, Laura saw Owen walking toward them, carrying a tray.

"I woke up early," Walter said, coming over to Laura, though he kept a wary eye on the mastiff. "I wanted to see how James was."

"Of course." Laura opened the door wider, stepping back. "Come in. But I fear he isn't awake."

Demosthenes took the opportunity to go to the bed and give James a nudge with his nose. James muttered something that might have been, "Good Dem," and rolled over on his side. Apparently satisfied, the dog padded back to Laura.

Walter didn't enter the room, just hung in the doorway, staring across at his brother. "Why is he here? I don't understand."

"I spilled water on the bed last night." Laura told him the story she had concocted, hoping that by the light of day it still sounded reasonable. Between him and Owen, who had come up behind Walter, the word would be all over the house in minutes. "I think we may remain for a while. It's easier for me to care for him here."

Walter didn't question her words, merely nodded. "Is he . . . any better?"

"He's holding his own." In Laura's opinion, it was better that the others in the house knew as little as possible about James's condition or her efforts.

As long as the would-be murderer thought James was at death's door, surely he wouldn't try to do him further harm. It was difficult to picture Walter, the youngest and mildest of the de Veres, plotting to kill James, but she wasn't about to let down her guard.

Owen slipped past the other man to set the tray on the dresser. "I brought you a bite of breakfast, ma'am. I'll take Demosthenes out now, if you like."

"Thank you, Owen."

Walter finally moved into the room, though he stopped at the foot of the bed. Laura followed Owen and the dog into the hall. Keeping an eye on Walter, she said in a quiet voice, "Owen, I need you to stay with James for a while when you return with Dem. James asked me to talk to his aunt." She was becoming frighteningly adept at lying.

"Yes, ma'am. Shall I have the carriage brought round?"

Laura nodded and went back into the room. Walter still stood at the foot of the bed, watching James. He turned toward her and summoned a smile. "I mustn't keep you from your breakfast. I only wanted to see how he was doing this morning."

After Walter left, Laura closed the door and crossed to James's bed. James opened his eyes. "Laura." His gaze went beyond her to the tester above him and he frowned, twisting his head to glance around. "Where—oh." He relaxed. "This is your room." He paused, his eyes narrowing. "We—we moved in here in the middle of the night."

"Yes, we did. So you remember."

He nodded. "You were—did you say someone wanted to kill me? Was that a dream?"

"No. It wasn't a dream."

"But how . . . why . . ." He frowned, raising a hand to rub his forehead.

"Mercury. They placed some under your bed. And it was in your tonic. You were breathing it in with every treatment."

"I can't . . . I can't think. Damn!" He pushed himself up. "I'm so bloody useless, Laura." He took her arm. "You must be careful."

"Don't worry. I haven't let on that I discovered the mercury; I said you moved in here because I spilled water on your bed. We're safely away from the poison, and Demosthenes will stand guard at the door." She took his hand between both of hers. "All you have to do is get better."

"I'm not sure I can."

"You can. You must." She leaned in closer, staring into his eyes. "James, I need you. You have to get better and help me figure this out. I'm all alone here, and you can't leave me." One thing she had learned about James in the past few days was his overriding sense of responsibility.

He gazed at her for a long moment. "I won't."

"Good. Now take this medicine." She mixed a measure of milk thistle with a tiny amount of water.

"What is it?"

"Bitter."

"Of course." There was a glimmer of his old self in his eyes.

"It's milk thistle. My father used it with success." Her father had always said that medicine worked better with belief.

He swallowed it without protest. It was harder work getting him to drink any of the cup of broth Owen had brought for him, but she managed that as well. Laura couldn't bring herself to eat anything. Her stomach was too tied up in knots. Going into her dressing room, she changed clothes, then sat down before the mirror to put her hair into some rudimentary order.

By the time she was ready, Owen was waiting on a bench in the hall, Demosthenes in his usual place. The dog made his routine check on James before returning to his spot at the door. Laura leaned over James, checking a last time for fever.

"James, I'm going to see about more medicine. I'll be

gone for a bit, but Owen will be here with you. He'll take care of you." His eyes didn't open; she couldn't tell if he was asleep. Fear tugged at her stomach. What if his life slipped away while she was gone? "I'll be back as soon as I can. And Dem is outside the door." Impulsively she bent and pressed her lips to his forehead.

"Please sit with him, Owen," she said as she pulled on her gloves. At his quick nod, she went on, "It's best if he sleeps. You might want to close the door to, um, shut out any noise." And discourage visitors.

It was a lovely spring day, but Laura was too wrapped in her worrisome thoughts to look at the view outside the carriage. It was much too early to be making a call, but that social solecism weighed little compared to seeking help from the wife of the man Laura had loved for much of her life.

Laura liked Abby. Indeed, when they had met by accident, unaware of who the other was, they had chatted like good friends. Abigail seemed a reasonable, fair person, but the heart didn't always follow one's head.

No matter how much Graeme loved his wife now, it did not change the fact that the first years of their marriage had been bitter—and his thwarted love for Laura was the reason he had turned away from his new bride. Any woman would find that hard to forgive.

So it was with some trepidation that Laura entered the front door of Lydcombe Hall. The Parr family's imperturbable butler, Fletcher, gave no indication that he found such an early morning visit odd, merely bowed and said, "Miss Laura. Lady de Vere, I should say. We are most grieved at the news of Sir James's illness. Lady Montclair—Lady Mirabelle, that is—is still abed, but I will tell her you are here."

"No, it's not Mirabelle I've come to see. It's Abigail." Laura hesitated. "If, that is, you think she would not mind."

Something like a smile lurked in the butler's eyes. "Indeed, Lady Abigail is, ah, quite at ease with informality."

Laura followed him upstairs to the sunny sitting room overlooking the rose garden. Within moments, Abigail rushed into the room. She was still clad in her dressing gown, a dramatic blue satin robe reminiscent of a Japanese kimono, richly embroidered, her black hair hanging in a loose braid down her back. In her arms, she carried a small bundle.

It was impossible not to be struck anew by the other woman's beauty. Tall and statuesque, with vivid green eyes and thick black hair, Abigail Parr was stunning. But now her face was creased with concern as she said, "Laura? What's happened? Is James—"

"No! Oh, Abigail, no. I'm sorry; I didn't think. I should have told Fletcher that James is . . . not worse. I didn't come here about—well, I did, but—oh—" She raised her hands to her face and realized they were trembling. "I'm sorry. I'm not making sense."

"Come, sit down. You must be terribly distressed. I'll ring for tea. Or would you like coffee? The staff has given in to my American love for coffee."

As she came closer, the bundle emitted a squeak and stirred, and Laura saw that the object in Abigail's arms was a baby wrapped in a blanket. An arm emerged, knocking back the blanket to reveal the rest of her. "Oh! I didn't realize. Is this—"

"Anna," Abigail said, beaming, and turned, tilting her so that Laura could see the infant better.

"My goodness." Laura peered down into the perfect features. All white and pink and dimpled, with a thick shock of black hair and huge blue eyes, the baby stared back up at Laura. "She's beautiful."

"Would you like to hold her?" Abby extended her toward Laura.

"Could I?" A smile lit Laura's face. "Oh, yes, if you don't mind." Laura settled the baby carefully into the crook of one arm, brushing a finger across Anna's petal-soft cheeks. "Such black hair . . . and those eyes. Graeme must be over the moon."

Abigail chuckled. "He is already tightly wrapped around her little finger. I'm certain he'll be the most doting father ever."

"I can see why." The girl took a firm hold on Laura's dress, making cooing noises. Laura bent her head closer, breathing in the sweet scent of baby. "She looks like you."

"Do you think so? Graeme says she does, but I can't see it—except for the hair, of course, but Graeme and his mother have dark hair, too."

"Yes, but . . . I can't identify it, really, but there's something of you in her little face." Laura raised her head, smiling at the other woman, and received a warm smile in return. Perhaps talking to Abigail would not be as hard as she feared.

At that moment, the baby's nurse bustled in to take Anna back to the nursery for a change, and Laura handed her over somewhat reluctantly. The butler, with his usual efficiency, had not waited for Abby to request refreshments, but swept in now with a tray of coffee, tea, and rolls.

Laura, unable to eat anything before she left, was suddenly starving. Abigail sipped a cup of coffee, waiting until Laura had consumed an air-light croissant before she spoke. "I'm glad to hear that James is not worse. But something must be amiss."

"Yes. I'm very sorry to barge in like this so early, but I—" Laura drew a shaky breath. "I need help."

"What can I do?" Abigail set down her coffee and leaned forward. "What do you need?"

"I think—I fear someone is trying to harm James." Abby gaped at her, and Laura rushed on, suddenly fearing that Abby would not believe her. "I found mercury in James's medicine."

"Mercury?" Abby looked even more astonished. "Quicksilver?"

"Yes. Do you know anything about it?"

"My father owned part of a quicksilver mine in California. I think they used it to extract gold from the ore."

"There have been doctors who prescribed it for some ailments. But not for a cough. I dropped a bottle of his tonic, and there was mercury in the liquid. That's not all." Her story poured out—the discovery of the pan beneath James's bed, Laura's fears, her father's cases. "It's very dangerous; one only has to breathe the vapors. It doesn't even have to be heated."

Laura finally wound down, the knot in her chest that had been her companion the past few hours loosening. Abby at first said nothing, still gazing at her in amazement.

"I know this must sound mad," Laura told her. "But I promise I am perfectly sane. Someone deliberately set out to harm James."

"No, I have no doubt about your sanity," Abby assured her. "It's just hard to take it all in." She straightened. "The two of you should come here. No one could get to him here."

"Thank you. You're very kind. But I'm afraid to move him. He is . . ." Tears glistened in Laura's eyes. "James is very ill. I put him in a different room, and Demosthenes guards the door."

"That should discourage any attacker." Abby smiled. "What can you do for him—will he recover?"

"I don't know. Some of my father's patients died, and others didn't. My father used milk thistle, and he thought it helped speed recovery. That's why I came to you. To ask you to purchase some for me. I have a little, but I need much more."

"I will, of course, but I don't understand. Why not send a servant to the village? Wouldn't the apothecary have it?"

"That's where his tonic came from."

"Ohhh." Abby's brows rose in understanding. "You suspect the apothecary of adding the poison?"

"I suspect everyone in the house, but I cannot rule out the apothecary. I fear if I bought it or sent a servant or, well, anyone in the house, the man would reason that it was for James, and if he is the person who contaminated the medicine, he might taint it, as well. But you are far enough removed that I don't think he would assume you were buying it for James. Also . . . I don't want anyone at Grace Hill to know about it."

Abby nodded. "I understand. I'll go there this morning. As soon as I have it, I'll come to call on you and Tessa. That would seem natural, don't you think? I'll bring Mirabelle with me."

"But you won't tell her, will you?"

"No. I won't breathe a word of it. It would upset her greatly, and she would be bound to tell her sister. I must tell Graeme, though."

"Yes, of course."

"He will be back before long. I wired him about James's condition, and he wired back immediately that he was returning. But Lady Eugenia insists on coming with him."

"The dowager countess?" Laura stared. "Why?"

"I don't know; I suppose she tyrannized James as well when he and Graeme were boys."

Laura half smiled. "I suspect she had a bit less success with James."

"No doubt. Anyway, she's got it in her head to come, and so of course he had to wait another day for her. Doubtless when I tell him, Graeme will want to charge over there and have at someone."

"I'd be happy for him to, if only we knew who. I'm hoping I'll see something in their faces or catch them checking on the mercury. Something that will tell me who it is."

"Just let me know if you need anything else from me. I'll do whatever I can. You have my word."

"Thank you." Laura smiled, and both of them knew that something more than Abby's help had been obtained.

chapter 18

Laura arrived home to discover that James's fever had returned while she was gone. Owen let out a sigh of relief when she entered, and he jumped to his feet. "I wasn't sure what to do. Sir James has been restless for a while. Well, ever since Mrs. Salstone and her ladyship were here to see him."

"Did they talk to him? Do anything?" Laura asked as she stripped off her gloves and began to untie her bonnet.

"Um . . . well, Lady de Vere cried." He looked puzzled. "Is that what you mean?"

"I thought perhaps they might have gotten him to eat or drink something."

"Oh. No. Mrs. Salstone was upset because the dog growled. You know how Dem is." Laura thought amusement lurked in his eyes. "Dem let them in, but then he came and stood next to Sir James and they couldn't get close to the bed. Mrs. Salstone said as how a dog shouldn't be allowed in a sickroom. But then Lady de Vere told her not to be silly, as Sir James would rather have Dem with him than anyone else."

Laura could not hold back a little smile. "I suspect that's true." She poured water into the basin and added a few drops of lavender.

"But then Mrs. Salstone began to cry, and her ladyship did, too. And Sir James said, 'Do stop sniveling.'" Clearly Owen had a good memory and a delight in storytelling, as well.

"Oh, dear."

He nodded. "Then Mrs. Salstone cried harder, and the ladies left. That's when he asked where you were, and then he began tossing and turning and talking like . . ." Owen frowned, looking as troubled as his round freckled face was capable of, and lowered his voice. "Well, you know, like somebody else was here talking back to him."

"Yes, I know." Laura wet a cloth and began to wipe James's face.

"Laura," James murmured, not opening his eyes.

"Yes, I'm here."

"I've been talking to your father."

Laura's hand stilled for an instant. "My father?"

"He says so. I think he's lying."

"Why is that?"

"His head is wrong." He gestured vaguely. "It's a deer."

"Then, yes, I would say that's not Papa."

Her answer seemed to satisfy him, for he fell silent. She coaxed him to drink a little of her headache tincture, followed by some water, and though he shook his head at the milk thistle extract, he swallowed that, as well.

"Knew you'd come back," he said softly.

"Yes, of course." She picked up the cool cloth again.

"How else could you torment me?"

"Exactly." Laura continued to wipe his face, dampening the cloth again and again. After a time, he quieted and fell asleep.

While James slept, she occupied herself with digging

through her father's papers. She had no luck in his journals, but when she thumbed through the doctor's correspondence, she found a letter from a doctor in Australia thanking Dr. Hinsdale for his recommendations regarding treatment of men who mined cinnabar ore.

Cinnabar, she remembered, was the ore that yielded mercury. The letter was two pages long and the handwriting cramped, but she waded through it, finding a list of foods the Australian thought helped his patients recover.

Laura wasted no time in giving Simpson the new requirements for James's menu. That was the easy part, of course. The trouble would come in getting James to eat them.

For two days, things went on much the same. James would be feverish, then chilled. His eyes were usually closed, though she wasn't sure how much he slept. Sometimes he talked in an eerie one-sided conversation. When he was awake, his eyes were often clouded and confused.

Laura watched over him, never leaving James alone unless Owen was there to help him and Demosthenes to guard him. True to her word, Abigail brought her the bottle of milk thistle under the guise of a call. Laura persuaded James to take it by cajoling or annoying him into it, whichever worked. She even managed to convince him to eat some food.

The members of James's family trailed in to see him at various times. Laura watched them, hoping to pick up some indication that one of them had planned James's demise. Claude's face was almost as difficult to read as James's. Walter seemed the most concerned. But was he afraid James would die or afraid he would live?

Patricia resented Laura's constant presence in the sickroom, which made Laura wonder why the woman wanted so much to be alone with James. It might only be Patricia's dislike of Laura, but perhaps it was something far worse. Laura hated the suspicion with which she lived. But none of it was as bad as the constant, draining worry that James had moved beyond the reach of her help, that he would never emerge from this semiconscious state.

James drifted. He knew who he was. He knew that something had happened to him and he hurt. That much was clear. He was less sure where he was. The sky above him was dark green, but that was wrong. Sometimes he burned and sometimes he was cold to the marrow of his bones. People he didn't want to see came in and peered at him. His mother cried over him. But, no, she cried because Vincent was gone.

Now and then the dog stuck its square head over the top of the bed and stared at him, frowning. Mags. He smiled to see his first dog. Only she was Dem, too, and that couldn't be right. But he liked having both of them there.

She was there. He knew who she was, though sometimes her name floated away from him. She gave him bitter things to drink, but her hands were soft and cool. She was lovely and the light glowed on her golden hair. Often her hair was in braids wound around her head, and other times it hung down over her shoulders and back like a waterfall. When he was hot, she bathed his face with cool water, and he felt better. When he was freezing, she held him. And that felt the best. He knew she was Graeme's. But, no, she was *his*.

That didn't make any sense at all. It was so difficult to think. He didn't really want to think, anyway. There was that dark thing, and it was best left alone.

Then all at once, he would wake, and everything was real. The green above his head wasn't the sky, but a canopy above a bed, and the room . . . the room was Laura's. She was his wife. It was Dem who watched him. Mags had died years and years ago. The pain in his body separated into all its various points. And someone wanted him dead.

It was better, really, to drift.

Now and then when he drifted, he wasn't even here. Once he was standing beside his father's desk, and it didn't seem odd that he was only a boy. James showed his father numbers on a piece of paper, but the numbers didn't matter. What mattered was that his father laughed, and his arm curled around James, enclosing him in his warmth and scent for an instant, as he said, "Who would have thought it would be the cuckoo in the nest?"

Another time, James stood in the doorway of that same study, older now and more wary, watching his father, who sat, head in his hands and a half-empty bottle and glass before him on the desk. James had heard the argument earlier in his parents' bedroom, and he'd trailed downstairs after his father stormed out, with some vague idea of making things right.

He knew deep down he couldn't fix things between his parents. Nothing could, for Mama was all sunshine and laughter and storms, and Papa was all stone, as his mother said.

He didn't know what they had fought about other than it had something to do with Captain Randall, whom James disliked because of the way he smiled and jovially patted James on the shoulder, as if he was a friend.

Laurence looked up and saw James, with that wry twist of the mouth James so often saw on him, and said, "Don't be a fool like me, boy. Don't let a woman tear you up inside."

But even being there was better than the other place he went to, where the darkness lurked across the nursery in the room where Mama wept and the doctor came and Nurse shooed James away. And Papa was not like Papa at all, but broken.

James was glad to hear *her* voice. Sharp and angry, it pulled at him, tugging him away from the darkness. Other voices rose against hers. Laura needed help. He must stop this nonsense and be himself.

James opened his eyes. The room was dim, the only light the lamp on the dresser. Laura stood in the doorway beside Dem, both of them taut as they faced the people in the hall. There the lights were brighter, illuminating his sister and her husband.

"It's very late," Laura said. "James is sleeping."

"What difference does it make?" That was Patricia; he'd heard that whine for nigh on thirty years. "He's always asleep."

"Yes. He's ill."

"But what's wrong with him? Nobody knows. Mother says it's something in his brain, but James never told us anything. Now you're always here, not letting anybody see him."

There was a moment of tense silence, then Laura said, "Very well. For just a few minutes." James closed his eyes so he wouldn't have to talk to his sister, but Laura said sharply, "Just you, Patricia."

James opened his eyes again, alert. Dem was growling, the hair on his ruff standing up, and Laura had crossed her arms.

"But Archie wants to see him," Patricia protested. "To say good-bye." Good-bye? No doubt that would be a conversation Archie would relish.

"Be that as it may, James doesn't want to see him."

"How would you know what James wants? He's *my* brother."

"I know him a great deal better than you if you think he wants to see the man he threw out of the house a fortnight ago," Laura shot back.

"How dare you?" Patricia's voice rose to a piercing shriek that was all too familiar. "How dare you sweep in here and tell us all what to do? I don't know how you tricked James into marrying you, but—"

"Tricked James?" Laura gave a humorless chuckle. "Do you honestly think anyone could trick James into anything? I *dare* to keep you from him because I am his *wife*. I am the mistress of this household. I will do whatever it takes to make sure James has peace and quiet. If you don't like it, you are, of course, welcome to leave Grace Hill."

Well done, Laura. James smiled to himself.

"This is all damned havey-cavey, if you ask me." That was Archie, in a tone that made James want to growl like Dem.

Laura, however, remained cool as ice. "No doubt you are more familiar with havey-cavey doings than I, Mr. Salstone. But whatever you think, you are not seeing James. I will not have you bothering him."

"Now, see here," Archie began. Beside Laura, Dem's growl deepened, and he bared his teeth. Salstone stopped abruptly.

James rolled up on his elbow and shoved aside the covers. He swung out of bed, reaching one hand to the bedpost and hoping he didn't crumple ignominiously to the floor. Then another voice joined the others in the corridor.

"Salstone." It was Claude. James relaxed. Whatever else Claude was—murderer came to mind—he disliked Archie Salstone as much as James did. "Don't be an ass, Archie. You've had too much port this evening."

Now Salstone stepped away, out of James's sight. He heard Claude saying cheerfully as they moved away, "I'd stay clear of that dog if I were you. I saw the leg of someone Dem went after. Not a pretty sight."

Laura turned to Patricia. The color in Laura's cheeks was high, but her voice remained calm. "Would you like to see James?"

Patricia let out a short wordless noise of frustration and stalked away. Laura and Dem stood in the doorway for a moment, still alert.

"How fierce you are," James said. "I scarcely need Dem."

"James!" Laura swung back around, her face alight. She rushed over to where he stood by the bed, reaching out to slip her arm around his waist. It felt familiar and right, and he curled his arm around her shoulders, pulling her in a little tighter. He let his head droop toward hers, breathing in the scent of lavender. His head still pounded and his very bones ached, but nothing hurt as much with her slender body fitted against his side. He was glad, though, that the bed was not far.

Dem butted his nose against James's leg and James reached down to ruffle his ears.

"What are you doing up?" Laura scolded in a way that somehow pleased him, another one of the many peculiarities he felt. "You should be in bed."

"I heard Archie and Patricia."

"Them," she scoffed as she steered him toward the bed. "You needn't have gotten up. I can handle those two."

"I saw." He sat down and leaned back against the headboard. He felt as if he'd run a race. "I thought I might have to stop you from laying them low."

She rolled her eyes and sat down on the bed beside him. "How do you feel?"

"Not dead."

"Well, that's to the good." Her smile was bright enough to make him almost believe he felt better. "You sound . . . you sound *here* again."

Laura took his hand, as she had many times before since he'd been sick. But it was different somehow; he no longer felt only the unspoken comfort. He was conscious of her touch now, just as he was aware of how near she sat, how at ease with him she was.

"I think . . . perhaps I am myself again," James agreed cautiously. "I feel like the devil, but I don't feel as if I'm trying to hold back the tide." He paused. "Are you sure? That it's mercury poisoning?"

"Yes." She stood up and went into the dressing room, returning a moment later with a battered journal. "My father treated men who had mercury poisoning. These are his notes." She began to read from the book, listing symptom after symptom so familiar they made his stomach churn. "You see?"

"What happened to those men?"

She looked him square in the eye. "They *lived*, James."

"All of them?"

Laura let out a soft noise of frustration. "That is so like you. No, not every single one, but more of them lived than died. You have a better chance than any of them."

Hope shimmered in his chest, but he dared not grasp it. "What were they like? Did they continue like this?" He circled his hand, indicating himself and the bed.

"No." She set the book aside and sat down on the bed again, leaning earnestly toward him. "They recovered. The symptoms disappeared. You're going to be yourself again."

"Christ," he muttered, not sure whether he was cursing or praying, and tilted his head back against the headboard, closing his eyes.

He was going to live. It had been so long. He had been so sure. Resigned. He hardly knew how to feel, how to act, what to say. If he wasn't careful, he thought he might start to shake until he fell to pieces.

Laura moved forward, sliding her arms around him, laying her head against his. James went still for an instant, then wrapped his arms around her almost convulsively, squeezing her to him, and buried his face in her hair.

chapter 19

Laura was sorry when James's embrace loosened; it was quite wonderful for those few minutes to be close, to share the sudden, sweeping joy and relief. It was as if the two of them had been through some small, fierce personal war together, and the victory was even sweeter because they held it together.

But she hadn't expected him to hold her long. There was around James some unseen barrier, a layer that stood between him and others. She wasn't sure why or what it was, but she knew that it would embarrass him to have relaxed his guard. Whatever James felt—and she often found it hard to know what that was—he hated to reveal it.

So when he relaxed his grip, his arms sliding away, she released him and stood up. "You should sleep now."

"It seems I've done nothing but sleep the past few days."

"You have a good many nights to make up for. You need to heal and regain your strength." She moved over to the bottles on the dresser and began to measure out a dose.

"Are you going to give me more of that noxious brown liquid?"

"I am. It will help you recover more quickly." Laura handed him the glass.

"I suspect people tell you they feel better just so you'll stop pouring it down their throat." He downed it quickly, his face screwing up in distaste.

"I'll ring for Owen to bring your cup of hot milk."

"That, too? Milk tastes bad enough as it is without making it hot."

"I'm going to take it as a good sign that you feel well enough to grumble." Laura smiled. "Milk will help you fight the poison."

Despite his complaints, he drank it down when Owen brought it, and within minutes he was asleep. Laura sat in her chair and let the tears come. She cried silently, not with sorrow but with release, for the first time allowing herself to admit the fear that had lurked in her for days, acidly eating away at her. The fear that it was too late, that James was doomed, that despite everything, he would lose his stubborn battle.

Then, drained, she lay down beside him as she had every night for the past week and went to sleep.

James spent most of the next few days sleeping. While his temperature fluctuated, he did not fall into another high fever. Laura was able to get his medicine down him as well as some food. Slowly but surely he was getting better. Because he was so often asleep, it was easy to hide his progress from his family. The only person who knew was Owen, whom Laura had sworn to secrecy.

Laura awoke one morning snuggled up against James, his arm thrown across her. She had become accustomed to waking up like this. Indeed, she found it was a pleasant way to awaken. Perhaps that was shameful of her, but there was something so warm and secure about it, so safe. The past weeks she had been grateful for every bit of safety and comfort she could find, no matter how illusory.

Laura started to slide away, but James's arm tightened around her and he mumbled something, burrowing his face into her outspread hair. Laura stilled, enjoying it for another moment. James cuddled her closer, his breath hot upon the nape of her neck. Something pushed insistently against her backside. Her eyes flew open, and just as realization began to dawn on her, James's arm suddenly tightened, then was yanked away just as quickly. Laura shot out of bed, her face flaming, and whirled to face him. He was staring at her, his face slack with astonishment or—or something. She hoped it wasn't horror. "I—I fell asleep. I've been, well, the past few days, while I've been here taking care of you, it just, well, it was easier." Laura knew she was babbling, and she forced herself to stop, pulling around her whatever remnants of her dignity remained. "I'll tell Owen to set up a cot."

"No, I, um . . . my fault." His eyes strayed down her form, and it occurred to Laura that she was standing there in only her nightgown. She fled into the dressing room.

Well, that had certainly been humiliating. Her fingers trembled as she tugged at the ribbons on the front of her nightgown. She had become so used to being with James these past days, so accustomed to touching him, helping him, being with him all the time that she felt at ease with him. But they were still strangers, really.

He felt none of that familiarity with her, for he had been asleep or in a fever most of that time. After her sharp statements when he proposed, vowing not to share a bed with him, he had awakened to find her cuddled up against him.

She dreaded what he must think of her—and what kind of acerbic comments he would make.

Reaching the top button of her bodice, she found that she had buttoned it wrong and had to start all over again. She drew a deep breath and pressed her hands against her heated cheeks, forcing herself into something resembling calm.

What had happened, happened, and she couldn't change it. She'd had a good reason for sleeping there. Obviously James was in no condition to take advantage of the situation—and in any case, she was married to the man, which made it perfectly acceptable to share his bed. Anyway, if you came down to it, he was in *her* bed.

She shouldn't feel ashamed. The only reason she did sprang from the knowledge that she *liked* lying in his arms. James wouldn't know that. He had no idea she looked forward to snuggling up to him when she lay down at night—indeed, she had done an excellent job of hiding that fact from herself until this very moment.

That was obviously something she would have to deal with, but she didn't have to worry about it this minute. Right now, her course must be to brazen it out. She would be like Graeme's wife Abigail, who went her own way, holding her head up and not caring what others might be whispering about her . . . or, at least, not showing that she did.

But when she emerged from her dressing room, her pose vanished, for James was up and leaning against the dresser, pale as a ghost.

"What are you doing?" She rushed to him, taking his arm.

"I'm getting up. Getting dressed." He set his jaw, keeping his gaze turned slightly away from her. "I refuse to spend my days lying about."

"Oh, for heaven's sake. You are the most impossible man. Get back in bed before you fall over."

"I am not going to fall over," he replied with great dignity. "However, perhaps I should . . . sit down." He sank into the chair beside the bed.

"You've been running a high fever on and off for days. Until last night, I was unsure whether you would live or die. You need to recuperate. Rest. If you overtax yourself, you'll bring back your fever."

"I refuse to be treated like a child."

"Then perhaps you shouldn't act like one."

He sat back, copying her pose of crossed arms, and looked at her so sulkily that it was all she could do not to smile. Finally, with a sigh, James dropped his arms and let his head fall back against the high back of the chair. He rubbed his hands over his face and pushed his hands into his hair, fingertips pressing into his scalp.

"I want to bathe," he said wearily. "I want to shave. I want to wash my blasted hair. I feel like something one scrapes off the bottom of one's shoe."

"I know." Her irritation vanished in sympathy, and she went to kneel by his side. "Does your head hurt?"

His only answer was a snort. Laura slid her hands gently into his hair and began to rub his scalp with her fingertips. It was something she had done many times when he was frowning in pain, and it had seemed to ease him. From the soft noise he made, she thought it did now, as well.

After a moment, he said in a low voice, "I'm sorry for snapping at you. I'm a dreadful ingrate."

"Are you?" she said mildly. "I wouldn't have said that. A terrible patient, perhaps, who will not do as he's told."

"Very well. I'm a terrible patient. I will admit to anything as long you keep doing that."

"Your headache is better?" But she knew the answer; she could see the lines of his face smoothing out.

He nodded. "Laura . . ."

"Yes?"

"I'm no good at this."

"At what? Being sick?"

"No. Well, I'm not good at that, either, apparently. But what I meant . . . what I'm trying to say is . . . thank you."

A pale flush started along the sharp edge of his cheekbones, and Laura realized he was embarrassed.

"You're welcome."

After a moment, he murmured, "I hate being weak. I hate them knowing I'm helpless."

"Then I would say you shouldn't go downstairs and risk falling down in a faint in front of them."

"True. That thought doesn't appeal." He sighed. "You're right. Of course. But I feel so useless."

"The most useful thing you can do is get stronger. Get well."

"I can't *make* that happen," he said irritably.

"No, but you can allow it. You can lie here and sleep, give your body time to heal itself. You can eat."

"You mean drink that blasted milk you want to pour down my throat."

"Among other things. It would be better if you stayed in bed . . . if the others didn't know you were improving yet."

He cocked an eyebrow at her. "Meaning that if they

think I'm dying they won't decide it's necessary to come in and smother me in my sleep?"

"Well, yes."

He studied her for a moment, then said, "Very well. I shall do as you wish . . . on one condition."

"What?"

"You needn't look so suspicious." He stood up. "Well, actually, two. One, I get clean."

Laura nodded. "I'll send Owen in to help you."

"And two, you will rest, as well."

"Me? I don't need to rest."

"You do. You have done nothing but look after me for I don't know how many days now. You need a change of scenery. Walk around the gardens. Go downstairs and have breakfast."

"With your family?"

"They may be murderers, but they'll take your mind off the sickroom."

"James!"

"No arguments. We have an agreement."

"I didn't agree to anything."

"You will. The only question is whether you say yes now or we stand here arguing about it until I fall into a swoon at your feet."

"Oh, very well," Laura said in exasperation, taking his arm and propelling him toward the bed. He went easily enough, and it seemed to Laura that his walk was already a little steadier, his color better. No doubt winning an argument raised his spirits. "But what if something happens to you while I'm gone?"

"Dem is ample protection. Owen can sit in here if it eases your mind. You've left me in his hands a few times."

He was right, she knew. A change of scenery would do her good. And, little as the prospect of dining with his relatives pleased her, she might be able to learn something useful. So once James was settled and had taken his medicine, she left him in the care of Owen and Demosthenes and made her way downstairs to the dining room. It was late enough that Tessa and the other ladies of the household were there, along with Walter and Tessa's admirer, Mr. Netherly.

Laura greeted the women, ignoring the glare Patricia sent her. At least Archie Salstone was missing, for which Laura was grateful. She gave them all a polite smile, reminding herself that she must treat them as she would have a week ago, as if she hadn't discovered that someone wanted to kill James. "Walter. How are you? Mr. Netherly. I hope you are doing well. I didn't realize you were still here." She did not add that a man of any sensitivity would have left days ago.

Netherly turned soulful brown eyes on her. "I could not leave Lady de Vere to bear this alone."

"Of course."

"How is dear James this morning?" Adelaide asked. "We are all so worried about him."

"Much the same," Laura answered vaguely. Anything she told Claude's wife would no doubt go directly back to him.

"I'm so glad you decided to come down to breakfast," Tessa told her, reaching out to pat her arm. "It must be dreadful, sitting at his bedside all day long." Tears welled in her eyes, and Tessa dabbed delicately at them.

"I am a little tired," Laura admitted. "I thought I might walk in the gardens."

"Lovely. You'll feel much better. The flowers are glorious now. The bluebells along the roadway are all in bloom." Tessa gasped, then beamed. "I know *exactly* what you should do! You should go for a ride through the countryside."

"Oh, no, I don't think . . ." Laura began to demur.

"Yes, yes, it's beautiful. I'll tell the coachman to take the back road toward Lydcombe. It's the long way round by the old castle—a bit farther, of course—but perfect for a ride. It's so picturesque."

"Bluebells line the road like blankets of stunning blue," Mr. Netherly intoned, apparently contemplating a new poem.

"And the old bridge over the river just past the castle!" Adelaide joined in enthusiastically. "Such a romantic vista."

"I could sit with Sir James while you are out," Netherly went on. "I'll read to him. Nothing lifts the soul like poetry."

That, Laura thought, would be certain to send James to his grave, but she said only, "That's very kind of you, but James is sleeping, and I don't wish to disturb him."

"It's a capital idea," Walter put in. "Going for a ride, I mean." He flicked a disdainful glance at Mr. Netherly. "You can take the victoria and fold the top back. Nice fresh air . . . scenery. I'll escort you if you like."

"Oh, Walter," Patricia said scornfully. "She won't want company. That's the whole idea—to have a few minutes by herself."

"Well, yes, of course, I mean, no, needn't go with you."

"Thank you, it's very kind of you to offer," Laura told him. "But it *would* be nice to have a bit of solitude." The idea of a drive by herself in the fresh air really was appealing. She hesitated at leaving James alone that long, but he was doing better now, and he would have Dem and Owen with him. The more she thought about it, the more she longed for a chance to get away.

"There! It's done." Tessa saw the acquiescence on Laura's face. "I'll tell them to have the carriage ready for you this afternoon."

So it was that Laura found herself getting into Tessa's elegant low-slung victoria a few hours later. As Littletree, the coachman, climbed up onto his seat, Laura glanced over and saw Claude walking out of the stable. She had a moment's panic that James's brother had decided to accompany her, but fortunately, when he turned and saw her, he merely tipped his hat and continued walking toward the house.

Laura let out a sigh of relief and settled back to enjoy the ride. The calash top was folded back, and though Laura had the parasol Tessa insisted she carry, she let it rest on the seat beside her, enjoying the caress of the sun on her shoulders. Though the team was spirited, Littletree kept them to a sedate pace, allowing Laura to fully enjoy the view.

Just as Tessa had described, thick swaths of vivid purplish-blue bluebells lined both sides of the country lane. The road wound around, coming back in a U to drop in a long dramatic slope to the old castle at the bottom of the hill. Beyond the castle lay the river and the quaint narrow wooden bridge Adelaide had mentioned. In the distance the lane curved out of sight around the hill. On her right Laura could see the roofs of Grace Hill above the trees, the gardens in between.

The descent was steep, and the coachman stopped the carriage at the top of the hill to jump down and attach the chained brake slipper to a rear wheel. They had just started down the hill when suddenly the right horse jumped and whinnied, shying to the side, startling its companion so that it, too, reared. They began to run.

The coachman pulled back on the reins, calling to the horses to stop, but just then a loud crack sounded beneath the carriage, and the brake slipper went tumbling down the road. The noise panicked the horses even further, and they leapt forward. Littletree braced his legs against the footrest and hauled back with all his might, but nothing could stop the headlong flight of the horses down the hill.

Laura grabbed the armrest beside her and held on tightly, her stomach seemingly left behind her at the top of the hill, along with her bonnet. As the carriage jounced and swayed toward the bottom, Laura's mind raced.

If the road had been straight before them, Laura thought the team would slow down once they reached the bottom. However, the slope ended just before the bridge and on the other side of the river the lane bent sharply around the base of the hill. The driver would have no hope of slowing the runaways before they took the curve, and the light victoria would overturn, sending its occupants flying.

"The river!" Laura shouted. "We have to jump!"

The driver swung halfway toward her, still hauling back uselessly on the reins. Laura crouched on the seat and grabbed the side of the carriage, muscles tensing, and prayed she wouldn't misjudge the jump and land bone-breakingly on the side of the road or be unable to clear the bridge. Prayed, too, that the water would be deep enough, the current not too swift. The endless frightening possibilities charged through her mind too quickly to even grasp them all.

The road leveled out, and the horses pounded onto the bridge. With another shout to the driver, Laura took a deep breath and launched herself from the carriage.

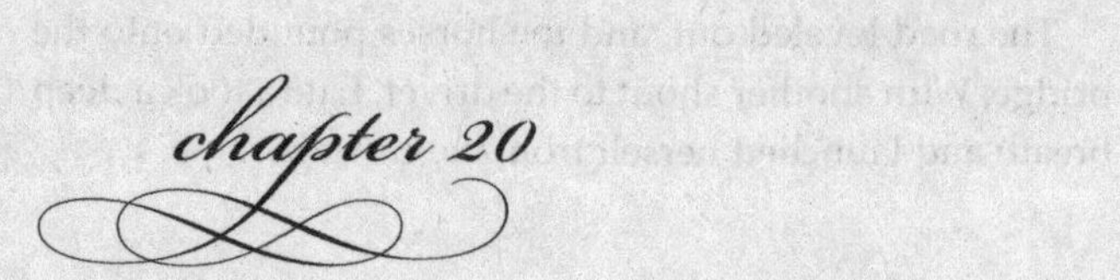

chapter 20

There was an instant of terrifying flight through the air before Laura hit the river. The water was another shock, cold despite the warmth of the day, and her momentum sent her deep enough that her feet touched the bottom. She pushed off with all her might, shooting up through the water.

Her head popped up on the downriver side of the narrow bridge. Water soaked her petticoats and skirts and filled her shoes, but fortune was still on her side, for she landed not far from the shore and the current was a lazy one.

She struck out strongly for the side. Reeds and ferns and even small trees grew along the gently sloping bank of the water, and she grabbed at them, pulling herself in until her feet finally found purchase in the mud.

She could see Littletree not far from her, nearer the shore and upriver, clinging with one hand to a slender sapling growing out of the bank. His other arm hung uselessly at his side; his face was white and contorted with pain.

Laura slogged toward him through the reedy water and mud, moving sideways and holding on to whatever plant or root was handy to help propel herself forward against the current. Littletree was obviously too dazed to realize that he could simply push his legs down and scramble up the bank.

She was only a foot from him when the slender branch he clung to finally ripped. He yelled in panic, but Laura was able to turn and reach out, blocking him. She held on to him with one hand, and with the other kept a firm hold on the root of a large tree that protruded from the dirt.

"Put your feet down. Climb." She hadn't the strength to hold him long against the current; her grip would soon slip from either him or the root.

But Littletree had recovered enough from his initial panic that he understood and fought for a toehold in the muddy bottom. With his good arm, he managed to grasp another of the roots, and they plowed forward onto the bank. Falling and stumbling, they dragged themselves up the muddy slope and flopped down on the ground, water streaming off them. Laura sat, gasping for air and trying to stop shaking all over.

"Biscuit . . . Binky. . ." Littletree moaned.

Laura looked at him in bewilderment, until she realized he must be talking about the horses. That would be his first concern, of course. "I'm sure they'll be fine," she told him bracingly, though she had her own doubts as to that. "They'll have to stop running after a while. If nothing else, the carriage turning over should slow them down."

"Ohhh." He let out another groan at this statement and brought his hand up to cover his eyes.

"You've hurt your arm. Is it broken?"

He nodded, his face so white the smattering of freckles on it stood out. "I think so, my lady. I hit it on something when I jumped. The bridge, maybe." He pulled his feet under him, starting to get up. "I need to find the team."

"You need to sit right here and do nothing," Laura corrected, putting her hand on his good shoulder to keep him down. "How do you think you'd handle them, anyway, with only one good arm?"

He nodded, seeing the sense of that. It might have helped that even starting to stand had made him look distinctly queasy. Laura rose, picking various leaves and twigs and a strand of some sort of vine from her clothes and hair. She wrung what water she could from her muddy skirts. Her legs were shaky, but at least the trembling in her fingers had nearly stopped.

"I'm going up to the road. Someone is bound to come along sooner or later."

"It's just a lane," Littletree said gloomily. "Not much along it. Just the back way to the hall."

"I'll walk to the house to fetch help, then. It's not that far if I take the path up through the gardens."

"No, my lady, I should go," he protested.

"Don't be silly. You have had a shock, and you're in no shape to climb a hill. Sit here and wait. I'll send grooms back with a wagon for you. They can find the horses, too."

Laura shivered as she walked, the pleasant breeze now cold through her wet clothes. Her hair had come loose, straggling wetly all over the place. She pulled out the remaining hairpins and squeezed out the water, thinking yearningly of a long warm bath. And a cup of hot tea. Another shudder shook her.

As she started over the bridge, she heard the sound of

a vehicle and team. She swung back around, wondering if the team, running loose, had turned to head home. If so, they were still moving at a rapid clip. But it was a different team that charged around the curve, a foursome of grays pulling a two-seater barouche. The driver was Lord Montclair.

"Graeme!" Laura cried, and hurried toward the carriage, waving her arms.

He was already pulling back on the reins, and when he drew to a stop, he dropped them and leapt down from the vehicle. "Laura! My God, what happened?"

Only seconds behind him, Abby got out of the carriage. "Are you all right?"

"Yes, I'm fine," Laura said quickly. "It's Littletree who's hurt." She pointed toward the coachman sitting on the bank.

At the sight of Graeme, the man shoved himself up to his feet and reached his hand up to sweep off his hat before realizing it was long gone. Instead, he bobbed his head respectfully. "My lord."

"Littletree!" Graeme strode over to him. "You're injured. Sit down, man, no reason to stand on ceremony. Here's a nice boulder." He guided the man toward a large rock.

"What happened?" Abby asked. "We came upon the carriage overturned. Mirabelle feared it was Aunt Tessa's."

Mirabelle climbed down from the carriage, as well, albeit more slowly, her face creased with worry. "Is Tessa all right?"

"Tessa's fine," Laura reassured her. "I was the only one in the carriage. We started down the hill, but something happened to the brake, and the horses ran."

"It was Binky, my lord; he took off," Littletree hastened

to explain. "I think a bee must have stung him. He started running, and of course Biscuit joined him. I had the brake slipper on, but the chain snapped. You know how it is on a hill like that."

"Of course," Graeme agreed. "Even if the brake had held, it couldn't stop a runaway team. I'm sure you did everything you could, Littletree." He glanced at Laura. "Were you thrown out here at the river?"

"We jumped when we reached the bridge," Laura explained. "I thought it would be a softer landing than crashing on the curve."

"Indeed. Quick thinking," Graeme said approvingly. "The carriage wound up on its side and lost a wheel. You two might have been killed if you were still in it."

A violent shiver ran through Laura, only partially from the cold.

"Here," an imperious female voice said, and Laura turned to see that Graeme's grandmother, the dowager Countess of Montclair, had joined them. She draped a carriage rug around Laura's shoulders. "No need to stand about freezing."

"Thank you," Laura said in a heartfelt voice, and remembered to give the older woman a little curtsey in greeting. Lady Eugenia was a stickler for courtesy.

"The horses, sir," Littletree said to Graeme, his expression pleading. "Are they all right?"

"Yes, yes," Graeme hastened to assure him. "They looked in decent shape. In a lather of course and standing there looking quite lost, but I didn't see any cuts, and neither seemed to be limping. I left Barrow to look after them, and I drove us on to see what had happened to the people in the vehicle. Thank heavens you were all right."

"Barrow." Clearly the idea of Montclair's coachman seeing to the team lifted much of the weight from Littletree's shoulders. "That's good. Thank you, my lord."

"Now," Abigail said firmly, "I think it's time we took these two home and got them cared for."

"Oh, yes," Mirabelle agreed, putting her arm around Laura's waist and leading her toward the carriage.

The others followed. The dowager countess seemed rather taken aback when she realized that Graeme was putting the injured coachman into the carriage with the ladies—as, indeed, did Littletree himself—but Graeme quelled whatever she was about to say with a firm look. Abigail wedged herself into the seat with Laura and Littletree so that the two older women had the forward-facing seat to themselves.

"I don't know what Sir James is going to say about this," Littletree said mournfully.

"Nothing," Laura said firmly. "Because he's not going to know about it." Laura fixed the driver with a stern look. "Do you understand? You are not to let a word of what just happened get back to Sir James."

"But, Laura, James would want to know." Graeme paused in the act of climbing up into the higher driver's seat. "No man would want to be kept in the dark if his wife had been in an accident."

"No doubt he would not," Laura retorted crisply. "But that doesn't mean he *should*. You didn't see how ill he's been, Graeme."

Graeme nodded, his eyes dark with worry. "He's no better? Abby said—"

"I hope he will improve," Laura said carefully, mindful of the coachman's presence and the likelihood of servant gossip. "But I won't have James fret himself into another fever because of some silly accident that he couldn't have done anything to prevent."

"No, you're right, of course." Graeme nodded. "We'll say nothing about it."

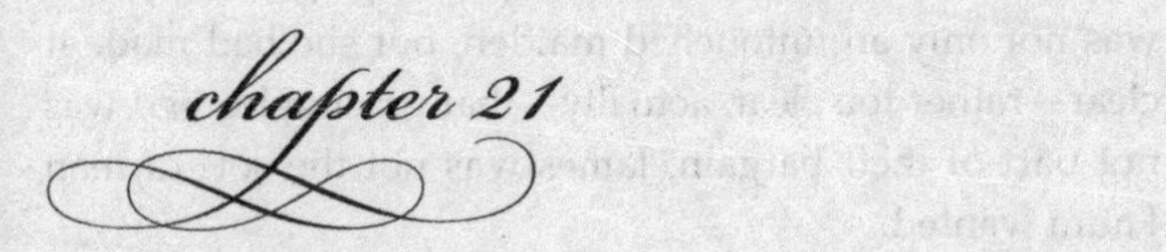

James walked from the bed to the dresser to the far wall and back again. He felt like a fool, tottering around his room like a two-year-old. But Laura was right. He must get stronger; he was useless as he was. So he would eat, though food still was tasteless at best. He would take Laura's bitter nostrums and drink the blasted milk. He would sleep—he'd already taken two naps since he awoke this morning.

And he would walk in the privacy of his room to regain his strength. At least he had rid himself of Owen after a brief argument over whether Lady de Vere would approve. Fortunately, a desire to remain employed overcame the loyalty Laura engendered in everyone. He had waited until Laura left before he started his treks.

Not that Laura would have been shocked at his weakness. Hell, he'd been flat on his back, it seemed, half the time she'd been here. Still, he had some pride. He had already embarrassed himself this morning when he awoke and found Laura's soft body snuggled against him—and his own body in a thoroughly aroused state. He'd been dreaming of her, and in that dream Laura was warm and willing, even eager, and he had no longer been ill or weak. He had been himself again, hungry and strong.

But even as the sweet pleasure flooded his body, he had realized how appalled Laura would be to awaken with the unmistakable evidence of his lust pressing against her. She was not only an untouched maiden, but she had made it clear—rather too clear, actually—that gracing his bed was not part of their bargain. James was not the sort of man Laura wanted.

Then he had made the situation even more humiliating by jumping back from her as if he were some maiden aunt. The result was that now he had permanently lost her sweet presence in his bed.

James cast a jaundiced eye at the cot Owen had set up for Laura on the other side of the room. It seemed a very poor place indeed for her to sleep while he took her large, soft bed. But she would never let her patient take the cot.

It wasn't really the inequity of the sleeping arrangements that bothered him. The thing was . . . he *enjoyed* waking up with her in his arms. He'd liked turning over in the night and feeling her beside him. He wasn't sure why, for he was a man who had always preferred to sleep in his own bed. Alone. He made it a point to leave a woman's bed, not linger through the night. He had no need to cuddle and utter honeyed, meaningless words.

But these past few nights had been different. Even though he had been in and out of consciousness, half the time not knowing what was real and what was not, he had been aware of Laura's presence. The slow gentle sound of her breath. Her softness. Her warmth. It hadn't been sexual. Or, at least, it had not been until this morning. James had the feeling he'd ruined things.

His less-than-happy thoughts were interrupted by a bark outside his door. James knew that particular bark, accompanied by several thumps of a large tail against the door. James turned, unsurprised when, after a short knock, Graeme opened the door.

More unexpected, however, was the square woman beside his cousin. "Lady Eugenia!"

"You needn't sound so surprised, James." The dowager countess stepped past Demosthenes, who was occupied with letting Graeme rub his ears. "One would think a beast like that wouldn't have a place in a sickroom."

"He keeps out unwanted visitors." James sketched a bow. "Naturally, that would not include you."

"Hmph."

"James . . ." Aunt Mirabelle rushed into the room and engulfed him in a soft, sweet-scented hug. "I've been so worried about you."

"No need to worry, you know nothing can kill me." He gave her an affectionate squeeze and kissed her cheek. "Though, promise me, you will not tell the others I am better."

"I won't, dear, I swear. Graeme already warned me they'd all be in here bothering you if they knew you were on the mend." She looked at him searchingly. "Oh, lovie, how thin you are." Mirabelle steered him toward the bed. "Come, sit down."

She fussed over him as the dowager countess took a seat on the chair and Graeme came over to shake his cousin's hand. "You look well, James."

James gave him a sardonic look. "No need to lie, coz. I look like I have one foot in the grave, but fortunately I'm pulling it out now, I think. Thanks to Laura."

"I knew she was the perfect wife for you," Mirabelle told him, patting his hand. "I'm so happy for you."

"I must say I was surprised when I heard you'd married her," Lady Eugenia said. "But I agree, she will make you an excellent wife."

"That's not what you said when *I* wanted to marry her!" Graeme protested.

James cast a jaundiced eye at his cousin. Graeme obviously was the sort of man Laura *did* want.

"Of course not. She wouldn't have been a suitable wife for the Earl of Montclair."

"But of course *I*," James drawled, "am lowly enough in station to make it perfectly acceptable."

"Don't be impertinent." Lady Eugenia fixed him with a gimlet eye. "The fact that you are ill does not give you license to be rude."

"Of course not." James bowed his head, properly chastened. "I beg your pardon."

"As for Laura's worthiness," Lady Eugenia went on. "She is of good family and quite unexceptionable in manner. We all know where her lack lay, and since James is swimming in money, it will not signify. She's a sensible girl. No doubt she has come to realize that marriage is a contract, and security is a far more important consideration than love."

Her words, James reflected, were frighteningly similar to the argument James himself had made to Laura. He wondered why it sounded so irritating when Lady Eugenia said it.

"I feel sure she will be an admirable influence on you, James," Lady Eugenia went on.

"No doubt."

"She already has been a wonderful influence," Mirabelle said, patting James's hand. "She saved his life."

"Indeed. I owe her a great deal."

Mirabelle smiled and gave him another pat. "I'll leave you to talk to the countess now, as I'll have many other opportunities to visit you, but Lady Eugenia will be here only a short while." From the look on his aunt's face, James suspected that the brevity of the dowager countess's stay was more a wish than a fact.

"Where is Laura?" James asked, looking toward the door.

"I am sure, quite properly, Laura is giving us the opportunity of a private conversation with you," Lady Eugenia told him.

"Yes, no doubt that's it," Graeme agreed in a hearty voice.

"For pity's sake, Graeme, sit down and stop fidgeting about," Lady Eugenia said. "You don't need to pretend all's well in front of me. I'm fully aware that someone is trying to kill James."

Ignoring Graeme's pained expression, she turned back to James. "I suppose it's Claude who wants you dead."

"Grandmother . . ." Graeme groaned.

"Don't be so missish, Montclair," his grandmother retorted.

"Yes, Claude is my first choice," James agreed.

"I always thought he was a sly boy," Lady Eugenia went on. "But handling it will be a delicate situation. You won't want any scandal."

"Naturally. I've thought of simply slipping a knife between his ribs one night."

"James . . ." Graeme rolled his eyes. "This is scarcely a time for jests."

"Who says I'm jesting?"

"That wouldn't do," the dowager countess put in. "It

would still be a dreadful scandal. And you wouldn't want to be sent to the gallows."

"That *is* a consideration."

Graeme looked pained, but the dowager countess appeared pleased with their exchange. She stood up, reaching over to lay her hand on James's shoulder. "I'm glad you didn't leave us." She gave him a little pat, completing James's astonishment, and stepped back. "I am sure you two would prefer to talk in private." She let out a martyred sigh. "So I shall visit with Tessa and Mirabelle."

James watched her leave the room, then turned to his cousin. "I think I may be delirious again."

"I told you Grandmother is fond of you."

"I would have thought anything more than not fiercely disapproving of me would have been a step up for Lady Eugenia."

"Are you all right?" Graeme moved closer. "I mean, really. Not for Mother's or the dowager countess's ears. Just me."

"I am beginning to believe I shall live, yes. In exactly what state of health, I'm not sure." James swung his legs off the bed and stood up. "I've spent the day walking back and forth across the room. So far I haven't managed to stay on my feet much longer than five minutes. But it's better than being flat on my back in bed."

"Perhaps you should come to the hall to stay for a while. We've plenty of room."

James gave him a sardonic look. "I'm not that feeble."

"You're not well," Graeme countered. "If someone here is trying to kill you, how are you to stop him?"

"I'm well protected." James waved toward the door. "Most of my family has a healthy regard for Dem's teeth."

He paused, then added with a grin, "Besides, you should have seen Laura bar the door to Patricia and Archie."

Graeme's expression lightened. "I imagine that would be a sight."

"All she needed was a flaming sword."

At that moment the door opened, and the subject of their conversation stepped in. Graeme promptly popped to his feet. "Laura."

"Montclair." She gave him a formal nod.

James glanced from Graeme to his wife. They looked equally uncomfortable. What did Laura feel when she looked at Graeme? Regret? Bitterness? Yearning? James sat back down, suddenly exhausted.

"I'm sorry. I shouldn't have interrupted." Laura turned toward the door. "Excuse me."

"No, no, pray don't go on my account. I was about to take my leave," Graeme assured her. He glanced back at James and away.

"Is it raining outside?" James asked.

"What?" Laura looked surprised. "No, it's quite lovely."

"I just thought . . . is your hair wet?" James looked at Laura's hair, not in its usual neat coronet of braids, but knotted loosely at the base of her neck and, yes, definitely dark with dampness.

"Oh!" Her cheeks flooded with color. "Well, when I got home I, um . . ."

"I should go," Graeme said at the same time. "No doubt you'll want to, uh . . ." With a vague nod, Graeme left the room.

James lay back against his pillows, linking his arms behind his head and idly watching Laura as she went to her vanity table. "That's a different dress."

"Yes. I bathed and changed clothes after I returned from the ride." Pink bloomed along her cheekbones.

"Ah. Then that's why your hair is wet." And no doubt that was also why she had stumbled on the words earlier; it wasn't the sort of thing to say in front of another man. But something a husband could be privy to. He wasn't sure why that thought pleased him.

"Yes." Looking into the mirror, not at him, she reached up and began to remove the pins from the heavy knot of hair at the base of her neck. It was only loosely done and it easily tumbled down, spilling over her shoulders. "I came to dry it by the fire."

"I see." His mouth suddenly dry, James watched her pick up a brush and comb and sit down in front of the fire. This, then, was another private intimacy afforded a husband, seeing the long fall of hair unbound, watching her brush it out.

"I'm sorry. I didn't mean to interrupt you and Graeme."

"Graeme was only fussing." He dismissed him casually, more interested in watching Laura comb through her dark honey locks.

She leaned over, turning her face toward the fire, pulling her brush through the strands of her hair to the ends and letting it cascade down. James watched her, eyes half closed, desire coiling low in his abdomen. He didn't mind the prickles of hunger. He welcomed the feeling of life stirring in him again, however little it would be satisfied.

This was enough for the moment, more than enough. He was alive and whole once more. And whatever lay in the past, whomever she had once loved, Laura was now his.

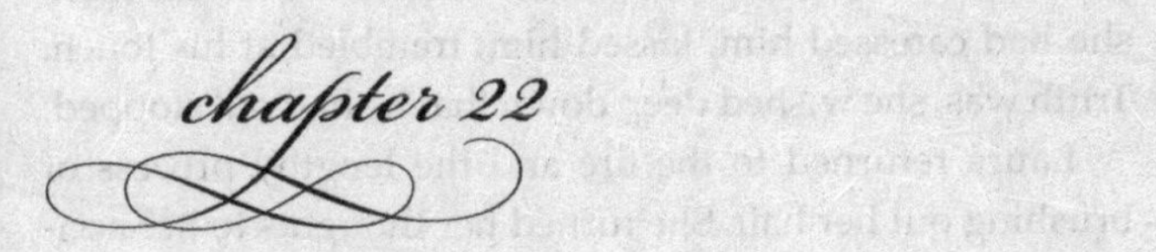

Laura glanced over her shoulder at the bed. James had fallen asleep. She tiptoed to his bed to pull the light blanket up over him. She studied his face. He looked vulnerable this way, his lashes long and dark against his cheeks, no mockery in his eyes or smirk to his mouth. She knew a momentary urge to stroke her fingers down his cheek. But that was foolish, of course. It might awaken him, and there was no need to touch him. Not really.

This new desire to stroke his face or brush back his hair must come from the days she'd spent nursing him back to health—judging his temperature with a palm against his forehead, washing his face and chest with a cooling rag to quell his fever, rubbing his scalp to ease a headache. Touching him had become familiar. Easy.

And she liked it. There was a deep sensual pleasure in running her fingers through his thick, soft hair, in pressing her fingertips against his scalp, and it gave her a visceral satisfaction to watch his face soften and relax as she did so.

It warmed her, too, to slide her arm around his waist, his side against hers all the way up and down. To drag a damp cloth across his chest, feeling the padding of muscle and hardness of bone beneath his skin.

She must be a sensualist, given to unladylike pleasures—look at the way she had responded to his kisses when he was in a delirium. Without any love for the man, she had caressed him, kissed him, trembled at his touch. Truth was, she wished deep down that he had not stopped.

Laura returned to the fire and the lengthy process of brushing out her hair. She turned her thoughts to her accident this afternoon. It was enough to make one suspicious, given the attempt on James's life.

However, it took only a few minutes' reflection to see how unlikely it was that someone arranged it. Perhaps, in the short time between Tessa suggesting the idea and Laura leaving the house, one of the others could have sneaked down to the stables and tampered with the brake mechanism.

But how could Claude or anyone else have arranged for a bee to sting one of the horses at the top of that hill and set it off on a run? The idea was ludicrous. And to what purpose? She doubted James had told anyone how much of his fortune he was leaving to Laura. They would assume she had only a relatively small widow's portion. No, she was simply starting at shadows. Thank heavens Graeme had not leapt to the same cynical thoughts, or he would have insisted on telling James about it.

She continued to brush her hair. It was a soothing, almost hypnotic ritual.

"I've kept you from practicing." James's voice from the bed startled Laura from her reverie.

She jumped, banging the brush against her scalp, and turned to him, fearful his mind was wandering again. "What?"

"Your music. Violin in the mornings. Piano in the music room. Sometimes I'd stop and listen."

"Why didn't you come in?"

"I didn't want to disturb you."

"I invited you one day, if you'll remember." Laura went over to the bed. "Do you like music?"

"I haven't any talent for it, but I enjoy listening. I'm fond of Mozart. Among current composers, I like Tchaikovsky."

"Really?" It came as no surprise that James would like the crisp mathematical precision of Mozart's music, but she would not have guessed he was drawn to the more florid, emotional Russian compositions.

"What? You thought I wouldn't enjoy a little bombast?" he asked, correctly interpreting where her surprise lay.

"Then you've heard the 1812 Overture."

"Indeed. In London a month ago."

"I should like to hear it. I've read about it."

"I'll take you. We'll go to London. See everything you want to."

"I'd like that." She bent over him, her loose hair falling down over his chest and arm, as she pressed her palm to his face. "How are you feeling?"

"Better."

"That's good to hear." She slid her fingers into his hair, fingertips rubbing his scalp. She was, she knew, giving in to her odd need to touch him, but there was no reason he had to know that. "Your head aching?"

James made a soft noise and closed his eyes, nestling his head against her hand. "Yes."

"Did you have a good visit with Graeme and the dowager countess?"

"I came out unscathed, which with Lady Eugenia means it went well. She gave me her thoughts on who was trying to murder me."

"I don't suppose it occurred to her not to upset you?"

"Graeme was a little upset by it." James shrugged and slid up to a sitting position, pulling away from her hand, and leaned back against the massive headboard.

She quirked up an eyebrow as she straightened and stepped back. "It didn't bother you at all, I take it."

"Sad to say, I'm apparently as insensitive as the dowager countess. I'll admit it took me back a bit at first to think someone in my family wants me dead." James's tone was light, but it sent a pang through Laura's chest. "I mean, not just in a general I-wish-you-weren't-here way, but in a very specific, final knife-through-the-heart fashion."

"We needn't talk about this right now. Later, when you're feeling better . . ."

"No, I think I must." He gave her a faint smile. "I'd rather they not succeed. So it would seem the only recourse is to find him and stop him."

"Very well." She sat down on the bed beside him. "Who—do you have any idea who it is?"

"As you're the one who stopped it, I think it's safe to assume it's not you."

"James! Don't even joke about such a thing."

"My guess is my loving brother. It's Claude who will inherit the title and the estate. Until I married you, he doubtless assumed I would leave him all the rest, as well—or at least the bulk of it."

"There could be other reasons. Other people."

"You're saying there are a number of people who would like to see me dead?"

"No." She grimaced. "I didn't mean that. But it would be careless not to look at other possibilities. The apothecary could have added the mercury to your treatment."

"True, but why? I hardly know the man. Besides, it would be rather hard for him to put the pan of mercury beneath my bed unnoticed. I think it must be someone here. Besides my family, that leaves only the servants. Any one of them could have been bribed, obviously."

"A big risk to take for a bribe," Laura pointed out. "They'd face the gallows if caught."

"That's one reason I'm inclined to put the staff at the bottom of my list. That leaves my family."

"And Mr. Netherly."

"The poet?" He snorted. "Yes, I suppose he could have done it, though I don't see how it would help him in any way. That leaves us with the family. It's the near and dear who would benefit most."

"I think we can exempt your mother."

"One would hope."

"But you left money for all the others. Even if it is in a trust, it would mean more money—and one could easily assume that the trustees might be easier to persuade than you."

"Yes. The same would apply for Sir Laurence's trust. If I am gone, it would fall to his attorney and our banker, with his friend Blankenship as the third trustee. Everyone knows Blankenship is a soft touch, and our banker is more or less putty in Mother's hands. No doubt she could talk them into any idiotic thing Patricia or Walter wants."

"Claude doesn't receive money from it?"

"No. Claude got his share. He was already twenty-one, and he's never been a spendthrift. Sir Laurence wanted to protect Patricia's funds from Archie. Walter was still quite young, and money goes through Tessa's hands like water. Those were his major concerns."

"Does that mean that Walter will get his portion when he reaches a certain age?"

James nodded. "At twenty-one, he gets one third, another third at twenty-five, then the rest at thirty."

"So he will be coming into money fairly soon. It would be easier, not to mention safer, to wait."

"True. But Walter's hallmark is his impulsivity. Maybe he's too impatient to wait another year. Besides, the amount he receives at twenty-one is subject to the trustees' approval. We have to agree that he's mature enough to handle it."

"Ah. He might fear you would withhold his money."

"If he was smart, he would. I've had to buy him out of enough scrapes to harbor some doubts on the issue. Remember, Walter is the one who usually brought my tonic from the apothecary, so he had the best chance to doctor it."

"Yes, but after he brought it home, it was sitting in the cabinet, where anyone could have added something to it. It's hard for me to picture Walter wanting to do away with you. He was the most concerned about your health. He offered to help; he looked in on you frequently."

"Maybe he wanted to make certain his scheme was working." James grinned faintly at her frown. "However, I'm inclined to agree with you that Walter is not our villain. I don't think he'd have the nerve." He tilted his head. "Who would be your choice for the culprit?"

Laura's response was immediate. "Mr. Salstone. He would control any money your sister inherits, wouldn't he?"

"Ah, yes, the inimitable Archibald Salstone." James's narrow smile was a little chilling. "I'd like it to be Archie, too." He toyed idly with the ruffle that ran around the hem of her skirt. Laura was tinglingly aware of his fingers, so close to her leg yet not touching her. "I would wager his dislike of me outstrips even Claude's. And because of our dear Archie, Patricia's trust was set up not to ever distribute the principal to her. It will continue for her children and eventually be given outright to them."

"So Archie's only chance of getting money is the good graces of the trustees?"

"Yes. And my graces are generally not deemed very good." He sighed. "The problem is, it's a subtle scheme, and subtlety is not something Archie possesses. Neither he nor my sister is clever. Now Walter *is* devious—look at all his pranks."

"Rather more harmless than plotting to murder one's brother."

"So . . ." Laura settled into a more comfortable position on the bed, resting her back against a post at the foot of the bed and stretching her legs out in front of her, so that she and James faced each other. "The fact is, all of them had a reason to do it. It needn't be a compelling motive, only compelling to them. Perhaps we should approach it from a different direction."

"Which of them had access to mercury?"

"Exactly." Laura beamed at his ready understanding.

"You're enjoying this, aren't you?" James chuckled. "Who would have thought you'd have such a taste for the macabre?"

"I'm not enjoying the reason for it," Laura denied, then admitted, "But, that aside, it's rather an interesting puzzle."

He leaned back, watching her, his lips curved in a way that sent odd sizzles through her. "So it is. Go on, fair sleuth."

Laura cleared her throat, doing her best to ignore the sensations he caused in her. "Why would any of them know the effects of mercury?"

"I can't imagine. I had no idea it was lethal, and I can assure you that I am a scholar compared to my siblings."

"I would think he must have had some experience with mercury."

"And possess patience. It's not a quick method."

"Not to mention a great capacity for cruelty," Laura added hotly. "If it was someone in this house, they were watching your illness progress. They knew full well how it made you suffer."

"Mm. I would think that was probably part of the reason for it."

"How can you be so calm about it?"

"Would it help if I were irate?" he asked reasonably. "Anger clouds one's thinking."

"Yes, but how can you make yourself not feel it?"

"Years of practice, my dear." James smiled and patted her leg. "I'll let you carry the indignation standard for both of us. You do it well."

His hand was warm, even through the layers of her clothes, and Laura was so conscious of it, it was difficult to keep her thoughts on the matter at hand. She wondered if James even noticed. No doubt he was able to divorce himself from that as ably as he did from other feelings.

Not, of course, that she wanted him to notice, much less to act upon it. Anger was not the only emotion that clouded one's thinking. It was better that he wanted her as little as she wanted him . . . except, of course, that she was increasingly unsure how little she wanted him.

Her thoughts went involuntarily to that night when he

had been out of his mind with fever, when he kissed her in a way that made her feel limp all over even now, just thinking about it. His hands on her body, firm and sure, his weight on her, pressing her into the soft mattress, as his mouth consumed hers. It was all very indecent—and even more indecent to be sitting here daydreaming about it.

James apparently noticed where his hand was, for he jerked it back abruptly. And that, she supposed, was a clear indication of how little his emotions ran in the same direction as hers. Good heavens, what was the matter with her?

She barely knew the man, had never liked him, and a few weeks ago she would have been shocked to her toes to even think of what they had done the other night. Worse, he wasn't well, as was obvious from his shadowed eyes and too-thin face—even if those things did give his face a certain tantalizing look of dissipation.

Laura dragged her thoughts from their wayward path to the subject at hand. "It's hard to believe one of your brothers could do that to you, no matter how much he might resent you."

"We're not a close family." He gave her a wry smile. "Claude and I have never done more than tolerate each other."

"Why not?"

James shrugged. "I suppose because after my older brother died, I was destined to inherit everything."

"I'm sorry. I didn't realize you had an older brother."

"Vincent died before you were even born. I don't really remember him, aside from a vague recollection of the night he died. The doctor coming . . . my mother crying . . . my father—" He stopped.

"Your father what?"

"Nothing." He shook his head. "Claude was several years younger than I. I always thought him an unnecessary nuisance."

"That could explain his dislike of you."

"It could," James allowed. "But more likely, it's because I'm not Sir Laurence's son."

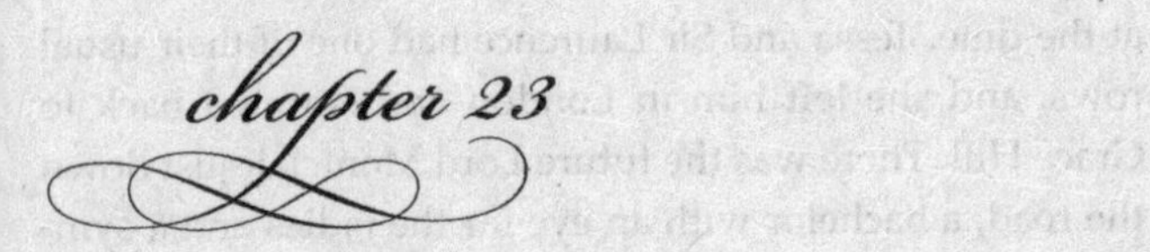

chapter 23

A stunned silence followed his words. "I—what?" Laura said at last.

James shifted his position, glancing away. "I'm sorry. I don't usually . . . I shouldn't . . . oh, the devil, I don't know why I told you."

"Because it's the truth?" Laura suggested.

"Yes, well, that's usually the reason something's secret."

"So you are saying that Tessa . . ."

"Had an affair. Yes." He leaned his head back, looking even more weary. "No doubt you can guess the father."

Laura began to shake her head. "How would I—" She stopped, sucking in a quick breath. "Not—Graeme's father? Are you saying Reginald was . . ."

"Yes. Helps to explain the close family resemblance, doesn't it?"

"I—I don't know what to say."

"Not much to say." He edged away, folding his arms. "I hope you will not think too badly of Tessa. I shouldn't have told you; I'm usually better at minding my tongue."

"I'm sure you are. I have no right to judge Tessa." She

paused, but couldn't hold back her words. "It's just—Mirabelle is her sister."

"To be fair, Reginald was not yet married to Mirabelle at the time. Tessa and Sir Laurence had one of their usual rows, and she left him in London and stormed back to Grace Hill. There was the future Lord Montclair just down the road, a bachelor with an eye for the ladies and a sympathetic shoulder to cry on. Mother had done her dynastic duty by producing a son and heir in Vincent. Where was the harm, Reginald doubtless thought. Tessa's reasoning would have been that it would serve Laurence right for being so heartless.

"A few months later, Aunt Mirabelle came to visit her sister and Reginald met *her*. Mirabelle hadn't even made her debut. I presume he realized he'd found a better version of the same woman—although no doubt my mother would claim that Reginald settled for her sister, knowing he couldn't have her."

"Or Graeme's father was just a rake who liked beautiful women."

"That, too. And Tessa is a woman who likes being liked." He shrugged. "My parents, or rather, Sir Laurence and Tessa, were the worst possible people to be married. Absolute opposites."

"It was a loveless marriage?"

James let out a bark of mirthless laughter. "Hardly. They were altogether too much in love. He was mad for her till the end. Anyone could see that. But they were nothing alike, and they brought out the worst in each other. Sir Laurence was a true de Vere, cold and logical, with, as Lady Eugenia would say, a deplorable talent for making money. My mother has little use for logic, and while she finds money useful for purchasing things, I think she believes it falls from the sky like manna."

"Ah. I see. They argued over money."

"Among a vast number of things. Sir Laurence was harsh and demanding; she was flighty and unreasonable. But at the base of it, it was all about one thing—love. Mother is an inveterate flirt. She lives to be admired, to beguile. Clearly there have been times when she went beyond flirtation, how often I don't know and frankly don't care to. Sir Laurence was jealous."

"It makes a bad combination."

"Bizarrely enough, in most ways he was much like me."

Laura suspected that the truth was more that James had modeled himself on the man he thought was his father, but she said nothing.

"He was ruled by his head, not his heart. He couldn't understand Mother's vagaries, her moods, her love of drama and passion. His one passion was her, and in that he was trapped. Hopelessly lost."

"Something you never wanted to be."

"Something I am not, and I thank God for it." His gaze slid over to her and away. "I don't know why I'm telling you all this."

"It does much to explain the gulf between you and Claude—between you and all of them. Have you always known?"

He shook his head. "When I was young, I thought Sir Laurence was my father. There was no reason not to, and everyone spoke of how alike we were. I had his head for numbers, his impatience, his . . . aloofness." He slanted a wry glance at her. "You may find it hard to believe, but I was not a loving child."

"No? I'm surprised. I would have thought you had a dog you loved."

"I did." James's face lit up. "Maggie. I was three years old and scarcely reached her shoulders. She adopted me; I think I was more her pet than the other way round. Everyone else was terrified of her. Nurse nearly had apoplexy when I brought her into my room. But there was no budging Mags once she'd set her mind to something."

"Or you, I'll warrant."

"Or me."

"You said her name when you were in a fever."

"I saw her— I suppose it was actually Dem. She was his grand—no, great-grandmother. Mother banished her from the nursery when Claude was born . . . even though I told her I was almost positive Mags wouldn't eat the baby."

Laura laughed. "I wonder why she wasn't reassured."

"Mags could be another reason for Claude's animosity. As I remember, he and Patricia were frightened of her."

"I'm sure you did nothing to dispel that fear."

"Laura!" He widened his eyes dramatically. "How can you say that?"

"Because I remember you when you were young."

"You do?" He looked surprised.

"Yes, you would come to see Graeme sometimes when Mama and I were visiting Mirabelle. I thoroughly disliked you."

"Was I unkind to you? I do beg your pardon. I don't remember."

"Of course you don't; I was merely that nuisance of a girl. When you were there, the two of you went off and did 'boy' things and I was not allowed to join you."

"Ah. So I stole Graeme away from you."

"Yes, you did, but I forgive you." She paused. "When did you—how did you—"

"Find out I was a bastard?"

"You're not."

"Not legally. Sir Laurence acknowledged me. He may have wished otherwise once Claude came along, but he would never have shamed Tessa. It was when I was older, maybe thirteen or so; I overheard one of the servants say something about it, just an offhand remark, making a joke. But I realized what he meant."

"I'm sorry." Laura took his hand in hers, as she had so many times through his illness. "It must have hurt terribly."

He shrugged. "It explained a lot of things. Why Sir Laurence often looked at me the way he did. Things he'd said that hadn't made sense to me at the time. How happy he was when Claude was born. I must have been a constant reminder of his wife's infidelity."

Though his voice was even, as it nearly always was, Laura sensed the pain that threaded through it. She squeezed his hand. "Yet you were the one he left in charge."

"Since he acknowledged me, I had to be the heir; I was eldest."

"Only the title and this estate. You told me that was all that would go to Claude. Yet Sir Laurence gave you everything, did he not? Except for that fund for the others, which he put into *your* care."

"I am the only one he could trust to handle the money wisely and not give in to their wishes."

"I would think having earned the trust of someone like Sir Laurence would mean a good deal," Laura said.

James glanced at her sharply, but he said only, "You

can see why Claude resents me—getting all the things he thinks should be his."

"If it's unfair, it's the law that makes it so—and Sir Laurence. It's not your fault."

"No. But he has to get rid of me to have what he thinks he's owed."

"True—but is he the sort of person who would kill his brother in order to get it?"

"Who else could it be? If the apothecary or a servant did it, it would have to be because someone paid them; I cannot imagine someone taking that kind of risk just because they didn't like me. And while you can make something of a case for the trust beneficiaries, it is Claude who has the strongest motive." He paused. "There's another factor to consider. I got sick in London. Someone must have put a pan of the stuff under my bed there, as they did here."

"Which would eliminate the servants—in both places. And anyone else who was at Grace Hill the whole time. Who was at the house in London at the time you grew ill?"

"I'm not sure. I was here when Graeme's baby was born, and I returned to London a week or so later. Within days, I was sick. It must have been placed there while I was at Grace Hill or as soon as I returned. I don't really remember who was in London then. Tessa, of course." He paused, thinking. "Walter hasn't been in the house in town since last year when he got sent down."

"What about the others?"

"Patricia and Archie doubtless were in London during the Season, but they would have stayed at Lord Salstone's home."

"They would have called on your mother, though."

"True. I can't remember when Claude was last in London. My memory is still cloudy, I'm afraid." He frowned.

"What about that man who's your partner? Doesn't he inherit something?"

"Caulfield?" His brows lifted. "Yes, the factory we own jointly will revert to him on my death. It was his family's originally."

"Then he profits by your death. Surely he calls on you in London."

"Yes," he agreed slowly, frowning. "He does. I have even sometimes wondered if he has a *tendre* for Mother."

"You said he was a hard man."

"Yes, he'd have the spine to do it and the intelligence. I wouldn't have thought he had the animosity—but I'm beginning to question my ability to judge one's character. He would be handy, wouldn't he, if not as satisfying as blaming it on Salstone? Still, half of a business doesn't seem enough for murder."

"Part of a *family* business."

"There are some people to whom that would matter quite a bit." He sent her a silvery glance, the corner of his mouth quirked up, in that look that did odd things to her insides. "Care to place a wager on it? My money's on Claude. Who's your man, Archie or Caulfield?"

"I don't prefer either one." Irritation sparked in her. "Really, James, you want to take bets on the identity of your murderer?"

"Would-be murderer, one hopes. Come, it will make it more entertaining."

"Entertaining!" Laura scrambled off the bed, her annoyance flaring into anger. "How can you—after all this—and you're *joking* about it? I have been here night after night, watching you struggle to breathe, listening to you converse with people who aren't there, worried every second that you—" Her voice caught, her eyes suddenly filling with tears. "Oh, blast."

She whirled to walk off, but James caught her wrist. "Laura, no. Wait." He stood up, tugging her back. "Don't cry. Please." His hand curved around her cheek, tilting her face up. "I'm sorry. I didn't think—I'm a wretch. An idiot." He smoothed his thumb across her cheek, wiping away the tear that trickled down. "I would not hurt you for the world. And yet somehow I always do."

"I realize you like to pretend that nothing matters, that you care for nothing, even your own life. But I *do* care. I've been so worried."

"I know. You are an angel. I promise you, I didn't mean to make light of what you did for me. I was just . . . being too much myself." His thumb caressed her cheek again. "Sweet girl. Don't waste your tears on me." His eyes moved over her face, his hand sliding down to her neck, cupping it. "Laura . . ." His voice changed, suddenly huskier.

He said her name again, little more than a whisper, and she felt the brush of his breath against her skin. Then he kissed her.

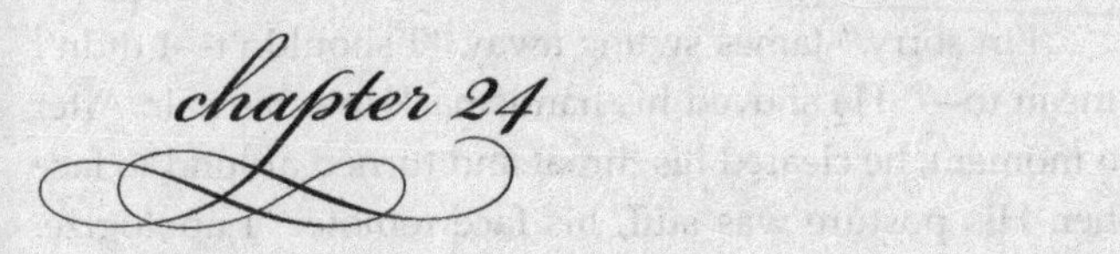

chapter 24

James curved over her, fitting her body to his, and Laura melted into him. His lips were warm and gently insistent, opening her mouth. He slid his hand down her back, following the curve in, then out, his caress as soft and inviting as his mouth. Their kiss deepened, his tongue tangling with hers, and Laura felt the surge of heat in his body.

His fingertips pressed into the soft flesh of her buttocks, and his other arm wrapped around her waist, locking her to him. Laura's heart pounded madly. She was awash in sensual pleasure, her mind a blank. James changed the angle of their kiss, his lips harder, fiercer. His hand strayed over her, coming up to cup her breast.

Laura's body responded, her nipple tightening beneath his touch and warmth blossoming between her legs. She wanted to touch him, to slide her hands over his chest and up his neck, to feel the glide of his hair through her fingers. The way he held her had shackled her arms to her sides. Laura shifted to pull one hand up through the circle of his embrace, pushing his arm aside a little, to reach his chest. James froze.

He lifted his head abruptly and stared down at her for a startled moment, his gaze the gray of storms. He jerked back from her with a low curse. Laura couldn't move, just stared at him with her lips still parted, too surprised, too full of conflicting emotions, to even think, let alone speak.

"I'm sorry." James swung away. "I shouldn't—I didn't mean to—" He shoved his hands back into his hair. After a moment, he cleared his throat and turned around to face her. His posture was stiff, his face remote. "I apologize. I have no excuse other than I am . . . not myself, as you know."

"Yes, of course." Laura's own face was so stiff she thought it might crack. She felt almost literally ill, her stomach fluttering with all the emotions that had torn at her for the past week, mingling with the desire and pleasure that had flooded her with his kiss. She was in a state of confusion, but one thing was perfectly plain—James regretted kissing her.

"It won't happen again." James pressed on, as if she had expressed disbelief. "You have my word. You are not . . ." He paused, as if casting about for something to say.

"I am not a woman whom you would consider in that way," Laura finished for him, her voice crisp. "I understand. The boundaries of our marriage were perfectly clear."

"No." He frowned. "I mean yes, I am clear about the boundaries. But—" He stopped, his face a study in frustration. He turned and strode over to the fireplace to stare moodily into its low flames.

Laura turned in the opposite direction and caught sight of herself in the mirror. She looked like a slattern, her hair loose and hanging all about. Reaching up, she braided her hair with trembling fingers. She wished she could bring her life into order as easily.

What a wretched day this had been—and how foolish

and selfish it was of her to think that way when James was so much better. Flushing with shame, Laura glanced at James, still turned away from her, gazing fixedly at the mantel.

"I, um, if you'll excuse me, I must see to some things." Without waiting for a response, Laura turned and fled from the room.

James sagged, one hand gripping the mantel. Demosthenes, who had entered the room as Laura left, trotted over to him, giving his free hand a helpful nudge. James glanced down and ran his hand over the dog's head. "I made an utter mess of that, didn't I?"

He hadn't set out to kiss her. Doubtless Laura would not believe it, but he had intended nothing except to apologize. He had been filled with an unaccustomed tenderness, a bittersweet regret at causing her to cry, combined with a pleased and amazed awareness that talk of his dying should upset her.

It had been sheer, unthinking instinct to kiss her, a soft reassurance and apology and expression of gratitude, all the things he could not bring himself to say. But then, touching her, tasting her, had been so sweet he wanted more. The flash of tenderness had turned to hunger, and he had responded as he had this morning in his sleep. Instinct was a dangerous thing.

It had taken Laura pushing against his arm, her palm on his chest trying to ward him off, to awaken him to reality, to realize that he had been on the verge of breaking his promises to her. Clearly his illness had affected his mind. How else to explain the absence of his usual control?

It was only natural to want her—what man wouldn't?

Laura was a beauty. That fall of golden hair around her shoulders, loose and soft and fine, beckoned one's fingers to sink into it. The curve of her lips . . . the curves of her body . . . the satiny skin, all cream and rose. A man would have to be a saint not to want her, and James was anything but a saint.

But he should have been able to conquer it. He should have thought, considered, weighed the rewards and the consequences. He was not an impulsive man; he wasn't ruled by his senses. He was always able to leash his hunger.

Today, though, kissing her had seemed so good, so right, that it bypassed his mind altogether. Perhaps, he thought, it was because the kiss had come from something other than mere physical desire. He wasn't accustomed to heat and hunger spreading through him from his chest rather than his groin. He wasn't used to such a wash of emotion.

And he didn't like it. The more he thought about it, the more he realized it was a distinctly uncomfortable feeling.

This strange turmoil inside him would change, surely, as he regained his health. His sickness had left him thin-skinned, his barriers lowered, too slow of thought to maintain his equilibrium. Soon he would be back to himself. But what was he to do right now?

His first thought—that damnable instinct again—was to find a way around those promises he'd made to Laura. He could try to woo Laura into his bed, convince her to change their agreement. Surely he was not incapable of charm if he set his mind to it.

But it made him uneasy to think of inveigling Laura into something she didn't want. The last thing he wanted was to deceive Laura or set her against him. After all she had done for him, it would be reprehensible to try to escape his part of the bargain.

From the start Laura had made it clear she didn't desire him—indeed, was repelled by him. Truth be known, it had stung to be told nothing would induce her to bed him, but it had been easy enough to agree to her conditions. It was a bitter irony that Laura's excellent care had brought him back to life, making him ache to ignore those boundaries. By saving him she had condemned herself to a lifetime with him.

No. He would not indulge himself at her expense. He would stick to their bargain and he would make that clear to her. James sank into the chair beside the bed, suddenly swamped with weariness. Dem settled his head on James's leg and watched him soulfully. James stroked the silky head, smoothing out the wrinkles in the way the dog particularly liked. What he must do was obvious. It was both foolish and unlike him to be reluctant.

When Laura returned to the room sometime later, James rose from his chair to face her. He found the words irrationally hard to get out, but he forced himself to say, "It's time for me to move back into my room."

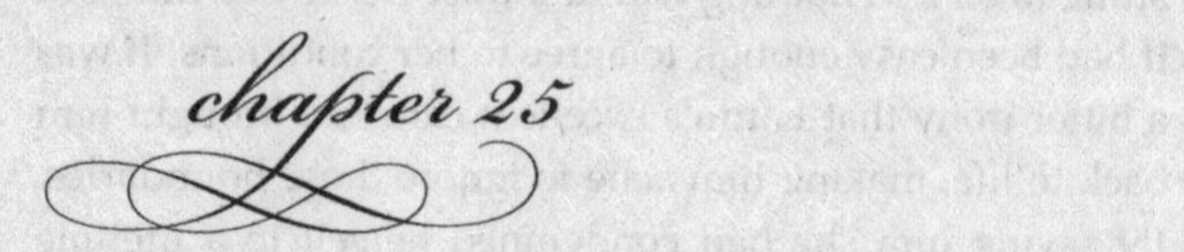

"What?" Laura stared, her stomach tightening. It had taken her several minutes strolling through the garden to even out her nerves, and already James had destroyed her calm. "No! It's not safe. I didn't dispose of the mercury."

"Then we must get rid of it. I cannot continue to hide in here."

Laura swallowed the protest that rose in her throat. He was right, of course; their life must revert to a normal state at some point. No doubt James felt caged and uncomfortable here. It was absurd, really, to feel this stab of hurt. "Still, you must give the room time to air out."

"In a few days then." James was all business now, the dispassionate man she had known before.

"Very well. You intend to reveal that we found the mercury?" Laura was determined that she could be as matter-of-fact as he.

"I suppose I'll have to." He frowned. "Though I'd like to have some proof of who is responsible before I do anything."

"What do you intend to do?" Laura asked.

"I don't know."

"It's good to see you have a well-thought-out plan."

A reluctant smile tugged at the corner of his mouth. "Clearly you're going to force me to think." He rubbed his forehead.

"Do you have a headache?" Laura took a step toward him. "Shall I massage your head again?"

James moved back a step. "No. Best not." He began to pace. "I'll go down to dinner tomorrow." He held up a hand to forestall her. "I know you think I'm too weak. But so do they, and I want to surprise them. I need to judge their reactions." Laura crossed her arms, jaw set stubbornly, and glared at him. He sighed. "Very well. I'll wait two days."

"I'll agree to that." Though James wasn't even close to fully recovered, Laura had learned how far his will could take him. And she would be there to help him if he had trouble. "You intend to keep everyone uninformed about your progress until then?"

"If possible. I've either been asleep or pretended to be whenever anyone comes in. So all they know is that I haven't died. You didn't tell anyone I had improved, did you?"

Laura shook her head. "No one except Graeme and his family. They wouldn't have said anything, knowing you are in danger, not even Mirabelle."

"Everyone views their visit today as a 'last good-bye'?"

"Yes." The words sent a shiver through Laura.

"I made it clear to Owen that he must not gossip with the other servants about my condition. I dangled a permanent position as my valet as a carrot, so I think he will keep his mouth shut."

"What about this evening? I imagine Walter will visit you again, and Tessa. Claude usually comes to see you in the evening, as well."

"Checking to see how his plan is progressing, no doubt."

"James, you don't know that."

"Why are you so protective of Claude?" He raised an eyebrow.

"I'm not. I just—I don't want it to be one of your siblings," Laura admitted. "Do you? Honestly?"

"Well, if you're going to insist on honesty . . ." He sighed, shrugging a shoulder. "No, I'd rather it not be one of them. But I cannot let sentimentality interfere with my thinking."

"I know."

"I shall just continue my pretense of sleep. That's easiest. What about you? Can you keep up the charade?"

"It's a trifle hard not to look lighter of spirit," Laura admitted. "But I managed it this morning." That seemed ages ago. "And, aside from your mother and Walter, I am not usually given to conversation with any of them."

"You won't have to hide much longer. Everything can return to normal."

"Aside from possible attempts to murder you."

"Yes, aside from that." He smiled at her. "But life always has its little ups and downs, doesn't it?"

When James and Laura strolled into the dining room two days later, every jaw in the room dropped. But if James had hoped to see an indication of guilt on any of the gathered faces, he was doomed to disappointment. Astonishment so stamped their features that there was little room for anything else. Even the butler stood in blank shock, staring.

Simpson, not surprisingly, was the first to recover. "Sir James. Please, allow me."

He whisked out the chair at the head of the table, in two

quick gestures sending one of the footmen to bring in more place settings and another to pull out Laura's chair. Tessa sprang to her feet, tears welling in her eyes, and went to her son, bending to kiss him on the cheek.

"James, love, I knew it." Tessa turned and sent a smile bright with triumph at the others. "You see, Claude? I told you he would be fine." She stroked her hand across James's hair and bent to kiss him again. Then she burst into tears.

"Mother . . ." James looked pained, but stood and took his mother's hand, patting it, and glanced over at Laura for help.

Laura went to her mother-in-law's side, curving an arm around Tessa's waist. "Of course you knew best. You are his mother."

"Yes." Tessa glowed at her. "Mothers always know, don't they?" Tessa pulled out a delicate lace handkerchief and dabbed at her tears.

Before she could sit down, Mr. Netherly shot up from his chair across from Cousin Maurice and went to Tessa, taking her hand solicitously. "Lady de Vere, this must be a shock for you. Let me escort you to your room so you can rest after this excitement."

"Careful, Netherly," James drawled. "Mother is far too young a woman to be laid low by a happy surprise."

"Of course." Netherly shot him a dark look. "I didn't mean to imply—it is just that Lady de Vere is so sensitive. So delicate."

"Thank you, Mr. Netherly." Tessa gave her swain a gracious nod, but disengaged her hand as she sat down again. "I assure you, I am not as fragile as I may appear." Laura saw a silvery flash of amusement in the older woman's eyes that reminded her forcibly of James. "Besides, we must celebrate." She raised her glass toward James. "Welcome back, love."

"Mother." James nodded to her, a grin tugging at his mouth, and raised his glass in return. "I am most happy to find myself still in the land of the living."

Laura had been watching everyone's faces since they entered the room, but she had caught no sign of anything suspicious. After the initial shock, they continued to eye James, some curious, others more wary.

Only Walter grinned. "I say, James, this is splendid. I thought for sure you were, well, you know . . ."

"Dying?" James asked, quirking a brow. "No. Sorry to disappoint everyone." James looked at Claude.

Claude returned James's gaze stonily. "Don't worry. We're all accustomed to that by now."

Adelaide looked sweetly puzzled, Archie laughed, and Tessa said placidly, "Now, boys."

"No, James . . ." Walter protested, looking appalled. "You know we were all worried. Terribly worried."

"Were you? How kind."

Claude's wife, Adelaide, offered a tentative smile. "It's so nice that you are feeling better, Sir James. Claude has been most anxious. We all were."

"Yes." Patricia appeared more aggrieved than anxious. "You looked positively ghastly. Don't tell me you were shamming all this time."

"No, Patricia, I assure you, I was not malingering. Thank you for your concern."

"Well, I *was* concerned. I came to see you several times. Whenever your wife would let me in." She turned an accusatory gaze on Laura. "She positively hid you away."

"Mm. I've found Laura to be quite dictatorial." He slanted a dancing look at Laura.

"James, you cannot mean it," Walter said anxiously. "Laura is the most pleasant, gentle . . ."

"Clearly she hasn't been forcing noxious liquids down your throat."

"Do stop teasing everyone, James." Laura sent a kindly smile toward her champion. "Don't worry, Walter. I've learned that Sir James is not nearly so fearsome as he would have one believe."

"No?" James raised his brows.

Laura raised hers in return. "No."

James held the supercilious look for another moment before his lips twitched and he murmured, "Clearly not to you." He turned his cool gaze back to his sister. "I am sorry, Patricia, that you were not allowed in the sickroom the numerous times you wanted to keep watch at my bedside."

Patricia, not fool enough to misunderstand his dry remark, fell back on her usual pout. "I would have been happy to. She would not let poor Archie in at all."

"Astonishing." James's eyes moved to the man in question. "And when Archie has been so kind to Laura."

Patricia colored and opened her mouth to retort, but her husband said, "Leave it alone, Patsy. You'll never induce James to like me."

"It's not fair," Patricia said, setting her chin stubbornly, but she subsided.

"Any other complaints?" James asked lightly, glancing around the table. "Walter? Cousin Maurice? I hope my illness did not discommode you."

Walter, correctly taking his question as rhetorical, said

nothing. Maurice replied, "Good heavens, no, no bother at all. I've been laid up all week with my lumbago."

James cut his eyes toward Laura, whose eyes were dancing, her lips pressed tightly together to keep from laughing. James clamped his napkin to his mouth, muffling a choked noise.

"James, what's the matter? Are you all right?" Tessa asked. "Claude, do something."

"No, no." James held up a hand. "I'm fine, Mother. I was just overcome for the moment by the joy of being back in the bosom of my family."

"Of course you were." Tessa gave him a sparkling smile. "Now that you are better, perhaps we should have a party. What do you think, Adelaide? We haven't had the chance to introduce Laura to everyone."

The conversation moved on as the other three women, ignoring Laura's protests, launched into plans for a party. Laura said little, spending most of her time studying the faces of everyone around the table, hoping for some look or gesture or words that would give someone away. Now and then she cast a glance at James, monitoring his condition.

When the meal finally wound to a close, Laura moved to head off the possibility of James lingering with the other gentlemen over port. As she rose with the other women, she gave a smile to the table of men and said, "I hope you will excuse me. I am rather tired. Dear?" She turned to James. "Will you escort me?"

Amusement flickered in his eyes. "Of course. Dear."

As they climbed the stairs, James leaned in to murmur, "You know they will all assume you are a shockingly demanding bride."

"Oh, hush." Laura could feel her cheeks heating. "Perhaps they are not as low-minded as you."

James chuckled, a deep rumbling sound that set up the same sort of tingles in her as his wicked smile. "They are men, Laura."

"Well, I couldn't rely on you to take care of yourself. And I don't think you're quite up to another sparring session with Mr. Salstone."

"You might be right. I'm not objecting, you understand. No doubt they are all green with envy."

"Come in and stop talking nonsense. Does your head ache? Sit down and I'll rub it for you."

"It's not necessary."

"I didn't offer because I had to."

James hesitated, then sank onto the stool in front of her vanity. Laura came up behind him and slid her fingers into his hair. She glanced in the mirror before them. James was watching her reflection, and he quickly looked away. Laura began to massage his temples. He closed his eyes, hiding their silver gleam. Laura felt his body relax, leaning back into her. His head was heavy against her stomach.

Anticipation coiled low in her body, a breathless sense of waiting. She thought of sliding her fingers over his neck and across his shoulders, down onto his chest. It was wicked of her, for he had amply demonstrated yesterday that he wanted nothing like that from her.

Then why had he kissed her? Why, in his delirium, had he caressed her and fitted his mouth to hers, his fingers seeking her breasts, his tongue hot and eager in her mouth? Even though she was inexperienced, Laura couldn't believe his actions had not meant that he was as hungry for her as she was for him.

It was pointless to deny her own passion. However wanton that made her, Laura wanted him. She wanted to be married to him in this most intimate way, to feel his heat and desire. Laura gazed at her reflection again. Her face was loose and soft, her eyes lambent. If James opened his eyes and saw her this way, he would know how she felt. It would be horridly embarrassing. She had to stop thinking this way. Feeling this way.

Suddenly James surged to his feet, taking a long step away from her. He dragged his hands through his hair, pulling it into some sort of order, and it seemed to Laura that he was trying to sweep away the touch of her hands. Had he sensed her thoughts? Her emotions?

She turned away, humiliation roiling in her. However much it might appear that James desired her, it was equally clear that he wished he did not. "I'll ring for Owen to help you." She yanked at the bell pull. "Since it's clear you don't want mine."

"Laura, no . . ." He took a half step toward her. "I didn't mean . . ."

"What nonsense. Of course you did. You seem to have acquired some notion that I am about to impose myself on you. Well, let me reassure you—the fact that I helped you when you were ill does not mean I want anything more from this marriage than we bargained for. I don't." She gave a sharp nod for emphasis. "Now. I am going for a walk and leaving you to yourself, since that is obviously the company you prefer."

Without waiting for a response, Laura whirled and stalked out the door.

Unsurprisingly, James attacked getting well as if it were a business. Laura watched him go through each day, methodical and persistent, taking the drafts she gave him and downing the food laid before him. He even forced himself to rest.

He was equally intent on rebuilding his strength. The first few days he limited himself to trips up and down the stairs and along the hallways, but he soon began to venture farther—to the terrace, then the gardens, increasing the distance with each trip. Sometimes he had to sit and rest on a bench before starting back to the house, but he doggedly kept at it.

At least the weariness made him sleep. Laura wished she could say the same for herself. She told herself she tossed and turned because the cot on which she lay was uncomfortable, but when they disposed of the mercury beneath James's bed and he returned to his own room, she found sleep even more elusive.

James, of course, was not bothered at all. He was smoothly polite, giving Laura his arm as courtesy demanded, but never touching her in any other way. He spent little time with her except at meals and in the evening, when they were surrounded by his family.

At first Laura reacted to his new aloofness by withdrawing into an equally stiff silence. It was not long, however, before she realized that this path led only to permanent separation. She could not bear to lose James entirely, as she had lost Graeme.

If their relationship could not be all she wanted, she could at least regain what they had had before. She forced herself back into her former amiable, light attitude, and James's manner began to relax.

Laura knew the evenings spent in conversation with the others in the household were deadly dull for James—after all, they were equally boring for her—so she strove to enliven the gatherings. Sometimes she played the piano and Tessa sang along with her, which had the advantage of making it difficult for all of them to snipe at each other.

She suspected from the twinkle in his eyes that James guessed her reasons for the musicales, but it served its purpose. Laura knew he liked to hear her play, and though he refused to join in their singing—unlike Walter, who surprisingly turned out to bask in the attention—it warmed her to see James happy amidst his family. Well, happy might be too strong a word, but at least comfortable.

However, the music gave her little opportunity to be with James, so she frequently suggested a game instead. She feared at first that he would not join in, for he was bound to be annoyed by the play of most of the others, but to her surprise, James readily agreed whenever she suggested it.

It turned out that their most frequent companions at the game table were Adelaide and Patricia. It was not an ideal arrangement, as Adelaide was a foolish player and Patricia a terrible loser, but at least Adelaide's saccharine conversation usually suppressed some of Patricia's sniping.

After a few evenings spent playing cribbage, however, Adelaide protested, "No, not that game again, please!" She turned large soulful eyes on Laura. "I can never keep up when James is playing. The pegs are moving so fast, and everyone's saying all those numbers."

"Whist, then?" Laura asked, glancing at James and his sister.

Adelaide nodded enthusiastically, James shrugged, and Patricia said sourly, "It doesn't matter. James will win whatever we play."

"You could partner with James," Laura offered, suppressing a grin at the look of alarm on her husband's face.

"Goodness, no, that's even worse. Then James is sitting there the whole time, judging my poor play."

"Is he?" Laura sent him a teasing glance. "I suppose I should worry, then."

"Not you." Patricia's lips thinned. "He thinks you're perfect."

Laura chuckled. "Hardly."

"Laura remembers which suit is trump," James told his sister with a pointed look. "Which makes it vastly easier to play with her."

"Claude's the same way," Adelaide put in, smoothing the waters as she often did. "He knows every card that's been played. He thinks I'm dreadfully silly." She seemed more pleased than not at this evaluation. "He prefers the play at the tavern in the village. That's why he took Walter and Archie there this evening."

"They're going to gamble?" Patricia's brows pinched together. "I thought it was just to have a drink."

"Don't worry, I doubt the play is very deep," James told her. "Not like in London. Claude won't let Salstone get into trouble."

"I wasn't worried." Patricia glared and began to deal out the cards.

Laura, picking up her hand, said casually, "I suppose you must miss London, Patricia." It made her feel a trifle guilty to probe an obviously sore subject for James's sister, but she could not pass up the opportunity to dig for information.

"Oh, yes," Patricia replied in the most heartfelt voice Laura had ever heard from her. Then she seemed to come to herself and glared. "I'm sure you know that."

Laura ignored her last words. "I haven't been to London often myself. What about you, Adelaide? Do you and Claude go there frequently?"

"No. I'm afraid Claude isn't fond of the city. Oh, look! I took that trick." Adelaide giggled and scooped up the cards. Laura was pondering how to phrase a more specific inquiry when Adelaide went on, "Actually, I don't believe we've been in London for a year now. Since last Season."

Laura glanced at James. If Claude had not been at the London house recently, that would exonerate him, wouldn't it? After all, that was where James had first fallen ill.

"You didn't come with him last time he was there?" Patricia asked. "We saw Claude, oh, it must have been two or three months ago."

"Oh! Of course. How silly of me. Claude did go to the city on some sort of business. How could I have forgotten? I suppose it was because I wasn't with him. Poor Robby had a terrible cough. I couldn't leave him." Adelaide sighed at the memory and shook her head. "You cannot imagine, Patricia, how hard it is for a mother to see her child suffering."

Pain bloomed in Patricia's eyes, and, not for the first time, Laura wondered if Adelaide was really as sweet as she appeared. Were her words artless or a barb about Patricia's childlessness? Whichever it was, it didn't make Laura like Adelaide any better.

Laura turned back to her hand, dropping her investigations for the moment. But later that evening, as she and James climbed the stairs to their rooms, James said, "Well, now we know that Claude had the opportunity to set up mercury in the town house as well as here."

"But several of the others were in London, too. Obviously Patricia and Salstone were there."

"Still championing Archie for the villain, I see." James smiled. "Yes, it could have been any of them. But it's another nail in the coffin for Claude. Or, actually, for me, I suppose."

"James . . ." They reached Laura's door, and she turned to him.

"Don't worry, I'm not condemning Claude yet."

Laura blushed. She hadn't been thinking of Claude when she'd said James's name. It had been merely a desire to stop him, to make him linger here with her, perhaps even come inside her room. But, of course, that was a hopeless endeavor.

So she smiled stiffly and said, "Well, then . . . good night."

He stood looking down at her, a heat in his gaze that made her hope for an instant that he was about to kiss her. But he stepped back, giving her a sharp nod. "Good night, Laura. Sleep well."

Little likelihood of that, Laura thought sourly as she went inside her chamber. It was ridiculous. She had spent her entire life sleeping alone, but now her room seemed empty without him there. She could not escape the constant humming memory of his kiss—the way his arms had gone around her, his body lean and hard against hers, his lips wonderfully soft.

How could James remain so indifferent? She had felt the passion in him; she could not be mistaken. But deep down she knew the answer to her question. James might desire her, but she was not the wife he wanted. Now that he was getting better, he realized what a mistake he had made in marrying Laura.

She could never hope to match the paragon of cool self-sufficiency that he had wanted for a wife. When he had first described his ideal wife to her, she had been amused. Now she found it difficult to laugh about it.

Other men might settle for something less, might let passion overcome their intentions. But not James. He would suppress whatever spark he might feel until it was utterly smothered. Laura supposed it was fortunate that she was no longer in his company as often. It would be easier for her to regain her equilibrium without him around.

The only problem was that being apart from James was the last thing she wanted.

Laura was sitting in the garden the following afternoon when she looked up and saw Abigail walking toward her. She jumped to her feet, smiling. "Abigail! How nice to see you."

Smiling, Abby took her hand in greeting. "When Graeme

said he was coming to call on James, Mirabelle and I decided to join him. We've been in the drawing room visiting with Aunt Tessa and the others."

"Is that why you fled to the garden?"

Abby laughed. "It *was* a bit dull." She slipped her arm through Laura's and they turned to stroll deeper into the garden. "How is Anna?" Laura asked.

"Delightful, of course." Abby grinned. "You must come visit us and see her again. It seems as if every day she's doing something new."

"Thank you. I shall."

"You know, I am quite determined we shall become friends."

Laura glanced at the other woman, startled. "I should like that, as well."

"I hope I'm not too blunt. I hate to hint at things."

"I don't mind," Laura assured her. "I prefer to be straightforward myself. And I would value our friendship. You've already done a great deal for me."

"We've . . . exchanged favors," Abby agreed. "But I would like there to be more between us. When I first met you, I thought, well, finally, here's a woman in England I could be friends with."

"I liked you, as well," Laura told her. "It's just—"

"Graeme. I know. It's awkward. But I'm hoping it doesn't have to be." Abigail came to a stop and gazed earnestly into Laura's eyes. "Graeme has told me what good friends the two of you were; you're important to him. So is James. I don't want there to be anything that hinders that closeness."

"I feel the same."

"Good." Abigail began walking again. "I will tell you

that I was jealous of you when I first saw you. So lovely and English and blond. So well bred."

"Oh, Abigail, no . . ."

"Don't worry." Abigail smiled at her. "Graeme has convinced me of his love for me. I'm not jealous. I wanted to make sure you know that. But I didn't know . . . whether the situation would be difficult for you."

"You mean, do I still pine for Graeme?" Laura asked wryly.

"Yes." Abigail turned her vivid green eyes on Laura, serious, even sympathetic. "I don't want to cause you pain. But now that you have married James, I hoped it meant you no longer felt the same about Graeme."

"Since you are so honest with me, I must be with you, as well. I'm not entirely sure how I feel about James. But I *am* quite sure I don't wish I was married to Graeme. Seeing how happy Graeme is, I could not feel any way but pleased."

"Really?" Abby's expression was one of such astonishment that Laura had to laugh.

"Yes. Really."

"If I knew that Graeme was happier with a woman other than me, I think I'd want to scratch her eyes out. His, too! No, I'd want to do worse than that to him," Abby mused.

"I think perhaps you love Graeme in a way I don't. A way I'm not sure I ever did. Graeme is dear to me; we were friends for years. But I didn't—I mean, when James—" Her words stumbled to a halt, her cheeks turning fiery.

"My goodness, don't stop there," Abby said. "When James what? Has he—I mean, I thought he was so ill he . . . I'm sorry. I'm too inquisitive. I beg your pardon."

"No, I'd—frankly, I'd like to talk to someone. But I can't

talk to Tessa about James. Or Mirabelle. And Patricia and Adelaide are . . . um . . ."

"No need to explain. I've met Patricia and Adelaide."

Laura smiled, but her cheeks were still flaming. "It's embarrassing. You probably don't want to hear such things."

"My dear, this is exactly the sort of thing I want to hear," Abby said, with such an easy droll manner that Laura relaxed.

"Very well." Laura took a deep breath and began. "Obviously, ours was not a love match. James and I weren't friends—just the opposite. I was stunned when he proposed."

"Perhaps he had been harboring a secret passion for you all these years?" Abby suggested.

"James?" Laura laughed. "You *have* met him, haven't you?"

"Well . . ." Abby shrugged. "I hoped it was something terribly romantic."

"Not at all romantic. But very kind. He's a good man, however much he tries to hide it. I have come to care for him."

"Do you love him?"

Laura hesitated. "I don't know. It's not the same."

"As it was with Graeme?"

Laura nodded. "I don't think James is wonderful or that he's a perfect example of a man, as I did Graeme. James is excessively irritating sometimes. He's aloof. He's very . . . sealed off, somehow. I don't *know* him; I'm not sure I'll ever really know him. He doesn't want anyone to. But I enjoy being with him. It makes me happy just to see him. And I feel—I have such—" A flush spread across her cheeks and she glanced at Abby, then away. "I want him." Her words came out barely above a whisper.

"Ah."

"I tell myself I shouldn't."

"Why not? He's your husband; it seems quite permissible to me."

"But I'm not sure that I love him. I *am* sure he will never love me. And that makes it just lust, doesn't it?"

"Perhaps it's not sacred. But it's legal." Abby smiled, her eyes twinkling. "And James *is* very pleasing to the eye."

Laura laughed, though her cheeks still burned. "He is, isn't he? It gives me shivers when he smiles in that wicked way, as if he knows something is sinful but he wants you to enjoy it with him anyway. His eyes light up silver, and he has such disgustingly thick black eyelashes. And when he kisses me, I—" She stopped, words failing her, and shook her head. "I shouldn't be talking about this."

"Oh, you should. You absolutely should," Abby told her. "So the situation is thus: you're married, and he wants you, and you want him."

"It sounds terribly silly when you put it like that, doesn't it?"

"No. I understand. You're like Graeme. You want to do what's right, and just because something is acceptable doesn't mean it's right."

"I'm not even sure James desires me."

"You just said he kissed you. I doubt it was charity."

"Yes, but it was when James was in a fever. He was delirious, out of his head. That's not very encouraging, is it?"

"He hasn't kissed you any other time?"

"At the ceremony, of course, and once here in the garden, but that was just for show. He didn't want his relatives to know how ill he was." Laura added in a rush, "And also the other day."

"Then he's kissed you four times. We'll dismiss the wedding kiss, and I'll even omit the one 'for show,' though it seems to me that kissing someone isn't necessary to prove you aren't ill. There's one when he's feverish, which is open for debate. That still leaves you with one kiss that was clearly intentional."

"Yes. Oh, yes."

"With no other motive than that he wanted to. Do you think James goes about giving out kisses indiscriminately?"

Laura laughed. "No, definitely not. But after he kissed me, he jerked away as if he'd touched a hot stove and began to talk about the boundaries of our agreement. Then he told me he was going to move back into his bedroom."

"Boundaries? What do you mean?"

"What we agreed to at the beginning—you know, that it would be a marriage in name only."

"But that was when he thought he was about to die. I cannot imagine he wants an entire lifetime of celibacy. Nor can I see why he would kiss you if he didn't want to."

"Then why did he pull away?"

"I don't know. Men are odd creatures. You said James doesn't want anyone to really know him. Maybe he's afraid that if he went further, he would be revealing too much of himself. That he would . . . I don't know, be handing you the key to unlock him."

"But he has slept with other women. I'm sure of it."

"No doubt. But there's a good deal of difference between a mistress and a wife. A man can lie with a prostitute and take the pleasure, but he doesn't give up anything of himself."

"It's a business proposition. A contract. James likes contracts."

"Exactly. It's an exchange: he gives her money and she gives him, well, you know. But when there are feelings involved, when you are close to someone, it isn't a barter, but a mutual sharing, and he would be giving you not money, but something of himself. Then he can be hurt."

"But so can I."

"True. It's a risky endeavor." Abby smiled. "But well worth it, I think. James wants you; all he needs is a little push."

"A push?" Laura looked at her, intrigued.

"Yes. An alluring dress. A little flirtation. That sort of thing."

Laura looked doubtful. "I haven't any alluring dresses." She waved her hand down her dress.

"Get some new ones. I doubt James would begrudge you a new wardrobe."

Laura laughed. "It irritates him that I haven't bought any new clothes. I believe he thinks I'm dowdy."

"Maybe he just wants to give you something."

"Maybe." Laura could not help but smile at that thought. "I haven't had the time to go to London on a shopping expedition. I'll be in mourning for months yet, and it seems wasteful to buy new clothes in black and then not wear them when the year is up."

"Hasn't Tessa told you it's never a waste to buy a beautiful dress?"

"No, but I'm sure she would agree."

"In the meantime . . . I have several black gowns that I wore after my grandfather's death. They're a little behind in fashion, but that won't matter. We'll have to hem them, of course, but Molly can do it in a trice. Trust me, you'll have James wondering why he was ever foolish enough to want a marriage 'in name only.'" Abigail linked her arm through Laura's. "Now, what do you say we sit down on this lovely bench and make plans?"

Laura grinned. "I think that sounds like an excellent idea."

James stood at the window and brooded. He had been in his office since luncheon, and so far he had accomplished nothing. He had been trying for the past two weeks to get back into the routine of business, but his efforts had proved largely futile. It wasn't that numbers still eluded him; in that sense his mind had been steadily improving.

The problem was that his thoughts kept stubbornly going in a different direction. All he could think of these days was Laura. Laura with her hair down. Laura curled up in bed beside him. Laura undressed. Her body beneath his, her legs parting to take him in.

With a growl, he turned away from the window. He would drive himself insane this way. He was beginning to think that the mercury had destroyed whatever part of his brain contained his willpower. Demosthenes, who had done no more than raise his head when James left the desk, now did not bother to do even that, just followed him with his eyes, then went back to sleep. The dog had become accustomed to James's recent fits and starts.

For the last two weeks James had sought the refuge of his office in the hopes that removing himself from Laura's presence would ease his hunger for her. It had worked as well as removing himself from her bedroom, which was to say, not at all. It just meant that he spent his time daydreaming about her like a moonstruck calf instead of having the pleasure of her company.

James was beginning to decide he was a fool.

There were voices in the entry and the clatter of footsteps, along with high-pitched feminine laughter. Someone had come to call on Tessa. When the knock sounded on his door a moment later, he muffled a groan. The last thing he wanted was to have to go out and make polite conversation with his mother and her friends.

In the next moment, though, he heard Graeme say, "James?"

He opened the door. "Graeme. Thank God it's you."

"Hiding in your office?" Graeme asked with a smile.

"Of course. Is Lady Eugenia here, too?" James cast a cautious glance down the corridor.

"No, thank heavens." Graeme bent to give Demosthenes the greeting he expected, then straightened. "I took her back two days ago. I'm not exactly sure why it was necessary that I accompany her. She had her maid with her."

"I'm sure the sole reason is that she knew she could bully you into it."

Graeme sighed. "She has a way of making it so that one has to be rude not to do what she asks."

"You should try it." James sat down, and Graeme took the chair across from him.

Graeme smiled faintly. "You manage to do it without resorting to rudeness."

"That's because she knows I will be if she presses."

"How are you feeling?" Graeme asked. "You're looking much better."

"I am better. I even managed to walk down to the castle and back without stopping the other day."

"Your insomnia's gone?"

"Somewhat." There was something else that kept him awake at nights now—but he could hardly talk to Graeme about Laura and his desire for her. "I'm better, Graeme. Really."

"You seem . . . different."

"Almost dying will do that to one." James moved restlessly.

"Have you found out anything more about who, um . . ."

"Tried to kill me? No, very little. I got a new bottle of tonic from the apothecary. Since there was no mercury in it, presumably the apothecary was not the one doctoring it. We haven't spotted anyone sneaking into my bedroom to check on the mercury. But of course I can hardly keep an eye on it all the time, and I daren't risk the gossip that would ensue if I told one of the servants to spy on it."

"How would anyone have gotten their hands on mercury anyway?"

"It's used for a number of things, from making hats to actual medicines. Scientists conduct experiments with it. It's in thermometers—though I doubt anyone would have broken that many thermometers and emptied them out."

"What are you going to do?"

James shrugged. "I'm not sure. As the dowager countess pointed out, it's a rather delicate situation."

"You can't allow a murderer to run about loose."

"I doubt he's going to kill anyone but me."

"I would think that would be enough."

"I've considered tossing Claude out of Grace Hill. That would hopefully relieve the immediate threat, but he could go after me in London or somewhere else. And while he seems the likeliest, it's possible it was one of the others. Laura is partial to Salstone as the villain."

"Archie? He's always been a bit of a scoundrel. You know he keeps a mistress in London."

"Worse than that. The man's a bounder, but little good it would do Patsy to tell her. Claude got into fisticuffs with him over it. The stick I used with him was financial. But the black eye didn't stop Archie for long, and when I hold back money, Patricia's the one who loses. You can bet Salstone takes care of what he wants first."

"But what would killing you get Archie? A different trustee who would be freer with the money? Would even Salstone murder a man for that?"

"If Archie had the nerve, I imagine he'd kill me for far less."

Graeme shook his head, looking worried. "I don't like any of this, James."

"I'm not fond of it myself. But I'll handle it. I don't think any of them are foolish enough to try something so soon after the first attempt."

"True. At least you'll have some time to decide what to do. Why don't you and Laura move to London?"

"The idea appeals," James admitted. He had thought about it more than once. He could take Laura to plays and concerts, indulge her in all the things she had never had the money to buy. Clothes and jewels. They could be alone together, without the annoyance of everyone else. But of course that was the problem, as well—he would be with her all the time, no distractions, his hunger growing by the day. His control was already tenuous at best. James shook his head. "Better to be here, I think, where I can keep an eye on them. The answer's more likely to be here, if I can just find it."

"If there's any way I can help . . ."

"I know. Believe me, I will call on you if I need it."

A silence fell on them. For one of the few times in his life, James felt vaguely uncomfortable with Graeme. The only other time there had been this constraint between them, the reason for it had been the same: Laura Hinsdale. No, Laura de Vere. (And how strange it was that he felt a little throb of satisfaction, even smugness, at the thought that she bore his name.)

At that time Graeme had been so furious with James that he had barely talked to him for weeks, and when they had conversed, there had been a certain wariness, a careful avoidance of the topic. James could understand better now the fury Graeme had felt. It would have been hard to lose a woman like Laura, to love her and know he must marry another. It made James doubly glad that he himself wasn't the sort to fall in love.

Any discussion of Laura seemed too fraught with past emotions to bring up with Graeme. What could he say? *Frightfully sorry I married the woman you wanted? And, by the way, do you mind if I tell you how soft her skin is or how good it felt to kiss her or how damnably hard it is to keep my hands off her? Do you think she'd despise me if I broke my vow not to insist on my husbandly rights?*

To cover his awkwardness, James reached down to scratch Dem's head.

"How is Laura?" Graeme asked, as if he'd been reading James's thoughts. "She looks well."

"Yes. She's fine." He looked up at the other man, his eyes narrowing. "Why?"

Graeme blinked. "I don't know. I just thought I'd ask after her."

"Well, she's fine," James repeated. He was silent for a moment, but he couldn't hold it back. "Did she say something to you?"

"What? No." Graeme frowned. "What do you mean? Say what?"

"I don't know. You're the one who mentioned it." James looked at the other man's astonished face. "Oh, the devil. I'm sorry, coz. I'm in a devilish humor. I, um, it's these headaches." He seized on the first excuse he could think of. Cowardly, of course, but better than the truth.

"You still have them?" Graeme was immediately concerned, which made James feel even lower.

"Yes, somewhat. Don't tell Laura," he added hastily. "I, uh, well, I just . . ."

"Don't want her to know?" Graeme suggested. He smiled. "I understand; wives tend to fuss. I think it means they care."

"Mm. I suppose."

"I shan't say a thing to Laura." Graeme rose. "You should go up and lie down, get rid of your headache."

"No, I didn't mean . . ."

"It's fine." Graeme smiled. "I'm the last person you need to play stoic with, James, you know that. I must pay my regards to your mother and the other ladies anyway."

James stood up and followed him to the door. It seemed craven to seize on Graeme's excuse. But maybe his cousin was right; things might improve if he lay down and slept. At least he could avoid being pulled into the drawing room by his mother.

He turned down the hall in the opposite direction,

Dem padding along behind him, and climbed the back stairs to the next floor. He thought about the way Laura would soak a cloth in lavender water and lay it across his forehead, and he wished he had one of those rags now. Even better would be to have Laura sink her fingers into his hair, rubbing his scalp in that way that turned him to butter. It was amazing, really, this new affinity for being coddled.

He had always considered himself so independent, so self-contained, so little in need of someone else's attention. He hated being cosseted. Why had it felt so good when Laura did it? Why did he miss it now?

James hesitated outside the door of his chamber. Dem tilted his head inquiringly. James looked down at him. "I know. I'm a fool, aren't I?"

He walked on to Laura's open doorway. Dem followed and squeezed past him into her bedchamber. Tail going at a slow pace, the mastiff trailed around the room, sniffing at this and that, reacquainting himself. James understood how Dem felt; he, too, had an urge to walk about the room, picking up her perfume bottle and sniffing it, trailing his hand along the cover of her bed.

Why had he insisted on going back to his room to sleep? It was much nicer here, really. All the reasons he'd told himself held, of course—his shaving stand was there, his clothes, everything. It was what he was accustomed to; he liked the comfort of his own bed. He liked to be alone.

But it was damned quiet and empty.

It wasn't like this room, which even in Laura's absence was filled with her presence. Her dressing gown was tossed across the foot of the bed. The cameo she often wore lay on top of her enameled jewel box. Her jars and bottles lined the vanity, the tortoiseshell brush and comb before them. Beside the brush set was a dainty glass dish containing the jumble of her hairpins. There was a squat perfume bottle of amethyst-colored crystal, with an arching metal spritzer and oblong bulb. The faint scent of lavender, Laura's scent, hung in the air.

The furniture was mostly the same, heavy and dark, but she'd made the place her own—a low rocking chair by the window, decorative pillows strewn across the bed, a delicate lace runner along the dresser. Everything seemed softer here, more inviting. Feminine and faintly mysterious and therefore alluring.

He thought of what it would be like to lounge on the bed and watch her brush out her hair or pin it up, spray a little mist of perfume at her throat, clasp a strand of pearls around her throat. He thought of putting the pearls around her throat himself.

Trapped in his unsatisfying thoughts, he roamed to the window to gaze out. Laura was climbing up the steps from the garden. She wore no hat, and her blond hair gleamed in the sun. James leaned closer.

She looked up at the terrace, and a smile broke across her face. Below him Graeme stepped into view. As James watched, Laura ran lightly up the steps, her hands held out to Graeme. Her face glowed; James knew that if he were able to see her eyes, they would be shining. Something in James's chest clenched, tight as a fist.

Did she still love the man? Graeme had pined for years over their blighted love; there was little reason to think Laura would not have done so, as well. And while Graeme had been pulled from that mire by his wife, had found love and happiness, Laura had never married. She had lived at home with her father, tending to him, helping him, no real life for her except in her music.

If he wanted to write a romantic tale of sorrow and lost love, with some wretchedly saintly heroine to suffer it all, Laura would be the perfect subject. The fact that Laura had faced her situation with a level head and a pleasant nature did not make her loss any less real.

James might dismiss the idea of love enduring over the years as maudlin sentimentality. But he was not the one who had to live this way, constantly reminded of what she had lost. He was not a woman of sensibility, artistic and loving and loyal.

Nor did it matter that James had not meant to put her in this situation, that he had tried to give her a rosier future than the one facing her. The result was still the same: Laura had saved James, and in doing so, had manacled herself to a marriage she did not want with a man she didn't like, let alone love.

And all he could think about was how much he wanted her in his bed. That, he supposed, said all one needed to know about the two of them.

Laura trotted up the stairs, humming beneath her breath. Her spirits had been so buoyed by her talk with Abby that when she ran into Graeme afterward, he had probably wondered if she'd lost her mind. A woman whose husband's life was in danger should be more worried.

She *was* worried. It was just that James was so much better now and so determined, so capable, that it was easy to let those troubles slide. Easy for her mind to stray to more frivolous thoughts, such as whether James would kiss her again or what it would be like to make love with him or if Abby's dresses would spark a light in his eyes.

Was Abby right? Could Laura lure James into becoming a real husband to her? And wasn't it amazing that only a month ago she would have recoiled from that possibility, not rushed toward it?

She was thinking so much about James that it didn't surprise her when she walked into her room and saw him standing there, idly fiddling with the objects on her vanity table, his mind obviously somewhere else.

"James!" She came to a halt, a smile starting on her face until she saw that he looked drawn and tired. "Are you ill?"

"No. Sorry. I shouldn't have come in here."

"Why not?" Laura frowned, puzzled. She couldn't put her finger on it, but there was something different about him, something more like he used to be.

"Without an invitation."

"Oh." She went closer. "Is something wrong? You seem . . ." He quirked an eyebrow, and she finished lamely, "I don't know."

"I—" He glanced around as if he might find his next words posted on her wall or wardrobe. "I apologize for putting you in this situation. I didn't mean to."

"I'm sure you didn't realize someone was trying to kill you," Laura said reasonably. Whatever was the matter with him?

"No, of course not." He paused, still not looking at her. "Or that you wouldn't let me die."

Laura had no answer for that.

"You could have." He looked into her face finally, crossing his arms over his chest.

"I could have what?"

"You didn't have to save me. You could have left me in there, done nothing."

Laura's jaw dropped. "Let you die? Have you gone mad?"

"Why not?" James shrugged. "It would have been easier. No one would have been any the wiser. You would have been rich and free. It wouldn't have been murder, you know. Simply appreciating the fortuitous aftermath."

"You're serious, aren't you? Of all the harebrained ideas . . ."

"You've disliked me for years."

"That doesn't mean I wanted you dead!" Laura wasn't about to admit her feelings for him had changed. At this moment, with anger rising in her, she had to wonder why they had.

"No? Perhaps it's just me, then. I've wished any number of people dead over the years."

"Well, one would hope you wouldn't have acted on it. Good Lord, James." Laura swung away, too angry to stand still. She turned back, fisting her hands on her hips. "Do you really think I could have done such a thing?"

He gazed at her for a moment. "No. Of course not. Not you."

"No doubt you consider me too straitlaced."

"No. But perhaps too selfless for your own good."

"I don't understand you. This is the most bizarre conversation I have ever had. And with you that's saying a great deal. You sound as if you *wish* I had let you die."

"No. Believe me, I'd rather be standing here than lying in the family plot. But you did yourself little good. And I—" He took a little breath. "I am sorry for that."

"So your apology is for not dying." The man was trying to start an argument, she decided. He was the most contrary person she had ever met.

"I promised you a widowhood. Wealth and future freedom. Yet here you are, shackled to me for life."

"It may surprise you to know," Laura said bitingly, "but becoming a widow was never my primary goal in life. I suspect any number of women would count themselves lucky to be plucked up and dropped into a life of ease. Unless your plan is to lock me up or beat me daily—"

"Laura!" He stiffened, his eyes flashing.

"Hah!" Laura jabbed her forefinger at him. "You see how unpleasant it is to have someone suggest you'd do awful things? Since clearly you want to have a disagreement, I will tell you my side of it. If you had not offered me your hand in marriage, I would be sunk in debt to a despicable man. I would have had to give up my home and most of my possessions and live in a governess's room or on my aunt's charity. You have put me in a lovely house; you have on more than one occasion urged me to buy new clothes."

"And will again," he muttered. "I cannot see why you are so stubborn about that."

"I'm not stubborn. I would love to have a new wardrobe. But I haven't exactly had a lot of time. Silly me, I thought trying to keep you from dying was more important than trotting off to London to buy new frocks." He moved to object, but with a sweeping gesture, she went on. "Don't try to distract me. I haven't finished."

"I'm sure you have not."

"I am living in luxury. I can spend my time on my music or whatever I want. I can go to London. See plays, the ballet, opera, museums, galleries . . ."

"But you won't have love."

Laura went still. It was surprising how much his words pierced her. She already knew he didn't love her; she thought she was armored against such emotion. She turned away to hide the hurt that must show in her eyes. "That's an odd thing for you to be concerned about, I must say."

"No doubt you're right," he retorted in a clipped voice. "I can't imagine why I even thought to consider your problems."

"I don't *have* a problem. Other than you." She swung around. "I'm beginning to understand the reason for all this nonsense. It's *you* who is regretting our marriage. You obviously think of marriage as chains. Imprisonment. You've lost your freedom."

"I beg your pardon? You think that I—"

"Wish you had not made that impulsive decision to marry me," she finished. "Yes. It was all very well to leave your money to a stranger as some bitter jest upon your expectant relatives. But the prospect of having to live with the woman you married is a different thing, indeed. You are ruing your hasty bargain."

"Don't be a fool. We were talking about you, not me."

"I don't know what you're talking about, but I am discussing *you*. You've realized you made a bad bargain. That you lost your chance at your perfect wife."

"Who?" His eyebrows soared in astonishment.

"Your dream bride." Laura injected the words with all the sarcasm she could muster. Anger bubbled in her now. "You told me how little I resembled that woman, if you'll remember."

"Oh, that," he scoffed.

"Yes, that. The woman of acceptable appearance and superior lineage. One willing to provide you with heirs but not offer any of those sticky inconveniences like feelings."

"I know I didn't say that."

"It was implied. In any case, your vision of an ideal wife was certainly not me."

"And yet I chose you," he said flatly.

"As I said, you made a bad bargain. You purchased a widow but you wound up with a wife."

"You may not count my life as worth very much," he shot back. "But it's rather important to me, so that would make marrying you a very good bargain, I'd say!"

"Naturally you're glad I stumbled upon the cause of your illness."

"You did a good bit more than that."

"Of course you're glad you're alive, but that doesn't change the fact that you are tied to a wife you don't want."

"Don't want?" He gave an odd little mirthless laugh. "When, may I ask, have you ever heard of me doing anything except what I want? It's a hallmark of my character, is it not?"

"No. The hallmark of your character is coldness." And now, suddenly, it came spilling out of her, a surging tangled mass built from weeks of worry and jangled nerves, of frustration and wounded feelings and dashed hopes. Why had she ever thought she could have a real marriage with this man? Why had she even considered it? "You don't care about anyone. Worse, you take pride in that fact! It's no wonder you wanted a bloodless cipher for a wife. Someone who wouldn't ask anything of you or want anything from you."

His eyes were silvery bright with anger, his body taut. "No doubt you're right. I am still the despicable man you told me I was years ago. Almost dying didn't change that. Didn't make me a paragon like—"

"Ohhh!" She couldn't stand it anymore. Laura flung out her hands, planting them flat on his chest, and shoved.

Taken by surprise, he staggered back a step. His eyes widened. "You think you can push me out?" He closed on her. "You're going to put me out of your life? Shove me away?"

"Yes! Yes!" Laura felt wild and somehow exhilarated, as if arousing his anger excited her. She knew in the back of her mind that she was not acting like herself, neither of them were, but another part of her, the one that yearned and wept and laughed, didn't care. That part was charging full speed ahead. "I want you out." She shoved at his chest again, though this time he was ready for it and it didn't move him. "Out! Out of my room. Out of my head." With each statement, she pushed him, not caring whether it rocked him back, just aching to do it. "Out! Out!"

He clamped his hands around her arms and jerked her to him. She came up hard against his unyielding body. He hooked one arm around her waist, imprisoning her, and he plunged the other one into her hair, dislodging hairpins and sending her hair tumbling. She barely had time to draw in a little gasp before his mouth was on hers.

There was none of the tenderness of the last time he had kissed her. This was all heat and fury and hunger. And she loved it. Laura responded in kind, wrapping her arms around his neck and pressing her body into his, meeting his kiss with fire of her own.

She clenched her fingers into his jacket. She wanted to meld herself to him, to crawl inside him. It was mad and wild and desperate, and it made her tremble. It was dangerous to feel like this, yet she rushed toward it. The kiss went on and on, and when finally his mouth left hers, he kissed his way down her throat.

James groaned, lifting her, and they tumbled back onto the bed. His hand went to the buttons down the front of her bodice, fumbling them open, and he delved inside, shoving her chemise down to cup her breast.

He bent to take her nipple into his mouth, and Laura jerked at the delicious surprise of it. She tangled her fingers in his hair, her breath catching in her throat. Every nerve in her body, it seemed, was alert, waiting, seeking each new pleasure. She loved this; she wanted more.

He came back to kiss her mouth, his hand caressing her breast. His leg lay over hers, pinning her down, and strangely, that, too, was exciting. She wanted—oh, God, she wanted so much and she wasn't even sure what it was she yearned for.

But James, she knew, was leading her to it. With each kiss, each stroke of his fingers, each breath that tickled across her skin, he was drawing her closer. She gave herself into his hands, aching for the end, but reveling in each moment along the way.

His kisses were no longer frantic but had turned soft and seductive. He tasted; he savored; he feasted. "Laura . . . Laura . . ." He mumbled her name against her skin as he worked his way down her.

A sudden "Eek!" of surprise brought them out of their erotic trance. James's head snapped up, and he turned toward the open door, where a maid stood, gaping at them. She quickly popped out of sight.

James let out a pithy curse and scrambled off the bed. Laura hastily rose to her feet, as well, her hand clutching together the opened sides of her bodice. Her cheeks flamed with embarrassment. This would be all around the servants' hall in ten minutes.

"God. I—uh . . ." James shoved his hand back through his hair. "Laura . . . I didn't mean— I— Forgive me."

He whipped around and strode from the room. Laura stared after him. What in the world had just happened?

One thing was certain. Whatever James might say, he wanted her. Just as clearly, he did not *want* to be drawn to her. He ran from it—literally today. The question was: What was she going to do about it?

Laura set her jaw pugnaciously. This time she was not going to sacrifice her happiness for what was good or right. This once she was going to go after what *she* wanted.

She yanked at the bell pull and began to rebutton her dress. When the maid answered, Laura asked, "Have Lord and Lady Montclair left yet?"

"No, ma'am, they just walked in from the garden."

"Good. Run down and tell them to wait." Laura grabbed up her bonnet. "I'm going with them."

chapter 29

James charged down the hallway as if someone were in pursuit, but he could not escape his thoughts. How could he have broken his word . . . again? And he hadn't just stepped out of line—he had grabbed Laura so tightly he must have left bruises on her arms. Then he had compounded his sins by tumbling her onto the bed like the veriest doxy.

Laura was bound to be furious. She hadn't asked for his kisses; indeed, only the moment before she had shoved him away, ordering him out of her room. It didn't matter that her mouth had been soft and yielding beneath his. What was important was that he had been angry and demanding, not thinking of her wishes at all, only of his driving need.

James wasn't aware of where he was going until he looked up and found himself at the stables. It had been months since he had ridden, but he realized that a long, hard ride was precisely what he needed right now. The groom looked surprised to see him, but quickly saddled James's horse. He took off, thundering across the countryside, jumping fences and hedges and ditches without care for life or limb, until he had ridden both his mount and himself into exhaustion. Dem, smarter than both of them, had stopped beneath a tree a few minutes from the house and lay waiting there for them to come back.

But no matter how hard he rode, he could not exorcize his demons, and finally he returned to the house. The first person he saw when he stepped inside was his mother. James let out a curse under his breath.

"James, love, there you are!" Tessa started toward him, beaming.

"Hello, Mother."

Tessa stopped, taking in his sweaty, disheveled appearance. "Goodness, love, what *have* you been doing? Do not tell me you've been out riding!"

"Then I fear I must keep silent. Mother, where—"

"But it's scarcely a fortnight since you rose like Lazarus from your deathbed."

"Hardly like Lazarus, since I was not yet dead. I'm fine." He wasn't; he was exhausted and sore, and his head was throbbing, but there was no need to tell her that. "I'm sorry, I haven't the time to chat. I must speak to Laura."

"But, dear, she's gone."

"Gone!" It hit him like a blow to the chest. Laura had left him.

"Yes, she went home with Mirabelle and the others." She frowned faintly. "Now I'm not sure of the number for dinner. Ah, well, Simpson will manage, no doubt."

"Damn Simpson," James said bluntly. Laura had gone running to Graeme. "Is she—did she say if she'd return?"

His mother looked at him oddly. "If she'd return! James, whatever is the matter? You look white as a sheet. I knew you shouldn't have gone riding!" Tessa linked her arm through his and steered him toward his study. "Come and sit down, dear. I'll ring for tea. No, maybe a brandy would be in order."

She directed him to a chair and bustled about, pouring a healthy dose of brandy into a glass and thrusting it into his hand. As he gulped down the liquor, Tessa shut the door and turned back to him. "Now. Tell me what is going on. What is the matter? This isn't just from your riding out, is it? Why did you say 'if she'd return'? Why wouldn't she? Oh, James." Tessa sank gracefully down onto her knees beside his chair and looked into his face. "What have you done?"

He intended to make his usual sort of sardonic remark, asking why she would assume he was the cause of the problem, but instead, he looked away from his mother's sympathetic face and said, "I've ruined everything."

"Surely not." Tessa took his hand in both hers. "Laura is a sweet girl. Whatever you've done, I am sure she hasn't left you. She didn't take any of her dresses, and no woman runs away without her clothes. Laura will forgive you. You haven't—was it one of the maids?"

"What?" He glanced at her, startled. "Good God, no. I haven't been sporting with a parlor maid."

"I didn't think you would, but men can do the most foolish things. Especially when they're in a jealous temper. Did you shout at her?"

"No! Honestly, Mother, what do you think of me? And I'm not jealous."

"Of course not, dear." She patted his hand. "Then what did you argue about?"

"We didn't argue. One cannot argue with Laura. She simply answers you calmly, then does whatever she likes."

"I know." Tessa sighed. "People like that are so irritating, aren't they? Just when you want a good healthy storm, they're doggedly agreeable. Mirabelle is like that."

"I didn't want a storm, healthy or otherwise." He frowned.

"No, it doesn't seem like you, but when a man's in love—"

"I'm *not* in love." James shot to his feet and strode away. Setting his glass down with a thunk, he stood for a moment, looking down at it, his finger circling the rim. "It was Graeme you meant, wasn't it? When you said I was jealous. You think she's still in love with him."

"Dearest, Laura would never—"

"I'm not worried about that—" He stopped, then sighed. "We didn't expect me to live, you see. When Laura agreed to marry me, we thought it would end soon and that she would be free. I didn't intend to trap her, but that's what happened."

"She wants to be free? To leave you?"

"She doesn't say so. Laura always makes the best of things. And I've kept to our bargain . . . mostly. Until today."

"Dearest, what did you do?" His mother's voice rose in alarm. "Surely you did not—"

"I didn't force myself on her, if that's what you're about to ask. I'm not quite a brute, at least not yet. But—oh, the devil—I cannot talk about this with you."

His mother laughed. "Surely you don't think you will shock me. I *do* have some knowledge of men."

"Well, Laura does not. She's an innocent. A lady."

"She's a woman, James. I'm sure she will forgive you if you were a little . . . overeager, shall we say?"

"You know I'm no good at apologies." James grimaced. He ached for Laura's forgiveness, but the thought of asking her for it filled him with dread. It always seemed as if the guiltier he felt, the harder it was to force the words out, and he invariably sounded stiff and insincere. And with Laura—well, with Laura it *mattered*. What if she looked at him coldly and turned away? "Besides, what can I say to her? I already broke my promise, then swore not to do so again—and I still couldn't hold to it. She'll never believe me."

"Then you'll just have to prove it to her. Honestly, James, if anyone can control himself, it is you."

"I would have thought so. But I can't think straight anymore. Blast it, I'm terrible at all this. I don't have the first idea what to do."

"Of course you don't. This isn't a matter you think through. Let me tell you something: I loved Laurence; I truly did. But he tried so desperately to make me into who he wanted me to be that he drove me away. I felt driven to show him that he could not own me."

"I don't want to *own* Laura. And I will *not* run roughshod over her as Father did to you."

"I know, dear. That is what I am saying. I think perhaps Laurence tried so hard to rule me because he knew he couldn't control himself. You must prove to Laura that you are in command of yourself. That you will not push her where she doesn't want to go. Laura has been sheltered; girls always are. Perhaps she still harbors feelings for Graeme—though how she could spend eleven years pining for a man, I cannot imagine. You must step back. Give her time and room to breathe."

"What if I'm not able?"

"You are able. Believe me. I've seen you be patient as a cat outside a mouse hole to get something you want. Accept these 'boundaries' of hers for the moment. Let her see that you are not Laurence. I can assure you that Laura is not me. She'll come around."

"Will she?"

"Trust me. I am an expert on women in love."

"I'm not after love."

"I know what you're after, dear." Tessa grinned, an impish twinkle in her eyes. "But with Laura, I think you won't get one without the other." She patted his arm and started toward the door, tossing back over her shoulder, "Apologize, James. Then suffer in silence for a bit. And flowers are never amiss."

Flowers.

In the city, it would have been easy—just buy them and have them sent to Laura's door. But what was he supposed to do here—pluck them out of his garden and take them to her door, clutching them in his fist like a grubby schoolboy? In the end, James resolved his dilemma by telling Simpson to make up a vase of flowers and take them to Laura's room.

Then he went upstairs to clean up and dress for dinner—and think of an apology. He could scarcely believe he was about to follow his mother's advice. Was she wiser than he thought or he more foolish?

As his mother had predicted, Laura returned home, arriving before supper. It settled James's nerves a degree to hear her footsteps in the hallway. Demosthenes, of course, went bounding over to greet her. James wished he could do the same, but of course he could not apologize in the middle of the hallway. And besides, he didn't have the words down quite right yet.

When it was almost time to go down for the evening meal, he went next door to her chamber. The door stood open, and he paused in the doorway. Laura stood at her vanity, dabbing on perfume, and though he could not smell it from here, he knew the scent and the thought of it made his abdomen tighten.

Laura turned. "James." Her voice was pleasant, but not exuberant; she offered no smile. Obviously she didn't intend to give him any help with this. She glanced at the dresser, where a bountiful display of flowers sat in a large vase. "Simpson brought in a lovely bouquet."

What was he supposed to say to that? *It was my idea? Do they make you willing to forgive me?* Somewhat lamely, he settled on, "I hope you like them."

"I do." As she strolled toward him, James realized that Laura looked . . . different. Her hair wasn't braided and coiled around her head in a neat knot, but swept up in a full, soft style that seemed too heavy for her slender neck. A few stray wisps had slipped out and clung to her skin in a way that made his fingers itch to touch them.

And where had she gotten that dress? He was certain he'd never seen it before. It was her usual mourning black, but the material was luxurious satin that would be, he knew, slick to the touch. Black lace edged the heart-shaped neckline—which, by the way, exposed a good deal more of her breasts than Laura usually showed. It was no more revealing than the dinner gowns Patricia or Tessa or Adelaide wore. But this was Laura, and the sight of her turned his brain to mush.

Had she raided his mother's closet? Or had she actually ordered dresses from London as he had urged her to? It looked like the sort of dress Graeme's wife might wear:

rich, fashionable, and a little bold, but it seemed unlikely that Laura and Abby would be girlishly sharing clothes.

The cameo on a simple black ribbon around Laura's neck was hers. She had worn it before, and he'd always admired it on her. However inexpensive and ordinary it might be, there was something about the black velvet against the creamy skin of her throat that did peculiar things to his insides. But tonight, with that dress, it was enough to turn a man into a gibbering idiot.

It was no wonder that his carefully worded apology flew right out of his head. "I . . . um, Laura . . ."

"Yes?" She waited, calm and unconcerned.

"I apologize for my behavior this afternoon," he said stiffly. "I assure you it will not happen again."

"Oh, James . . ." Laura sighed.

Clearly he'd bungled it. The speech he had labored over earlier had sounded far better, but he could hardly go back and start over. He half turned away and crossed his arms, aware of her eyes on him. Finally he said, "Well, say something, will you?"

"What do you want, James?"

He scowled at her. "I want things to be the same. I want you to stay."

"Stay!"

"Bloody hell, Laura, you know what I want."

To his surprise, a smile curved her lips. She stepped forward, tucking her hand in his arm and starting for the door. "Yes, I rather think I do."

Laura stayed, certainly enough, but things were *not* the same. She had apparently acquired a whole new wardrobe of alluring dresses, and she favored softer, fuller hairstyles that looked as if they might tumble down at a touch. And he wanted very much to touch them.

But it was more than lower necklines and beckoning curls. It was the way she would lean forward over the table, giving him a clear view down the front of her dress, or climb the ladder to search for a book on a high shelf when he was in the library, or stand close to him as she talked, looking up into his eyes.

Her goal, he decided, was to break him. She was testing his control, punishing him for breaking his promise. It surprised him that Laura was capable of this cruelty. Perversely, the fact that she did it to tease and torment him only made him want her more. Equally twisted, he chose to endure it. Foul as his temper was, he did not remove himself from her presence. Indeed, he sought her out. It was worse not to see her.

Every night he waged an internal battle, pacing around his room, and thinking of going to her door and . . . what? Seduce her? Grab her and kiss her, as he had before? Prove once more that his lust for her was greater than his honor?

He was beginning to think his mother was as wrong about this as she usually was about money. Laura seemed entirely unaffected by his display of patience and control. And, really, Laura had never shown the slightest inclination to be intimidated by him. Why would she suddenly have become shy and wary? But if Tessa was wrong, if this didn't work, then it meant that Laura was simply uninterested. And what was he to do then?

Finally, after a torturous week of her campaign, James walked into his room to find Laura sitting in the chair by the window, waiting for him. She was wearing a blue dressing gown, the ruffled neckline of a white cotton gown peeping between the open V at the top. Her hair hung in a long, thick braid that he ached to wrap around his arm.

Lust surged in him. His tongue cleaved to the roof of his mouth. Finally he managed to get out a strangled, "Laura."

"James." She stood, her face pale but set. He was suddenly afraid again that she was leaving him, and he felt even more certain of it when she went on, "I want to talk to you."

"Very well." He was a trifle amazed that his voice came out as steady as it did.

"When you proposed our . . . arrangement, you compared it to a business agreement, a contract of sorts."

James stuck his hands into his pockets so she wouldn't see them clench. "What is it you want?"

"I want to amend our contract." She lifted her chin, looking almost defiantly into his eyes. "I want a complete marriage."

chapter 30

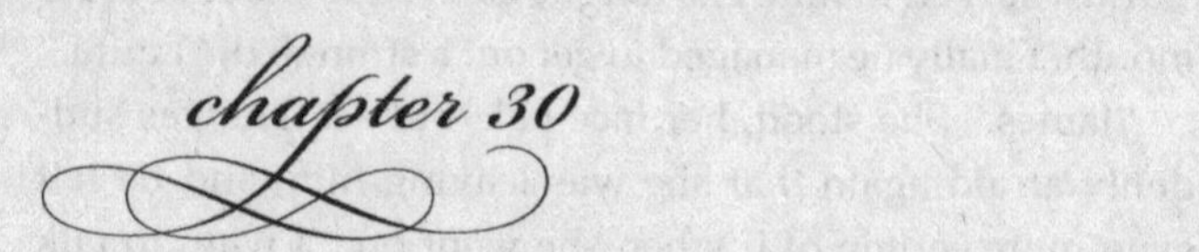

"I beg your pardon?" His voice came out a croak. Laura could not mean what James thought she did.

She made a little moue of exasperation. "You heard me. Please, if you have any gratitude, any friendship, do not make this more difficult for me."

"I have no desire to upset you, I assure you." He held himself rigidly, stifling his willful, idiotic hope. "Just say it, Laura, and be done with it."

"Very well." She drew a breath. "I have no desire to spend the rest of my life in some kind of marital limbo. Neither one thing nor another. Lady de Vere but not your wife."

"You are both."

"No, not really. I realize that I am not the wife you would have chosen had you not been in a desperate situation."

"Nor would you have taken me."

"No," Laura admitted. "Probably not. But those people, those lives, are not a possibility. All we can deal with is what we have. Don't worry, I am not asking you for love. But I would like to"—pink started along her cheeks—"to have what other married women have. I don't want to grow old, knowing I've missed out on . . . well, on so many things."

James clamped down on another stab of desire, waiting

for whatever hook would come at the end of her statement.

Laura went on, not looking at him, "I know you must think me terribly bold, but I have been trying and trying to entice you, but it hasn't worked. So I realized that I must just ask you. I wouldn't do so if I did not think that you—the other day you seemed to feel some desire for me." She lifted her head, setting her chin.

"Some desire." He let out a little huff of a laugh. "You might say so."

A hope he'd hardly dared to consider was now careening around inside him, and even as he tried to hold it down, he could feel the expectation, the hunger, bubbling up in him. James moved toward her, his steps slow and controlled. His eyes traveled over her face, taking in the delectable flush on her cheeks, the mingling of anticipation and uncertainty in her blue eyes. Her beauty made it hard to breathe.

"And what about you?" he asked, his voice low and husky. "The other day, did you feel some desire?"

Her blush deepened rosily, and now she could not meet his eyes. "Yes, of course. I hope you don't think I go about kissing just any man that way."

"I'm glad of that." He crooked his finger under her chin, tilting her face up so that she gazed into his eyes. "But I gave you little choice, as I remember."

"I didn't notice."

His gut tightened at her words, at the soft, almost dreamy expression on her face. He stroked his finger lightly down her throat. His blood was roaring in his ears. "I wouldn't hurt you for the world."

"I know." Her answer was so simple, her voice so clear and sure, it shook him.

"Laura . . ." The word was only a whisper as he bent and kissed her, his lips as soft as his voice. He raised his head and studied her as he cradled her face. His fingers trembled on her skin.

James's eyes went to the thick braid of golden hair that draped over her shoulder. Reaching out, he curled his hand around it and slid his hand slowly all the way down. The rope of hair was softer than silk. When he reached the feathery ends, James tugged on the ribbon that tied it, opening the bow and pulling it from her hair. He tucked the ribbon into his pocket.

"My ribbon . . ." she protested.

"Uh-uh." He grinned. "It's mine now." Freed from its restraint, the plait began to loosen. He twined his fingers through it, hastening the undoing. "You don't know how long I've wanted to do that."

A smile curved her mouth. "Unbraid my hair?"

"Mm-hm." His eyes were on his hand tangling through her hair, separating the strands and letting them whisper through his fingers. He rested his hands on her shoulders, thumbs tracing the line of her collarbone. "You see, I am a man of simple pleasures."

"Are you?" Laughter threaded through Laura's voice, and it made the hunger tighten and coil deep within James.

"Yes." He brought up his other hand and cupped her face between them, his long fingers edging into her hair. "All I ask for is simple . . ." He bent and kissed her upper lip. "Utter . . ." He kissed her lower lip. "Perfection." His mouth settled on hers.

When he lifted his lips from her, she said a little breathlessly, "Perfection? That's a rather steep requirement."

He shook his head slowly. "No. It is precisely what you are."

James kissed her again. He would be slow and careful. This time, this woman, were important. He had never been, he hoped, a hasty or completely selfish lover. The journey was all the sweeter if one took one's time, the pleasure greater when it was shared. But in the end, it had been that burst of satisfaction for himself he sought, and anything else had been incidental.

But Laura . . . Laura was different from any woman he had ever bedded. She was innocent, untouched. He had to get it right; he had to make it good for her. He could not let the desire that clawed at him make him rush. Much as he wanted to drink deeply, he knew he must sip. Woo her in a way he'd never wooed before.

He rocked his mouth against hers, giving, inviting, teasing. The little noise she made deep in her throat, the way her fingers dug into his shoulders, were his reward and his temptation, making his heart slam in his chest, his nerves sizzle.

Their kiss deepened; it was she who stretched up to him, her lips insistent, her tongue eager. James jerked the tie of her robe undone, pushing the dressing gown back and down so that it fell from her. Now there was only the thin material of her gown between them, a barrier so flimsy it was more arousing than any sort of protection. He slid his hand down over her back, feeling the heat of her skin through the fabric. It was the most delicate, delicious torture.

He kissed her mouth, her cheeks, her throat. He took the lobe of her ear between his teeth and worried it gently until

Laura's breath hitched and she pressed her body into him, her hands sliding beneath his jacket and roaming over him. It was all he could do not to throw her back on the bed and take her right there and then.

James stepped back, ripping at the impediment of his clothes, wanting more than anything to feel her hands on his bare flesh. Jacket, shirt, shoes all came off haphazardly. His hands went to the buttons of his trousers and then stilled as he watched Laura reach down and take her nightgown in her hands, pulling it up and off over her head.

The simple cotton gown slipped up over her skin, more tantalizing than the boldest display of flesh, revealing her to his eyes inch by inch. The cloth snagged for an instant on her nipples, and that alone was enough to send a shudder of desire through him. Then her breasts were in full view, rounded and soft, centered by pale pink nipples, already tightened with arousal.

She stole a glance at him, her cheeks bright pink, her expression a curious mixture of embarrassment and pleasure. James came closer, his hands reaching out to cup her breasts. His voice was low and thick. "You are so beautiful."

He slid his arms around her, pulling her gently against him. He kissed her again, and this time his mouth was hungry and insistent, drinking her in. He slipped a hand between them, gliding down over the satiny skin of her stomach and stealing between her legs. Laura started in surprise but did not pull back, instead parting her legs a little to accommodate him. He smiled against her mouth. Her willingness, even eagerness, ratcheted up his passion.

He was hard as a rock, aching to plunge into her, to feel her close and tight around him, but he held back, stroking and kissing, teasing the slick satiny folds until she moved against his hand, mutely urging him on.

Sweeping her up in his arms, he laid her on the bed and, quickly divesting himself of his remaining clothes, he lay down beside her. Her wide, solemn blue eyes were on him the entire time, warm and faintly dazed. Her mouth was rosy from their kisses, soft and faintly damp. It made him surge with the need to kiss her again.

He settled in to kiss her, as if he could spend the rest of his life on this only, but as his mouth moved on hers, his hand explored her body. Finally, when he felt he must shatter under the force of his desire, he slipped down her body, his mouth finding and caressing every place he had touched her.

Laura's hands moved restlessly, her nails digging into him when he took her nipple into his mouth. She moaned, her pelvis circling. "James."

"Again," he murmured, his lips against her ear, and nipped at the fleshy lobe. "Say my name again."

"James," she responded. "James, James, James . . ." She curved her hands down over his back and dug her fingertips into his buttocks, surprising a groan from him. Laura turned her head, pressing her lips to his shoulder. He buried his face in her neck, stifling the words that threatened to flood from his mouth.

He moved between her legs, and she opened to him. As he began to slide into her, Laura tightened for an instant, but James continued to caress her, his hands light, his mouth soft and coaxing on her breast, and she relaxed. Again he moved, and he felt her give, and then he was deep inside her, her body clamped around him, so tight and hot that he went still, struggling to hold on to his control.

He hung there for a moment, poised on the edge between instinct and restraint. Laura slid her hands up his arms onto his shoulders, her touch tender, and it filled his chest with such an odd sweet feeling he could hardly bear it. He bent his head to kiss her and began to move within her. He heard her sharp indrawn breath, and he almost stopped, thinking he'd hurt her, but that was followed by a low hum, almost a purr, and she smiled up at him, her eyes lambent.

Now, at last, he let slip the leash of his control, stroking in and out in an ever-building rhythm. He felt as if the world were hurtling through him, sweeping him toward some other unimaginable realm. She was soft and yielding beneath him, her heat drawing him in, surrounding him. And when she let out a soft cry as the pleasure took her, he surrendered to his own surging passion.

James collapsed against her, holding her tightly. He knew he was probably crushing her, should release her, but he could not move, could not let her go. Laura made no effort to pull away, only curled her arms around him and rubbed her cheek against his shoulder. There was no reason for that to make him feel so . . . well, he wasn't even sure what it was he felt. Fierce, somehow, and strong, as if he could do anything, defeat anyone.

It was, he decided, the rush of life in him, the strength and health returning to him after so long. He was himself again. It had been days since a headache or a tremor. He no longer had to brace himself to go up or down the stairs, didn't have to assume a mantle of ease. He'd returned to riding, and just the other day he had walked all the way down to the castle and back, not even thinking about it.

Tonight had been more evidence of that. The explosion

of joy and release. Pleasure that he had thought he would never have again. The bone-deep satisfaction. Of course, he could not remember ever having felt quite this way before. It doubtless would not continue.

But he wasn't about to give it up now. James rolled to his side, his arms tight around Laura, taking her with him. She nestled into his shoulder as he pressed a kiss into her hair. Closing his eyes, he drifted into sleep.

chapter 31

Laura lay listening to the quiet sound of James's breathing, aware of the rise and fall of his chest against her back. She didn't want to sleep yet; it was much too nice to drift in languid contentment, hugging her happiness to her.

She had taken a gamble tonight, knowing her hopes could crumble into dust with one harsh comment from James. But she had had to try it. And she had received more than she had expected or hoped. It had been worth the risk, the embarrassment, even the flash of pain. She had never realized that she could feel so much, want so much. Certainly she hadn't imagined the paroxysm of pleasure that had rocked her.

It had been more than pleasure. It had been—she searched for a word that would adequately express what she had felt. *Fulfillment*. That was it. She had felt a wholeness, a completion—even though before now she had never noticed there was something missing.

James's hold had loosened in his sleep. One arm lay thrown across her. She stroked her finger across his hand, tracing the underlying framework of bone and sinew. He was still too thin. Of course, the taut, honed look suited him—all sharp edges and cold intensity.

He had always borne the look of something coiled and waiting. Years ago, that had been all she saw. Those qualities were still there; James would never be cuddly. But now she saw beneath them to the man inside.

Or maybe it was just that she had been admitted to the small circle of those he cared for. Would he ever come to love her? Laura had no idea. It wasn't something he believed in. Perhaps her heart would bruise over the years, banging up against the solid wall of his self-containment.

But Laura had no interest in wasting her time thinking about what might or might not happen. The future would take care of itself. Right here, right now, she had everything she wanted. And Laura planned to enjoy it.

When she awakened the next morning, Laura was alone in James's bed, which was a little disappointing. Still, she could hardly expect him to loll about, waiting for her to wake up. It felt peculiar being in his room all by herself.

Laura rolled over, her face against his pillow. In some small, indefinable way it smelled like him. She nestled there, looking around the room. It brought back memories of those dark, fearful days when James had been so ill. But there were other things about it—his shaving soap and mug on the high shaving stand, the silver-backed masculine brush and comb on the dresser, the flat teak box, standing open to reveal cuff links and tie pins—that were all such reminders of James that they made her smile.

She slipped out of bed. Her dressing gown and night shift were folded neatly on the chair. It made Laura blush a little, wondering if Owen, now James's valet, had picked them up and placed them there. Or had it been James's fingers straightening and folding them? That made her blush a little, too, but in a better way.

Pulling on the shift, she belted the dressing gown around her and started toward the door. There, sitting on the dresser, was a tray with covered plates and a pot and cup. Picking up the covers, she found the plates filled with a sampling of the foods usually on the buffet downstairs. She smiled to herself as she poured a cup of tea. She was certain this tray had been sent by James. He was certainly thoughtful for a man who claimed to lack sensitivity.

There was too much food here, even as hungry as she felt this morning. She made a dent in it, though, before she left the room. Fortunately, she did not run into anyone as she slipped down the hall to her room. She wished there was a connecting door between their chambers.

As she bathed and dressed and pinned up her hair, she wondered when she would first see James today. No doubt he had already eaten breakfast and was in his office. How would he look at her when he saw her again? She hoped it would not be in front of other people; she feared everything that had passed between them would show on her face. Of course, she had the uneasy feeling that everyone would be able to tell that anyway as soon as they saw her.

Would he smile at her? Laura hated to think that he might look at her with that cool mask she had seen on his face many times. She thought of the light in his eyes last night, the way his lips had curved sensually. Just the memory of it sent warmth snaking through her.

As it turned out, she didn't have to wonder long. As she reached the bottom of the stairs and turned down the hallway toward the dining room, there was a clatter of nails on the floor from the opposite direction, and Laura turned to see Demosthenes loping down the hallway toward her.

Laura bent to greet the dog, and when she raised her

head again, she saw James in the doorway of his office, shoulder propped negligently against the doorjamb. He was watching her, a smile curling up one side of his mouth, eyelids drooping down over the unmistakable heat in his eyes.

"Laura." He levered away from the door and strolled toward her. "Did you have a pleasant sleep?"

She went to meet him, Dem trotting along beside her, tail wagging, tongue lolling out in a foolishly happy expression. Laura sympathized; if she wasn't careful, that was the way she would be looking at James.

"I did," Laura replied, unable to completely keep a smirk off her lips.

"That's good to hear." He stopped in front of her. The smile on his lips was faint and slightly sardonic, but the heat in his eyes was anything but casual. James propped his hand on the wall, leaning against it, and loomed closer. "One hopes you will continue to do so."

"I suspect I might." Laura linked her hands behind her back and smiled up at him flirtatiously. "Of course, it all depends."

"And upon what does it depend?" Laughter lurked in his voice, but threaded through it was a fiercer, more urgent tone.

She curled her hands around his lapels, her face tilted up to him. "You, I believe."

He ran a finger down the line of her buttons. "Does it? Then there's little need to worry." He hooked his finger into the waistband of her skirt, tugging her toward him. "For I intend to do all I can to help you."

"Really?"

"Mm." He bent and brushed her lips with his. "Really."

"I'll look forward to it."

Her words sparked a brighter light in his eyes, and he kissed her again, his mouth hard and fierce and full of promise. When he straightened, he took a quick step back, shoving his hands into his pockets. "Blast. It's a devil of a long time till night falls." A rueful, vaguely puzzled smile flickered across his face. "You do the damnedest things to me."

"Do I?" Laura grinned, her spirits soaring. "I'm glad to hear it."

"I'm sure you are." He leaned against the wall, gazing down into her eyes. "You delight in tormenting me." His voice sounded amused, and the look in his eyes was still the one that turned her insides to mush.

"Tormenting you! I never—"

"Really?" James grinned. "What about those dresses you've been wearing the last week? The ones with the necklines down to here." He reached out and ran a forefinger in a curve across the tops of her breasts. His eyes darkened. "And what about the times you leaned closer so I could see how utterly delicious you looked? How luscious you smelled."

"I didn't think you'd noticed." Laura could not keep from leaning toward him. She would have liked nothing better than to let her body curve into his. Why did there always have to be so many people around? Anyone could come upon them—though at the moment, she wasn't sure she would care.

"Not notice!" His eyebrows shot upward, and he let out a funny little groan of a laugh. "How could I not?" He toyed with one of her buttons. "I thought I would go mad from wanting you."

Laura stared. "But you never said a thing. You never—why did you not kiss me?"

He looked, not at her, but at the button between his fingers as he said in a low voice, "I didn't want to break trust with you."

"James . . ." She took his hand between hers, touched.

He looked into her eyes. "I promised you. You told me how little you wanted to share my bed."

"People change."

"So I've heard." His hand curled around hers and he raised it to his lips, pressing a kiss on the back of her hand. "I didn't dare hope you had."

"Perhaps I could make amends for your suffering."

"Oh?" He didn't let go of her hand, but pulled it against his chest, his thumb making lazy circles in her palm. "How is that?"

"We could take a walk to help pass the time."

"That sounds . . . promising."

"I could ask Cook to make a basket lunch to take with us."

"So it would be a long walk. Even better."

"A long walk," she agreed, her smile inviting. "Down to the old castle, perhaps."

"I like the castle." His eyes danced.

"You could show me the ruins. We could take a blanket and have our lunch."

"Hmm. I admit it sounds like ample recompense for my suffering. There's just one thing . . ."

"What's that?"

He wrapped his hand around her wrist and whisked her up the hall into his study. Closing the door, he put his hands on her waist, pulling her against him. "I think that first a small sample of your offering would be in order."

"I have no objection to that." Laura smiled and linked her arms behind his neck.

"Make that a large sample," he murmured, and his mouth came down to take hers.

James gathered her up in his arms. Laura clung to him, lost in his kiss. When at last he lifted his head, his face was slack, his eyes dark with desire. He pressed her body into his, his hands traveling slowly over her, and nuzzled her neck. "In fact . . ." He roamed back up the tender skin of her throat, his lips evoking bright shivers all through her. "I believe we might not go to the castle at all."

He reached back and locked the door. Then, sweeping her up in his arms, he strode over to the rug in front of the fireplace and set her down. His fingers went to the buttons at the top of her dress. Laura's eyes widened. "James! Here?" She glanced around. "Now?"

"Here. Now."

She laughed and went to work on his waistcoat. They undressed each other, pausing to kiss or caress the flesh that they revealed bit by bit. It seemed wanton and daring to do this in the light of day—and thoroughly exciting. James kissed her until she trembled, his hands busy on her skin, seeking out all the most pleasurable spots. Laura had never before realized how many places on her body were so erotic.

She could not hold back a moan when his fingers slipped between her legs, exploring that most intimate spot. She leaned her head against his chest, her legs suddenly weak. "Oh, James . . . I . . ."

"Mm?" He was kissing his way across her collarbone. "You what?"

"I don't know. You make me feel . . ." She shook her head, blushing. "I can't describe it. Shivery." She lifted her head, looking into his eyes. "I hardly feel like myself."

His grin was slow and wicked. "You feel very much like yourself to me." To emphasize his words, he curved his hand over the fleshy mounds of her buttocks. "And that, by the way, feels very, very nice." He dropped a kiss on her shoulder as his hand returned to tease between her legs again.

As his fingers opened and stroked her, flooding her with desire, he trailed his mouth down to the curve of her breast. His tongue circled her nipple, making it harden even more. Everything in her ached for more. She wanted his mouth to take her nipple, to feel the warm, damp suction tugging at her. She wanted him inside her, filling her. But the long, slow building was a wonderful torment, enhanced by the fulfillment she now knew awaited at the end.

And when at last he closed his mouth over her nipple, the wave of intense pleasure that washed through her made it worth the wait. She stroked his arms and shoulders, running a hand up the back of his neck and sinking her fingers in his thick hair. She delighted in the heat that flared in him at her touch, the sharp inhale of his breath, the faint tremor in his skin.

James slipped a finger inside her, his thumb settling on the little nub of flesh, and Laura gasped at the new sensation. The heat and urgency inside her flared even higher. Her knees felt like melting wax; Laura thought she would have simply oozed down to the floor if it had not been for his arm around her waist. James raised his head, gazing down at her intently, as his fingers continued to work their magic.

Laura suspected she ought to feel embarrassed under his gaze, but she was too deeply caught up in her passion, too near that shattering explosion of bliss, to care. Her eyes fluttered closed as she felt it begin to take her, and then it rampaged through her. She shuddered, letting out a moan.

When she opened her eyes, she found James still watching her, his eyes glowing, an almost smug satisfaction mingling with raw hunger on his face. She looked at him a little wonderingly. "But, James . . . you haven't—" Her eyes went down involuntarily to his still heavily engorged state. "Don't you—"

"Oh, yes, I do." His voice was husky. "Don't worry. I'll have mine. But I wanted to see your face as it took you." He pressed his lips to her forehead. "It was a beautiful sight."

Laura felt herself blush and she turned her head, pressing her lips to his chest. His skin twitched beneath her lips and she felt his hand tighten on her waist. Emboldened, she traced his flat masculine nipple with her tongue, then took it in her mouth, pulling gently. He let out a low, choked noise, his skin flaring with heat beneath her lips.

She kissed her way across his chest, her hands roaming over him. She was eager to know him, to taste and touch him, to learn each hidden spot that gave him pleasure. There was something intensely gratifying about wresting each small noise or shiver or sigh from this normally implacable man.

A shudder rippled through James and he grasped her arms, pulling her down to the floor with him. His kiss plundered her mouth. Laura could feel the need in him, the almost palpable hunger, and she opened to him gladly.

He sank deep within her, filling her in the most satisfying way. He began to move in a timeless rhythm, each thrust fulfillment and enticement, the pleasure building with the longing until they mingled in an aching, wordless anticipation. At last he reached his peak, shuddering against her, and buried his face against her neck to muffle his hoarse cry.

Laura clung to him, feeling her own blissful answer to his ecstasy. And holding him like this, her arms locked around him and his as tightly clamped around her, was its own deep joy.

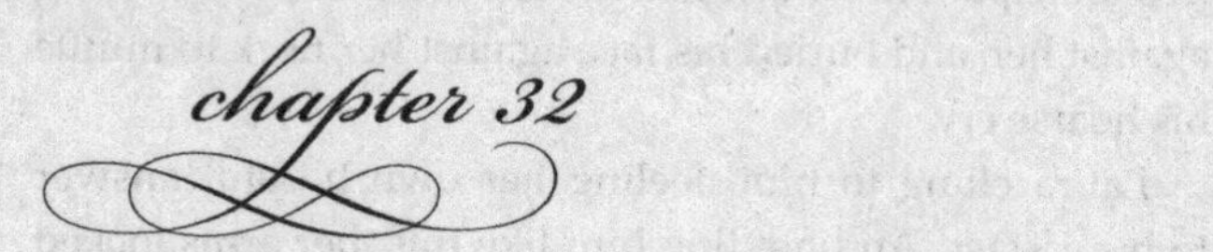

chapter 32

Laura lay curled against James's side, her head on his shoulder. Everything was perfect, she thought, then hastily retreated from that thought with a shiver. Such a notion was probably tempting fate.

"Cold?" James murmured, and draped his jacket over Laura. He kissed the top of her head. "Though it seems a shame to cover up such beauty."

"Flatterer." Still, she smiled.

"Ah, but you know I am distressingly blunt, so you may take what I say for the truth."

"Or at least the truth as you see it." She rose on her elbow to gaze down at him.

"Which naturally makes it correct." James grinned, his face the easiest and most relaxed she had ever seen it.

"Naturally." Laura made a little face at him. "If true, then we would be a matching pair."

"In bluntness or superior discernment?"

"Both, of course, though I was referring to beauty. You are a handsome man, you know."

"I am?"

"Of course. Don't pretend you haven't noticed the looks women give you. You just want to hear me compliment you."

"Feel free to do so." James linked his hands behind his head, as if settling in for a story.

"Well . . . first there is this hair." Laura ran her fingers lightly through his thick black locks. Sliding her forefinger down his forehead, she traced the line of one eyebrow. "And these brows." She laid a gentle kiss upon the eyebrow in question. "These eyes." Her finger curved down, coming to an end on the prominent bone beneath his eye. "These cheekbones." She kissed that, as well. "And most of all . . . this perfect, perfect mouth."

Her kiss lingered there before she sat up, smiling down at him. He gazed back at her, heat mingling with amusement in his eyes. "I see. You married me only for my looks."

"Not entirely." She tilted her head as if considering the matter. "I also have it on good authority that you are a man of some wealth, with a gracious home, and a respectable, even honored, name."

He began to laugh. "Touché. I should know better than to try to trade barbs with you."

"Where you're concerned, I have a good deal of ammunition."

"You do, at that." His eyes lit with mischief. "But you haven't my skill in distracting you."

Laura let out a little shriek as he lunged up, his fingers going to her ribs to tickle her. She giggled, twisting. "Stop that."

"Very well." His arms slid around her and pulled her to him, his lips meeting hers. After a long moment, he raised his head. "Now that might be the best way to deflect your arrows."

Laura rested against him, listening to the heavy thump

of his heart beneath her ear. She would have liked to linger, but she was certain that with a man like James, one needed the lightest of touches. With an inward sigh of regret, she pulled away. "I must go. I promised to help your mother with the invitations."

"What invitations?"

"For the ball she's planning. Don't you remember?"

"Ah, yes. Thank God I recovered so she could host a party."

"James! You shouldn't be unkind about your mother. I saw how she felt when you were so ill. Tessa loves you. And you love her, admit it."

"Of course." He paused in the act of buttoning his shirt and glanced up. "Though I do hope you won't let anyone know."

"It will remain our secret." Laura struggled to restore order to her hair, twisting to see her dim reflection in the glass door of a bookcase. "This would be much easier if you had a mirror in here."

"Thoughtless of me." James leaned against the wall, watching her. "Oddly, the occasion's never arisen before."

She tossed him a teasing glance over her shoulder. "You mean you aren't accustomed to ravishing women in your study?"

"Ravishing! I like that."

"So did I." Laura flashed a grin and returned to fixing her hair.

Behind her she heard James draw in his breath sharply. Suddenly he was right behind her, his hands sliding around her waist, and even in this poor reflection, she could see the unmistakable light in his eyes. He nuzzled her neck. "You'd best have a care or you'll find yourself having to dress and do your hair all over again." He nipped lightly at her earlobe.

His hands slid across her waist and up to cover her breasts. Laura leaned back into him, closing her eyes, but then, with a sigh, she slipped out of his arms. "No. I'd best get to it. Addressing invitations with the others will offer a splendid opportunity to find out things."

"What things?" He frowned. "Laura, I don't want you poking about, trying to expose a murderer."

"That's a fine thing to say, when you and I have done the very same thing."

"Yes, but it was both of us."

"What difference does that make?" Laura pulled away to look at him indignantly. "Are you saying I'm not capable of learning something on my own?"

James laughed. "No, no, no, my dear, I'm not that foolish a man. But I don't want you dealing with a murderer all by yourself."

"First of all, I won't be by myself." Laura held up her fingers. "Half your family will be there."

"That is scarcely reassuring," James said drily.

"Second," she went on, giving him a repressive look, "I'm not going to be obvious about it. And, third, surely the culprit realizes it would be suspicious to kill me after they've tried to poison you. Even you must be safe from another attempt, at least for a while."

"Hopefully." James smiled, reaching out and curling his fingers around hers to lift her hand up to his lips. "If I thought otherwise, I would have to take action. I wouldn't have the luxury of waiting and searching for proof. Claude's not stupid. I'm relying on that."

"Besides, he would know he won't get the full inheritance now that you are married. That would discourage him, as well." Laura frowned. "James? Are you all right? You looked quite odd."

"What? No, I'm fine." He gave her a perfunctory smile. "Just thinking."

Laura suspected there was more than he let on behind the look that had flickered across his face. It would be a pointless exercise, however, to try to pry any information out of him. She merely smiled and went up on tiptoe to kiss his cheek. His eyes widened a little, and Laura was pleased to see that she had put him somewhat off balance with the impulsive gesture.

Laura started out the door, then stopped and turned, sending him a provocative glance over her shoulder. "I hope I haven't disturbed your morning too much. Enjoy your account books."

"Little likelihood of that," James murmured as he strolled after her into the hallway and stood watching Laura walk away. He had felt an icy trickle down his spine at her words a moment earlier. He hadn't really thought until now about the fact that Laura now stood between Claude and his inheritance. But, no, surely Claude would not go so far as to hurt Laura. It was one thing to despise James and wish him gone—no doubt Claude felt some justification there—but quite another to actually kill an innocent woman. Claude would not, could not do that.

It was foolish that his palms had started to sweat, idiotic to feel an urge to hurry after Laura and walk with her, as if someone were going to jump out at her with a knife. No one but Laura and his attorney knew the terms of his will; Claude would doubtless assume that James would leave

Laura only a reasonable widow's share, not the bulk of his fortune. Even if Claude suspected Laura would inherit a good deal, he would know that the title and the land would be his. That was what Claude wanted—his father's title and Grace Hill, the de Vere estate that he so resented going to James.

The others would benefit little from Laura's death—surely not enough that they would resort to murder. Still, it might be best if he made them all believe he was leaving Laura nothing upon his death. He could tell his mother that he had given Laura a sum of money of her own when they married. That much was true enough; the only lie would be saying that he therefore would not be leaving her an inheritance. Tessa could be counted on to gossip with everyone else.

James would keep a more careful eye on Laura. He could set Dem to guarding her whenever James himself was not with her. His chest eased. Laura would be safe. He'd make sure of it. His alarm was unwarranted, nothing more than another example of the bizarre emotional turmoil he'd experienced since his return from the edge of death.

No doubt it was a result of the illness; the poison had, after all, seemed to afflict his nerves and brain most. These ups and downs, these hammering needs and fervid hungers, would disappear, just as the peculiar dreams had. He would return to his usual calm.

And that was a good thing.

However exciting it was, however shatteringly sweet it had been to make love to Laura, it was not the sort of thing that happened more than once. Or twice, actually. Well, it wasn't something that occurred on a regular basis. No matter how much he might want it to.

It was all . . . unsettling.

James had never felt this way before, as if he were not quite in command of himself—eager and edgy and hungry and yet somehow *happy* in that feeling. It was absurd. On the other hand, what did it matter if it didn't last? He had almost lost everything—all joy, all beauty, all sorrow, all lust. He could have died without ever feeling as he did now, without tasting Laura's kiss. Without knowing what it was like to sink into her softness, her heat, to feel her tight around him, her body soft and yielding beneath his, his own heart hammering till he thought it would burst out of his chest.

Laura turned the corner and was gone from his sight. He lingered in the corridor for a moment, lost in thought. A man's voice pulled him roughly back to reality. "Beautiful woman, Lady de Vere. Easy to see why you married her."

"Archie." James turned to see his sister's husband lounging against the newel post of the staircase, smirking.

James started back into his study, but Archie continued to talk, strolling down the corridor toward him. "I'm surprised you don't keep a more careful eye on her."

James swiveled back around, his jaw clenched and a look in his eyes that would have silenced a more intelligent man than Archie Salstone. James knew he should simply walk away—giving Salstone any sort of attention was always a mistake—but he could not do it, not when it was about Laura.

"Beautiful women like that. Most men would be jealous. Funny thing is, I never took you for a trusting sort of man."

"Have a care, Archie." James's voice was as quiet as his face was stony, but the threat in it was more lethal than if he had shouted. "You might remember that you are here only on Lady de Vere's sufferance."

"Oh, indeed. I am most grateful that your wife is such a . . . generous woman. And the extent to which she has softened your nature is a wonder to us all. Though one can scarcely believe that a man such as yourself would turn a blind eye to the way his wife runs over to Lydcombe Hall at every opportunity."

Something hot and fierce speared up through James's chest. It was a feeling James was unaccustomed to, but he recognized it. It was jealousy, corrosive as acid, hungry as wildfire. He shoved it down ruthlessly, but what he had felt must have shown on his face, for the other man smiled slyly even as he retreated a step.

"Where my wife goes and what she does is none of your business, Salstone." James advanced on him. "And if I learn that you have been spreading rumors about her, you'll find yourself in a far worse state than merely evicted from this house. I can make your life hell in so many ways your limited mind cannot even imagine it."

Archie's mouth twisted. "You're a bloody tyrant. It's no wonder someone tried to kill you."

James grabbed the other man's arm and shoved him back against the wall. "Was it you, Archie?"

"No. But I wouldn't have shed any tears over it, I'll tell you that." He started to leave, but James planted his hand on his chest, holding him there.

"Who was it? How do you know about it if you weren't involved?"

"I *didn't* know. I just guessed. It seemed likely—mysterious deadly disease, a man your age, and then a miraculous recovery. I assume someone poisoned you. But then that damned doctor's daughter came along," he finished sulkily.

"Yes, she did. Sorry she spoiled your fun." James studied him for a long moment. "You know, an astute man would try to curry favor with the trustee who controls the money he wants. While astute is not a term I'd apply to you . . ."

"I don't know who did it!" Archie snarled. "I don't know who or how or anything about it. I didn't even know it was true until you attacked me."

"Believe me, if I had attacked you, you would feel a good deal worse now. This was nothing more than a friendly warning." James stepped back, lowering his arm.

Archie tugged at his lapels and tried to pull his hauteur back into place. "I presume the killer must be Claude, since he's your heir." He narrowed his eyes shrewdly. "But you've no proof."

James snapped, "Don't make something up. And don't conceal anything, either. If I find out you did either, it'll go worse for you."

"I don't know anything," Salstone repeated, his voice bitter. "I'm sure there are any number of people besides Claude who would like to see you dead."

"You are the one I would have put in first place if I thought you had the brains for it." James turned and walked away.

chapter 33

James passed his study and headed toward the gardens, too restless now to sit. It was absurd to feel jealous. Damn Salstone anyway for putting such thoughts in his head.

There was no reason for it. Even if Laura had once been in love with his cousin—hell, even if she still loved him—she would never dishonor James or herself that way. For that matter, neither would Graeme. No doubt Archie had exaggerated the number of times she went there. And what did it matter anyway? She could have been paying a call on Aunt Mirabelle or Abigail.

Well, perhaps it was unlikely for her to be friends with Graeme's wife, but Laura had long been a particular favorite of Aunt Mirabelle's. Even if she saw Graeme, conversed with him, it would lead nowhere. James would regret it if Laura were pining after Graeme, but only because he disliked seeing Laura unhappy.

He was *not* a possessive sort of man. Never had been. He hadn't felt as if he owned any woman, any more than he owned his solicitor or his man of business. It was all a matter of agreement and exchange.

Marriage was another form of contract. Both he and Laura knew that, accepted it. As for all that talk of a married couple becoming one, James didn't believe in such nonsense. After all, he had seen firsthand how very separate a man and wife remained. Laura bore his name; she was entitled to his respect and support, his protection, but James certainly would not presume to say she belonged to him.

The problem, he realized in surprise, was that in some gut-deep, primitive way, he felt Laura *was* his. She had become his the moment he slid the ring onto her finger. He told himself the feeling was only because by marrying him, Laura had entered that small circle of people under his protection, like his mother and his annoying half siblings.

Except that the way he felt about Laura was in no way like the responsibility he carried for the rest of his family. It went core deep and it was . . . passionate.

Demosthenes whined at his side, and James glanced down, realizing that he had been standing for some minutes on the terrace, staring out blindly. "Sorry, boy." He reached down and patted the dog's side. "Be glad you're a dog."

James started down the steps, still sunk in thought. Feelings were bothersome things, but at least normally they were in the places they belonged, not spilling over and twisting through everything to complicate his life. But with Laura, it seemed impossible to keep himself in order.

He thought about waking up this morning with Laura in his bed. It was an odd experience for him. He always left a woman long before dawn. But he could hardly have tossed his wife out of his bed last night. After this, he would have to handle it differently; he would go to Laura's room, where he would be able to leave when he wanted to. Laura's bedroom was a more enticing place anyway, everything soft and feminine and smelling of her.

For several minutes after he awoke, James had just lain there, studying Laura's face as she slept, taking in all the details as he would have liked to many times before but could not without embarrassing himself. She was curled up beside him, her hair spreading out over her pillow in a silken jumble. The pale morning light coming through the slit between the drapes cut a swath across her face and turned her hair to spun gold.

He had wanted to trace his finger over her brows or brush back the lock of hair that tumbled over her forehead. But it would have been unkind to awaken her just so he could touch her, and anyway, he would have looked damned silly lying there mooning over her sleeping form.

The sheet had slipped down, exposing one shoulder and skimming low over her breasts. That, too, was tempting. But he'd made himself leave the bed, moving quietly so as not to wake her.

Her dressing gown and nightshift were on the floor where they had been dropped last night; the sight of them sent an erotic twist through his abdomen—as did everything these days, it seemed. James picked them up and folded them, resisting the urge to fondle the soft cloth, and set them on the chair.

He considered ringing for a tray of breakfast. That was impractical and unnecessary, and anyway, he'd decided not to awaken her. He went downstairs to eat. Afterward, he thought about filling a tray and taking it up to her. It was very strange, this urge to bring her food.

Perhaps she would rather have the time alone. A lady might very well be embarrassed this morning after the intimacy last night. Besides, he knew where seeing her would lead, and that was something else a new bride might not want so soon.

In the end, he wound up sending one of the maids with a tray for Laura. It wasn't until he saw the amusement in the servant's eyes that he realized he was going on at too great a length about not awakening Laura and suggesting this or that food.

He was aware he was being altogether foolish. But still, he had kept the door of his study open, as he usually did not, and his attention had been more on footsteps in the hall than the correspondence in front of him. He realized it was also peculiar that he had recognized her footsteps. He couldn't have said if it was his mother or sister or Adelaide walking along the corridor, but Laura's steps brought his head up, much as they had Demosthenes'.

He smiled, remembering her walking toward him. Just seeing her made his heart begin to race. Her manner had been light and provocative, guaranteed to arouse him. The thought that she had wanted to do so, that she had deliberately cast out lures, had been as seductive as anything she said.

Just thinking about their lovemaking this morning was enough to make him ache. And really, who gave a damn if she went to talk to Graeme? James was the one who would be in her bed tonight.

Laura found it difficult to keep her mind on her task. She kept drifting off to thoughts of James and this morning in his study, only to come to her senses and realize she'd dripped a great blob of ink onto the pristine white notepaper. Fortunately, the number of invitations was perforce small since their rural location greatly limited the guest list.

It was boring work, but Laura preferred it to sitting with Adelaide and Tessa, making plans for the party. She could not help but hear all the details, from refreshments to decorations to a deep discussion of what clothes and jewelry they would wear. It seemed that they were determined to have a "theme" for the ball; both agreed that it was too bad midsummer's night eve had already passed, yet it was too soon for a harvest ball.

When Adelaide, in a burst of inspiration, suggested a masquerade ball, Laura had to cough to cover her laughter. She could well imagine James's reaction to the idea that he wear a costume. Idly she pondered what would best suit him. A Roman soldier might be good—James did have very nice long legs.

Laura jumped, startled, when Walter said her name. Blushing, she looked over at him. "Good afternoon. Pray have a seat and keep me company." She motioned toward a chair sitting near the small secretary where Laura was working.

"Gladly." He sat down, lowering his voice conspiratorially. "I was afraid I might get pulled into arrangements for the party. Either that or have to sit with that Netherly chap." He glanced toward the dark-haired man who sat by the window, staring across the room at Tessa and Adelaide.

"Hmm. Scylla or Charybdis," Laura agreed, matching his tone.

"Who? Oh, yes, those Greek folks. Never cared much for ancient gods and all that. Everyone always died. What good is that?"

"You're absolutely right." Laura chuckled. "What do you suppose Netherly is doing—admiring your mother or concocting poetry?"

"I'd wager he'd say both. He's fond of calling her his muse." He frowned. "Never understood poetry, really. All that rhyming seems unnecessary."

"I thought Tessa said you were poetical."

He goggled. "Me?"

"She mentioned once that you were frequently in your room writing."

"Oh. That." Walter reddened. "That's just . . . well, not poetry. It's, um, some stories."

"Really?" Laura asked, intrigued. "What sort of stories?"

"Oh, well, nothing important, really. Um, just tales of adventure. That kind of thing. James would say it's foolish."

Laura laughed. "James would no doubt say that about a number of things. *James* can be quite foolish that way."

She startled a laugh from the young man, but he shrugged. "I do it to pass the time. University is so boring, you see. I rather like history, but philosophy and Latin . . ." His face turned gloomy.

"Those things do sound dull."

"They are." Walter perked up a bit at her agreement. "Now, knights or cavaliers are ever so much more interesting."

"Is that what you write about? Days of yore?"

"Well . . . yes, sometimes." He blushed again. "A couple of them."

"How many have you written?"

"I don't know. A few. That's what I do instead of studying most times. Well, or helping the other chaps with pranks."

"Do you ever let anyone read them? I'd like to read one."

"You would?" He gaped at her. "Really? Yes, of course, that would be grand! I mean, if you really want to."

"Of course." Laura smiled at his eagerness. Walter could not, absolutely could not, be the person who had tried to kill James. "Walter . . . when you used to fetch James's medicine from the apothecary . . . were you always the one to pick it up?"

"I think so. I like getting out. It's easy to think when I'm riding or walking. I suppose one of the servants might have gone sometimes if I wasn't around."

"When you brought it home, did you put it away in that cabinet in his room?"

"If his door was open, I set it on his dresser. If not, I'd put it on the table outside his room—didn't want to disturb him, you see." His brow knitted. "Why? James asked me the same question." He leaned forward. "You don't think—was there something wrong with the medicine? You can't think someone, well, tampered with it. Do you?"

"There would be little reason for it," Laura said, avoiding his question.

"No, of course not. The servants like James well enough, I think." He looked thoughtful. "I can't imagine Barkens would have anything against James, either; couldn't be him."

"Who?"

"The apothecary. His name's Barkens. He seems a good enough chap. Claude and Archie and I played cards with him awhile back."

"Oh, yes, I remember." Laura hoped she had hidden her start of surprise at his words. "He's one of the men Claude plays cards with in the village."

"Yes. Poor play. Old Arch was disappointed, I'll tell

you." Walter let out a crack of laughter. "But, you know, not much choice in the village."

Laura struggled to think of some other topic to distract Walter before he could think too much about the apothecary and Claude. Fortunately, Patricia stormed into the sitting room at that moment, drawing everyone's attention.

"Where is he?" As the occupants of the room swung toward her, Patricia waved the straw bonnet in her hand at the women on the couch. "Look at this! He ruined my new hat! And don't you dare try to tell me he didn't mean to. Robbie's an absolute menace with that slingshot, always creeping about taking potshots at everything! He could have taken out my eye, you know, instead of crushing my hat. I bought this in London just last winter," she ended in a moan.

Adelaide sprang to her feet, her eyes flashing, but before she could say anything, Tessa exclaimed, "Oh, my dear, your lovely bonnet!" She curved an arm around her daughter's waist, taking the hat to examine it. "No wonder you're upset. But, look, see, it's not crushed. The dent comes right out and we can replace this feather and the grapes easily enough."

"That still doesn't excuse that little brat for—"

"Now, now, Patsy." Tessa overrode her daughter's voice, steering her toward the door and walking with her to it. "I know Adelaide is devastated about this."

Laura thought Adelaide looked more furious than devastated, but Adelaide forced her face into a smile and said, "Yes, of course. I shall speak to Robbie about it, I promise. It's very naughty of him to be playing with that slingshot so close to people. No doubt he's run away to hide in shame over what he did. He wouldn't harm you for the world, Patricia. You're his favorite aunt."

Laura suspected that was true, since Patricia was Claude's only sister, but this statement seemed to mollify Patricia, for she let her mother propel her out of the room.

"Poor Robbie." Adelaide turned back. "I'm sure he is most distraught over this."

"Dear Mrs. De Vere, you must be so distressed." Mr. Netherly came over to take Adelaide's arm and help her to the sofa, as if she were too fragile to manage it on her own.

"I should rather think it's Patsy who's distressed," Walter pointed out. Privately Laura agreed. Little as Laura liked James's sister, what the boy had done was dangerous.

"You're right, Walter," Adelaide agreed earnestly. "I do hope you won't think badly of Robbie. He *can* be thoughtless, as young boys so often are."

"Thank heavens Lady de Vere was here to comfort Mrs. Salstone," Mr. Netherly volunteered. "She is an angel, of course."

"Of course." Walter gave the other man a look of contempt. "I'm surprised you didn't rush to help Lady de Vere, Netherly."

"You're right." The other man appeared much struck by his statement. "I should go to her."

"Lot of good he'll do," Walter muttered as the other man hurried off.

Adelaide turned to Laura and Walter. "I'm sure Robbie was not aiming at Patricia. He just didn't think." She sighed. "Poor Patricia. I know she wouldn't normally get this upset at Robbie. She's quite fond of him. It's what happened in London, of course."

Laura moved closer, saying casually, "What happened in London?"

"Oh, well, I probably shouldn't speak of it. Perhaps it

isn't true." There was a gleam in Adelaide's eyes that was at odds with her normally saccharine attitude. "But I cannot help but think it explains why Patricia has been so . . ."

"Mean?" Walter suggested.

"Now, Walter, dear . . . Patsy isn't mean; she's merely unhappy."

"That's Patsy's natural state," Walter responded carelessly.

"I'm sure you don't mean that." Adelaide smiled up at him. "Patricia has ample reason to be unhappy, especially now. It's said that Salstone has run up so many debts in London he isn't welcome among his peers anymore. It's a terrible disgrace; I'm sure Patricia is humiliated."

"But surely his father will pay his debts, won't he?" Laura asked.

"That's just it." Adelaide shook her head gravely. "Lord Salstone washed his hands of Archie. Said he's not going to keep throwing good money after bad. That's why they're here rusticating."

"Why not go back to that castle Patsy's always bragging about?" Walter asked.

"I gather the castle is a mite *too* rustic. And Archie's mother is still very much in charge of the running of it." Adelaide sighed and shook her head. "One cannot help but feel for poor Patricia. It's no wonder she gets overwrought now and then."

It was not long before Tessa returned, Mr. Netherly devotedly by her side. Laura quickly excused herself to return to the unfinished business of the invitations. She noticed that Walter, too, had recalled an urgent task that needed doing.

Adelaide's revelations about Patricia and Archie certainly opened up new avenues of thought. Laura was eager to talk it over with James. Perhaps he would drop into the music room to listen to her practice this afternoon, as he sometimes did. Or tonight when he came to her bedroom . . .

If he came to her bedroom, Laura reminded herself. She could not count on desire bringing him to her tonight, especially after this morning in his study. Laura couldn't hold back a secretive little smile as she thought about that. James might be content now, even sated. Perhaps it was because she was so new to the experience that she was already humming with eagerness to be in his arms again. Or perhaps—a lowering thought—she was more licentious than other people.

In any case, she could not expect him to come to her. Would it be too forward of her to seek him out? In the past she would have thought nothing of going to talk to him. How strange that their new intimacy had the result of making her feel shyer with him. It was, she realized, because now she had something to protect—a new green shoot of a relationship to nurture.

The knot of nerves in her stomach grew all through supper. She had taken extra care with her appearance, and it seemed to her that James's gaze strayed to her many times throughout the meal and in the drawing room afterward. There was a heat in his eyes that stirred an answering warmth deep within her, but when she retired to her room, she was still uncertain.

As she readied herself for bed, her thoughts tumbled all around—what she should do if James did not come to her, how she should react if he did, what she should say or do or think. When at last there was a knock on her door,

Laura's mouth went dry, and she had to try a second time before she could get out a response.

Then the door opened and James stepped into the room, and in an instant, Laura was in his arms, all questions and doubts vanishing.

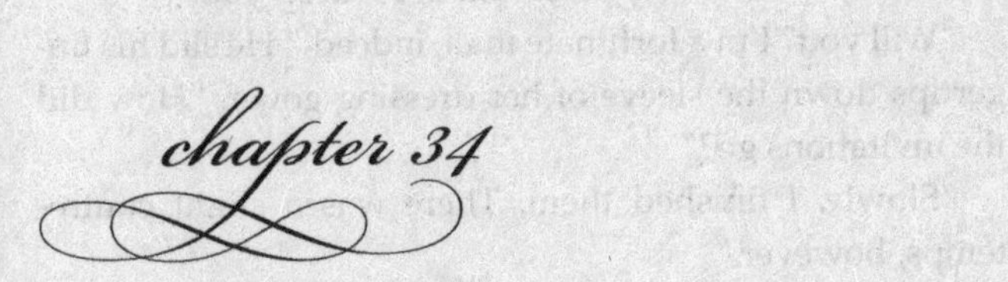

chapter 34

James had found it difficult to keep his mind off Laura all day. Truth was, he had completely failed at it. He wanted to talk to her, touch her, take her in his arms. He wanted to be naked and in bed with her again.

But strangely, when he entered her room and Laura rushed into his arms, he wanted just as much—well, almost as much—to simply hold her against him. An uncoiling started deep inside him.

James kissed his way down her face and nibbled at her neck, relishing the leap of her pulse beneath his lips. Then, sweeping her up in his arms, he settled into the chair by the fireplace. Laura snuggled up against him, and he indulged in the pleasure of simply holding her, anticipation of what would come later simmering beneath the surface.

"Have I told you how lovely you are?" James murmured.

"Yes, but you are welcome to do so again."

"You are lovely," he said obligingly, then went on, punctuating his words with haphazard kisses all over her face. "Beautiful. Radiant. Comely. Exquisite." Laughter bubbled from her throat, and James smiled at the sound, kissing the tender flesh of her throat. "Utterly transcendent."

"Oh, my." She sighed, idly tracing the pattern of his silk waistcoat. "That's very nice. I think I'll keep you."

"Will you? I'm a fortunate man, indeed." He slid his fingertips down the sleeve of her dressing gown. "How did the invitations go?"

"Slowly. I finished them. There was a slight contretemps, however."

"Indeed?" He enjoyed hearing her talk, but more than that, he liked . . . knowing her, learning what she did, what she thought. James spread out his fingers over her stomach, watching his hand glide slowly over her body.

"Yes." She stretched like a cat, arching back as if offering more of herself to his touch. He obliged, smoothing his way up and over her breast as she went on to describe Patricia's stormy entrance into the drawing room.

His blood heated, clouding his brain, but he retained enough wit to keep the conversation going. "Patricia has always enjoyed making an entrance."

"Yes, but here's the thing." Laura sat up, dislodging his hand, and turned to face him. "After she left, Adelaide told us Patricia was upset because Archie had run up so much debt in London they'd had to leave. Lord Salstone's washed his hands of him."

"So that's why they're here." He sighed. "Now I'll never be free of them. Certainly that gives Archie an urgent need for money. Perhaps that was enough to spur him to get rid of me, even though they wouldn't get a large amount."

"I thought so. Except . . . it seems too complex and *planned* for him."

"Yes, Archie's intelligence, or rather lack thereof, brings one up short. Sad to say, I doubt Patricia has any more brains than he. What about our other suspects? What else has your sleuthing uncovered?"

Laura sighed, reluctant to tell him. "Walter told me that one of the men Claude plays cards with is the apothecary."

"Ah." A bleakness flickered in his eyes and was gone. "So Claude is friends with a man who could provide him with mercury."

"Acquaintances," Laura amended. "That doesn't mean the man was willing to conspire in a murder plot."

"No, but enough to purchase mercury for him, I imagine. It's not illegal."

Hoping to turn the conversation to a lighter mood, Laura went on. "Sadly, I was able to find out little else of value. Aside from your Cousin Maurice's headaches, digestive problems, and aching joints"—she smiled at James's groan—"I also managed to determine that he hasn't visited London in almost a year."

"That's one reason I spent much of the last year in London."

"I doubt he's a realistic suspect anyway, since I can't see that he stands to gain anything from your death."

"Maurice needn't resort to poison. He intends to plague me to death with his presence. I suppose he's completely run out of funds. But I offered him the use of the cottage in Scotland, and he wouldn't take it."

"Goodness, no. He wouldn't want to be stuck up there all by himself. James . . . he's lonely."

"Of course he's lonely. Hard to attract friends when all one talks about are bunions and ague and lumbago," James retorted.

"Not if one was staying at a health resort. Bath, say,

where he could partake of the waters and discuss illnesses with the other guests."

"Are you serious? You think I should pension him off to Bath?"

"Why not?" Laura shrugged. "At least for some of the year. You would be happier. He would be happier. It'd satisfy your sense of responsibility for your family, and while it might cost you a little more than his living here, wouldn't it be worth it?"

"It might at that." James grinned and picked up her hand to kiss it. "Tell me how to be rid of the rest of them."

"Well . . . I think your mother is growing bored. She may be tiring of Mr. Netherly's attentions."

"No surprise there. The man's too saccharine for Mother. Too practiced. There's something . . . off about him. I've wondered if he's more interested in having a free roof over his head than in Mother's charms."

"Perhaps. But Patricia intimated Mr. Netherly was well-to-do; she said his family was in trade."

"Ah. That could be what's 'off' about him."

"I wouldn't be surprised if your mother decides to go back to London after this party."

"You're probably right," James agreed. "Planning the party will reinvigorate her love of socializing and at the same time remind her how much more the city has to offer."

"Netherly will follow, so that will be two more gone."

"Now if only I could persuade Salstone to leave."

"I feel sorry for Patricia."

"Why?" James quirked an eyebrow. "She's not been kind to you."

"No, but that doesn't mean I relish her misery. Look at

her life: She's married to Archie. She has no children. She isn't the mistress of her own home; Lady Salstone apparently is tightly in charge of that castle, and here Tessa is the lady of the house."

"Actually, you are the lady of the house now."

"That makes it even worse—an interloper who's no older than she. She tries to make herself happy with clothes and parties and such, but those are fleeting pleasures. She's tied for life to a foolish man who fritters away their money and is never faithful."

"Patsy knows about that?" James's eyebrows shot up.

"I would think so. Your mother is the one who told me." Laura gave him a wry smile. "Just because you men try to hide information from women doesn't mean we don't hear about it. Some unkind soul in London is bound to have 'accidentally' let it slip to Patricia. Imagine if you were having to leave London because your husband's so deeply in debt he's in disgrace, and you know that he has been supporting a mistress."

"Poor Patsy. I thought she had no idea about his women."

"I'm sure she's angry and humiliated, as well as heartbroken. Difficult as it is for me to conceive of it, Patricia must once have been taken with Archie."

"I think Patricia was most taken with his title."

"Still, she thought she had more and discovered that she had far less."

"How fortunate for me that you knew you had very little to begin with."

Laura laughed and put her hands on either side of his face. "How fortunate for me that I was mistaken." She leaned forward and kissed him. James didn't move, just savored the damp, sweet heat of her questing mouth and let her take the kiss where she would.

Her fingers slid back into his hair, slowly separating the strands and sending chills through him. His desire for her was an ache within him, but he held back, wanting to experience her tentative explorations. He wanted to know her inside and out—her pleasures, her needs, her responses. Not only to take but to give. To see her eyes flare with heat and hear her moan of satisfaction.

When she slid her searching hand beneath his jacket, he was quick to unbutton his waistcoat and shirt so that she could roam over his bare skin. Her trailing fingers left fire wherever they touched, and when Laura bent to press her lips against his chest, a shudder ran through him and his hands went to her hips, digging into the folds of her dressing gown.

Laura raised her head and gazed down at him, her blue eyes warm with passion but also thoughtful, even analytical. She was, he thought, gauging him, studying his reactions.

"Why do I feel as if I'm the subject of an experiment?"

"Not that." She laid a light kiss on his lips. "But, perhaps, an education." She bent to kiss his throat. "Do you mind?"

"Mind?" He let out a little laugh. "I find it arousing. Of course, I find almost everything about you arousing."

Her throaty chuckle sent another sizzle of desire through him. "I like that."

"So do I." He bit back a groan as her fingers found his nipple and began to toy with it. How was it that Laura could do things to him that other women had done, yet it was ten times more exciting with her?

There was something almost frightening in the way she could bring out of him a flood of sensations and feelings. Even as he kissed her, as the pleasure swamped him, it carried with it a frisson of alarm, as well, a hint of danger lurking below the surface. And, bizarrely, that dark undertow lured him most of all.

His hands dug into the soft folds of her robe, pushing her firm bottom more tightly against him. She kissed him now deeply, urgently. He delved under her dressing gown, wanting her bare flesh beneath his hands. With an impatient noise, Laura pulled herself back from their kiss and turned on his lap, settling astride him.

That was enough to send his hunger spiraling almost out of control, and he roughly pulled her dressing gown open and shoved it back off her arms. Freed of that impeding garment, Laura reached down and grasped the hem of her nightshift, stripping it up and off over her head.

He took her in his hands, gliding over her legs, her hips, her narrow waist. The low golden light of the lamp flickered over her pale skin, shadows and light shifting on her as if caressing her. Words crowded his throat, so jumbled and eager he couldn't say anything. He wanted to tell her how beautiful she was, how deeply desire struck him, but nothing could adequately express it.

So he kissed her, his hands urgent on her body, and they came together in such a rush of passion that he did no more than shuck off his trousers before Laura sank down upon him, taking him into her with a slow deliberation that had him digging his fingers into the arms of the chair.

She began to move on him, a lazy up and down that drove any thought of control from his mind and hurled him, mindless and aching, into a furious explosion. He gazed into her face as the orgasm took him, watching her as the sensual joy swept over her, and it made his own rush harder, longer, more complete.

Laura collapsed against him, breathless. James wrapped his arms around her, unwilling to separate his flesh from hers. Finally, when the air began to grow cold on their damp skin, James carried Laura to her bed. He thought of leaving, the familiar instinct to separate himself tugging at him. But Laura smiled at him, the bedcovers pulled back invitingly, and he lay down beside her.

Later. Right now he was too drowsy and content, the thought of lying with Laura too pleasant. She nestled against his side, one palm resting against his, fingers laced together, and lazily they talked, their conversation haphazard and tinged with laughter, punctuated now and then with a kiss or idle caress.

James awakened some hours later. He had rolled over onto his side, and Laura's body was a pleasant warmth against his back. He should return to his room now. He sighed, pushing aside the covers, and swung out of bed. He began to gather up his clothes. It seemed a great deal of effort to dress and return to his room. And, really, there was no need for it. He glanced over at the bed and Laura's sleeping form. Then he tossed the pile of clothes onto the chair and, turning out the lamp on the dresser, he crawled back into bed.

To Laura's astonishment, a dressmaker arrived on the morning train from London, bringing with her an assistant loaded down with a bag of sample materials and dress designs.

"You simply must have a new gown for the ball," Tessa explained. "I had thought we might run up to London to order one, but I know you're reluctant to leave James." Tessa's eyes twinkled merrily. "So I thought, why not bring the clothes here instead of the other way around?"

Laughing, Laura agreed. Though she had never been especially interested in fashion, she was not immune to the lure of new dresses. She had enjoyed wearing the gowns Abby had lent her, but a larger variety of gowns made just for her was even more appealing.

Tessa and the other ladies retired to Tessa's bedroom, shutting the door against the household men, and indulged in an orgy of fashion. While Laura stood for a seemingly interminable time with the dressmaker's assistant crawling all around her, measuring, the other women clustered on the chaise longue, examining fashion books.

The dressmaker arranged a profusion of materials across the bed for Laura to choose from—because, as Tessa pointed out, while Laura was still in mourning, it would not be terribly long before she could move to half mourning, and wasn't this light shade of purple luscious?

Laura was at first reluctant to order so many clothes at once; it would be a large expense, and really, she had no need of so many. She had to remind herself that she no longer had to watch pennies, and, given his frequent comments, James was more than willing for her to buy new frocks. Still, she could not be as extravagant as Tessa urged.

Even Patricia was convivial as they bent their heads over the drawings of elegant dresses and discussed bustles and bows and trains. And since Tessa decreed that all of them must order something new for the ball, it was a cheerful group that went down to supper that night.

Preparations for the party went on apace. Laura had wondered how they could possibly need three weeks to put on a ball, but after she saw the frequency with which Tessa changed her mind, she understood why. Laura was content to leave the other women to it. She preferred a walk in the garden or a quiet hour alone with a book or visiting Abby and the baby. Most of all, she preferred spending time with James.

It was this new closeness with her husband, not the prospect of a grand party nor the anticipation of a new wardrobe, that wreathed her days in happiness. While a walk in the garden was pleasant, it became so much more if James strolled with her, holding her hand or draping an arm over her shoulders, stopping now and then to steal a kiss.

James insisted that Laura learn how to ride, for he had in mind to buy her a horse, so they spent part of each morning on horseback. When he first announced his intention, Laura had a few qualms. James, she feared, would be an impatient teacher who required perfection, and she not only had never ridden but was faintly uneasy around horses.

However, he turned out to be surprisingly easygoing, more apt to smile at her mistakes than to lecture. When she expressed her surprise, James looked taken aback, then gave her a wry smile. "Am I really such a tyrant?"

"No. A bit impatient. And perhaps not entirely given to sympathy."

"Mm. Not entirely." They rode on in silence for a moment, then he said, "You think I expect too much from people."

"No. Actually, I think it's just the opposite. You expect very little of people."

"And I am rarely disappointed."

"There. You see? That is just what I mean. You don't demand that others be responsible; you don't even assume they could be. You are so good at everything." He snorted derisively, and Laura frowned at him. "You are. You told me yourself that you understand numbers."

"Well, yes, I'm good at that. Business things. Not feelings."

"No, you are rather leery about those. But it's not merely numbers. You're good at anything mental. You're well read; you can debate on numerous issues."

"Not a habit that necessarily makes one a welcome companion, I fear."

"You know a great deal about art and music. Look at you; you even ride well. I suspect you waltz perfectly."

He shrugged. "I manage to get around the floor."

"You demand perfection in what *you* do. But you set such a low bar for everyone else that they are failures from the start. You don't ask for affection or even friendship from anyone. Indeed, it's only those who force it on you like Graeme whom you will admit into your affections."

"Graeme. Of course." His lips twitched in irritation. "But then Graeme is perfect, isn't he?"

"Don't try to distract me. We're not talking about Graeme. We're talking about you."

"I am well aware of that fact," he retorted drily.

"Have you ever expected Patricia to be anything but silly and flighty? Or for Claude not to be envious? Have you ever asked him for help or advice?"

"No. Why would I?"

"Because he's your brother."

"He's not—"

"Don't tell me he's not your brother. So what if you have a different father? You have the same mother. You grew up in the same household. You're brothers."

"You think he wouldn't have tried to murder me if only I'd told him not to?" He raised his brows in cool inquiry.

"First of all, you don't know that he is the one who did it." Laura began to tick her points off on her fingers. "Second, that supercilious tone of yours won't deter me. Third—" She let out a little shriek as his arm lashed out and clamped around her waist, pulling her off her horse and onto his.

"*Last*, I know that there's no way I can win an argument with you except this . . ." He kissed her.

Laura made no objection, merely twined her arms around his neck and enjoyed his kiss. When he lifted his head from hers, she smiled up into his eyes. "That's not winning; that's just delaying."

James began to laugh. "I surrender." He kissed her again, and after that, all other thought fled.

It was the way many conversations between them ended. Whether they argued or laughed or teased, heat and hunger were never very far beneath the surface for them. But later, as they rode home, James said, "What of Walter? How is it I have failed him?"

"You haven't failed him." Laura reached out to lay her hand on his arm. "You haven't *failed* any of them. Sir Laurence left you with a great deal of responsibility, and you have done everything you could to live up to that trust he had in you. You aren't to blame for whatever might be amiss with them. I only meant that you have shouldered too much, perhaps, and not left enough of their burden on them."

"Walter was still a lad when Sir Laurence died. I never knew what to do with him." He glanced at her. "If only I had been wise enough to marry you then, no doubt he would have come out better."

"There's nothing wrong with Walter. And no one can blame a young man for not knowing what to do with a stripling boy. He admires you, James."

"Walter?" James looked startled. "He scarcely talks to me."

"He is, I think, a little in awe of you. He's not a confident young man, and I think he's afraid of displeasing you."

"If he was so afraid of that, one would think he would try harder to stay in school. I don't understand him. He's not unintelligent. He used to always have his nose in some book or other."

"I get the impression he's bored."

"School is always boring."

Laura laughed. "Not all his subjects bore him. He likes history. But he's uninterested in most of the others."

"It's clear he's not destined to be a scholar, but I cannot see that he has the slightest aptitude for anything else, either. He hasn't any sense for money. He'll buy a book or go to a play when he hasn't enough left of his allowance to eat. He'll lend money to anyone with a sad story."

"He has a good heart." Laura paused, then took the plunge. "He wants to write books."

"He what?" If she had hoped to startle him, she had more than succeeded. "Books? History books?"

"Stories set in the past, certainly, but more . . . tales of derring-do."

James stared at her blankly. "Good Gad." He absorbed the news and let out a laugh. "Walter? Really? Sir Walter Scott sort of tales? Stevenson?"

"Dumas. Yes."

"Who would have thought? He was ever the most timid of us."

"I gather it's more the thinking of it than the doing he enjoys."

He gave her a considering look. "He has come to you, I take it, to intercede? He'd like to leave university and take up residence in a garret in London and write?"

"He didn't ask me for intercession, and I doubt he wants to live in an attic anywhere, but yes, he would love to leave university. Writing books seems to be what he's interested in, at least at the moment. He is still young."

They rode the rest of the way in silence, but after they dismounted and were strolling toward the house, James said, "Have you read Walter's stories? Are they any good? Can he do it?"

"As for 'can,' he already has written two, as well as some shorter pieces."

"Two? Really?"

Laura nodded. "I enjoyed them. As to whether or not he will find someone to publish them or becomes a famous author, I don't know that I can judge. I'm not sure that's really the point. It's what he wants to do."

James took her hand. "Tell me, my wise Laura, what should I do?"

Laura glanced up at him and was surprised to see the uncertainty in his face. "That's up to you and Walter, isn't it?"

"You have no opinion?" He cocked a disbelieving eyebrow. "There's a first."

"My opinion is that you should talk to Walter. Find out for yourself what he thinks, how he feels. What would mean the most to him is for you to pay heed to him. He would appreciate knowing you are more interested in him than in his record at school."

"I don't give a damn about his school record. Or how he lives, really. I merely hate to see him fritter away his life, playing the fool."

"Telling *me* that does little good, since I am not Walter."

"Bloody hell, Laura, you know I have no facility with people."

"You're able to talk to me well enough."

He grimaced. "That's because of you, not me."

"Flattering as that is, I don't think it's true. I think it's that with me you are more yourself."

"That makes absolutely no sense." But he was smiling down at her as he said it.

"Doesn't it?" She sparkled up at him.

They had slowed as they walked, and now he pulled her to a stop and bent to give her a hard, quick kiss on her mouth. When he lifted his head, he sighed and said, "And now, I suppose I must talk to Walter."

His hand tightened around hers for an instant, then he turned and walked up the steps and into the house.

Laura watched him go.

"A tender scene."

She lifted her head at the sound of the woman's brittle voice and saw Patricia sitting on the shadowed terrace. Determined to be pleasant, Laura smiled and strolled over to her.

"Good afternoon, Mrs. Salstone."

"You might as well call me Patricia. Clearly we're going to be stuck here together forever."

"Surely not that long." Laura smiled. "But it would be nice to be Patricia and Laura, not Mrs. Salstone and Lady de Vere."

Patricia gazed off into the garden, not looking at Laura, as she said in a quiet voice, "James seems . . . happy."

"I hope he is."

"What about you?" Patricia narrowed her eyes at Laura. "Are you happy? Is this what you wanted? Or did you hope he'd die?"

Laura started to snap back an angry retort, but caught herself. "I never hoped for James's death. I'm not sure what I wanted or expected. I didn't envision the life I have now. But, yes, I am happy."

She refrained from adding "far happier than you," but there was no need to; the truth hovered in the air between them.

Patricia's mouth pursed into its usual pout. "James loves you." There was an almost wistful note in her voice. "The way Graeme loves that American."

Laura's heart squeezed in her chest. She managed to say, "I would like to think he holds me in regard."

Bidding the other woman a quick good-bye, Laura turned and walked on to the house. Her thoughts tumbled wildly about in her head. Did James love her?

There were times when she thought so, when he made love to her with such tenderness that she almost cried or when he turned and saw her approaching and a smile broke across his face like the sun rising. But he had never come close to expressing anything more than the assertion that she was beautiful. Of course, pulling a confession of love from James would probably require torture. He was so closed off, his emotions shielded behind an impenetrable wall, that she sometimes feared James could never love her. And what was she to do then?

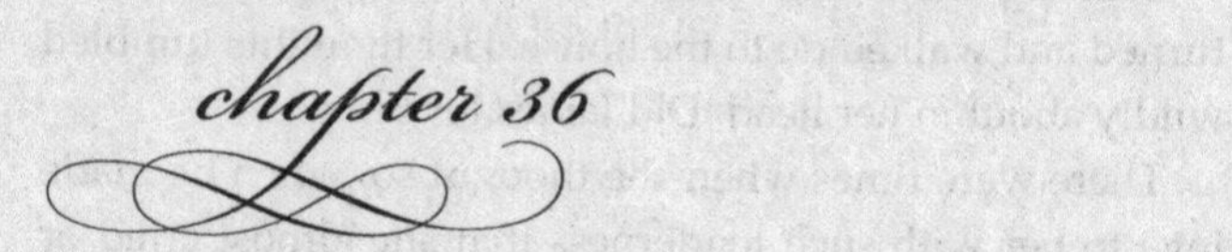

chapter 36

James watched his wife circle the ballroom with Graeme. She was beautiful, her face alight. James wondered how much of the glow arose from the fact that she was waltzing with Graeme. James glanced over at Abigail, in animated conversation with Tessa and Aunt Mirabelle. Obviously Graeme waltzing with his first love didn't disturb her. It was foolish to let it nibble at him.

The difference, of course, was that Abigail knew she held Graeme's heart in her hand. Whereas Laura . . . but that was nonsense. It was absurd to have this cold feeling in the pit of his stomach, this sense that something was lacking. Laura was his and his alone. She'd never been in any other man's bed, never felt anyone else's touch, never taken another into her warmth as she had him. If there was any lack, it was only love, and he was not some weak milksop of a man to sit about whining about romance. And how unfair, unkind, to wish he had Laura's love, when he could not offer it in return.

James was fully aware that he did not love deeply. Heartache was foreign to him. Indeed, it was vaguely unsettling even to think about it.

There was nothing wrong in Laura dancing with

Graeme. Nor was it worrisome that Laura visited Lydcombe Hall frequently. It was only . . . Laura never mentioned her visits to James. She had not once asked if James would like to accompany her. In fact, she seemed to call on them when he was not around—the day he had gone to Tunbridge Wells, for instance, or of a morning when he was in his study working. The thought that Laura didn't want James with her left a slender thread of emptiness in its wake.

"They make an attractive couple, don't they?"

Salstone, of course. The man had a knack for showing up when James least wanted to see him. James turned, polite inquiry on his face. "Who does?"

Salstone gave an irritating chuckle. Blast the man; it was he who had first put this maggot of doubt in James's head. For that reason alone, James ought to dismiss the idea.

"I've been meaning to talk to you," James said with a little fillip of satisfaction at the wary look that entered Archie's eyes.

"Talk away." Salstone surveyed the room as if he hadn't a care in the world.

"I understand you've run up a bit of debt in London."

Archie shot him a look out of the corner of his eye. "Where'd you hear that?"

James gave him the smile he'd perfected over the years, a thin lift of the lips that contained a predatory anticipation. "Archie, dear fellow, do you think I don't keep up with what you've been doing in London? Don't you know roulette's a fool's game?"

"The house cheated; the wheel was fixed."

"No doubt you're right."

"I know better than to go back there now."

"That shouldn't be a problem, since I daresay they won't let you in anymore."

His brother-in-law shrugged in a semblance of nonchalance.

James went on, "More worrisome, of course, are your notes to Cuddington and Lord Welborne. Not paying your gentlemanly debts will turn everyone against you—but you are already aware of that, aren't you?"

"What is your point?" Salstone flushed with anger.

"Just this, Archie: I am prepared to pay off your debts."

Archie's eyes widened. "I—I say, de Vere, that's damned decent of you."

"There are conditions."

"I might have known," Archie said with some bitterness.

"First, you will give up your women on the side. I refuse to allow you to treat Patricia with so little respect."

Archie bristled. "Patsy doesn't know."

"*I* know. Half the peerage knows. My *mother* knows. Do you honestly think Patricia isn't aware, no matter how much she may pretend otherwise?"

Salstone glared at him, but finally he said grudgingly, "Yes, very well. I agree."

"*All* of them, Archie. No mistresses, no prostitutes, no chasing the upstairs maid about. And if you believe I won't know, think again."

"You have no right!"

"Just as I have no obligation to pay your debts. If you want one, you take the other."

"Yes!" Salstone ground out. "Yes, I will give them up."

"Good. Now, for the rest of it—"

"There's more? What the devil do you want from me?"

"I want you to be a decent man, or at least as much of one as you can be. You are also to give up gambling. I have a house in York where you and Patsy may live."

"York! You're exiling me to York?"

"My first thought was Scotland, but I suspected Patricia might have hysterics."

"I should think so. Why even bother to clear up my debts if I can't go back to London?"

"You can go to London *if* you limit yourself to one month a year. That will give you and Patsy an opportunity to visit without taxing your resolve to abstain from your vices. York is large enough that you and Patricia will have ample entertainment and society. And the two of you will have a home of your own. Patricia can be mistress of her own household. You won't have to live here or at your father's. You can be your own man."

"My own man! To do what?"

"I don't know, Archie. I suppose you will have to figure that out."

"But . . . York! Why York?"

"For one thing, because I happen to own a house there."

"Because it's far away from you," Salstone shot back.

"That does add to its appeal," James agreed. "I have corresponded with your father, and he has agreed to increase your allowance since you will have a household of your own. I will also set up a regular payment from the trust—income only, you understand."

"And what if I don't agree to this . . . this . . . prison?"

"A rather luxurious prison. And one which you yourself will have the running of. I cannot force you, obviously. But if you want the income from your father and from Patsy's trust, if you want a place of your own in which to live, if you want your present debts paid so that you can show your face in London, then you will do this."

"I haven't got much choice, have I?" Salstone asked bitterly.

"You have a choice. It's just that one option is not very agreeable." James leaned closer. "And, believe me, Archie, if you break trust with me, I will find out. Then you are finished. I will never pay another debt of yours. Your father will cut off your money, and I won't give you a cent from the trust. You will no longer be welcome in my home."

"Patsy's your own sister!"

"Patsy can live here. Not you."

"You're a bastard."

"You aren't the first to say so. Do you agree or not?"

Salstone stared at him for a long moment, then burst out, "Yes! Yes, damn you, I agree."

James gave him a short nod and turned away. The waltz had ended, and Laura and Graeme were wending their way toward him. James went to meet them, his dark mood lifting, as it always did, when Laura smiled at him.

"I believe the next dance is mine," he said, and led her out onto the floor to take her in his arms.

Later in the evening, as the ball began to show signs of winding down, James and Graeme made their way to James's study to enjoy a glass of brandy. Graeme leaned back with a sigh, stretching his legs out in front of him. "Aunt Tessa's party was a success, it seems."

"I'm sure she's pleased." James took a sip of brandy as he watched his cousin. Despite his cheerful words, Graeme was frowning slightly, his gaze on his hand as he turned his glass around aimlessly. James waited a moment, then said, "For pity's sake, Graeme, out with it."

"What?" Graeme turned toward him, feigning confusion. "I don't know what you mean."

"You're the one who suggested we have a drink away from the party, and I doubt you were intent on complimenting my mother's party. You've something on your mind. Say it and have done with it. I promised Laura another waltz."

"Well, um, actually, it's about Laura."

"What about Laura?" James frowned.

"Nothing, really." Graeme set down his drink. "It's just . . . I wanted to ask you to . . . please be careful."

James's eyebrows soared. "What the devil are you on about? What do you mean, be careful? Of what? Who?"

"I would hate for Laura to be hurt."

That brought James upright from his casual pose. His tone as icy as his eyes, he said, "I beg your pardon. Are you suggesting that I would harm Laura?"

"No, of course not," Graeme replied hastily. "I know you would never try to hurt her."

"So it's just that I am likely to do so without trying? Is that it? That I am so unfeeling, so boorish, I will mangle her and never even notice?"

Graeme stared. "No, of course not. Good Lord, James. Calm down."

"I am perfectly calm. Dead calm. Despite what you and others might think, I don't delight in kicking puppies and pulling the wings off flies. I have no interest in making Laura unhappy. I cannot change the fact that we are married. I didn't set out to tie her to me irrevocably, to force her to spend her life with me. But—"

"Bloody hell, would you stop putting words in my mouth?" Graeme snapped back. "I never said any of that. I know you married her with the best of intentions."

"It is just the result that makes her unhappy." The rush of anger drained out of James as quickly as it had come, leaving him empty and faintly sick. He set his mouth grimly. "Did she come to cry on your shoulder? What is it Laura wants? She could have told me herself."

"No! Good Lord, James, why would you assume that? You misunderstand. Laura has said nothing to me. She's not unhappy about your marriage. Not at all. It's just the opposite; she seems very happy. Giddy, almost."

Relief flooded James. "Then what the devil are you talking about?"

Graeme sighed. "James, you know I want the best of everything for you. I'm glad you married Laura. My sincerest hope is that you find the same sort of happiness Abby and I have. But I worry a bit because Laura is the sort of woman who puts her whole heart into everything she does. I hope you won't, um . . ."

"Break her heart," James said flatly.

"Exactly."

"It's none of your business."

"You're right. But I'm fond of Laura."

"I am rather fond of her myself, as it happens," James said drily.

"It's obvious you are. But I know how you feel, what you think about love. And I know the . . . the sort of relationships to which you are accustomed."

"You think I'm going to treat her like a mistress? That I'll toss her aside one day with a note and a bauble?"

"Not exactly."

"Not at all. Laura is my *wife*—and, I must point out, *not* yours."

"James!" Graeme's face flooded with red.

"I don't need you telling me Laura's too good for me. I already know that. I realize she will never have what she wants, what she deserves, in a husband." James swung away. "And sooner or later she will realize it, too. But I can hardly stop her from doing that."

He downed the rest of his drink and slapped the glass onto his desk. When he turned back, his temper more firmly in control, he found Graeme staring at him, stunned.

"You love her, don't you?" Graeme said in awe.

"Don't be absurd," James scoffed.

"I'm not. You have fallen utterly, madly in love with Laura." His cousin began to grin.

"Come, Graeme, you know me better than that."

"I do know you. And I have never seen you act like this over any woman."

"I don't know what you're talking about. I'm not acting any way."

"No, not at all." Graeme's eyes danced. "You aren't jealous or anxious or angry at me."

"I *am* angry at you. You're pushing your nose into my business. It has nothing to do with how I feel about Laura."

"And how do you feel about Laura?"

"The same as I always have," James retorted, beleaguered. "She's an admirable, intelligent, lovely woman who was foolish enough to fall in love with you and even more foolish to marry me."

"That's what you think. What do you *feel*?"

"I feel damn sorry I ever walked into this room with you, that's what. I'm leaving." James turned and strode to the door. "I am going to dance with my wife and do my best to forget this entire conversation."

A smile played at the corner of Graeme's mouth. "I wish you luck with that."

James made his way down the corridor toward the ballroom. He realized he was scowling when one of the footmen walking toward him took one look at him and hurriedly ducked into an open doorway.

Making a conscious effort to clear his forehead and unclench his jaw, James continued to the ballroom. There were still a few people dancing, though some had left and many were sitting about in small clumps, chatting. He glanced around, but Laura was nowhere to be seen.

He looked across the room to the double doors leading outside and saw Laura standing on the flagstone terrace. She leaned against the stone balustrade, hands braced on the wide stone rail, gazing out across the garden. James stepped through the doorway, saying her name, and she straightened and turned toward him, smiling.

There was a harsh scrape of stone against stone on the balcony that formed the roof of the terrace. Instinctively James glanced up and saw a large, dark shape hurtling down from the balcony above. He shouted Laura's name, his insides going cold as ice as he desperately lunged for her, knowing he could not possibly reach her in time. Laura flung herself forward, falling to the ground, as a large stone flowerpot crashed onto the railing where she had been standing.

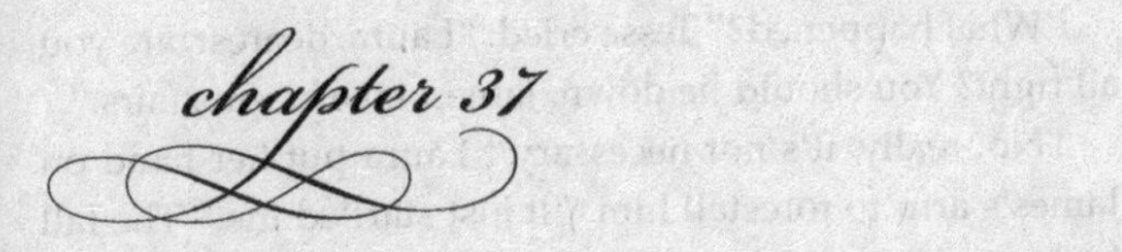

It was the flash of fear on James's face that sent Laura rushing toward him. The enormous crash came a fraction of a second later, and something thudded into her back, knocking her down. Then James was there, saying her name and going down on his knees beside her.

"Laura, Laura, are you all right?" His hands swept over her, searching for damage. "Are you hurt? Did it hit you?"

Laura blinked, momentarily numb with shock. "What? What happened?"

"A bloody urn fell from the balcony, that's what happened." James's voice was shaky, his hands cold. "No, don't get up. You may have broken something."

"I'm fine. It didn't hit me. Let me up."

Instead he swept her up in his arms and stood. She had a glimpse of the stone balustrade, a large crack running across it, and pieces of stone, dirt, and plant scattered all over the rail and floor, before James turned and carried her inside.

"James, I'm all right. Really," Laura protested, but she was secretly glad he ignored her words. She felt both numb and shaky, and it was comforting to be held in his arms.

James set her down on one of the chairs and knelt beside her, holding her hands in his, his face pale. Mirabelle and Abby came to her other side, and everyone crowded around, all talking at once.

"What happened?" Tessa cried. "Laura, dearest, are you all right? You should lie down. James, take her upstairs."

"No, really, it's not necessary." Laura put her hand on James's arm to forestall him. "It just startled me." The fall had jarred her and the spot high on her back was beginning to throb, but she wasn't about to be tucked away into bed yet.

"You were hit." James's hands were gentle on her shoulders as he turned her. He brushed a hand lightly over her back. "Your dress is marked here. Are you sure you're all right? Where's the doctor anyway?" He glanced around.

"He and his wife left some time ago, dear," Aunt Mirabelle answered. "Should we send someone after him?"

"No, please, really, I'm sure nothing is broken," Laura assured them. "I'll fix a poultice to take away the ache."

"You'll do nothing," James said flatly. "Someone else will make a poultice." The color was rushing back into his face now. His eyes glittered. "What I'd like to know is how the hell a great urn like that could fall from the balcony."

No one had an answer to that. Graeme, who had wedged his way through the others, said, "Laura! Good Lord. Are you all right?" Without waiting for a reply, he went on, "This puts an entirely different light on your other accident."

James's head snapped toward him. "Accident? What other accident?"

"You never told him?" Graeme asked Laura, ignoring the elbow Abigail dug into his side.

"No. She never told me." James shot a short, sharp glance at Laura, then fixed his gaze on Graeme. "I repeat, *what* other accident?"

"It was while you were ill. It was nothing, just an accident," Laura said soothingly.

"The horses bolted, and the victoria's brake slipper failed on the hill down to the castle," Graeme explained.

"*You* were in the carriage when Littletree crashed it?" James surged to his feet. He stared down at Laura.

"Yes, but I wasn't hurt." Laura rose to her feet to face him. Something more was roiling beneath James's surface than mere surprise, and she sought for words to reassure him, but could only repeat lamely, "It was only an accident." She looked toward Graeme for help.

But Graeme, his face furrowed and arms crossed over his chest, provided none. Instead he said, "Two separate accidents seems unusual, especially given . . . the rest of it." He glanced significantly at James.

Laura stared at Graeme. "But why would anyone—" She swung toward James. "You don't really think—"

"I think that I have been a fool." James's face blazed with fury. "Why didn't I realize?" He swung around, searching the room. He focused on Adelaide, standing a few feet away, and growled, "Where is he?"

Adelaide stared at him, wide-eyed and speechless. Laura, guessing his intent, jumped up and reached out to grab his arm, but James was already gone. Shoving past the knot of people around them, he charged out of the room.

"Graeme! Why did you tell him that now?" Laura threw an angry glance at Graeme and ran after her husband. James was already heading up the stairs, shouting, "Claude!"

There was no answer, but James did not pause. Laura lifted her skirts and ran after him. Graeme passed her, taking the steps two at a time, and Walter pelted after him, but James had too great a lead on all of them. As Laura reached the top of the stairs, she saw the door to Claude's bedroom open, and he stepped out, scowling.

"What the—"

James barreled into his brother, knocking him down, and began to pummel him. Graeme and Walter reached the struggling pair and grabbed James's arms, hauling him up. Claude lashed out, hitting James, and Walter threw himself between them. Walter warded off Claude as Graeme wrapped his arms around James, struggling to hold him back. Mr. Netherly and two other men helped pull the two men several feet apart.

"Let go." James shook off Graeme's hold. "I'm not going to kill him. Not yet."

"What the hell is the matter with you?" Claude glared at his brother.

"What do you think is the matter?" James returned hotly. "You tried to *murder* her. It's one thing to go after me, but when you try to hurt Laura—"

Claude stared. "What are you talking about?"

"An urn fell from the balcony, almost hit Laura," Walter explained.

"What?" Claude's eyebrows shot up and he turned his head, looking past the men to where Laura and the other women of the family were clustered. His face closed down and he turned back to James, saying bitterly, "So of course you decided it was me."

"Who else would it be?" James retorted. "Bloody huge stone urns don't just slip off the balcony. It was pushed."

"Now, James, you don't know that," Graeme began reasonably.

"I *know*." James glared at his brother. "*He* knows. I'm telling you, Claude, this stops. Now. If anything happens to her, I will kill you."

"James . . ." Walter began nervously.

"Stay out of it, Walter."

"James, calm down," Graeme urged. "You don't mean that."

"The hell I don't." James turned to Graeme. "Don't you understand? He tried to kill Laura. Twice. You think I could possibly ignore that?" He swung back to Claude. "I should have gotten rid of you as soon as I recovered. I foolishly hoped it was someone else, not my own brother, who wanted me dead."

"I've wanted you dead a hundred times," Claude shot back. "But you're daft if you think I ever tried to kill you. And why in the bloody blue blazes would I pitch an urn down on your wife?"

"Because she stands in your way!"

The corridor went deathly quiet. It was Graeme who broke the silence. "James, this is absurd. Stop and think. You have no proof."

"I don't need proof." James swung his head toward his cousin, his eyes implacable. "Who else would try to kill my wife?" He swept his hand toward the other people watching in stunned fascination. "All of them might hate me enough to kill me, however small the benefit. But no one would kill Laura except for profit . . . and Claude is the one who would profit. He would have to act quickly, you see, because once I survived, he'd know she might provide me with an heir. Then he would lose all chance of inheriting." He looked back at his brother. "Wouldn't you, Claude?"

Claude crossed his arms and regarded James stonily.

"I may not have enough proof for a judge, that's true," James went on. "Nor do I wish to upset Mother with the scandal. So this is what I intend: I am going to hire an assassin."

"What?" A chorus of voices rose up around him.

"If Laura dies, if I die, he will kill you." James jabbed his finger at Claude. "Do you understand?"

"I understand that you're a bloody lunatic."

"James, that's mad," Graeme protested. "You can't just go about hiring someone to kill your brother!"

"Can't I?"

"Stop and think about this. Consider the consequences. What if something happened that Claude had nothing to do with? If it was just an accident?"

"Then I'd say that Claude has a vested interest in making sure Laura remains well." James turned and strode away, leaving everyone in the hall staring after him in shocked silence.

Laura whirled and ran after her husband. The remainder of their guests were clustered at the foot of the stairs, buzzing with curiosity, but Laura hardly glanced at them as she ran past.

When Laura entered the study, James was standing at his desk, tucking a sheaf of banknotes into an inner pocket of his jacket. She knew he had heard her enter because, if nothing else, Dem turned to wag his tail at her, but he did not acknowledge her. "James?"

He looked up then, and she saw that his lip was cut and

bloodied. Laura pulled out her handkerchief, going to him to wipe away the blood.

He jerked his head away, his expression cool and remote. "I'm going to London."

At the rebuff, Laura's hand fell to her side and she took a step back. She tried to match his demeanor despite the fact that her heart was still racing and her nerves jangling in the aftermath of her fright. "Why?"

"To hire an assassin," he said as calmly as if he'd told her he was going to buy a suit. "As I just told Claude."

"Are you serious?" She stared. "You really intend to hire a killer?"

"Of course. Did you think I was joking?"

"I presumed you were bluffing," she retorted, irritation blooming in her chest. "It's a trifle extreme, don't you think?"

"Trying to kill you was a trifle extreme," he answered. "I don't intend to sit around and wait until he's successful. This is the most efficient way to assure your safety."

"James, no! He's your brother." Laura's eyes widened as he pulled a small pistol out of the drawer.

"I don't have a great deal of brotherly love for the man right now." He stuck the pistol into the waistband of his trousers and pulled his coat closed over it. "I'm leaving tonight, and I'm taking Claude with me."

"You think he will be willing to go with you?"

James smiled thinly. "I'm not giving him a choice." He walked over to the liquor cabinet and poured a shot of whiskey, then drank it down.

Laura watched him, baffled. From the moment the urn had almost hit her, he had been roiling with emotion, first panic, then rage. Now he seemed utterly calm and in control. But why wouldn't he look at her? "I don't understand. Why do you want Claude to accompany you?"

"Do you think I would risk him being near you?"

Laura started to point out that James could just as easily take her to London with him and leave Claude here, but he seemed suddenly so cool, so much a stranger, that she felt embarrassed to do so—as if she would be begging for his attention. As she watched, he poured another drink and downed it.

"James, why are you acting this way?" Laura's legs began to tremble, and she had to lock her knees for fear she might crumple to the floor. Her chest was tight, and tears pushed at the edges of her eyes. She had almost died a few minutes ago. All she wanted right now was for James to hold her, to feel his strength and warmth all around her. Instead, he was as remote as a stranger. "This is madness!"

"Madness?" He whipped around, his composure cracking. "It's madness to feel I should protect you? I'm your husband, damn it, however little you may regard me as such."

Laura's jaw dropped in astonishment. "What?"

"Why in hell didn't you tell me?"

"Tell you what?"

"About someone trying to kill you! Or perhaps I should say the first time someone tried to murder you. Maybe there are a number of attempts you haven't seen fit to share with me."

"No, just the one." Laura struggled for calm, reminding herself that James had received a fright tonight, too, and was also on edge. "I didn't tell you because it was only an accident. We weren't hurt. We were able to jump into the river as we crossed the bridge. I wasn't even in the carriage when it crashed."

"Jumped into—" He cut off the words and swung away, slamming his glass down on the cabinet. "You could have been killed. Was that not important enough to speak of? Or perhaps *I* just wasn't important enough for you to tell."

"This is absurd. You were ill. Just starting to recover. I wasn't about to burden you with news of a carriage accident. I was fine, and there was nothing you could have done about it anyway."

"No, certainly not. I was too weak and useless to protect my wife. But of course you could tell Graeme. *He* was able to help."

"For pity's sake," Laura said, exasperated. "I didn't tell Graeme. He was there."

"He was *with* you?" For some reason, this seemed to incense him even more.

"No. He came along afterward."

"How convenient."

"What does that mean?" Laura was past being patient. Her own anger rose up in her, and she braced her hands on her hips, glaring at James. " What is wrong with you? Why are you being so obnoxious?"

"It's my natural state, remember?" His eyes glittered. "Forgive me. I'm sorry to be a bother about a little thing like someone trying to kill you! No doubt I should be calm and amiable about the fact that everyone knew about this except *me*."

"It wasn't everyone!"

"No, just Graeme. Your stalwart champion."

Laura let out a noise that sounded much like a growl. "God give me strength. They're right—you've gone mad."

"Yes, no doubt. I'm sure it's quite mad for a husband to think his wife might come to him if she was in danger. That she would think he had the right to take care of her, instead of some bloody fool who didn't even have the courage to marry her!"

Laura stared. "My God . . . you're jealous."

"I'm not jealous!" James turned away and suddenly, with a wordless roar, he swept his arm across his desk, sending the things on it crashing to the floor. Demosthenes, who had been watching them warily, now jumped to his feet and let out a bark. James cursed beneath his breath and braced his hands against the desk, just standing there for a long moment, not looking at Laura.

Understanding dawned on Laura. "You're running away."

James whipped back around. "What did you say?"

"You aren't going to London to hire a killer. Or to keep Claude from killing me. You're running away!"

"I beg your pardon." He scowled. "I've never run from anything."

"No?" Laura stepped forward. "You *are* running. From me."

"From you? Don't be absurd. You think I'm afraid of you?" James gave a scornful laugh.

"I think you're afraid of how you feel," she retorted. "You want to stay alone and locked up, secure in your isolation."

"Rubbish."

"I don't think so." She faced him, eyes bright, the truth burning like a flame in her. "You almost lost me tonight, and it scared you. That's why you're so angry. So wild."

"That's nonsense."

"Is it? Then why are you trying to escape? You're scared of the emotion you feel. Scared to death of it. You're afraid to admit it, even to yourself."

James curled his lip. "Afraid to admit what?"

"That you love me."

James went still, his silence filling the room. Finally, in a voice as cool and final as death, he said, "That, my dear, is where you are wrong."

He strode from the room, leaving Laura standing in numb silence behind him.

chapter 38

James sat across from his brother in the carriage, pretending an icy calm he didn't feel. Claude, after muttering, "Don't see why we have to flee in the night like criminals," contented himself with crossing his arms over his chest and glowering at James. Claude's resentment and anger didn't bother James; the hard, cold knot in the pit of his stomach did.

He was furious at everyone—at Claude, at himself for having placed her in danger, at Graeme for being there to save her when James himself was helpless to do so, at Laura for turning for help to someone other than him. And overlaying it all was the cold, sick terror that seized him as he saw the urn tumbling toward her, the emptiness that lurked beneath his fury.

His mind skittered away from that thought. Better to dwell on Claude and his perfidy. Concentrate on what he needed to do. First he must find where Claude had hidden the mercury in the town house and dispose of it. Since he could not watch his brother constantly, he should hire a detective to follow Claude when he left the house. And, not at all the least of it, he needed to locate someone who would carry out his threat against Claude.

James had considered simply bluffing about the assassin and trusting that it would keep his brother in line. But James wasn't the sort of man who left anything to chance. Besides, if Claude managed to harm Laura—he could feel that hard lump in his stomach clenching even more tightly—James wanted him dead.

He turned his eyes to Claude, and something of what he was thinking must have shown in his gaze, because Claude shifted in his seat, the sullen expression on his face flaring into anger.

"You're a fool, you know," Claude growled. James didn't answer, merely lifted his brows in that condescending way he knew infuriated his brother. "If your wife is really in any danger, which I doubt, you've just left her unprotected."

"Demosthenes is with her, in case you've hired someone to do the job you bungled."

"I didn't do anything to her. It's ludicrous. I'm sure it was only an accident."

"Two accidents in the space of what, a month, six weeks? I think not."

"You don't *know* that anyone deliberately pushed that urn. Someone could have stumbled and fallen against it. They'd have been too bloody scared to admit it once you started ranting and raving. Or maybe the weight of it broke the railing."

"I checked; the railing is sturdy. The urn's too heavy for a mere stumble to overset it. And you were missing from the ballroom. In fact, you were on the upper floor."

"Everyone else was in the ballroom at the time it happened? I suppose you noted every face there." Claude sneered. "No. You just looked for me—the man you wanted to accuse."

"The man who had a motive."

"How do you think I arranged a carriage accident? Brakes fail all the time, and that hill is steep. Horses bolting at just the right moment is a bit chancy for a murder method, don't you think?"

"I don't know what made the horses bolt. There are several things that could do it. Perhaps a loud noise startled them or you threw a rock at them."

"Threw a rock! You think I was standing beside the road, tossing rocks at them, and no one noticed me? Why in the hell would I want to kill your wife? I know nothing about the woman other than that she was foolish enough to marry you."

"Why? Because she stands between you and what you want. You would have been content with killing just me, but when I married her, I put her in your way."

"Now I'm supposed to have tried to murder you, as well? I somehow gave you a brain tumor?"

"You provided the poison that nearly killed me. You were in the London house when it was hidden there."

"Poison! What do you mean, 'hidden'? Where?"

James ignored him, plowing ahead. "Unfortunately I was too foolish and blind to believe you would go after Laura next. I thought your lifelong hatred of me had driven you more than greed. I should have realized that you would find Laura a grave danger to your plans. All she has to do is bear me a son, and the title is no longer yours."

Claude stared at him for a long moment. "You believe I would kill two people in order to get the title? Murder my own brother?"

"It isn't as if we have a close fraternal bond."

Claude snorted. "How could we? You had no interest in

any of us. All you ever cared about was your *true* brother. The mighty Earl of Montclair. You were really a Parr, much too good for us mere de Veres."

"What?" James's eyebrows soared upward. "When have I ever laid claim to being a Parr? You think I liked being one of 'Randy Reggie's' by-blows? Knowing that Sir Laurence hated the sight of me?" James heard the rising sound of his voice and clamped his mouth shut.

"Father hated you? Oh, poor James. How unfortunate your life has been. You inherited a title you didn't deserve, not to mention a house and estate. Our mother doted on you because you were *his* son, the man she truly loved. And Father favored you in every way imaginable. *I* am the oldest de Vere; *I* should have been the one to inherit. But he would never disclaim you. You were his prodigy, his shining son."

"What drivel. I was nothing to Sir Laurence but a daily reminder of his wife's infidelity."

"Then why did he claim you as his own even though it would make you the heir?"

"He would never have shamed Mother that way. He loved her."

"He didn't have to set you up to run everything, to oversee the trust, to manage his money, the businesses. That would have been no shame to her. He did it because you were his favorite. Because you are the one who resembles *her*. Every time he looked into your eyes, he saw the woman he loved more than anything else in the world."

"You don't know anything. Vincent was the child he loved. You weren't around when he died. I was. I saw the way Sir Laurence looked at me. I watched him weep for Vincent. I heard him say, 'Now I have no son.' I have no idea how he felt about you. But I know how he felt about me. I was, much to his chagrin, the one most like him in thought and temperament. The one he knew who would take care of the finances properly, even advance them. The only one he trusted to be hard enough to handle the trustee's duties. He gave me the responsibility, but he never gave me his love."

James looked away, all the anger that had carried him gone, leaving him exhausted. Claude, too, seemed out of words and wrath. The brothers were silent the rest of the way into London.

Laura awoke feeling sore all over. Looking at the emptiness beside her, she wished she could close her eyes and go back to sleep. How completely her life had changed in the course of one night.

James's words had pierced her. She suspected he was lying—whether to her or to himself, she wasn't sure—but it had cut deeply to hear him say he didn't love her. Worse, he didn't *want* to care for her. He wanted to be far away from her.

She was tempted to avoid breakfast, but she knew she had to face the aftermath of last night's events. Besides, she was mundanely hungry—clearly she hadn't the makings of a tragic heroine.

Breakfast was as bad as she feared it would be. Adelaide, unsurprisingly, was sullen and quiet. Tessa, red-eyed, kept dabbing her handkerchief to her eyes while Netherly tried to console her with poetic words. Archie seized the chance to hold forth on James's unfairness, Claude's slyness, and the unlikelihood that anyone had tried to kill Laura.

Walter finally slammed the butt of his knife down on the table. "Stop! Good Gad, Salstone, can't you keep your mouth shut?"

The uncharacteristic outburst so startled Archie that he lapsed into silence. Adelaide gave a sob and jumped up from the table and ran from the room. Patricia followed her, presumably to provide comfort. After that the others began to leave, as well.

Laura started to rise, too, but Walter said, "No, Laura, please stay. I'd like to talk to you, if I may."

"Of course."

Walter moved over to sit beside her. "I am so sorry about . . . everything."

"Thank you."

"Please don't take it amiss, but I cannot believe that Claude tried to kill you."

Laura gave him a soft smile. "That's only natural; he's your brother. I'm not sure myself. I hate to think that James's brother would try to kill either of us, but he is the one who would profit most by our deaths. And he *was* upstairs when it happened."

"But there were other people who weren't in the ballroom, including me. The party was breaking up." He sighed. "I do wish James hadn't taken off with Claude like that. It's not like him to be so impulsive."

"I'm not sure James was thinking clearly last night."

"No, of course not. He was distraught about you. The thing is, I don't believe Claude did it, which means whoever did it is still here. And James is gone! I don't know what to do. You're in danger, and God knows how much help I'd be."

"James left Dem here."

"Yes, I saw him in the hallway. But Dem couldn't have protected you from those other 'accidents.'"

"Neither could James," Laura pointed out.

"That's why we must find the culprit before he tries again. Even worse now, if he succeeds, it'll mean two deaths, because James will blame Claude."

"You really think James would do that?"

"I imagine so," Walter said matter-of-factly. "He's rather fierce, you know, about the people he loves." He gave her a half-sad smile. "I tell myself that's why he gets angry with me for getting into trouble."

Laura wasn't sure she qualified as one of the people James loved right now, but she said only, "I'm sure he loves you. James just . . . isn't very good at showing it."

"He asked me about my manuscripts the other day," Walter said shyly. "He said he would read one of them." His grin broadened. "And he told me I didn't have to go back to school if I didn't want to. I nearly fainted."

"You see? He cares about you. All of you. I think that's why he hasn't done anything before now about Claude; he couldn't bring himself to accuse Claude, no matter how logical it was."

"Claude wouldn't kill him. He certainly wouldn't do it in cold blood. And to do it in such a way, seeing James die by inches. No. Claude can be hard. He resents James and he's often bitter, but he's not cruel."

"Then who could it be? That's the sticking point. Who else would benefit from James dying? I have no trouble accepting that Mr. Salstone is that cruel, and he might be wicked enough to murder just to gain a laxer trustee than James for Patricia's funds. But why would he try to kill me? It would gain him nothing, and it seems a large risk to take merely because he dislikes me."

"It was a risk certainly. Someone could have seen him going in or out." He sighed. "Unfortunately, no one did."

"Perhaps they really were accidents."

"It seems unlikely that urn would have fallen by itself. And we know someone plotted James's death." His face took on a determined expression. "I must investigate it. I can't let James and Claude be at odds. Even if it turns out it was Claude, I have to know."

"I'll help you." Laura stood up. "Where shall we start?"

They went first to the balcony, which lay off a little-used sitting room near the nursery wing. At the sound of their footsteps, Robbie popped out of one of the rooms farther down the corridor. "Hullo!"

"Hullo, Robbie," Walter greeted him cheerfully. "Learning anything yet?"

"No," Robbie returned proudly as he trotted down the hall toward them. "Will you take me down to the castle this afternoon? Miss Barstow says I cannot go alone, and Papa's gone to London with Uncle James. I heard Uncle James and Papa had a mill last night. Did they?" He lifted his fists and launched into a pantomime of punching.

"Who told you that?" Walter asked.

"Nobody. I heard Mr. Netherly talking."

"You hear entirely too much," Walter responded. "Hasn't anyone told you not to go listening at doors?"

The boy laughed, showing his gap-toothed grin. "Then I wouldn't learn anything!"

The governess rushed down the hall after Robbie, looking harried. "Robbie!" She bobbed a curtsey to Walter and Laura. "Beg your pardon, sir. Ma'am."

She hauled the boy back to his studies, scolding him in a low voice. Walter, watching them go, said, "He's not a bad little chap, whatever Patsy says. He just gets bored."

As they continued down the hall, a man trotted up

from the back staircase and emerged into the hallway. He paused, looking startled, when he saw the two of them, but he recovered quickly. "'Ah, what light through yonder window breaks . . .'" He swept an elegant bow toward Laura. "Lady de Vere. What a pleasure to see you."

"Netherly," Walter replied sourly, and turned away, steering Laura into the sitting room across the hallway. "Jumped-up poseur," he muttered under his breath. "I don't know how Mother puts up with him."

"What's Mr. Netherly doing up here?" Laura wondered.

"Dropping in to flirt with Miss Barstow, I'd guess. You heard Robbie repeating something he said."

"He's flirting with the governess? What about his mad passion for your mother?"

Walter snorted. "Mad passion for foisting himself on society, I'd say. Miss Barstow's not the only female he pursues. He's always sneaking about, bothering the maids. I even heard Adelaide dressing him down about it the other day. Insult to Mother, but of course, nobody wants to hurt her by telling her about it."

He turned around, surveying the bland room where they stood. "We're right over the ballroom. Balcony's out those French doors." He pointed. "Easy enough to nip up here if one used those back stairs Netherly just came up. Of course, the culprit would risk being seen by the servants."

"The servants were busy running back and forth to the ballroom. I doubt they would have paid any attention to the stairs."

"He could get back to the ballroom quickly afterward, too. People might not even notice he'd been gone."

Laura nodded. "Which makes one wonder why Claude would still be hanging about upstairs if he was the culprit."

"Very true."

Walter opened the double-paned doors and they stepped outside. The balcony was built on the roof of the terrace. Slightly more narrow than the terrace below, it made a perfect spot to drop something onto anyone standing at the balustrade beneath it. There were four square stone posts, and all but one held round stone urns filled with red geraniums.

Walter pushed tentatively at one, but it didn't even budge until he put his shoulder into it. "You'd have to push it hard. Bound to be intentional."

They left the balcony, deep in thought. Finally Laura said, "But how did they manage to wreck the carriage? It was done on the spur of the moment. No one knew I was going for a ride, including me, until that morning."

"They had two or three hours. Plenty of time to sabotage the brake slipper. It wouldn't take much—just damage the chain so it comes off under stress."

"Wouldn't someone notice a member of the household sneaking about in the carriage house?"

Walter shrugged. "No one would think anything about it if he was dressed for riding. Just nip into the carriage house when no one is looking."

Laura's mind went back to that afternoon. She'd seen Claude outside the stables. Were she and Walter merely fooling themselves about Claude?

"Tougher to make the horses bolt at just the right moment," Walter mused. "But he knew you would take the road past the castle. He could hide in the shrubbery beside the road beforehand. No, in the garden somewhere. Parts of it aren't far from the lane, and he'd be concealed by the trees and bushes. When he saw the coachman set the brake and start down the hill, he just had to startle the horses."

"How? There weren't any loud noises. The driver thought one of the animals was stung by a bee. That's a bit difficult to arrange."

"Let's look around the gardens."

Taking the back stairs, they went out to the gardens, going in the opposite direction from the waterfall steps. More shrouded in trees, it did not offer the splendid view of the other path, but at last Laura caught a glimpse of the road.

Walter gestured in front of them, saying, "There's a clearer spot ahead." He stopped before a tree trailing vines and lifted the strands to let Laura pass under them. "It wasn't this overgrown when I was young."

"Oh!" Laura stepped into a small shaded glade, bordered on three sides by shrubs and a large flat rock. On the fourth side lay the road and castle. Sunlight filtered through the leaves of the trees, casting dappled shadows on the mossy ground. "How charming."

It offered a narrow view between the tree and a large rhododendron bush, but she could see the road quite clearly. It was astonishingly close.

"Yes, it's lovely. I used to like to sit here and daydream." Walter sat down on the flat rock, and Laura joined him. "I haven't been here in years."

"Someone has." Laura pointed to something on the ground beneath one of the bushes. "A cork from a bottle of wine."

"The moss looks trampled, too." Walter wandered around the perimeter. "Look!" He squatted down and came up holding a folded square of wool. "A blanket. Someone's made themselves comfortable here."

"So the murderer sat here waiting for the victoria," Laura mused. "If only we could figure out how he got the horses to bolt." She glanced up at Walter. "How would you do it?"

"What? Me?"

"Yes. If you were writing this in a book, how would you have your character engineer it?"

"Oh. Well . . ." Looking pleased, he sat down again. "Something simple, but effective. Not a gun because there was no noise. A peashooter wouldn't carry far enough." After a long moment, his face brightened. "Young Robbie's slingshot!"

"You're right!" Laura straightened. "If you were a good enough shot, it would be perfect. No noise. It stings the horse as if he's bitten, and he bolts. But wouldn't you be easily seen?"

"Not if you're wearing dark clothing and standing a bit back from the edge. It's well shaded, dark to anyone out in the sunlight. And who would be looking up here when they have that view spread out in front of them?"

"It's uncertain. Several things could make it fail—as it did."

"But nothing lost if it didn't succeed," Walter pointed out. "Small chance of being caught."

Laura sighed. "The problem is . . . the slingshot belongs to Claude's son. This doesn't clear Claude at all."

chapter 40

James was in a black mood when he arrived in London, and nothing in the days afterward lightened it. It was a new and thoroughly unwelcome state. He had never considered himself a jolly sort, but—aside from the painful weeks of his poisoning—he had spent most of his life feeling comfortable. Content.

He hadn't awakened in the morning wishing he had not, as he did now. Nor had he required two or three brandies in the evening before he could face his bed. If he had few friends, that was by choice. If he felt the stirrings of desire, he would seek out his mistress. It had been a good life, in its way.

At least he had not been lonely, hadn't felt as if he were rattling around in this house like a marble in a box. At least he hadn't had this constant annoying heat, this unsatisfied, indeed *unsatisfiable*, lust deep inside him. At least he hadn't spent every day missing something, as if he had left a vital piece of himself somewhere.

He got through the first day in the city well enough, doing the things he'd intended. He located the pans of mercury in the small room where he stored his illuminated manuscripts. It was a perfect spot. He had spent hours in that small space, windowless to protect the fragile documents. He hired a detective to follow Claude whenever he left the house. He visited his shadier business acquaintances, making inquiries about men who could be hired to carry out his threat.

Claude's dark, resentful presence was unavoidable, of course, but at least he avoided conversation with James. And James gleaned some bit of pleasure in knowing that Claude was as miserable as he himself was.

It took another night in his solitary bed to realize that nothing, not Claude's anger nor even the knowledge that he had nullified the danger to Laura, lessened James's own unhappiness. Within another day, he was beginning to suspect that he would never be happy again.

Why had he ever thought he liked sleeping alone? His bed was cold and empty, and for the first time he realized how much waking up beside Laura had set his day on a good course. He missed sitting in the music room in the afternoons as she played the piano. Hearing the sound of her laughter in another room.

He tried to fill his days with activity. He pored over his account books and harassed his business agent until he suspected the man took to ducking out a back door when he saw James coming. He went to his club, where he spent most of the time glowering at anyone who approached him. It would have been kinder to everyone concerned if he had just stayed at home. But it was unbearable to sit there, the house huge and empty as a mausoleum around him, his only company a brother who hated him.

He even called upon the dowager Countess of Montclair, who looked at him as if he were quite mad when he asked her for news from Lydcombe and Grace Hill.

"Weren't you just there?" Lady Eugenia asked. "Why would I have any word from Grace Hill? Mirabelle's letters are filled with the most useless and minute of details, but I doubt Tessa ever picks up a pen. If you want to know about home, I'd suggest you ask your wife."

Of course, that was the one thing James could not do. The silence from Laura was deafening. Much as he might wish that Laura would smooth everything over in her usual way, he knew that wouldn't happen this time. He had shown her the worst of himself.

Once his fury had died down, he realized with an appalled clarity just how badly he had mucked it all up. Laura had almost been killed. No doubt she had been shaken and scared—God knows, he had been. But instead of comforting her, he had lashed out at her. He had lost all his vaunted control and stormed about like a child in a tantrum. Worse than that, he had coldly, cruelly denied that he loved her.

It was the truth, of course. He didn't love her. He wasn't capable of the emotion and never had been. He was the son who held himself stiffly in his mother's arms, unable to return a hug. The one who stood dry-eyed and hollow at his father's funeral while all around him cried. The one who knew you didn't marry some winsome girl if it meant financial ruin.

He admired Laura and enjoyed her company. She was amusing and clever and lovely to look at. He desired her—good God, how he desired her. He wanted to protect her, to cherish her, to fight her battles and right her wrongs. But none of that was *love*.

Love was weak. Love was messy. Love was irrational. He wasn't about to fall into that trap. He would not be a man like Sir Laurence, a slave to love, torn by jealousy and vulnerable to every hurt.

No, he did not love Laura. But why had he been such an idiot as to *tell* her that? Not only that, he had done so publicly. The door had been open and people were bound to have heard them. She must have been humiliated. He thought of the look in her eyes as he turned away, and his insides roiled.

He had ruined everything. He had made himself miserable and earned Laura's animosity. He was . . . oh, hell, he was ashamed of himself. Guilty and wrong and sorry. More than that, he felt hopeless. He had the awful, icy feeling deep in the pit of his stomach that he couldn't make things right with her again. He wasn't even sure how to start.

One gave gifts as apologies, he knew. His mother's hurt feelings were always soothed by a new piece of jewelry, and a bauble softened whatever anger or resentment popped up in a mistress. It seemed wrong to do the same with Laura, who was on an altogether different level from other women, but he didn't know what else to try.

So James stopped by a jeweler's. He'd never enjoyed shopping; he found it a waste of time and energy. But now he discovered that it was strangely addicting. He spent almost an entire afternoon in the store and wound up buying two bracelets, a set of earrings, and a variety of gemmed hair ornaments, which he had them send to Laura. And the next day he visited another shop.

It was difficult to find the perfect piece for Laura. It must be elegant, of course, and beautiful, one of a kind. But it could not be ornate or flashy, the sort of thing that drew attention. That wouldn't suit her. Diamonds were too glittering, too obvious. Even rubies seemed wrong. Pearls fit her—lustrous, warm, subtle. Deep blue sapphires to match her eyes.

They were all inappropriate, of course, for she was still in mourning, but he bought them anyway. She could wear them later. Right now she would wear jet or onyx, so he bought those, as well. Brooches, earrings, bracelets, rings.

He soon realized, however, that there was only so much jewelry one could buy. And, really, jewelry was so . . . expected. Ordinary. The sort of thing anyone might buy for any woman. The problem was that there was nothing large enough, expensive enough, to atone for his failings or indicate the depth of his regret for wounding her.

It was then he hit upon the idea of books, and the next day found him in bookstores, searching, discussing, pondering what she might like to read. Of course, it was all utterly ridiculous. Did he think Laura would forgive him if he showered her with presents? He had the uneasy suspicion she might be shoving everything he sent her into some empty drawer.

But he could not seem to stop buying things for her. He could not stop thinking about her. He felt as if he were in exile. The worst thing was, he had only himself to blame.

James sat at his desk, studying the name in front of him. He'd gotten it two days ago from a tavern owner he knew in Southwark, who had assured him the man's skills at all manner of death were well worth the price. Now all he had to do was hire the fellow, and he would have the means to keep Claude in line.

It was stupid to delay it. Foolhardy. It would not happen unless Claude hurt Laura, but still . . . the idea of hiring a man to kill his brother chilled him. He kept remembering things he'd rather not think of, like teaching Claude how to climb a tree, and the day a few weeks after that when Claude had fallen out of one, the breath knocked from him, and James had been swept with panic, certain he'd killed him.

Maybe James's threat of retribution would be enough to keep Claude in check. "Contemplating how to get rid of me?"

James glanced up, startled, to see Claude standing in the doorway. "Actually, I was remembering the first time I saw you."

Claude's brows rose. "I suppose you recognized me as a devil straight off."

"No. But I did think you were a distinct disappointment, doing nothing but lying there and crying all the time. I would have preferred a new pony."

"No surprise there." Claude stood for a moment, arms crossed, leaning against the doorjamb. "I'm tired of this. I have someone looking for a house for Adelaide and Robbie and me. We'll move out of . . . your home soon."

It felt strange to hear Grace Hill called that, as if it had not always been Claude's home, as well. James stood up abruptly. "I'm not asking that. I don't care where you live. All I want is Laura's safety."

"That's not up to me." Claude held up his hands, forestalling James's reply. "No, I know you don't intend to listen to reason. You've got your hard head set; no one can change it." He straightened and moved a little farther into the room. "Have you hired your assassin yet?"

"Naturally." James was not about to tell Claude that he hadn't even talked to one yet.

"What made you think I tried to kill you? I know what

you hold as proof for your wife, the accidents you think were not. But how did someone poison you? How did they make it seem an illness?"

James gazed at him levelly. "You really mean to play this out? Do you think I'll believe you innocent if you pretend you don't know the method?"

"No." Claude glared at him. "I know I've no hope of that with you. You're bound and determined I'm the villain of the piece. I just want to know how it was done."

"Why?"

"Because how else can I prove who really did it? You're bloody certain it was me. I presume everyone else will fall in with your thinking because that's what they're accustomed to. And you're going to wind up *dead* because of it."

"As if you'd care."

"It's my head if you do," Claude retorted. "Don't you think I have a vested interest in the matter?"

James sighed. "Mercury."

"What?" Claude looked at him blankly.

"Mercury," James repeated, uneasiness beginning to coil in his stomach. "Quicksilver."

"Someone put quicksilver in what, your food? How?"

"My medicine. And beneath my bed."

"Under your bed!" Claude gaped at him. "I don't understand. You don't have to swallow it?"

James was growing tighter every moment. Could Claude possibly be this good an actor? "You breathe it in."

"That's it? You just breathe it and it makes you have . . ." He waved his hand toward James in a vague, encompassing gesture.

"Coughing. Tremors. Nightmares. Headaches. Insomnia. Weakness. Hallucinations."

"Hallucinations!"

"Yes. Visions." James leaned forward, bracing his hands on the desk, his voice harsh. "I saw your father. I saw Mother's dead cat, of all things. You lose your memory and your mind and eventually your life. It's a long, lingering, bloody awful way to go. It would have been kinder to have shot me."

Claude swallowed, looking ill. "James . . ." He shook his head. "James, I didn't . . . Good God, you honestly think that I could do such a thing? That I'm that low? That . . . that desperate and cruel?"

"I didn't want to think it." James heard the pain in his own voice and forced the emotion back down. "But you were in London at the right time to place it here. And you were at Grace Hill at the right time."

"So were a number of others."

"But who among them had the wits to do it?" James said with finality. "Archie? Patsy?"

Claude's snort was answer enough to those possibilities. "Well, I didn't have the wits to do it, either. I know nothing about mercury. How should I know you get ill just from breathing it? How would I even get it?"

"You play cards with the apothecary. He would know. He could get it."

"I barely know the man; we play cards every once in a while. That's scarcely reason enough for him to help me murder someone." He ran his hands back through his hair, his eyes a little wild. "James, I swear to you. On anything you like. I'll swear it on the life of my son. I did not do this."

"Then *who*?" James's voice was raw with desperation.

"I don't know. Why does it have to be one of us? Why not someone who—well, I don't know, but someone else.

A number of people are in and out of this house during the Season, visiting Mother."

"But not at Grace Hill, as well."

"Why not? There are visitors there, too."

"You think one of her beaus did it?" James asked sarcastically. "The poet, perhaps?"

"Netherly," Claude said in disgust. "No, someone else, someone with reason to want you dead. I'm sure there must—" He stopped. "Wait. Netherly . . . his family. Netherly's grandfather was in trade."

"So?" James shrugged. "How could he benefit from—"

"No, no, listen to me. I haven't the slightest notion why he would do it. But his family owns a factory. It makes gauges and things like that. Thermometers. They make thermometers."

The room was suddenly as silent and still as the grave.

"Good God." James's voice was hushed. "I left her there. He's with Laura."

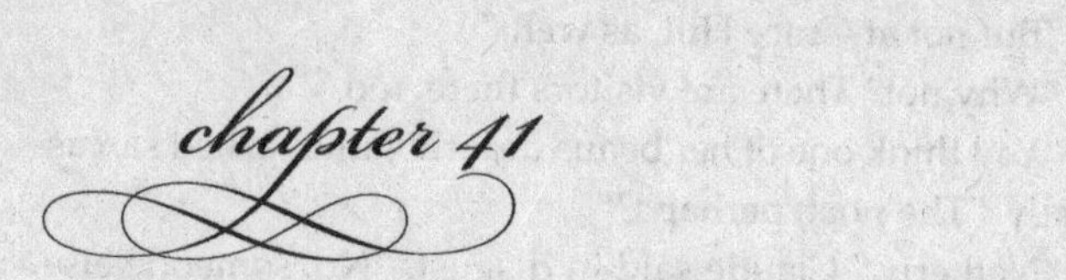

chapter 41

"I don't see why we have to move to York," Patricia whined. She had been reiterating this point for the past week. Now she had a new audience since Abigail and Mirabelle had come to call on them.

"What's wrong with York?" Abigail asked.

"What isn't?" Patricia responded. "It's provincial and staid and . . ."

"You've lived there before?" Laura feigned innocence.

"No! Of course not. I've never been there at all." Patricia flushed, apparently realizing that she had undermined her own argument, and added, "I don't know anyone there."

"It will give you an opportunity to make a new set of friends," Mirabelle said.

"But I don't want a new set of friends. I like the ones I have."

"I am sure you will enjoy making more," Adelaide told her brightly. After Adelaide's initial bout of melancholy and tears over Claude's absence, she was once again her sunny self. "One can never have too many friends. Isn't that so?"

"There are tall ships and small ships, but the best ships are friendships," Mr. Netherly said in a grand way.

Laura's lips twitched at that statement, and she was careful not to glance at Abigail.

"Yes, thank you, Mr. Netherly," Tessa said flatly.

"York is so far away." Patricia was not to be diverted from her grievance. "I think James is being mean."

"It's mean to offer you a house to live in?" Laura asked sharply.

"Well, no, but . . ."

"Did you not tell us James also agreed to pay off your husband's debts?"

"They weren't much," Patricia said. When Laura's eyebrows sailed up, she added hastily, "Anyway, I don't know why he said we couldn't live in London."

Laura's fierce gaze did not move from Patricia's face, and her voice was heavy with meaning as she asked, "Don't you?"

James's sister had the grace to blush. "Of course, I'm grateful for James's help."

"Naturally, dear," Tessa said with an approving nod.

"James has always been a good boy," Mirabelle added. "So kind."

"Don't let him hear you say that," Laura murmured.

"I wouldn't dream of it," Mirabelle assured her.

Conversation stopped as one of the footmen entered the room with a parcel in his hands. He carried it to Laura, saying, "A package for you, ma'am."

"Another one?" Patricia exclaimed.

Tessa began to laugh. "Laura! What in the world did my son do? I have never seen such an attempt at atonement."

The footman set the small wooden-slatted crate on the floor and cut the twine from around it. Laura took off the lid. "Books! Oh, my." Tears stung her eyes.

"Books!" Patricia repeated in an appalled tone. "James sent you *books*?"

"Oh, dear." Tessa turned a dismayed eye on the book in Laura's hands. "Whatever was he thinking?"

"He was thinking that I love books." Laura's throat closed up. She smoothed a hand over the cover.

Even the eternally cheerful Mirabelle frowned in puzzlement, but Laura looked over at Abigail and saw the understanding in her eyes. Abigail smiled. "Why don't I help you carry them up to your room?"

"Yes, thank you." Laura smiled at her friend.

The footman insisted on carrying the box upstairs for her, but Laura held the book she had picked up, cradling it to her chest as she and Abigail climbed the stairs to her room.

"I take it James has sent you other presents?" Abigail said.

"Every day, it seems. I don't know what to make of it."

"*Is* he trying to atone for something?"

"I'm not sure what he's doing," Laura replied a little grimly. "You know what happened at the party."

"Yes, and Tessa told us James dragged his brother off to London with him. Is he really going to hire someone to kill Claude if either of you is murdered?"

"He seemed rather intent on it. He thought threatening to do so was the best way to deter Claude. I suppose he might be right. And you know James, pragmatism outweighs sentiment."

"I suspect there's some sentiment involved, as well, given that you were almost killed," Abigail pointed out drily.

"Yes, I suppose so. Not," she added bitterly, "that James would ever admit to feeling anything for me."

Abigail studied her friend. "A flood of gifts smacks of feeling something for you, I'd say."

"It indicates his desire to cajole me out of anger."

"Oh, my, it sounds as if he does need to dig himself out of a hole."

"He told me he didn't love me."

"What?" Abigail turned to her, astonished. "He just offered that up?"

"No." Laura heaved a sigh. "I was foolish enough to tell him he loved me."

"Mm. I can see that would be a mistake with James."

"I should have known better. But it just dawned on me all of a sudden. After that urn almost hit me, he was angry, as if *I* had done something wrong."

"A typical male response."

"Probably typical of anyone. How many times do you see a mother scold a child because he was almost hurt?"

"True. It frightens one so."

"Exactly. I realized that he was angry because he was scared. So he was running away to London. Unfortunately, I blurted that out."

"Oooh."

"You can imagine how well he received that notion." Laura smiled wryly. "Then, to compound my mistake, I went on to say that he loved me and that his love was what frightened him."

"It was all true, I imagine."

"Maybe. But not exactly tactful."

Abigail chuckled. "I would think James de Vere, of all people, would understand a lack of tact."

"Receiving it is different from dealing it out."

The footman had set the box of books on the chest at the

end of Laura's bed. But Abigail was drawn to the smaller boxes piled on the dresser. "Are these his other presents?"

"Most of them." Laura set down the book on the bed and came over to show Abigail the jewelry inside the boxes.

"Oh! What beautiful drops!" Abigail held up a set of earrings that cascaded small sapphires, moving on to examine an onyx and ivory mourning brooch, a strand of lustrous graduated pearls with matching earrings, a filigreed gold hair ornament.

"Yes, they're all lovely." Laura opened an enameled box lined with red velvet and filled with more jewels. "He even sent this jewelry case to hold them, but as you can see, I haven't nearly enough room for them all. Look at this."

Laura went into her dressing room and returned wearing a hat, charmingly turned up on one side and lined with deep blue velvet.

"A Gainsborough!" Abigail exclaimed in delight. "It's beautiful. That color makes your eyes so wonderfully blue."

"I love it," Laura admitted, giving in to the temptation to admire her image in the mirror.

"I'd be tempted to forgive him, just for that hat." Abigail cast her a teasing glance. She went on more seriously. "Surely this shows the depth of his feeling for you."

"It shows the depth of his coffers," Laura replied lightly. "The excellence of his taste."

"I cannot help but think there's more than that to these gifts. James doesn't seem the sort to spend hours prowling about jewelry stores."

Laura laughed. "No. I'm sure not."

"Look at these; they're perfectly suited for you. These sapphires, that cameo, all of them indicate a great deal of knowledge of you—your looks, your taste, your nature. Not to mention a sizable amount of time spent choosing them." Abigail chuckled. "And what must it have taken for Sir James to go into a milliner's and buy you a hat!"

"I wish I could have seen it," Laura admitted.

"Some men—some *people*—have trouble saying how they feel. But it doesn't mean they don't feel it. Sometimes they can only express their love in what they do. They give you things. Protect you. Provide for you."

Laura walked over to the bed and reached down to touch the book James had sent her. Tracing the gilt lettering, she said, "I can put the other things down to his liking for beautiful things, to knowing what *should* be done, to having enough money that it's no hardship for him to buy them. But this . . ."

"What is it he sent you?"

"A book on Baroque music." She glanced at Abigail and grinned. "Not the thing to capture most women's hearts."

"Or even their attention."

"But it's something I would like, and he knew it. This is a thing he spent time and effort to purchase, something he thought about. And it gives me hope."

"Do you love James?" Abigail asked quietly.

Startled, Laura's eyes flew to her friend's. "I—I'm not sure. I thought I would be fine with the sort of marriage I could have with James. I'm practical. Sensible. No longer young and starry-eyed. I wasn't eager to give my heart to anyone, and James would never ask for it. It seemed a reasonable bargain. I like him; he's easy to converse with. He has a wicked sense of humor, which I am wicked enough to enjoy. A bit difficult at times, but who is not? And he is, I think, worth the trouble."

"But?" Abigail prodded.

"I've found I want more. I think I *have* fallen in love with him." She sighed. "He's not the only one frightened. I don't want to be hurt again. I don't want to love a man who will never love me back. And I'm afraid James never will. He's wrapped himself so tightly around with protection—hardness, indifference—I don't know if anything can ever penetrate that."

Abigail was silent for a moment, then said, "I cannot pretend to know how James feels or what he will do. But I do know hard men. My father was a harsh and callous man, far worse than James ever thought of being. But, despite all that, he was capable of love. He loved me. And from everything I've ever heard, he loved my mother."

"But James doesn't want to love me. Or anyone. He's determined not to feel the way his father did, not to act as Sir Laurence did."

"What a person wants doesn't matter when it comes to love. Graeme never wanted to love me; sometimes I thought he never would. But . . ." She shrugged. "He couldn't help himself, any more than I could. Love just reaches out and grabs you."

Laura smiled faintly. "Unfortunately, James is slippery as an eel."

The day crept on, just as it had every day since James left. Little appealed to Laura, but one must get through it. Abigail and Mirabelle had enlivened this afternoon with their call, but after they left, things settled into their usual quiet.

Laura and Walter had made little progress in their investigation. Walter had spoken with Robbie again, but his studiedly offhand questions about the boy's slingshot had yielded little information other than that his father had taken it away from him and put it on a high shelf for a week after Patsy complained.

Her music was some release, but this afternoon Mr. Netherly decided to drop in and listen, as he had on another day or two, so she cut the period short. She would have gone for a walk, but Netherly announced his intention of seeking inspiration in the gardens and suggested she join him, an invitation Laura quickly declined. She felt low enough without having to listen to Netherly prattle.

Dinner was deadly dull, as was the evening spent with the family in the drawing room afterward. Laura couldn't keep her mind on the conversation. She kept thinking about Abigail's words this afternoon and wondering if her friend was right. Did James love her and was simply unable to express it, as she had been so sure of the night of the dance? Was he even capable of love?

He was clearly determined to keep a barrier between Laura and himself. His lack of communication the past ten days had been further proof of that. Yes, he had sent her lovely gifts, and the arrival of the books today had shown a personal touch, but still, those were easy enough. What he had not done was write to her—not even a note to reassure her he had reached London safely, much less a letter of apology or explanation. How could she believe he loved her if he would not even pick up a pen to write her?

It was a relief when it grew late enough that she could retire to her room. Owen had taken Demosthenes for his nightly run, so Laura started up the stairs by herself. She had grown so accustomed to the dog's presence that it felt strange not to have him at her side.

Behind her, she heard the sound of footsteps, and Mr. Netherly said, "Lady de Vere."

Suppressing an inward groan, Laura turned toward him with a forced smile. "Mr. Netherly?"

"Allow me to escort you upstairs."

As if she could not find her way on her own—or perhaps he had appointed himself her protector, as Walter had. "No, please, I wouldn't want to take you away from the others."

He let out an indulgent little chuckle as he offered her his arm. "You must allow me to play the gentleman."

She could do nothing but take his arm. "I am sure Lady de Vere will miss your presence."

"Her ladyship knows my heart is firmly in her hands. She is my muse. My inspiration."

He continued in this vein as they climbed the stairs. They were almost to the top when the front door slammed open. Laura jumped and dropped Netherly's arm, whipping back around to see who had so rudely entered the house.

"James!"

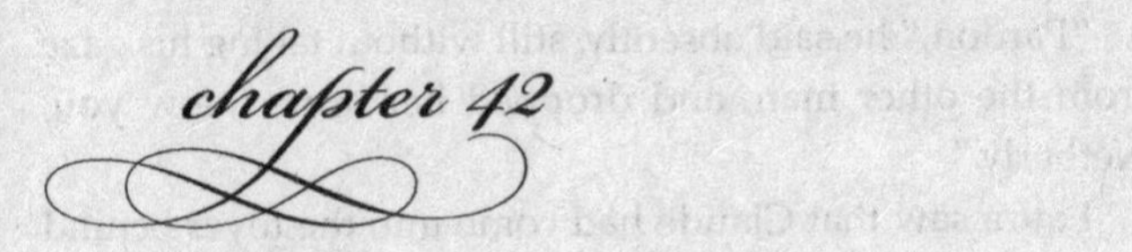

James's head snapped up at the sound of her voice. "Laura!" The word was almost a shout. "Come down here."

"I beg your pardon." Laura bristled. Gone over a week, having parted on unpleasant terms, and now he offered not even a greeting, just a short, sharp demand, as if she were a dog.

Down the hall, the other members of the family emerged, drawn by James's loud voice. He paid them no attention, just continued to glare at Laura. He moderated the volume of his voice but increased the intensity in his brief command. "Laura. Come. Here."

Laura thought about turning her back and stamping up to her room, finishing with a slam of her door. But there was something so strange about his tightly held posture, his burning gaze . . . and however blunt James could be, he was never so rude, at least not to her.

So, after a moment's hesitation, she suppressed her resentment and took a step down. From the corner of her eye, she saw Mr. Netherly's hand twitch, almost as if he was going to reach for her, but he did not. Oddly, she noted, James did not watch Laura as she came down the stairs, but kept his eyes fastened on Mr. Netherly. When she reached the bottom, James lashed out with one hand and wrapped it around her wrist like a manacle, pulling her behind him.

"James! You're hurting me."

"Pardon," he said absently, still without taking his gaze from the other man, and dropped her arm. "Now you, Netherly."

Laura saw that Claude had come into the foyer behind them. He, too, was watching Netherly. What in the world was going on? Mr. Netherly's eyes flickered from James to Claude, and after a moment's hesitation, he began slowly down the steps.

James waited. Laura saw that his right hand was curling into a fist. She wanted to blurt out a question—or a dozen—but the silence was too fraught with tension. She dared not distract James.

Netherly paused again on the bottom step, and James tightened all over, like an animal about to spring. At that instant a series of joyous barks erupted from the far end of the hall, and Demosthenes, fresh from his walk, charged down the hall to greet James. Startled, he glanced toward the noise. Netherly seized that moment to leap past him.

James whirled, reaching for the other man, but he was too late. Netherly grabbed Laura and jerked her back against him, one arm holding her tightly against his chest and his other hand encircling her throat.

"Don't." He tightened his hand around Laura's neck, cutting off her air. "I'll kill her."

James stopped, raising his hands in a peaceful gesture. "I'm not going to do anything. Just let her go."

Strangely enough, the uppermost emotion in Laura was not fear, but irritation—beginning with her initial annoyance at James and fueled by her anger—equally divided between Netherly for grabbing her and herself for standing there flat-footed and getting caught. She wasn't sure what was going on—impossible as it seemed, surely it must be that Tessa's poet was the man who had tried to kill her—but she refused to let him use her to escape.

"Get away from the door." Netherly's words were for Claude, who stood between him and the entrance, but he kept his gaze on James.

James gave a short nod to his brother, and Claude stepped aside. Demosthenes had come to a halt beside James, greeting forgotten as the dog lowered his head, growling, his lip curling up from his teeth.

"Stay," James told the dog, his voice carefully calm. "He's not going to hurt her. Are you? So far you haven't managed to actually kill anyone. You don't want to murder a woman in front of a houseful of witnesses."

"No," Netherly agreed, ignoring the numerous gasps from the spectators down the hall. "So do as I say, and Lady de Vere will be fine. Open the door."

At a nod from James, Claude opened the front door. Her captor began to move backward, dragging Laura with him. As he stepped into the open doorway, Laura threw herself down and to the side as hard as she could. Netherly's hand clenched, clamping off her breath, but the sudden violent shifting of her weight sent him lurching against the doorjamb. James sprang forward. Netherly flung Laura at him, then took to his heels.

James caught Laura and bent to peer into her face. She gasped for breath, nodding to assure him that she was all right. They turned to look out the door, as all the other occupants crowded into the foyer behind them, exclaiming and asking questions.

Mr. Netherly was running away across the wide lawn, with Claude chasing him, but neither of them could match the speed of the huge dog that bounded after them. Demosthenes passed Claude and launched himself at Netherly, landing with all his nearly two hundred pounds and knocking Netherly to the ground.

James smiled, his arm tightening around Laura, but he called, "Hold! Dem, hold!"

Demosthenes, standing with his front paws firmly on the recumbent man's chest, cast James a look so full of disapproval that Laura almost laughed. Claude tried to haul the man to his feet, but Dem was disinclined to budge. Finally, James, who had not yet let go of his tight hold on Laura, heaved a sigh and handed her into his mother's care, then went to shift Demosthenes off the prone form. He didn't hurry.

Demosthenes was rewarded with a large meaty bone in the kitchen. Claude and James hauled the wobbling Mr. Netherly back into the house and into the drawing room. Everyone else crowded in after the three men.

James cast a quick glance around, seeking Laura. He could still taste the sick fear he'd felt at seeing her in Netherly's grasp, the man's hand around her throat. He had to clamp down hard to keep fury from surging up and overwhelming him. His eyes found Laura standing beside his mother, the two women's arms around each other's waists. He wasn't sure who was supporting whom, but with Walter hovering around them, too, he trusted that Laura was in safe hands.

His business was with Netherly. Shoving the man into a chair, James stepped back, leaving Claude beside his mother's erstwhile swain, a heavy hand on his shoulder. The man's eyes flickered around the room, doubtlessly hoping to find support. The room fell silent, but James waited, idly tugging his cuffs into place, letting the tension build in his quarry.

"What do you want?" Netherly snapped at last.

James smiled to himself at the show of frayed nerves. "The constable should be along in a moment. I left word for him in the village as we drove through. It will go easier for you, I imagine, if you confess."

"Confess to what?" His quarry struggled to achieve an air of outrage. "I have no idea what you're talking about. You went after me without any reason. No wonder I ran."

"James, what is going on?" Tessa asked. "What has Mr. Netherly done?"

James glanced at his mother. "He tried to murder me." He turned back, his gray eyes now steely. "Worse, he tried to kill Laura, as well."

Though that was the obvious reason for the struggle, his words still brought gasps from most of the women there.

"You accused Claude of that the other day!" Adelaide cried out. "Now you're saying it was Mr. Netherly?"

"Your mother's admirer?" Cousin Maurice added doubtfully.

"Yes," James said shortly. He gave a nod to Adelaide. "You are quite right to be upset. I wronged Claude."

"Not for the first time," Claude put in, but his tone was more amused than resentful.

"Mm. Probably not the last, either," James retorted.

"But why do you think it's this chap?" Archie asked.

"How did he try to kill you?" Patricia's question came right on the heels of her husband's. "I don't understand."

"Why would he want you dead?" Walter's question was the one that still puzzled James.

"I don't know, but hopefully he will enlighten us." When Netherly did nothing except sneer in response, James went on. "He tried to poison me with mercury, but fortunately Laura figured it out and stopped it."

"You are so clever, darling." Tessa squeezed Laura's arm.

"I assumed Claude was behind it," James continued. "But when we began to discuss the matter . . ."

"When you were willing to listen to me," Claude corrected.

"When I *listened* to Claude, or more to the point, when I described the method to him, he informed me that Mr. Netherly's family owns a factory that manufactures various gauges, including thermometers. Which contain mercury. Your poet, Mother, was the only person in the place with access to mercury, and he had ample opportunity to place the poison both in London and here."

Tessa sucked in a sharp breath, tears glittering in her eyes. "How horrible!" She turned a look on Netherly that did not bode well for the man. "How could you!"

"I did nothing of the kind!" he denied hotly. "You're mistaken, de Vere. Your brother has manipulated you into believing lies. I have no reason to harm you. And the fact that my grandfather owns a factory which uses mercury doesn't prove I had any or that I planted it in the house. How could I have put it in your medicine? It was Walter who picked that up at the apothecary. You should look to your brothers, not me."

James smiled a trifle evilly. "I said nothing about the mercury being in my medicine. Odd that you should know it was if you weren't the one to put it there."

Netherly began to splutter, but was unable to come up with a defense. He cast a desperate glance around. "I don't know anything about mercury. I wasn't brought up in the family business. I was raised to be a gentleman."

"Pity they didn't do a very good job of it." James reached inside his jacket and pulled out a folded piece of paper. "I visited with your uncle this afternoon, and he was pleased to tell me how smart you were, how you had absorbed knowledge about the family business even though you were too fine to work there. He was also gracious enough to allow me to see his records."

James unfolded the paper slowly, confirming Laura's suspicion that he had inherited a bit of his mother's flair for drama. "I must commend your uncle's bookkeeper; the man keeps meticulous records." He read a date and an amount from his notes and he looked back to the captive. "You are listed as the purchaser of that quantity of mercury on that date, shortly before I fell ill with mercury poisoning. Rather a large amount; your uncle was puzzled why you would need so much. But I suppose it would require quite a bit to contaminate two houses, wouldn't it?"

The room erupted into chatter. James turned away, making his way toward Laura. He needed to be with her, touch her, as if to assure himself that she was there and well. Tessa said something to Laura, and she pivoted to face James.

She held herself erect, her expression guarded, and it crashed in on James that whatever he felt, whatever had happened, things were still not well between them. He stopped short and shoved his hands into his pockets. Neither of them spoke.

"James!" Tessa was quick to take up the conversational

slack. "Darling! This is astonishing. Why on earth would Mr. Netherly try to kill you?"

"I've no idea. I can only assume he hoped to persuade you to marry him and thought I would be an impediment."

"But I would never have married *him*!" Tessa said, astounded. "I assure you, I gave him no encouragement to think so."

"It's puzzling, but the evidence was clear."

Tessa continued to chatter, and Walter was full of questions. James shifted impatiently. All he wanted was to get Laura away from everyone so that he could talk to her in private. Annoyingly, Laura continued to regard him in that assessing way . . . which could not possibly be a good sign.

"Laura, I want to talk to you," he said abruptly, abandoning any attempt at subtlety, and took her arm.

As he did so, his mother exclaimed, "Of course you do. Laura was such a heroine! I could scarcely believe the way she pulled away from that man."

"Yes, and it was a damned foolish thing to do." James scowled at Laura. "You could have been killed."

Laura's brows shot up. "*That* is what you wanted to say to me?"

She jerked her arm away and whirled, rushing from the room.

chapter 43

Cursing under his breath, James hurried after her, catching up with Laura in the hallway. He grabbed her arm and pulled her into the nearest room, locking the door behind him. "Damn it, you are going to listen to me."

Laura pulled her arm from his hand and pointedly walked away. She faced him, straight as an arrow, chin high and her face bright with challenge. Just the sight of her was like a punch in the chest to him. James wanted to kiss her, to shake her, to beg her to forgive him. All the rage and terror of the past hours surged up in him, mingling with love and lust in a potent mix that momentarily robbed him of speech.

Laura apparently did not have the same problem. "After all this time, after all that's happened, after *abandoning* me and running off to London, not bothering to write a single time, not even to let me know Claude hadn't murdered you en route—"

"I didn't abandon you!"

"No? I don't know what else you would call leaving me here, not even considering taking me with you. You obviously didn't want my company."

"That's mad." How had his attempt to apologize turned into this? "Of course I—I always want—damn it, you had plenty of company."

"Much as I appreciate Demosthenes, a dog is not a substitute for a husband."

"You have Graeme! You run over there all the time anyway. I just gave you more time to spend with him."

Laura gaped at him. "Graeme! I don't spend time with Graeme."

"Oh. My mistake." His voice dripped sarcasm. "No doubt you visit Lydcombe all the time because you're bosom friends with the woman he married instead of you."

"I cannot understand why you are jealous of Graeme when I am of so little importance to you."

He stared at her. "So little importance! Good God, do you really think that I—"

"I *know*"—she cut through his words, taking a step forward, arms stiff at her side and hands clenched—"that you are indifferent to me. That you don't love me. You told me yourself."

"And you *believed* me?" He gave a short, bitter laugh.

"It's what you said."

"I lied!" James flung his arms wide. "You know I lied. You knew it even then."

"No," she said quietly, her eyes steady on his. "I only hoped."

"Then you got what you wanted." James swung away. He couldn't bear to look at her face. The emptiness that had been gnawing at him for the past week flooded out, consuming him. He gripped the mantel with one hand, as if it would help hold down the storm inside him. "Of course I love you. When I saw you almost killed, it terrified me.

I am hopelessly, idiotically in love with you. As big a fool as my father ever was. Worse. I'm eaten up with you, and I spend every day dreading that you will—"

He broke off with a growl of disgust. "Damn it!" James lifted a porcelain dog from the mantel and hurled it onto the hearth, where it shattered. "Damn it. Damn it. Damn it." He followed the first statue with its mate on the other end and finished with a heavy stone elephant that did not smash but only chipped its tail and put a crack in the slate hearth.

Laura stood, openmouthed, watching him. James refused to look at her, crossing his arms over his chest, hands tucked beneath them, and set his jaw. It had gone from bad to worse; now he'd made a perfect idiot of himself in front of her. Again.

"Well," Laura said after a silence that stretched his nerves. She let out a breathy little laugh. "That was the most graceless declaration of love I would ever hope to hear."

James flicked a black look at her. "I am well aware that I have made myself a figure of fun."

"James . . ." She laid her hand on his arm. He flinched, but did not pull away. "Do you mean it? You love me?"

"Of course I mean it. How many times must I say it?" He kept his head turned, unable to face what he might see in her eyes.

"Only a few thousand more." Laura slid her hand up his arm soothingly. "Why do you make it so hard? Why do you hate it that you feel something for me?"

"It's not 'something.' It's everything." James could not keep from turning to her even though he knew all he felt must show on his face. "I am lost. I've given my heart utterly into your hands. And I know—"

"What? What do you know?" She moved closer, gazing up into his eyes. "What is it that terrifies you?"

"You will never feel for me what you did for Graeme," he said roughly, pulling his arm from her grasp and taking a step back. "I know that I will never have you, that you will always wish, deep down, that I were he."

James started to move past her, but Laura grabbed the front of his waistcoat, and though she could not have held him, he stopped. He fixed his gaze on the back of the chair beside him, painfully afraid that if he looked at her, he might break down and beg her for her love.

"James. Look at me." Laura took his chin in her hand and turned his face to her, gazing straight into his stormy eyes. "I am not like your mother."

He half shrugged. "I know. It's not in your nature to be unfaithful." Slowly, as if the words were pulled from him, he went on, "But I won't *have* you. You'll never be truly mine."

"Of course you have me. All I am is yours. You say you have given your heart into my hands. Well, I have done the same. I have put everything into your keeping—my heart, my soul, my happiness. Every day without you has been bitter."

He watched her warily.

"Listen to me." She tugged sharply on the lapels of his jacket. "I loved Graeme many, many years ago. People change; feelings change. I still care for him as one cares for a . . . a cousin, say. But I don't love him as I love you."

He sucked in a nearly inaudible breath, his heart stuttering in his chest. "Do you?"

"Love you? Of course I do. Surely you must know I love you."

"No."

Laura took his hand in both of hers and lifted it, laying a soft kiss in his palm, then cradling it against her cheek. "Then you're right, you *are* a fool. I've loved you since . . . well, I won't say from the start, because you were excessively aggravating. But I've loved you for a long, long time. Since those long, awful nights when I sat there and listened to your breathing, so frightened it would stop."

"That was pity." He struggled to hold down the hope rising inside him.

"It wasn't pity. It was admiration for the strength of your spirit. Your refusal to give up."

"My stubbornness."

"Yes, your stubbornness. And your heart. I fell in love with you. The you inside, the one who loves art and music and beauty, the one who wanted to give me a future."

"Ah . . . the mawkish one." Everything began to loosen inside him. "Lady Eugenia would tell you that comes from my mother's side of the family."

"It comes from your heart," she corrected, poking her forefinger into his chest to illustrate. "And do not quote the dowager countess to me."

He trailed his fingertips down the side of her face. "That was the part of me that was ill."

"It's always there. You were simply too sick to hide it then. I was able to see past the substantial armor you usually have in place. I know there's more to you, much more. And you see, I love all the men you are."

"All?" A smile began in his eyes. "My. You must be a woman of diverse tastes."

"I am." Laura's face glowed. "I love the man who is a cynic, who cuts through pretense like a sword. I love the pragmatic man who makes sure all his business is wrapped up before he dies and the kind man who does that in order to ease the pain of those he leaves behind."

"I think you attribute some undeserved qualities to these men, but go ahead." James hooked his arm around her waist, holding her loosely against him. "Tell me more about your lovers."

"Well . . ." Laura linked her hands behind his neck and leaned into him, enjoying the spark that leapt in his eyes. "I'm very fond of the fellow who loves his dog, as well as the one who understands numbers. The one who makes me laugh. But most of all, I love the one who touches me just so." She stretched up, sliding her body over him. "Who kisses me"—she pressed her lips softly against his mouth—"in all those different ways. Who knows just where and when and how to turn me into a wanton."

"This fellow must be a man of many talents," he murmured, moving his hands down and pressing her pelvis more firmly against his.

"He is," she agreed solemnly, sliding her hands beneath his jacket.

James made a low noise, half laugh, half groan, and pressed his lips to the side of her neck. "God, I've missed you. I'm sorry. I'm sorry I hurt you. Will you forgive me?"

"After all those presents you sent me? How could I not?"

"Did you like them? I have more; I was too embarrassed to send them all."

Laura nodded. "I loved them. Especially the books."

He grinned. "I knew that would be the thing to win you, if aught would." He took her lips in a long, deep kiss, then raised his head to gaze intently into her eyes. "Did you mean it? Tell me the truth. I can bear anything but that you lie to me."

"The truth about what? That I love you? That I'm not in love with Graeme?"

He nodded. "Either. Both."

"I love you." Laura placed her hands on either side of his head and said firmly, "Not Graeme. I love only you. I will always love only you. And if you ever run from me again, I will track you down and make you rue it."

"Good. For if I ever left you, it would mean I had lost my mind." He lifted her up, kissing his way down her throat, repeating, "I love you. I love you. God help me, Laura, I love you."

Laura laughed in a throaty way that made every nerve in his body sizzle. "Perhaps you could show me how much." She sank her fingers into his hair.

His lips had made it down to the tops of her breasts. "I plan to."

"Wait." Laura wriggled out of his grasp.

"Laura . . ." he protested as he let her go. "You said—"

"I said . . ." Laura stopped his words, placing her finger over his lips. "I want you to make love to me."

"Then—"

"But not here. I mean to make a long, slow time of it." Her other hand trailed down his chest, fingers teasing at the waistband of his trousers. "I want to see you, to touch you everywhere," she whispered into his ear. "I want you to undress me and kiss me and give me your complete attention."

"You have that, believe me." James bent and swept her up into his arms, starting for the door.

"James! There are people out there. You can't carry me off in front of everyone."

"Can't I?" He cocked an eyebrow. "I'll just tell them my delicate wife fainted from all the frightful events."

"And what about that mess you made?" She waved vaguely toward the fireplace. "You ruined your mother's china dogs, you know."

"For which everyone should thank me."

Laughing, Laura reached down to open the door, then laid her head upon his shoulder and let him carry her away.

Their lovemaking was everything Laura had asked for, and more. They undressed each other, coming together in slow, delicious kisses in between removing this article of clothing and that. When at last they lay naked on the bed, James made a long, languorous exploration of her body, kissing, caressing, awakening every nerve, including some Laura wasn't aware she possessed.

She reveled in his touch, in the way his mouth traveled over her skin, teasing and awakening. He murmured endearments as he kissed her, as if now that the dam had broken, they could not be contained. "Beloved," he termed her, and "my love." "My heart."

And those words from this contained man were as wonderful, as pleasurable as his caresses. She returned his passion, stroking his arms, his back, his chest, emboldened by his love. This, she thought, was heaven—to have him, hold him, kiss him without the concern that she would violate some unknown barrier.

James was open to her and she to him, and whatever happened in the future, whatever disagreement or irritation or pain and loss, they would have this shining perfection at the heart of their marriage. And so, when at long last he came into her, Laura cried out at the intensity of the sweetness, the complete union of their selves.

He moved within her, slow and sure, stoking their pleasure and anticipation, extending the shimmering glory, until at last they reached the pinnacle they sought, shattering in a storm of pleasure that left them drained and utterly content.

James gathered Laura in his arms then, holding her close, and before they drifted into sleep, he murmured in her ear, "I have no home without you."

Laura awakened to James's kisses in the pale light of dawn, their lovemaking gentle and drowsy, and afterward she snuggled into his embrace, falling asleep. When next she awoke, it was much later, and James was gone.

She lay for a moment, smiling to herself, her hand idly smoothing over the sheet beside her where he had lain. Laura was almost reluctant to leave the sanctuary of her room. There was no unpleasantness here. She suspected that could not be said of the rest of the house.

She could not delay forever, though. However much she might dread dealing with Tessa's tears and everyone's questions and speculations, she had to do it. There was also the prospect of spending time with James. He would probably be embroiled in matters concerning Mr. Netherly a good part of the day, but perhaps she could persuade him to take a stroll through the gardens with her this afternoon.

Laura went down to breakfast, Demosthenes padding along beside her. She was disappointed not to find James there, but Tessa greeted her eagerly, and Claude even rose to pull out her chair. Surprisingly, Tessa was not in tears,

Claude was almost affable, and even Patricia and Archie were so enthralled with the mystery of Mr. Netherly's motives that they greeted Laura with delight and began to bombard her with questions.

"I have no idea why he would do it," Laura told them candidly. "I'm not sure even James does."

"He doesn't," Claude assured her. "The magistrate and constable were just here. They said Netherly's refused to answer any questions." A faint smile tugged at his lips. "Apparently he just quotes poetry."

"He would," Tessa said darkly.

The discussion of Mr. Netherly continued, though Laura contributed little, more eager to finish her food and go find James than to speculate on the poet's obscure motive. When she finished the meal, she was surprised to see that Claude followed her into the hall.

"Lady—that is, Laura . . ." When she turned back to him, Claude went on. "James told me you argued that I wasn't the culprit. I wanted to thank you. And . . . well, I should apologize that I was not more welcoming when you arrived."

Looking at his stiff demeanor, Laura thought he had more in common with his brother than either thought. She smiled. "Thank you. I hope that we can—all of us—become better friends."

A faint smile lightened his stern expression. "I'm not sure James and I can ever be *friends*. But perhaps we can be better brothers. I—James has changed since he married you. You've filed down his sharp edges."

"I'm not sure I deserve the credit, but I believe he looks at things a little differently now."

He nodded, offering nothing further, and somewhat awkwardly they parted. Laura watched as Claude walked down the hall to James's study. She had planned to see if James was there, but now she felt embarrassed to do so. She didn't want to appear too bold, especially in front of James's brother. James could, after all, come looking for her.

Feeling at loose ends, she strolled out to the terrace, Dem trailing along after her. Robbie was perched on the top step, and he jumped up at the sight of Demosthenes, coming forward to pet him.

"No studies this morning?" Laura asked lightly.

He shrugged. "Miss Barstow's in her room, crying."

It took Laura a moment to remember that Miss Barstow was the boy's governess. "I see. She's unhappy?"

"Mum was mad at her. But Mum left, so she'll feel better soon." He brightened. "You want to see something?"

Laura nodded and followed him into the house, feeling a trifle sorry for the boy, who often seemed lonely and bored.

"I found it yesterday," he went on as he led her and Demosthenes up the back stairs. "Miss Barstow said I mustn't disturb it." He frowned. "She's not a bad sort. I hope Mum doesn't send her away, but she was frightfully angry."

"At Miss Barstow?"

"Yes. But before that she was mad at Uncle James. She said Papa was a fool to trust him." He paused at the top of the stairs. "Then Mum heard Miss Barstow tell me Mr. Netherly was a wicked man who tried to kill Uncle James. Did he really?"

"Yes."

"Mum said Miss Barstow didn't know what she was

talking about and she shouldn't gossip about her betters. It was because she likes Mr. Netherly."

"Miss Barstow does?" Laura remembered the time they had seen Netherly coming up the back stairs and heading toward the nursery.

"No." Robbie laughed. "*Mum* likes him. He's her friend. But it's a secret." Robbie turned to Laura anxiously. "You won't tell her I said that, will you? I swore not to tell."

"No. I promise."

Mr. Netherly was Adelaide's *secret friend*? Was Claude's wife having an affair with Tessa's admirer? Perhaps she had become too cynical, living with James. Maybe it was just flirtation, or he simply showered Adelaide with the same sort of flowery comments he gave Tessa. Still . . .

"Robbie—" Laura began as she followed the boy into the sitting room over the ballroom. "Did Mr. Netherly ever borrow your slingshot?"

Robbie cackled. "No, he doesn't do things like that. He's *boring*." He crossed the room and opened the doors onto the balcony. "Come see what I found."

She stepped out onto the balcony after him, alarmed when she saw the child loop his arms over the balustrade and pull himself across it until his head was hanging over the edge. Dem let out a sharp bark, and Laura exclaimed, "Robbie! Be careful!"

"I'm fine," he said, shooting her a scornful glance. "Look." He pointed downward.

Laura planted her elbows on the stone railing and peered over the side. There, on a narrow lip, tucked in against the wall of the building, was a nest of twigs holding three small speckled eggs. Laura laughed, delighted. "Bird eggs!"

"I *thought* you'd like it. You're nice. Like Uncle Walter."

"Thank you, Robbie." Laura's mind was racing. "Robbie, did *anyone* ever borrow your slingshot?"

He glanced at her curiously. "No. Do you want to borrow it?"

She smiled. "I'm afraid I don't know how to use it. It's not a toy girls often have."

"My mum did," he said with pride.

Laura went still. "Your mother can use a slingshot?"

"Sure. She's capital! She learned it from her brothers. She's the one taught me."

"Robbie!" His name came down the hall in a high, slightly wobbly voice.

"Miss Barstow." Robbie shot Laura a guilty glance. "I better answer."

He took off, leaving Laura standing on the balcony, staring numbly after him. Adelaide?

Laura sank down, sitting on her heels on the floor. Demosthenes, after an inquiring snuffle against her ear, lay down beside her and laid his giant head on her lap. Absently, Laura petted him as she contemplated the news she'd just learned. Had fluffy, silly, sugary Adelaide tried to kill her?

If James died, Adelaide's husband would inherit the title. She would be the lady of the manor. And her son would someday inherit it all—sooner rather than later if Claude, too, suffered some mysterious illness.

Laura thought about Netherly, Adelaide's "secret friend." She remembered the small, shady spot hidden deep in the garden and the blanket she and Walter had found there. Secluded and sylvan, it was a perfect place for a lovers' tryst as well as for an expert to aim a slingshot at a passing horse. That day that she and Walter had seen the man climbing the back stairs perhaps he had been going to meet Robbie's mother in some unused room, not the boy's governess.

It made sly, slimy sense. Two people to commit the crimes. Netherly to obtain the mercury and plant it in London when he called on Tessa and Adelaide to frighten the horses into bolting, sending Laura's carriage down the treacherous hill. He would have pushed off the urn and probably crawled under the carriage to loosen the brake slipper. Either of them could have laced the medicine with mercury or put it beneath James's bed.

Claude's wife, she was beginning to think, must have been the brains behind the scheme. After all, she was the one who benefitted. Netherly, presumably, had done it for love—or at least for lust. Laura wondered whether the man had been an admirer of Tessa's and strayed into an affair with Adelaide, or had been Adelaide's lover from the beginning and only pretended to be one of Tessa's swains to disguise his true interest.

"Come, Dem." Laura rose to her feet. She must discuss all this with James.

James's study, however, was empty except for Claude, who rose politely at her entrance. "Are you looking for James? He hasn't returned yet."

"Do you know where he is?" Laura asked.

"He was going for a walk, I believe, but that was some time ago." Claude frowned. "But I'm sure there's no reason to worry, now that Netherly's locked up."

"Yes, of course." She could hardly confide her suspicions about Claude's wife to him. She forced a smile. "Perhaps I'll run into him in the garden."

Suddenly Demosthenes let out a bark that reverberated through the hallway and charged down the hall. Fear flooded Laura. She ran after the dog, and Claude followed her curiously. When Laura opened the back door, Dem shot across the terrace, cleared the steps in a single jump, and tore off down the path.

Her heart thundering in her chest, Laura took off after him in a run. Claude was right behind her.

James climbed the steps from the road, his head down in thought. After the magistrate left, James had walked along the road, trying to ascertain where and how someone had caused Laura's carriage accident. It wasn't necessary, of course, but it still bothered him that her would-be killer had so little motive for what he had done. James was a man who liked to have all the details.

But he had found nothing—no broken shrubbery where someone might have hidden, nothing that might have been used to frighten the horses and they tossed aside. Finally, admitting defeat, he started back to the house. Perhaps Laura would have some ideas. The two of them hadn't spent much time in conversation since he'd arrived home.

He was smiling at the thought—until he looked up and saw a woman sitting on the bench at the head of the stairs. When he saw the blond hair, his heart leapt, but then he realized that her hair was too bright a gold, the curls done up in blue ribbons to match her frilly blue dress. It wasn't Laura, but Adelaide. No doubt she wanted to take him to task again for having doubted Claude. He suppressed a sigh. He must be polite and listen to her; Laura would wish it.

"James," she greeted him gaily, rising to her feet. "I hoped I would catch you."

"And so you have." He reached the clearing at the top of the steps and paused politely.

"It's such a lovely day. I thought we might take a walk down to the ruins." She moved toward him, her hands by her side, half hidden by the voluminous folds of her skirts.

"That sounds charming," James lied. "However, I must get back to work." There was, after all, only so much sacrifice a man could make, even for Laura's approval.

He started to pass by her, but Adelaide stepped into his path and raised her hand from the concealment of her skirts. In her dainty gloved hand was a pistol, aimed straight at his chest.

Well. He hadn't expected this.

Adelaide raised an eyebrow. "What? No sardonic retort?"

Gone were the dimples and gracefully fluttering hands, the huge limpid eyes, the bright smile, the soft, pliable posture that made her look smaller than she was. Instead she stood straight and firm, the gun steady in her hand. Her face was cold and decisive. She might have been another person, distinctly out of place in her ruffles and ribbons.

"So it was you," James mused. "I must say, this comes as a surprise."

"I know. Poor, silly, vapid Adelaide." Her voice dripped scorn. "So dear, so sweet. So *boring*. It's quite useful."

"I can see how it would be." James moved closer. "You teamed up with Netherly, I take it. Or, no, I imagine it was more that he worked for you. What did you repay him with—money, your doubtlessly lovely body?" He took another step.

"Oh, no." Adelaide took a step back, waggling the pistol at him. "Don't think I won't shoot you. Or that I'll miss. I'm an excellent marksman. My brothers made sure of that." Her smile was sly. "I'm even better with a slingshot."

James's eyebrows rose. "So that's how you frightened the horses. Impressive."

"You always discounted me. I knew you made fun of me. It made me laugh; I was the one making fools of all of you."

"What's your plan now?" he asked in a conversational tone, edging forward. "I take it you've returned to targeting me."

"You're the important one. If you're gone, Laura will be unprotected, and I'll have plenty of time to deal with her afterward."

"That's reasonable." His cool tone concealed the surge of rage inside him.

"Stop talking. We're going to the ruins." She gestured with the gun.

"The thing is . . . don't you think people will find it a mite suspicious if I am shot after the other attempts on my life and Laura's? Say you kill me, you'll still have Laura to murder, and, well, I'm assuming from your use of Netherly that your ultimate plan is to do away with Claude, too. That's a great many bodies to explain."

She shrugged. "No one will suspect sweet little Adelaide." She batted her eyelashes mockingly, then reverted to a cold, commanding tone. "Now start walking."

"No."

"What?" Adelaide took a threatening step, the gun aimed straight at his chest. "I have a gun. Start walking or I'll shoot you right here."

"Very well." He spread his arms out. "Go ahead. Shoot me here. Rather close to the house, though. They'll hear the shot and be here quickly. How do you plan to explain my body lying bleeding on the ground? You won't be able to get away in time. Everyone will know."

"I'll throw the gun away and go into hysterics because I found you lying here."

"Mm, it might work." He tilted his head consideringly. "Sure it's worth the risk? I understand gaol is not a pleasant place to live."

Light flared in her eyes, and James thought she would fire. He tensed to jump. But at that moment something crashed through the shrubbery behind them, and a large, dark shape hurtled into the clearing. Demosthenes, teeth bared, flew straight toward Adelaide.

Adelaide heard the noise and whirled. James leapt forward, shouting, "No!"

He was too late. The gun roared, and Demosthenes went down. In the next instant, James grabbed Adelaide's arm and grappled for the weapon. It went off again, firing harmlessly into the air.

In the distance he heard Claude's bellow and Laura screaming his name. Adelaide raked her nails across his face, but James wrenched the gun away from her and hurled it into the fountain. He shoved Adelaide away, sending her staggering backward to land on the ground. He ran to Dem and dropped down on his knees beside the inert body.

Gently, he reached out to touch the dog's bloody head.

Behind him, Adelaide scrambled to her feet and picked up a rock, rushing at him. James flung himself aside, dodging the blow, and rolled to his feet.

"Adelaide!" Claude stumbled into the clear and came to a dead stop. "No!"

She paid him no attention but swung at James again. James grabbed her wrists, holding her off. Claude ran to them and wrapped his arms around Adelaide, pinning her arms to her side.

Laura raced into the clearing. "James!" She flung herself into his arms. "Are you all right?"

"I'm fine. I'm fine."

"I heard the shots, and I thought—" She broke off, her voice choking with tears, and hugged him again.

"I'm all right. It's Dem—"

"Dem!" Laura released him and whirled around. "Oh, my God, Dem!" She ran to the dog, her tears flowing. "No, Dem, please."

The dog's tail gave a thump against the ground, and he opened his eyes, twisting his head up to look at Laura.

"Oh! Thank God, you're alive. But all this blood . . ."

James knelt beside her, pulling his handkerchief from his pocket, and began to clean the wound. "I think the bullet just creased him." He gave a shaky laugh.

Laura threw her arms around James again, smiling and crying all at once. "I've never been so scared in my life."

"Shh, now. It's all right." He closed his arms around her. "It's over now."

Behind them, Adelaide snapped, "Let go of me. Let go this instant."

Laura and James turned to see Adelaide twist out of Claude's embrace. She faced her husband, her eyes stormy, but face cold and calm. "How dare you? He hurt me. I'm your wife. You should defend *me*."

"Adelaide . . . I saw you." Claude gaped at her. "What in the name of heaven are you doing?"

She tilted her head proudly, tugging her sleeves into place and smoothing down her hair. Her voice was crisp. "I am protecting my son's future. It wouldn't have been necessary if you had stepped up and acted like a man. Since you refused, I had to do it myself."

"You had to do what? Kill my brother? Are you mad?"

"No, I'm not mad. Just not a coward like you. I dare anything!" With that, she turned and sprinted for the steps down to the road.

Her action took them by surprise, and for a moment everyone just stared.

"Adelaide!" Claude shouted and began to follow. "Adelaide, stop!"

She reached the top of the long tiers of stairs and started down them at a run. Her feet slipped on the stone and she wavered, arms windmilling, then tumbled out of sight.

"No!" Claude roared and broke into a run.

James and Laura followed, stopping abruptly at the top of the stairs. Adelaide sprawled across a landing halfway down, unmoving, her head bent at an unnatural angle. Her bright hair had come loose and spilled over the stairs into the shallow water at the edge. Claude knelt beside her body, his hands over his face, his body racked with sobs.

James and Laura went down to him. James sent Laura a helpless glance, then reached out one hand and laid it on his brother's shoulder. With his other hand, he reached back to take Laura's. As they stood there, Demosthenes came up to stand with them, leaning his head against Laura's leg.

James thought of Laura lying in this place, lifeless, and a shiver ran through him. He pressed a kiss against her head. "It's over now, love. It's done. You're safe."

And he would make sure she always would be.

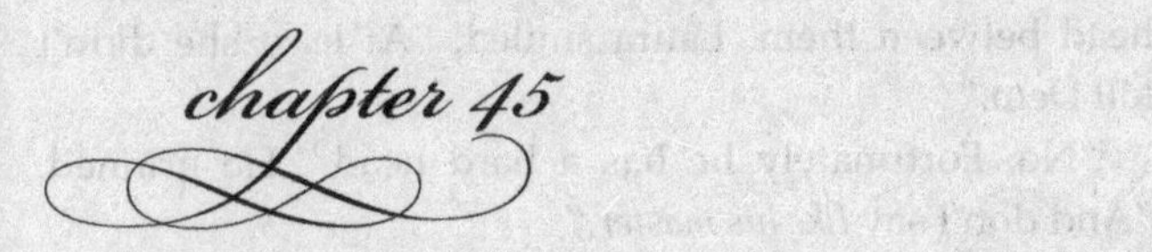

Laura slipped quietly into James's study. He stood at the window, staring out. Adelaide's funeral had been two days ago, and the house was draped in full mourning, gloom hanging in the air. The suddenness, the violence, the madness of it all, had left everyone stunned.

He turned and smiled, and she went to him, sliding her arms around him and leaning against his chest. "How are you? Have you spoken to Claude this morning?"

"I'm well enough. I saw Claude earlier. He's devastated. Hard as it is for me to fathom, he really loved the woman. He said to me, 'I never really knew her at all.' His whole foundation is shaken."

"He must be in dreadful pain."

"Now that she's gone, Netherly broke down and confessed. Adelaide persuaded him to help her do away with me—or, as he puts it, he was 'so in love I would have moved mountains for her.' They charged him with only an attempt on my life. I agreed, the stipulation being that he keeps his mouth shut about Adelaide. I won't let her actions taint Claude and Robbie."

"Yes, of course. It's bad enough that they've lost the

woman they loved, without having the scandal hanging over them all their lives." She looked down at Demosthenes, who, tail wagging, was trying to edge his massive head between them. Laura smiled. "At least she didn't kill Dem."

"No. Fortunately he has a hard head." He grinned. "And don't say *like his master*."

"I wouldn't dream of it." Laura laughed and pulled away from him. "I thought we might get away this afternoon."

"I would be happy to. What did you have in mind?"

"I thought we might visit Lydcombe. Do you want to see why I visit there so often?"

James eyed her a trifle warily. "I'm not sure. Do I?"

"I think you should." She knew he could not resist the challenge in her eyes. "Since my visits there have caused you concern."

"Laura . . . I promise you I don't doubt you. In any way."

"I know. But, still, I'd like for you to come. Will you?" She held out a hand to him.

"Of course. Anywhere."

Laura's attitude of amused anticipation continued throughout their ride to Lydcombe Hall, rousing James's curiosity. Once there, she led James upstairs and into a comfortable sitting room, where they found Aunt Mirabelle, knitting and chatting with Abigail.

James glanced around, then back at Laura, confused. "You just came to see Aunt Mirabelle and Lady Montclair?" Abigail laughed, and he looked over at her, abashed. "Not, of course, that the two of you aren't ample reason to visit."

His aunt joined in the laughter, rising to greet him. "James, dear boy, I should probably leave you twisting in the wind for that remark, but I will cut you free. Convivial company though Abby and I are, we are not who Laura loves to visit." Laura immediately began to protest and Mirabelle patted her cheek, smiling fondly. "Believe me, dear, we understand." She turned toward the door, and her smile grew even brighter. "Ah, here is the one Laura comes to see."

James turned, expecting Graeme. Instead, to his astonishment, a servant stood in the door, carrying a baby. The child's eyes were bright blue and her hair a cloud of dark curls, and he realized this must be Abigail's and Graeme's child. He had not seen her since she was a red, squirming infant. Now she was a chubby-cheeked girl with dimples and a strawberries-and-cream complexion, old enough to sit up.

He scrabbled to remember how old she was—it must have been five months since he saw her. Six? Worse, what was her name?

The child began to squirm and make babbling noises, reaching out to Laura. Laura took her, settling the baby comfortably on her hip. "Here's your Cousin James, Anna."

The baby popped two fingers in her mouth and regarded him assessingly.

"It's a pleasure to make your acquaintance." James gave her a bow, feeling something of a fool, but having no idea what else to do.

Fortunately, this seemed to tickle her, for she giggled and blew a few bubbles around her fingers.

"Isn't she beautiful?" Laura looked up at him, her face glowing in a way that made his heart swell in his chest.

"Yes," he replied, his eyes on Laura's face.

"Would you like to hold her?" Laura held the child toward him.

James's eyes widened, and he looked at the child in consternation. He cleared his throat. "Well, ah, I—"

Laura simply handed the baby to him, and he could do nothing but take her or drop her. The little girl seemed far less uneasy about the situation than he. Anna grabbed his lapel in a firm hold, crumpling it in her wet hand, and wriggled until she was firmly in the crook of his arm. She was heavier than he had expected, more substantial, which reassured him somewhat that he wouldn't accidentally break her.

She was a pretty thing, he reflected, looking into her huge blue eyes. He tried to imagine her with soft blond curls, her eyes in Laura's shade of blue. Anna leaned closer to him and grinned as if they shared a delightful secret, and he couldn't help but chuckle.

"Hello, Anna." James stroked his knuckle down her cheek. It was, he discovered, incredibly soft. He looked over at Laura, watching him with a smile. "Um, I'd better hand her back to you now."

Laura took the baby, and they sat down to visit. Anna was passed about from one woman to another, all of them obviously entranced by her. Graeme came in and joined in their admiration. James spent most of the time watching Laura. He wondered uneasily if this had been some sort of test. Had he passed or failed?

Later, as they walked out to their carriage, he took Laura's hand and said, "That was truly why you visited here? To see the baby?" At her nod, he went on, "Why didn't you tell me? Or ask me to escort you? It seemed you visited when I was busy elsewhere."

Her brows lifted. "I didn't imagine you were interested in cooing over a baby."

"Mm. You might be right."

"So I called on them when you were busy or somewhere else so that I . . ." Her cheeks reddened. "So I wouldn't take away time that I could spend with you."

He glanced at her, surprised and warmed.

Laura went on quickly, "I didn't say anything because I was afraid you would find me silly and sentimental. Maudlin."

"Don't," he said, his voice almost fierce, and he stopped, staring into her eyes. "I know I am cynical and even caustic, but I would *never* not want to know what you think or feel. I would hate it if I made you fear me in any way."

"I don't fear you," she said firmly. "It was embarrassment I worried about, and that came more from myself than you. I didn't want to reveal how I felt about you, how much I wanted a life with you." She sighed. "I told you that you were a coward, but I was, too. I was scared, so scared, of giving you my whole heart. It hurt before to love someone, but I knew it would be so much worse to love you and not have your love in return."

"Laura." He cupped her face in her hands and bent to kiss her gently. "You never have to worry about that." He continued to gaze at her for a moment. "Do you want a child? My child?"

"Oh, yes. More than anything."

He would, he thought, give her anything when she looked at him like that. "Then we're in luck, because I'm happy to spend many, many hours on the task."

He kissed her again, until finally she pulled away breathlessly, saying, "James . . . we're on the front drive. Everyone could be watching us."

"I have no shame where you're concerned." As if to prove it, he went down on one knee.

Laura stared. "James! What—"

"Shh. Let me get this out. I've been trying ever since I returned, but I hadn't yet worked up the courage."

Laura nodded, waiting. He took her hand between his.

"Before, when I asked you to marry me, I botched it. I can only be glad that you were desperate enough to take me up on it. I gave you a number of reasons why I wanted to marry you and why you should be willing to marry me. They were all, in retrospect, quite worthless. So I want another chance."

"You want to propose?" She lifted her brows. "Even though we're already married?"

"Yes. I want to get it right this time. I've been a fool far too many times and I suspect I'll prove myself one again before long. So I want you to be certain of my feelings for you—no matter how many times I might say the wrong thing or not understand you or lead with my head instead of my heart. I realized finally that there's only one good reason to marry you, and that is because I love you. You are the center of my life, and everything I have would mean nothing if you were not with me. You're all I want, all I need. This time I want to pledge to you not only my hand but my heart. I want to be with you the rest of my life . . . and forever after that, as well. Laura, will you do me the very great honor of marrying me?"

Laura nodded, tears welling in her eyes. "Yes. I will marry you. And I give to you the only thing I've ever had to give, myself. Heart and soul, I'm yours. I love you."

"It's a far better bargain this time." James stood, pulling Laura up and into his arms.

Fall in love with a great romance from Pocket Books!

Pick up or download your copies today!

XOXOAfterDark.com